A Murder of Wolves

GARY J. COOK

A Murder *of* Wolves

Gary J. Cook

Inari Publishing | Bloomington, Indiana

This book is a publication of

Inari Publishing, LLC
804 North College Avenue, Ste. 101
Bloomington, Indiana 47404 USA

www.inaripublishing.com

Telephone orders	800-536-5481
Fax orders	812-332-3154
Orders by e-mail	mike@inaripublishing.com

For more information on Inari Publishing books, see our website:
http://www.inaripublishing.com

Cover photo by Jackson Adams, with assistance from Patrick Adams.

♾ The paper used in this publication meets the minimum requirements of the American National Standard for Information Sciences—Permanence of Paper for Printed Library Materials, ANSI Z39.48-1992.

Manufactured in the United States of America

ISBN 978-0-9850833-1-1 (paperback)
ISBN 978-0-9850833-2-8 (e-book)

I am a brother to dragons,
and a companion to owls.

JOB 30:29

It is better to die in battle than of old age and sickness.

OLD BLACKFOOT PROVERB

Prologue
Dragons

The elk was on its side in the ferns and grass next to a muddy, well-trampled wallow. On the slope above the wallow a new road had been cut into the hillside—one of the many temporary roads gouged into the mountains that summer to help combat forest fires.

From where she stood on a rock the size of her pickup truck, she could see the shudder of two blue and white fletched arrows protruding from a mound of blond hair.

The rock was surrounded by tightly spaced fir and thick bushes. To her right, a well-used elk trail snaked its way through a forest of larch and lodgepole.

She looked up. The sky above the trees was a uniform gray.

In a few minutes, she would go over and make sure the elk was dead. If the meet didn't go down until it was supposed to, she would have the elk gutted and quartered and hidden in the trees before anyone showed.

The leaden sky promised rain—maybe even snow.

It was going to be after midnight before she got the elk down to the truck—maybe morning if it rained or snowed. Five trips, minimum. Say, three-quarters of a mile one-way. She could call someone to come help, but this was her first elk. She'd get it out by herself, even if she had to build a fire and rest between trips.

The good news was that it was downhill all the way and most of the slope was open. The bad news was that most of the slope was open. If it snowed or rained the ground would become slippery and the quarters would slide too easily. Once an elk quarter began moving, it would take on a mind of its own, and all she would be able to do would be to let go of the rope and get out of the way. Several hundred pounds of elk surfing down a steep slope is no joke.

With her right hand she reached back and shifted the pistol and holster sewn on the buttpack belt higher on her hip.

Something fluttered on the road above the elk.

The road dead-ended above the wallow in a large turn-around/staging area for firefighters. Maybe someone's shirt or blanket had blown off the last truck out. Might as well go check it out, she thought. Let the elk die in peace.

She turned to jump off the rock on the uphill side and, as she did, heard a tiny scraping sound at her feet. She caught a glimpse of her cell phone sliding off the rock where she'd set it when she'd nocked another arrow.

She knelt, taking care not to snag the razor-sharp broadhead in the bushes, and looked over the edge. Damn. The bushes were so thick it would take a machete to get to the cell phone.

With a dull grunt the elk raised its head. One eye rimmed in white stared in her direction. She froze, careful to not look directly at it.

The elk eased back down into the grass and ferns. Holding the bow high with her left hand, index finger keeping the arrow tight to the arrow rest, she stepped off the uphill edge of the rock, breasting through a thicket of young fir. Her cell phone would just have to wait until after the elk died.

She sidehilled away from the meadow, fifty yards up through a stand of old-growth larch, to where the ridge met the road and the embankment was only a few feet high.

Stepping onto the road, she walked back around the curve, into the turn-around, walking on the inside so that the elk could not see her moving on the road above.

A red and black plaid shirt and a pair of brown hiking boots had been left in the middle of the turnaround. The shirt moved and jerked.

She kicked a rock toward it, and two chipmunks streaked from underneath the plaid material and disappeared into rocks and torn branches at the edge of the embankment.

With the tip of the arrow, she plucked the shirt off the ground, and dropped it onto the boots. A power bar that must have been in the shirt pocket lay torn and shredded on the ground.

Judging from the tracks two vehicles had recently been in the turnaround. A narrow road tire on a small wheelbase, and a much wider, cleated, all-terrain truck tread. Both vehicles had left in a hurry. Dirt and rocks had sprayed in arcs as the vehicles had made u-turns and, in the case of the smaller track, fishtailed out of the turnaround.

Bow hunters, probably. They'd seen the herd of elk she'd followed up the ridge, and had left in a hurry hoping to head off the elk down the road. In their excitement, they'd forgotten about the shirt and boots on the tailgate.

She walked to the edge of the embankment, careful to keep as still as possible. The elk was a blond lump in the grass and ferns, difficult to recognize if she hadn't already known what it was. Its antlers looked like branches blown out of a tree.

To her right, she heard the distant sound of a vehicle slowly negotiating the twists and turns in the crude road.

She turned and ran back to where the ridge met the road, down the embankment, and onto a soft carpet of pine needles beneath the stand of big larch. The arrow caught on the trunk of a larch, and was jerked out of her hand, onto to the ground. She ignored it, holding the bow in front of her face, as she forced her way into the thicket of fir next to the large rock. She could hear the sound of a truck diesel knocking on the road above. Through the stand of larch, she saw a faded rust-red Volkswagen Rabbit drive into the turn-around and stop.

She couldn't see the truck, but she heard its diesel stop and doors open. "*Run again, motherfucker, and I'll—*" The rest was lost in the grate and squeal of door hinges on the Rabbit.

A man wearing the same camouflage she was wearing stepped out of the driver's side of the Rabbit, his face streaked and mottled with black and gray greasepaint. He walked around the back of the car, and she could see what looked like an MP5 submachine gun in his right hand. A long fat silencer tube nearly doubled the length of the barrel.

Through the trees she could see two other men dressed in camouflage escorting another man, shirtless and, from the gingerly way he was walking, barefoot. His skin was pale white, farmer's tan at arms and neck, blue jeans low on bony hips, long red welt across his shoulder and upper back.

Both men were wearing the same woodland pattern that she and the man who'd gotten out of the Rabbit were wearing. One of the men had on a black baseball cap and matching black wraparound sunglasses; the other wore a floppy bush hat. Their faces were streaked and mottled the same as the man who had gotten out of the Rabbit. Both had holstered black semi-automatic pistols in black pancake holsters high on their right hips, and both wore black, fingerless gloves. To anyone seeing them drive by they were just another group of bow hunters headed for the mountains.

The shirtless man stumbled, and then half hopped, half limped to regain his balance. Reddish-blond hair swung lank against both sides of his face. A scraggly goatee and beard only served to emphasize how young he looked—younger even than he had looked when she had watched detectives interrogate him at the Sheriff's Department a few days ago.

She caught movement to her right. The elk had raised its head and was straining to look uphill. It was only a matter of time before one of them saw it.

The man with the sunglasses said something to the man with the MP5, and the man with the MP5 went back to the VW and opened the passenger side door. He walked around to the driver's side and, the hinges once again grating and squealing, opened that door, too. His head and shoulders disappeared into the interior of the car, and she heard music turned loud—Jack Johnson, it sounded like . . . something about banana pancakes.

She couldn't keep up with what was happening.

The sunglasses man reached down and pulled a thin black knife from a scabbard strapped below his knee, and put the knife to the young man's eye. Even over the music, she could hear the intensity in his voice.

The music was incredibly irritating. She didn't like Jack Johnson much in the best of times; she sure as hell could do without him right now.

The man wearing the floppy bush hat set up a spindly-looking tripod, small black camera mounted on the tripod.

She reached behind to the .44 in the nylon holster, but changed her mind and, hands shaking, pulled another arrow from the quiver attached to the bow and nocked it. Why she did that, she didn't know.

She had to do something. It felt like she was about to witness a traffic accident and there was nothing she could do about it.

She edged out of the stand of fir, keeping a giant larch between her and the men on road, and clipped the release hanging from her right wrist onto the bowstring. She turned sideways, one hand holding the bow and the arrow, the other hand clipped onto the bowstring, and leaned forward, peeking around the side of the larch.

The man with the sunglasses and baseball hat was dragging the young man by the hair over to a large rock at the edge of the embankment. All three men were intent on the young man, and had not yet noticed the elk, its head twisted up toward the embankment, mouth opening and closing in agony.

Jack Johnson coming out of the mouth of a mortally wounded elk, she thought.

The man with the silenced MP5 walked behind the man with the tripod, around behind the young man and the man with the baseball hat and sunglasses, to the edge of the embankment.

He stomped his right foot firmly into the embankment, his boot sliding part way down in a small cascade of rocks and dirt before it was firmly anchored, left knee on the edge of the embankment, head and shoulders tilted forward, the MP5 firmly in his shoulder, cheek on the stock, fat barrel aimed at the chest of the young man.

The man wearing the floppy bush hat stepped around the tripod and walked to the sunglasses man and handed him a long-barreled, western-style revolver of some kind, and then walked back behind the camera.

The sunglasses man said something, and the young man lowered himself to the edge of the rock.

The man spoke again. Louder. A command. She couldn't make out what he was saying over the music, but she could sure hear the venom in his voice.

The young man lifted himself with his hands and arms so that he could sit Yoga fashion and look out over the valley far below. His nearly hairless chest was sallow in the gray metallic light.

The sunglasses man placed the long-barreled revolver in the young man's hand. He said something, and the young man's hand tightened around the grips.

She tasted bile, swallowed hard.

The man grasped the young man's elbow with his left hand, and with his right twisted hand and pistol so that the barrel of the pistol was at the young man's temple.

He released the hand and elbow.

The barrel sagged toward the ground.

He leaned forward, close to the young man's ear, talking intently.

The song was winding down.

She didn't know what to do. She didn't know if this was real. If it wasn't real, then it would be over in a minute, and they would have made their point, whatever it was, and be on their way, leaving the young man to pick up the pieces of his sanity.

She didn't know if it was real or not because what they were doing was not so different from what she and her crew had done many times when they were inducting someone new into the gang.

She could try to put a stop to it. But if it *was* real, then anything she did to try and stop it could get her killed, too. Her bow and the revolver against two semi-automatic pistols and a submachine gun was no contest at all. Especially since the guns were in the hands of men who looked like they knew how to use them.

The music ended. Thank God for small favors.

The sunglasses man again bent the young man's arm and hand so that the end of the barrel was at his temple, shaking the arm and hand to make sure the gun was firm against the temple.

The man with the MP5 leaned toward the young man, finger on the trigger.

She felt her right eye tremble. This was going down. It wasn't a bluff.

The sunglasses man said something, and the young man sat up straight, his eyes locked on the far horizon.

The man cocked the hammer, the double clack of the hammer coming all the way back loud in the still mountain air. He made sure the young man's finger was on the trigger, and then stepped quickly back, well out of the MP5's field of fire, and out of view of the camera mounted on the tripod.

The man with the floppy hat bent toward the camera.

The young man stared straight out at the valley. Even from where she stood she could see the sadness and, worse, the acceptance in his eyes.

The sunglasses man picked up a large rock and threw it hard at the young man, hitting him in the back. The young man flinched and the gun went off, a gout of skull and blood and brain matter spraying from the left side of his head. He toppled backward off the rock.

The sound of the gunshot was like two boards slapped together, immediately absorbed by the trees and the mountain and the sullen sky. She could see the sole of one foot on top the rock, twitching to the beginning riffs of another Jack Johnson song.

The man with the floppy bush hat folded the tripod and put it over his shoulder and headed back toward the truck she couldn't see.

The man with the black sunglasses and baseball hat picked up a dusty pine branch and began to sweep footprints from the vicinity of the body.

The foot continued to spasm.

She turned, feeling the roughness of the bark against her back. Her heart hammered. She couldn't get enough air.

The sound of the gun going off reverberated in her mind.

The man with the MP5 shouted. She took a deep shuddering breath, and let it out slowly. He shouted again, and she forced herself to turn and peek around the trunk of the larch.

He was aiming the MP5 at the elk. The elk had somehow managed to stand. Head tossing spastically, it took a halting step toward the trees on the other side of the wallow. Muscles shivered in waves beneath its hide.

Sure as anything, someone was going to decide that this was all her fault, she thought. If not for the feel of the bark, the smell of the forest, her hand wrapped around the bow—

The man with the MP5 fired a long burst into the elk, the sound of the action cycling back and forth clearly heard over the sound of the music, brass spewing from the receiver, the rounds stitching the elk from shoulder to head, bits of antler and ear and hair flying off the head.

Nose first, ass up, like a camel kneeling, the elk folded to the ground, and fell over onto the arrows embedded in its side, its back toward her, head and neck twisted by one antler stuck into mud and grass.

And unknown to her, she snarled deep in her throat, green eyes turning dark, much as the eyes of a cat will turn dark when it is angry or about to kill something.

She stepped back, sideways to the tree and to the men at the top of the embankment, and pulled back on the release attached to her wrist, finger to the side of the release trigger, the effort of the 63-pound pull barely registering.

The cams let off, and she took a breath, exhaled half of it, and stepped forward and rotated the bow and the arrow and her upper body toward the man with the MP5. As he turned toward the other two men, his arm and hand holding the MP5 straight out and pointed back toward the elk, she centered the fifty-yard pin on his chest and squeezed the release, the arrow rotating between the trees and across the opening at 293 feet per second, the razor edges on the broadhead slicing into his body below the armpit, the entire arrow, fletches and all, disappearing, as if sucked into his body, skewering him from side to side, the three razor edges on the broadhead cutting through skin and bone and muscle, veins and arteries, emerging out the other side of his body below the shoulder.

She turned the instant the arrow hit, knowing she had just killed a man, elated and terrified at the same time, and fought her way though thick bushes at the base of the rock, vaguely aware that there was only music behind her, when there should have been shouts and commotion, around the rock to the elk trail, running as hard and as fast as she could, hurdling rocks and fall-down, hearing the whine of bullets ricocheting off the large rock, snicking into trees to her right, part of her mind horrified by the speed with which one of the other men had reacted to the flight of the arrow—a blur at best coming across the opening—and picked up the MP5 and changed magazines and fired in her direction. As she half-ran, half-leaped down a steep portion of trail, around another large rock outcrop, she heard un-silenced rapid fire from a semi-automatic—a .45 or .40 caliber from the sound—but by then she was over the brow of the hill and no longer in danger of being hit by a stray bullet.

She slowed, working her way down the trail with short, fast, choppy steps, knees up, like a football player running rows of tires, using the toes of her boots rather than her heels to dig into the loose dirt and rocks.

The trail began to go sidehill, and lengthening her stride and striking the ground with her heels she leaped off the trail and bounded straight down the mountainside, trying not to think about the jagged rocks and dead, broken branches sticking up like punji stakes out of the grass, through clumps of bushes, jerking her bow free of branches, forced to run back uphill for fifty meters, around a tangle of downfall that looked like a giant pile of pick-up sticks thrown onto the hillside, back down the slope between two rock outcroppings.

The hillside turned steep and, as she moved to her left onto the beginning of a south-facing finger ridge, the undergrowth cleared and the trees were larger, the space beneath them more open. Through the trees she caught glimpses of the valley far below. Ranches and farms. A network of roads and highways leading between small towns.

Three hundred meters or so above the cut in the road where the Nissan was parked she stopped and concealed herself behind a screen of trees and rocks, breathing hard, and looked back the way she had come. Far uphill she could see the coordinated movement of two men leapfrogging their way down the steep slope.

She put the bow down, and reached back and drew the four-inch .44 magnum, and stood, and holding the magnum in a two-handed grip fired six rounds in the general direction of the two men, the explosions numbing her ears, the recoil bruising the web of her hand and hurting her wrist. She opened the cylinder and with her left hand ejected the spent shells, and with her other hand unzipped a small pocket on the side of the buttpack belt and pulled out a speedloader. She rotated the pistol barrel down, inserted the speedloader and twisted the knob, the six rounds falling smoothly into the cylinder, and snapped the cylinder closed. The smell of cordite was sharp and acrid, alien in the clean mountain air. She put the speedloader in her pocket. And even though she knew she should not waste the time or the rounds she raised the gun two-handed and fired all six rounds, spacing them evenly in a tight arc across the upper slope, aiming ten feet above where the figures had gone to ground, hoping that despite the distance and the steep slope at least a few of the rounds had hit close enough to slow the two men.

She jammed the pistol back into the holster, snapped the thumb-break closed, picked up the bow, and ran downhill as fast as she was capable of running, out of control and unable to stop at the lip of the road cut, and jumped, flinging the bow toward the truck while she was in mid-air, landing feet slightly spread and knees flexed, rolling onto her shoulder across the weed-strewn road.

She continued the roll, coming smoothly to her feet at the far edge of the road, and turned and sprinted toward the truck, picking the bow off the ground and throwing it into the bed of the pickup.

As always, she'd parked the truck facing back down the road—a little piece of paranoia that right now she was glad she carried around with her.

She opened the door and climbed in, ignoring the butt pack that jammed her forward in the seat, stomach and chest nearly against the steering wheel, foot stabbing for the clutch, fingers searching for the key under the rubber gearshift boot, hurrying, but not hurrying so much she'd fumble the key.

She found the key. Inserted it. Muttered a plea that the engine would turn over on the first try. Turned the key. The engine coughed once—and then caught and held. She floored the accelerator and popped the clutch and the door slammed shut, the tires spewing gravel and rock and weeds, as the truck fishtailed toward the first corner. She shifted into second, and let up slightly on the gas, around the first corner before they could have gotten close enough to see the truck and the license plate, no matter how fast they ran downhill.

Something pinged inside the truck bed, and two holes appeared in the roof to the right of her head, the rounds impacting into the far corner of the dash.

Sonofa*bitch!*

Who *were* these guys?

The truck slewed around the next corner, a high cut on her left protecting her from any further shooting.

"Fuck you!" she screamed at the windshield.

She forced herself to think. If they'd covered that much ground downhill, it meant she would be off the mountain and lost in traffic long before they could climb back up the mountain to their truck.

Dead. He had to be dead or about to be dead, beyond help, or the two of them would not have come after her.

A simple meet. The exchange of information, that's all it was supposed to be.

When the frail young man—*she couldn't remember his name*—had described where the meet would take place, she'd realized that she knew the area and had decided to come herself.

The location had given her pause. She hit the steering wheel with the heel of her hand. *Of course it had given her pause.* There was no reason to meet at the end of a road in the mountains.

She felt tears of anger on her cheeks.

But this was Montana, *damn it!* What did reason have to do with it? Montanans, especially if they were not really from Montana, were nearly always infected with what Mrs. W called a Cowboy-of-the-Mind attitude. And among those who had lived outside the law before they came to Montana, there was no accounting for the unique kinds of drama and paranoia that the constant juxtaposition of wilderness and civilization produced in such people. She'd passed the location of the meet off to someone's idea of being all rugged and Ramboesque. Macho bullshit, that was all.

She hadn't taken any of it seriously—had instead used it as an excuse to get out of the office.

And then, driving in, a herd of about forty elk had run across the road, the herd bull near the front.

She'd been so excited to get out of the truck and up the hill to the wallow that she'd left the camera in the truck.

And then she'd accidentally kicked her cell over the edge of that rock.

And *then*, as if that hadn't been enough fucking up for one day, she'd lost her mind and shot one of the bastards with an arrow. With an arrow! She should have put a cap in his ass with the .44, that's what she should have done. And she shouldn't have stopped with just one of them, either. She should have capped them all.

In her mind she heard bullets whine off the rock, snick into trees to her right.

And she knew in her gut and without the shadow of a doubt that had she used anything but the bow they would have reacted even faster and she probably would not have made it out.

Kill them she might want to, but if she was brutally honest with herself—and this certainly seemed an appropriate time to be brutal—kill them she could not. Whoever they were, they were special. She was lucky to have put an arrow into one of them. She was lucky they were arrogant and had not bothered to check out the area first.

No. That's not right. They probably *had* checked out the area. The young man had run, and they'd had to go after him, chase him down, and bring him back. There had been no reason for them to check out the area again, because they already knew they had the place to themselves.

A jolt of adrenaline made her face feel hot.

She knew in her bones the man she had shot was dead. She could feel a connection to him the same as she'd felt a connection to the elk.

Fuck him. She'd do it again. Kill them all . . . They had no idea who they were dealing with. She'd find out who they were, and then she'd manufacture a way to . . .

But what to do now? By the time she found a phone and called nine-one-one, they'd be long gone and, as stretched thin as law enforcement was in this State, there'd be virtually no chance of finding them—especially not guys as well trained as those three obviously were.

A gout of blood and bone and hair flew from the side of his head, his face one big wince.

A simple suicide.

A young man depressed.

A young man listening to Jack Johnson , while he looked out over mountains and valley.

And put a pistol to his head and blew his brains out.

The pistol must have a hair trigger. He'd flinched when the rock hit him in the back, and the flinch had been enough.

Tears of frustration and rage ran down her cheeks. Fucking animals. Absolute fucking animals.

Call it in or not?

Her eyes glittered.

She didn't know who the three men were. Maybe with pictures it would be possible to ID them—though with the camouflage it would be problematic, even with the new software. But she had no pictures. She hadn't even seen their truck, let alone gotten the plate. And this being Montana, their truck was probably nothing if not generic.

In her mind she saw the arrow rotate lazily across the clearing and disappear into the camouflage material below his extended arm, and she felt the rear end lose traction and the truck slide ass end around the corner. She braked hard, the truck broadsiding to a stop sideways in the middle of the road.

She opened the door and holding on to the door handle leaned out and vomited.

She spit, and with her free hand wiped tears from her right eye. She spit again, and sat up. She closed the door, and put the truck in gear, and headed down the road at a more reasonable speed. All the dead people she'd seen, she'd never thrown up before.

She looked at the bullet holes in the dash, looked at the holes in the roof. *That close.*

She'd write it up. Wait for instructions.

The elk was still up there, she thought.

By morning there'd be birds and scavengers of all sorts. Bears knew what gunshots this time of year might mean. Hunters would probably find the young man's body within a day or two—most of the animals would stay away that long.

In her mind she saw the two figures working their way down the mountain. Apparitions more than men, appearing and disappearing in the trees and bushes and grasses, keeping an interval of about fifty meters, using bushes and trees and rock formations so that most of the time only one of them was in the open, each time closer than the last—like watching a movie that jumped frames. She'd never seen anyone come down a mountain like that. Like spiders on the carpet. But then she was a city girl at heart. She was no stranger to violence, but she was not trained for this kind of work. She'd messed up, no doubt about it. She should have delegated to people who knew what they were doing—to people who were as well trained as those two figures flowing down the mountain.

The young man's eyes were ineffably sad as he looked out over the valley, the pistol pressed to his temple.

Animals, she thought.

Well-trained animals.

She smiled, her eyes glittering.

Well, she had a couple of those, too.

1
Wolves

Three in the morning and Barney's vastly modified World Rally Blue Subaru bug-eye wagon droned through the long, curving sweep of the Interstate into Hellgate Canyon.

Joe Big Snake Person, aka Joe Big, yawned and hauled himself upright. Beyond the glare of the headlights, one wall of the canyon loomed massive and black, a faint tinge of indigo delineating the ridgeline against the lighter black of the sky.

Barney shifted gears and the sound of the engine dropped a couple of octaves.

Joe Big pushed the window button and the window lowered. The night smelled of pine and mown hay and of the river that coursed hidden off to their right in the murk of the canyon wall. He closed his eyes and leaned his head out the window, feeling the wind against his face, pulling at his braid.

"Kiss my ass, world!" he shouted into the wind.

Barney smiled. "That's the spirit," he said, and gently depressed the throttle, the whine of the turbo barely heard over the deepening tone of the exhaust. The g-forces, as the car tracked the long curve, pushed Joe Big against the door, his head out the window, braid stretched out and fluttering in the wind.

"Yee-aahh!"

Up ahead between the Interstate and the river the blurred outlines of a new condominium complex shone gray and white.

The Subaru decelerated as they came out of the curve and out of the canyon, headed for the Blackfoot.

Joe Big sat back, braid trailing down the right side of his chest. With both hands, he rubbed his face. "Ahh, damn," he said. "I love riding in this car."

"Buy a used one, and I'll help you modify it."

Joe Big slouched down in the seat. "If I had a car like this, I'd probably be dead in a week."

"You can jump out of perfectly good airplanes, from totally unreasonable heights, drive four-wheelers at speeds and in conditions that still give *me* nightmares, but you are afraid to drive this car . . ."

Joe Big stared at Barney for a moment, at Barney dressed in a black AudioSlave T-shirt, ratty old Grenade baseball cap pulled down to his ears. "You look like a cop trying to not look like a cop," he said.

"Thank you."

Joe Big leaned forward, peering into the darkness past the headlights, pensive, as he stroked the fine hair of his soul patch.

"Man . . ." he said.

"Yes?"

"I don't know what I wanted to be when I grew up, but I don't think it was this."

"Grow up?" Barney downshifted, and floored the accelerator, and the car leaped forward, engine winding up at an incredible rate, the torque snapping Joe Big back into the seat, head pressed against the headrest.

"You'll never grow up!" Barney shouted. He snapped the gearshift back, all four tires chirping, the car accelerating as if it were on rails. "GET SOME, MOTHERFUCKER!"

Joe Big laughed. "Help," he said.

A FEW MINUTES later, Barney pulled the WRX off the highway onto an old road overgrown with weeds and grass and a few tiny fir trees. "The beauty of all-wheel-drive," he said, as they bumped and scraped their way across a meadow toward a little bluff that overlooked the Blackfoot River.

"You hurt my neck again," Big said.

"So sue me."

"I'll have to see the acupuncture lady again. Hey, take it easy, will you? I'm not kidding."

The car coasted to a stop, and Barney killed the lights and the engine. "Whine, whine, whine. The only thing wrong with your neck is what's sitting on top it."

He opened his door and they could hear rapids, the slap of water against rocks invisible in the hard, moving blackness of the river.

He released his seat belt and leaned his head back against the headrest.

"I love it out here," he said. "When I worked uniformed patrol—graveyard shift—and things were slow, I'd come out here and sit and listen to the river."

Underneath the sounds of the rapids they could hear water against the riverbank—could feel the steep mountains of shale pressing in against each other, leaving little room for anything but the water and the highway and an occasional hay field or meadow at a bend in the river.

"Dark," Joe Big murmured, looking up at the dense mass of mountain. "Really dark in here."

He opened the door and got out. His movements as always smooth and controlled, leaving Barney with the sense that something had just uncoiled from, rather than merely exited the car.

Barney sighed, and climbed out. He picked his way through rocks, up onto a small mound, next to Joe Big. Black fast-moving water chuckled against the hollowed out embankment beneath their feet.

A breeze, inexplicably warm and moist, rippled up the canyon. The pines at the edge of the meadow shifted, creaking and groaning in the darkness.

"Hear that?" Barney said. "That's the ghosts of your ancestors, setting up to ambush the first Salish or Pend D'Oreille or Flathead that happen down this canyon." He picked up a small rock and threw it. They waited, but the sound of its splash was lost in the white water in the middle of the river.

Joe Big leaned back and spread his arms and took a deep breath, smelling the canyon and the trees and the river. He looked up at the black ridge etched against the star field.

"What're you doing now?" Barney asked.

"Getting in touch with my spiritual side, what do you think I'm doing?"

Barney laughed.

"Let's go do it," he said.

"GRAVEYARD," JOE BIG said as they pulled slowly back out onto the deserted highway. "I used to like graveyard, too. Only you and the assholes out and about late at night, early in the morning. Whole different world when the citizens aren't around to watch. Make up your own rules."

"Graveyard Rules," Barney said.

"Indeed."

"Indeed? Is that an Indian word?"

"Indeed."

The Subaru puttered around a sharp curve. Bright specks of emerald gleamed out of the darkness at the edge of the light from the headlights. Barney flicked on the brights and the aftermarket projector beams lit up three deer standing frozen in the gravel and on the pavement at the edge of the road. He downshifted and swerved out into the middle of the highway, the sudden whine of the turbo causing the deer to bolt from the road.

"You're under arrest," Joe Big shouted out the window. "Lurking with intent to commit mopery."

"Crazy deer," he muttered. "Never around when you want to shoot one, but the rest of the time they're everyfuckingwhere . . ."

"Might as well have one of those beers in the back," Barney said.

"We're almost there," Joe Big said. He pulled the SIG Sauer from the holster at his hip and pointed it out the window and, reaching across with his left hand, pulled the slide back far enough to see that there was a round in the chamber. He eased the slide forward and replaced the pistol in the holster.

The Subaru grumbled down a long, straight stretch, tall pines and firs crowding out of the shadows on both sides of the blacktop, making it seem as though they were driving through an alley in the forest. A metal guardrail unraveled out of the darkness. Squat metal posts flicked by like railroad ties seen in the shadow of a moving train.

"This part of the canyon just doesn't feel right," Joe Big said. "Even Blackfoot warriors didn't hang around in here long. But these days every little gulch and ridge has grown a rich-man's house. I have no idea how such people sleep at night. You can almost feel the blood—"

"Feel the blood." Barney said. "There you go again."

"You know what I mean, man. Spirits. Bad air. Whatever. Some of those valleys in Afghanistan and some of those islands in Indonesia and the Philippines had the same feeling."

Barney raised up slightly off the seat, and farted—a long wet sound. "There. How's that? That get rid of some of the bad air for you?"

"Man . . ."

"We're here," Barney said, his voice abruptly all business.

He turned the Subaru off onto a dirt road that led into a rest area, past a handful of paved parking spots designed for fishermen who wanted to stay overnight, the parking spots wide enough for a vehicle and a boat or raft trailer. His-and-her outhouses loomed at the periphery of the headlights. "Doesn't appear to be anyone here tonight," Barney said.

The Subaru cruised through to the far end, and then followed a little used, moss-covered track up the hill, across a small ridge, and up a rocky embankment, small rocks pinging off the undercarriage, onto a large well-constructed logging road.

Barney goosed the throttle and stayed on the clutch, sliding the rear end around, and followed the road back up over the same ridge they'd crossed coming up the hill, into a large, recently-graded turn-out about fifty meters wide by a hundred and fifty long, a massive deck of fresh logs and a dusty yellow Caterpillar tractor at the far end.

"Well, this is certainly fucked," Joe Big said.

Barney swung the Subaru in a tight arc, and backed in next to the deck of logs. Behind them at the edge of the cleared area was a rock about twice the size of the car, a large bull pine next to the rock. He shut the engine off.

The exhaust ticked and popped in the silence.

They could hear the faint rush of the river on the other side of the highway.

Joe Big released his seat belt, and opened the door, and got out. He walked a few steps away from the Subaru, and unzipped his fly. The ground was dusty, strewn with tiny pieces of branches crushed by logging trucks and by the big Caterpillar tractor. His urine made a plopping sound as it hit the thick layer of dust.

"It's enough to piss you off," he said, and snickered.

"What is?"

"Oh, I don't know. The fact that people back here were busy raping this place—building condominiums and houses for the rich and the retired, logging off these ridges—while we were dicking around in The Great Kitty Litter Box On The Other Side Of The World."

"You sound bitter."

"I *am* bitter."

"You did three tours, Big. Not counting ops you pulled in other parts of the world. You did the full five plus some with Force Recon. You got no one to blame but yourself."

"That's not why I'm bitter."

"So why're you bitter, then? Jesus, how long are you going to piss, anyway? You must have a bladder the size of a beach ball."

Joe Big zipped up. "I'm bitter because I'm supposed to be bitter, that's why I'm bitter."

Barney got out of the car, and walked around the back toward the big rock and the pine tree. "Only you could make that sound like perfect sense."

He stood looking into the darkness beneath the trees. He turned to Joe Big who had silently come up next to him. They both could feel it. Someone or something was in there.

"What it is," Joe Big said, "is your dad and mine, they went to Vietnam, and for ever after, beneath their humor and their good manners, they were angry and mean as snakes. They knew they'd been conned by their government into fighting a war in the wrong place at the wrong time for the wrong reasons. And now here we are, the products of *even more* fucked up wars."

"Are you saying we're supposed to be pissed off?"

"That's exactly what I'm saying. It's in our genes."

Barney laughed.

"I hope they don't bring that silly cunt with them," he said.

"Eye candy," Joe Big said. "You got to like that."

"Little Miss Earth Liberation Front . . ." Barney's voice trailed off as they heard the sound of a vehicle approaching, still about a mile away, and still on the highway.

"How do you want to work this?" Joe Big asked, still looking toward the darkness beneath the trees.

"Like we talked about. Play it by ear. See what happens. These guys are supposed to be friends. *Despite their paranoia and bad manners,"* he said, loud enough for anyone hidden in the trees to hear. "You stand behind the back end, and I'll stand on the driver's side next to the front fender."

They could hear the vehicle slowing for the rest area turn. A powerful engine. A truck with a modified exhaust system. Lights hit in and out of trees across the river as the truck negotiated the final curve before the rest area.

The lights disappeared and they heard the truck turn into the rest area and rumble slowly through the small campground. The sound of the engine deepened, the revs coming up as the truck turned onto the track leading from the rest area up to the logging road. They heard a brief bellow, the spinning of large tires as the truck fought for purchase on the logging road, headlights bouncing through the trees on the ridge.

A large pickup, abnormally high off the ground, yellow fog lights on the front bumper, headlights on bright, blasted around the corner.

"All right!" Joe Big said. "Get. It. *On*."

"Dipshits," Barney said.

The truck downshifted and roared into the other end of the open area, brakes locked up, gravel and dirt, dust and twigs and rocks billowing from the fat off-road tires. It stopped thirty yards in front of the Subaru, engine burbling like an inboard-boat motor.

Dust washed over them and over the Subaru, the yellow fog lamps baleful through the fog.

A man tall and big climbed out of the passenger side and walked up even with the front bumper. "That you, Barney? Big?"

"Sure 'nuff is," Barney answered.

Southern syrup, Joe Big thought.

"Y'all bring the green?" Barney asked.

"Well, hell, boy. You think we're out here this time of night to go fishing?" The big man laughed and went back to the cab. He opened the passenger-side door and pulled out a briefcase made to look like stainless steel.

"C'mon over here," he said. "See if this meets with your approval."

Barney walked from beside the blue Subaru to the big man. Joe Big moved up even with the rear door and the shotgun that was on the backseat, thumbs hooked over his belt. Barney was a tad over six feet tall, stocky and very fit, but he was at least a head shorter and fifty pounds lighter than the other man. Puny in comparison.

The man opened the briefcase toward Barney. Squinting against the glare of lights, Joe Big could not see what was in it.

The big man reached in and said something to Barney, and Barney's back went rigid, his arms perfectly still at his sides, and Joe Big, his stomach abruptly hollow, reached for the SIG, as two aircraft running lights, mounted high on the pickup's roll bar, exploded on, blinding him.

"Freeze, you Hiawatha motherfucker!" a female voice, high and shrill, shouted from his right, and a short, incredibly loud burst of automatic-weapons fire—an M16, he immediately knew—cracked and snapped and impacted into the deck of logs, the explosions echoing across the river and against the mountains. He raised his hands, and looked down at the ground. The dirt and gravel were sterile-white in the intense light. His eyes blinked rapidly.

"Put your hands on your head!"

The smell of cordite hung in the air.

He put his hands on his head, and heard the driver get out of the pickup and walk toward him, gravel crunching under heavy boots. Two nearly new hiking books halted in the dirt in front of him, the driver's body momentarily blocking the lights. The SIG was jerked out of the holster, a dull thud as it landed somewhere inside the Subaru.

"Up against the car," a nervous voice said, "You know how to do it," and giggled. "I always wanted to say that."

"The Intel chips are not here. We're not that stupid." Joe Big could hear the bluff in Barney's voice, his Cajun accent gone.

"Shut up, you fascist fuck!" the female voice screamed. *"Homeland Security slime!"*

"Homeland Security?" Joe Big said. He laughed.

"Left hand," the man said to him, "Give me your left hand." Joe felt the hard edge of a handcuff encircle his left wrist, heard the ratchet sound as it tightened. "Now the other one."

All the pickup lights except the fog lamps went out. Joe Big blinked, looking down at the Subaru's rooftop. White and red spots pulsed in front of his eyes.

"Turn around," the nervous voice said.

Joe Big turned, and leaned back against the car. "Harold. I thought that was you, man."

Harold was short and muscular, his head shaved bald to hide a receding hairline. White T-shirt. Oversize plaid shirt. Baggy jeans. A twenty-something computer-techno-freak-weight lifter with male-pattern baldness trying to look like a barrio gangbanger, Joe Big thought. In Montana, no less. "Whassup, Homes?" he asked.

Harold giggled.

"They never knew I was here!" the female voice said. "They got out and took a pee and never knew I was here!" A slim figure wearing a jumpsuit mottled with the brown and tan patterns of desert camouflage walked toward them from beside the big rock, her long dark-brown hair gleaming even in the yellow light. Joe could see the barrel tremble. Her eyes glittered with excitement.

"Desert camouflage," Barney muttered.

"Tanya." Joe Big grinned. "Don't you look fetching—"

"Shut up! Just shut the fuck up, Big!" The barrel of the M16 jerked toward him. "I heard you talking about me!"

Barney laughed, slumping against the bumper of the truck, arms behind his back.

Tanya walked over to Barney. "How about I shoot you in the balls?" she said, her voice quiet. "Then gut shoot you so that you take all night and most of the day to die? Wouldn't that just give you something to laugh about?"

Barney stopped laughing. "Fuck you, bitch."

"Enough," the big man said from the shadows next to the truck's bumper. "Well done," he said to the woman. He stepped over next to Barney and shoved him hard out into the space between the truck and the deck of logs.

Barney took two faltering steps, hands cuffed behind his back, but unable to keep up with the force of the shove, he fell, chin and chest skidding in the dirt and rocks and branch fragments. Dust swirled in the yellow light.

Barney rolled over onto one shoulder, arms behind his back, knees pulled up to his chest, and pushed off with his shoulder and rose to his knees.

"Laugh now!" Tanya said, and kicked him in the small of the back, slamming him chest down into the dirt again.

The big man walked over and grasped the chain that held the two handcuffs together and effortlessly picked Barney up. Joe Big could see pain ripple across Barney's face as his arms were pulled straight back, shoulder blades nearly touching. Barney staggered upright, pants and shirt and lower face dark with dirt.

Harold herded Joe over next to him.

The big man stroked his walrus moustache, one side and then the other, studying the two men. His eyes narrowed.

"You drank with us," he intoned. "You shared food with us." Freckles on his balding head and round face made his skin appear blotched and unhealthy in the yellow light. "You even smoked weed with us," he said to Joe Big.

Barney and Joe Big watched him.

Tanya's breathing was almost a pant.

Harold giggled.

"A warning," the big man finally said. "That be all this is."

Joe Big smiled.

"Tonight be our word against yours," the big man said. "And you know who be our lawyers." He paused, frowning at Joe.

He reached out and gently grabbed Joe's soul patch. "You asshole," he said, shaking Joe's face from side to side, and jerked hard, tearing most of the soul patch from beneath Joe's lip. "You think this is a game?" His other fist came up and twice in rapid succession smashed into Joe's mouth.

The big man waited a moment as tiny droplets of blood formed on the skin beneath Joe's mouth, and blood welled out of his lower lip, and then, one more time, hit Joe in the mouth—a short punch delivered with the kind of speed and force that only a boxer could deliver.

Joe Big's head snapped back. Blood arced into the yellow light.

"Oh," Tanya breathed. "Yes."

Joe Big's eyes were unreadable, obsidian in the sickly light.

"You don't look so fucking sleek now, do you?" Tanya said.

"Do you understand?" the big man asked.

Tanya reached forward and with the barrel of the M16 firmly rapped Joe's crotch with the flash suppressor. "Now would be good time to answer the man, lover."

Joe Big's head slowly swiveled to look down at the M16.

"We heard you," Barney said.

"Move back," the big man said to the woman. He grasped Barney and Joe by the shoulder, and turned them back-to-back. "Sit," he commanded, and pushed down, forcing them to sit on the ground, legs sprawled out in front.

Harold removed Barney's hat, and put it on.

The big man took the M16 from the woman. He pressed the flash suppressor against Barney's temple.

Barney jerked his head away.

The big man chuckled, and moved the flash suppressor in front of Barney's face, waving it gently, like a snake about to strike, barrel pointed toward the far end of the open area, and fired a burst, the muzzle blast and flash blinding Barney, causing his head to reflexively snap back, the back of his head thunking against the back of Joe Big's head.

The woman and Harold laughed.

The big man pressed the flash suppressor against Joe Big's head, pushing harder as Joe Big sat unmoving.

"Joe Big Snake Person," the big man said, and jabbed the flash suppressor several times against Joe's temple. "Blackfeet warrior. Ladies man. You don't look so big now, Joe Big."

Joe Big's neck muscles tightened, holding his head rigid.

The big man considered him for a moment.

"You're going to be a problem, aren't you?"

He stared at them for a moment.

"I ought to do you right now," he said. "Both of you."

"He won't be a problem," Barney said.

The big man's hand tightened around the M16's pistol grip, the large muscles of his forearm in sharp relief. He moved the flash suppressor fractionally above Joe's head and fired the remainder of the 30-round magazine, the barrel climbing as the rounds cracked into the darkness.

Cordite reeked in the yellow light.

The three of them stared down at Barney and Joe Big sitting rigid, looking straight ahead.

The big man abruptly wheeled. "Do it," he said to Tanya.

Tanya stepped forward, as the big man and Harold walked to the truck, and flicked open a large black knife. "Lean forward," she said to Barney, pushing him forward and down with her left hand.

She grabbed Joe's braid, and pulled it taut. And placing the blade sharp side up underneath the braid, with one, strong, upward slice, severed the braid from the back of his head.

She folded the knife and put it in the pocket of her jumpsuit, and walked around in front of Joe Big. She waved the braid in front of his eyes. Brushed it back and forth across his face. "How's it feel to be scalped?" she asked. "Too bad it's not your dick."

She put the braid in her pocket, walked to the truck, and climbed in. The engine rumbled to life. Headlights and aircraft lights exploded into white incandescence, and the truck backed up, bellowing, all four tires churning and digging, throwing rocks and pine needles, branches and dust over the two figures sitting in the middle of the large open area. The truck turned away, lights sweeping across the deck of logs and the Subaru and the trees, and accelerated to the end of the opening, and disappeared over the ridge, light again bouncing through the trees.

They sat silent, dust sifting down around them.

Rubber squealed as the truck reached pavement. They listened to its howl fade down the highway.

To the east, in the direction the truck had gone, the star-filled sky was turning deep violet above black mountains.

Their ears were numb and buzzing, but they could once again hear the river and the pines, smell the water and the forest. Smell the dust. All of it overlaid with the stench of cordite and the stink of their sweat: that sour sweat.

"I don't suppose you've got a handcuff key," Barney said.

Joe Big spit blood and dust from his lips and gums.

"In my back pocket."

2
Exoskeletons

The sky had lightened, the trees and buildings of the city become distinct and gray. Joe Big stared out the window, only dimly aware of vacant city streets sliding past, his eyes automatically checking alleys, cars parked on the street, all the little nooks and crannies where someone might hide an Improvised Explosive Device.

Going to be one of those early Fall days, Barney thought. Hot, dry, only a few clouds in the sky. One of those days made for fishing and drinking beer—one of those days that made it easy to remember why he'd traded Louisiana for Montana.

"We can't just go kill them," he said.

"Oh, yes, we can."

"No, we can't." Barney turned the Subaru into the alley, "This is not some sand-flea infested never-never land," and made a quick turn behind a screen of blue pines onto an ancient concrete driveway. Tree roots had cracked and heaved the concrete, and they bumped, nearly scraping bottom, to a stop. "This is America. This is where we live."

"All the more reason."

Barney shut off the engine, and leaned back, head against the headrest.

"Look," he said. "We've got options. But the options don't include killing them. Put all that out of your head right now."

Joe Big was silent. They both stared at the back of the old brick building.

Over a hundred years old, the house had been built for a well-to-do family. The top third or so of the big bay windows at the front and on the street side had leaded stained-glass murals. The rooms had hardwood floors and dark cherry and maple bookshelves and dressers built into the walls. But the bathroom and the kitchen on the ground floor had been remodeled to conform to Federal Government standards, the juxtaposition of Government Issue bland with the inherent warmth of old hardwood floors and crown molding and stained-glass windows a travesty to both of them.

"You're too—*we're* too pissed off, right now," Barney said. "We need to give it some time."

Many of the neighboring houses had long ago been converted into medical and legal offices. Across the street, hidden from their view by the screen of pines, and by ancient maples that lined every block in this, the old part of the city, was a one-story medical complex. Several blocks beyond that, rising above the maples, was the City-County-Federal office complex—a disconcerting combination of 60s functional and beautiful old domed courthouse.

Joe Big closed his eyes. The early morning breeze coming through the open window felt soft on his face.

Time.

Once upon a time, his grandmother and his father had both grown up in this neighborhood; he'd lived in it until the seventh grade.

As a child his favorite thing to do was to run the cracked and heaved sidewalks beneath the maples, through fall leaves, down to the courthouse, where he'd run along the top of the concrete wall that bordered the courthouse lawn.

Fat and tall that wall, when he was a little kid. Barely up to his shins now.

Run along the wall to the corner, and look up at the statue of the World War I doughboy attacking, rifle in one hand, grenade in the other.

Born to run. Always running.

"Look at that Chink kid run," old man Lavoie, a scrawny old French Chippewa-Cree, used to shout. "Lookit that Chink kid go."

He smiled to himself. His grandmother, all five-feet-ten inches of her, and a piece of work when she wanted to be, had finally one Fall day—a day exactly like this day was going to be, as a matter of fact—stomped over to old man Lavoie's fence and explained in language that any Marine Corps drill instructor could appreciate that her grandson was not a "Chink"; he was half Blackfoot.

"Humph!" old man Lavoie had said. "If you say so. But I seen a lot of Chinks in my time, and he sure looks Chink to me."

The wind shifted, and he could smell the lilac bushes that took up most of the lawn between the house they sat behind and the house next door.

The lilac bushes and the thick hedges of pine scattered throughout the neighborhood had been filled with secret tunnels and passages. He wondered if the tunnels and passages were still there, now that the neighborhood was no longer filled with children.

He eyed the house.

The back porch was new. Concrete steps on one side, the other side a long concrete ramp for handicap access, ugly black wrought-iron railing along the outside edge. Shiny new aluminum screen door.

"Fuck a bunch of time," he said out loud. "What are we doing *here?*"

"Our fearless Leaderette will want to know where the computer chips are. We need to put them back in the safe." Barney rubbed the stubble on the side of his face. He gingerly touched his chin. "And as long as we're here we might as well get the report over with."

"Why didn't they take the chips?"

"Either they believed me when I said we didn't have them—or they never wanted them in the first place."

Joe Big looked at him. "What do you mean?"

"Well, they sure seemed to know who we are, didn't they?"

He opened the door, and climbed out.

"What're you going to put in the report?" Joe Big asked, as he got out the other side.

Barney put his hands at the small of his back, and stretched. "As far as anyone else is concerned, they didn't show. We waited around. Drank some beer. Got in a pissing match with each other. Wrestled in the dirt." He rotated his torso from side to side. "You know. The usual."

"Why say anything?"

"Well, we won't, unless someone asks. Shouldn't be anyone here this time of the morning, anyway—unless your not-so-sweet Irish colleen stayed the night again."

"Wouldn't that just make the day complete."

"Man, I wish you two would get it over with. You're like two cats in heat, and it's starting to get on everyone's nerves." He paused his stretching, and eyed Joe. "Just please don't have any kids, okay?"

"It's impossible for different species to breed," Joe Big said, as he walked up the handicap ramp.

"The spawn of Alien verses Predator." Barney laughed.

Joe Big waited at the door for Barney. "You people really don't get it, do you?"

"*Us* people? Oh, you mean as in, us-people-who-don't-have-Injun-blood people. Us people who don't have a *spiritual* bone in our bodies."

"Fuck you. I never said that. I never even *think* that. You know what I mean."

"Know what you mean? Are you shitting me? I have no idea what you mean. I never know what you mean. In fact, *no one* ever knows what you mean."

"She's got a stone for a heart, man. I don't understand why the rest of you can't see it."

Barney opened the screen door. He unlocked the back door and pushed it open. "Who says we can't?"

"Who's there?" a female voice called from inside the house.

"Ah, fuck," Joe said. "I'll be in the car if you need me."

With both hands Barney grabbed him by the front of the sweatshirt and leveraged him into the kitchen. "It's us," he yelled. "The Lone Stranger and Pocahontas."

Joe Big turned toward him, but Barney lowered his shoulder and bumped him, forcing Joe to hop on one foot, arms flailing, into the center of the kitchen.

"How did it go—my God, what happened to you two?"

"We happened to each other," Barney said.

"I've got to take a piss," Joe muttered, and shouldered past her, down the short hallway to the bathroom.

Her hand went to her mouth, eyes wide. "Your hair . . ." she said.

Barney smiled to himself. Peas in a pod, he thought. Quinn McBride, tall and thin and athletic-to-the-max. Boston Irish to the core. But Black Irish, and looking Spanish with her long raven-black hair pulled back in a severe ponytail, green eyes watching Joe Big, sans braid, hair all raggedy and greasy looking, ghost toward the bathroom. Late 30s, early 40s, but looking mid 20s. Eyes and skin glowing with so much good health it was flat disgusting. Madame Fed. Their very own Leaderette. Every "i" dotted, every "t" crossed. Inherently bureaucratic, as only a Fed could be. But make no mistake, he reminded himself, she was also a product of some seriously mean Boston streets. According to the Sheriff, who'd heard it from his former buds in the FBI, she'd been a gangbanger when she was in her teens.

He watched her eyes narrow as she watched Big go into the bathroom. Having her around was sort of like having a water moccasin somewhere in the house, you just never knew where.

Better to tell her nothing, than to tell her something, he thought. Better to piss her off than to take care of it her way—the by-the-book way.

"What happened to his hair?" she asked, her green eyes boring into him—into his brain, looking around in there—the tone of her voice implying that, whatever had happened, it was his, not Joe Big's, fault.

He shrugged. "Not my place to say, ma'am." She was dressed to go running, shorts and tank top and jog bra under the tank top, her arms and legs long and tanned and lean. Not much need for the jog bra, he thought. She was built like a boy up top . . . well, that wasn't quite fair, but with the jog bra that's how she looked.

"What happened to your face and chin . . ." She put her hands on her hips. "Please tell me something did *not* happen to the chips."

Barney held his hands up, palms out. "The chips are fine. Nothing happened. Nobody showed."

She stared at him.

He put his hands in his back pockets. "We, ah . . . We stood around for hours on that logging road I showed you on the map." He smiled. "Well, it seemed like hours, anyway. You know how it goes. Bored out of our minds." He shook his head. "We had a few beers, and, um, well, Big, he started pissing and moaning, like he always does when he drinks too much . . ." He frowned at her. "I guess you don't know about me and Big when he drinks too much?"

"No. I don't."

He shrugged. "Well, like always happens, we started wrestling around. Him and his boxing. Me and my judo. And I accidentally threw him too hard and he . . . well, you know. Like that."

"What happened to his hair?"

"His hair . . . Yeah, well, you know, that's what started it. He started ranting about him being nothing more than an apple—you know, red on the outside, white on the inside—"

"I know what an apple is."

"And all of a sudden he pulled out that knife of his, and before I could do anything he'd sawed off his braid . . . Which kind of set me off, I'm embarrassed to say—not about him cutting off his braid, I don't mean that—but about him feeling so fucking sorry for himself . . . s'cuse the French—"

"You were wrestling around in the dirt, while Joe Big, one of the best knife fighters on the planet, had a knife in his hand?"

She walked across the kitchen, into his personal space, and peered, unblinking, into his eyes. He was a shade over six feet, taller than her, but she made it seem as if they were eyeball to eyeball.

He knew there was a reason why he liked small women.

"Bullshit," she said.

"No, ma'am." He tried to make his eyes guileless. "That's pretty much how it went down."

"Pretty much went down," she repeated, her eyes narrowing. "Please tell me again the chips are okay."

"The chips are okay."

She brushed past him and strode to the door and pulled it open. "Write it up before you leave."

"You got it, Boss."

She hesitated in the doorway, screen door held open, and turned toward him. "We both know how much control I *don't* have over you two," she said, her voice almost friendly. "But you lie to me on paper the way you just lied to my face, and I'll see to it that your Sheriff assigns you to the security detail at the stockyards." She smiled. "Where you will have a chance to shovel shit for real. Do I make myself clear, deputy?" Her eyes were like shards of green glass.

"Yes, ma'am. You surely do. And may I just say how darlin' you look in your cute little jogging outfit."

Her eyes flashed, and all expression left her face.

Uh-oh, he thought.

She considered him for a long moment, her face and eyes unreadable. She nodded, as if they had agreed to something, and turned and went out the door, careful to latch the screen door behind her.

Barney crossed his arms across his chest. He shook his head. "Well, that went well," he said to the empty kitchen. He looked around. "Where is he," he muttered. He dropped his arms to his sides. "Why is it there's never an Indian around when you want one . . ."

"Hey!" he shouted down the hallway. "Cowardly redskin. You can come out now."

IN THE BATHROOM, Joe Big stared in the mirror at the image staring back at him. *Joe Big Snake Person. Look at you.* Dirty hair lank and falling in ragged edges to below his ears and jaw. Dark eyes and long lashes and an inexplicably small nose—a Chinese nose. Swollen lower lip. Dried blood and a few wispy hairs where his soul patch had been. Pock marks on both cheeks from the bad acne he'd had in high school.

He hated his looks. With his soul patch gone and his hair like that, he looked more Chinese than Blackfeet. Old Man Lavoie hadn't been mean or racist; he'd simply been accurate.

His mother and father, all their clan had big noses, proud noses. And they were all big people. White guys always thought that a big Blackfoot must get his size and height from the white-side blood. But when white men first came to Blackfeet country, the average Blackfoot had been at least five-ten, the average white about five-five.

He'd always been the "pretty" one. Six-one and lean as a snake, when he was in high school. Not much heavier now. The fastest runner, the best boxer—more out of a sense of survival than anything else. In his family if you weren't big and tough, you had to be fast and sneaky—mentally as well as physically.

He ran water into the sink.

He'd had the braid since he'd gotten out of the Marines. Not sure why. *That bitch . . .*

He splashed water on his face, but the water only served to spread a film of oil and dust evenly over his face.

He hadn't felt like this since Afghanistan.

Holed up in the rocks for days, his only company creatures that featured exoskeletons instead of bones. A few snakes. Hot and dry to the point of desiccation during the day, freezing his ass off at night. Waiting. Watching. No need to say much because most of what he saw was beamed to a satellite or to a plane or to a drone orbiting out of sight and out of hearing. As easy as one, two, three:

Paint a target.

Ordnance arrived.

People ceased to exist.

One moment there was a file of men with rifles, some carrying machine guns and mortars and RPGs, and the next there was a flash and a ball of smoke and a delayed, rolling thunder, and when the thunder had passed and the smoke and dust had cleared, the file of men had disappeared.

Mr. Magic, the Afghani kid had called him, and the name had stuck. Joe Big Snake Person, a Force Recon sergeant sneaking around arid mountains and unbelievably humid island jungles, using magic to make people and things vanish.

His war hadn't much resembled his father's and his uncle's war in Vietnam, that was for sure. He'd only killed a handful with his knife. And even that had pissed off the Gunny. "Billions of dollars in technology and weapons systems, and you have to fucking use your knife, like some God-damn bush nigger . . ." The Gunny was a rail-thin black man from Detroit and, in the Gunny's words, "was thus permitted linguistic choices that were not otherwise afforded Wiggers and niggers." The Gunny insisted on addressing him not as Magic, or Big, or Chief, but simply as Person. "Person, where you at?" he'd ask, and chuckle to himself—some kind of personal joke associated with calling a person, Person.

He smiled at the memory of the Gunny. A piece of work the Gunny. Not up to the standards of his uncle, but no one he'd want sneaking up on his ass, that was for sure. He splashed more water on his face. Barney was yelling at him. Quinn must have departed for her morning run.

He wiped his face with a pink hand towel from the towel rack next to the sink. The bathroom was institutional—two shitters with gray, swinging doors, a single urinal with an automatic flusher, standard-issue mirror and sinks—but Quinn had tried to make it less institutional by adding potted plants on the window sill and real towels on a bamboo stand next to the sink. Some days the towels were pink, some days they were blue. Some days they even had flowers embroidered on the edges.

Well, why not? The whole world was out of its collective mind, why should this place be any different?

His eyes were puffy from the dust generated by that truck. *"That big motherfu—"*

Don't think about it.

Barney was right. Give it some time. Keep things in perspective.

He wet one end of the towel, dabbed at his lip.

Perspective.

The Gunny had trained them to think about perspective. The perspective of the people they were tasked to kill: tough mountain people fighting the latest in a series of foreign invasions that stretched back through all of recorded history. He didn't understand them. Didn't want to understand them. Didn't understand their politics or their religion or their culture. Didn't want to. *Perspective is not the same thing as understanding, the Gunny had explained. Perspective is all about balance. Perspective is about seeing your weaknesses through someone else's eyes. Proper perspective is what will keep you people alive.*

He'd scoffed. They were there to find and kill the kind of people who flew airplanes into towers full of civilians. The only perspective he needed was what he saw through the scope on his sniper rifle.

A classic case of find them, fix them, and kill them. Except that most of the people he watched—and killed—had never been to a city, never been on an airplane. They could field strip and clean their weapons in the absolute darkness of a cave, but most had never seen a flush toilet or a sink like the sink in front of him that, government issue or not, had hot and cold running water—so much water, in fact, that you could waste as much of it as you wanted to waste.

He glared at himself in the mirror.

Counted coup on him, that's what she'd done—they'd done. It hadn't been spur of the moment, either. They'd planned it. Scalp the Indian: what a great story. *Where was his braid now? Hanging on the wall above the fireplace?*

"Hey! Dickhead! Stop abusing yourself, and get your ass out here."

Joe Big stared at his image in the mirror.

"C'mon. I want to get out of here before she gets back."

"All right, all right. Damn . . ." He turned away from the mirror. "You sound like my grandmother, sometimes."

"What?"

Joe opened the door. "I said you sound like my grandmother sometimes."

Barney stepped back away from the door. "You missed the part where I told our fearless Leaderette how good she looked in her jogging togs."

"Togs?"

"Yeah, you know, her . . . fuck you."

Joe headed for the dining room. "No, fuck *her.* We don't have to take any shit from her."

The dining room had been converted into office space, with three gray metal desks arrayed in a big L along two walls, an expensive-looking copier/collator/fax machine just inside the large opening connecting the dining room to what used to be the living room—now Quinn's office. Potted plants and flowers adorned the window bay and the tops of small wooden tables and nightstands scattered around the room. A large plasma screen connected to the Internet and to the computers on the desks was mounted on the wall opposite the desks. A cork bulletin board on the wall next to the screen held the usual assortment of government announcements and regulations. Dried wildflowers were fastened to the top corners of the bulletin board.

"Yes, we do," Barney said. "We have to kiss her ass because the Sheriff likes her."

"Yeah, he likes her because she's a Fed, and he used to be a Fed."

"And because she can shoot, and he can shoot."

"But she's breast-challenged, and he likes big ta-ta's."

"Hmm," Barney said. "I never thought about that. Old guy that he is, the Sheriff probably needs something softer than her tough-as-beef-jerky body to lay his weary head on."

"You're comparing a body like that to beef jerky?"

"I'm hungry. What can I say?"

Joe Big pulled a chair out from behind one of the desks, and sat, legs sprawled to the front, arms akimbo at his sides. "Did you put the chips in the safe?"

Barney took a seat behind the desk next to Joe, and booted up the computer. "I thought maybe we'd hang onto the chips for a few days. See if anyone shows up to take them away from us."

Joe swiveled his head to look at Barney. "You think someone around here is talking to them? Is that what you're saying?"

Barney shrugged, and began typing. "Only one way to find out. For sure *someone* is talking to them."

Joe Big stared at him.

Barney glanced at him, and then back at the computer screen. He continued to type. "It's only about seven hundred fifty thousand dollars worth of chips. The Feds spend that much every day on toilet paper."

"You think maybe it's someone in the Sheriff's Department?"

"Only the Sheriff knows we've been assigned to this so-called Anti-terrorism Task Force. Everyone else thinks we're working undercover narcs."

"So someone here, then?"

"Maybe . . ." Barney stopped typing and peered at the screen. "How's this sound: Deputies J. L. Lambier and J. Big drove to a deserted logging road off Highway 200, near mile marker 27, at approximately 0230 hours, 23 June, to meet members of a local group suspected of terrorist/drug cartel/ultra right-wing ties (see report #46905, 10 May). Members of the group did not show up. Officers RTB, returned to base—I thought I'd better explain RTB to our Federal comrades. Officers did not return Intel computer chips to safe because suspects may have continued interest in acquiring said chips. Officers went home at 0721 in the morning."

"In the morning is redundant."

"Hah. Redundant R Us."

"I don't remember writing a report on these people."

"I threw that in to make it look professional."

The copier across the room came to life, and a sheet of paper silently came out the top. Joe Big stood and walked over to the copier and retrieved the paper.

"Sign it," Barney said.

"Sign it, sign it," Joe Big said, making his voice sound like some sort of jungle bird. He laid the paper on the desk, and picked a pen out of a cup full of pens, and signed the paper, and handed the paper to Barney.

"What's this?"

"My name in Chinese."

"Sign your real name, asshole. You want to upset your girlfriend?"

"That's the realest name I got at the moment . . . and stop with this whatever it is you think is between us."

Barney signed the report with a huge illegible scrawl. "If it's you and it's female, there's always something—"

"Way to go with the signature, Barn. Nothing like fostering inter-agency cooperation and all that."

"Ah, who gives a rat's ass," Barney said. "What's she going to do? Send us back to the Sheriff's Department? The sooner the better, if you ask me."

"Well, we don't want to go back until we—"

Barney held up his hand. "Until we get some sleep," he said, pointing to his ear and looking around the room.

Joe Big's eyes darkened as he caught Barney's meaning.

Barney shut off the computer, and stood. "Let's get out of here," he said, and without further conversation they walked down the hallway, Joe Big trailing Barney, and went outside, down the steps to the car.

"Is that beer still cold?" Barney asked, as they climbed into the car.

"Should be." Joe reached behind the seat and opened a small plastic cooler on the seat next to the shotgun. He fished out a couple of long-necked bottles, other bottles tinking and shushing against the remaining ice and each other. He sat forward, the bottles dripping water and ice, took a church key and popped off the tops. "Moose Drool," he said. "You must of thought there was going to be cause for celebration?"

"Shows you how smart I am."

The sun was over the top of the pines, the Subaru about to lose its shade.

Both of them took a long drink. "Ah, damn . . ." Barney said. He started the car, and backed out of the driveway.

"What are we going to do now?" Big asked.

"What we are going to do now is we are going to go over to your place and pick up some fly-fishing gear and then drive out to Bear's place. Drink a few more beers and fall asleep in the shade of a tree. Wake up and catch enough fish to eat for dinner. And then probably get drunk and crazy and shoot at pinecones and shit so we won't do anything rash that we might regret later. How's that sound?"

"Sounds good."

Barney put the car in gear and they headed down the alley to the cross street.

Joe Big drained his beer.

"How'd you explain my hair?" he asked.

3
Not A Chance

What did you do to your hair?" she asked.

Joe Big opened his eyes. Miss Mouse, the cat, dusty-gray even on her paws, sat sharing the windowsill with four or five dead flies and a precarious-looking pile of books. Dust motes floated in yellow-white beams of sunlight.

Miss Mouse yawned, exposing her teeth and throat, and stretched, careful of the dead flies.

"I thought you had to work all week," he croaked. He cleared his throat.

"The door was wide open." She was behind him, fooling around with something in the dresser. "Did you know someone shot a hole in your television?"

"Barney."

"*Barney* shot a hole in your television?"

"He was watching the news. What are you doing?"

"Oh, well, that explains it—watching the news."

"That's my private stuff you're digging through?"

"Why is it men always hide stuff in dresser drawers?"

Miss Mouse jumped from the windowsill and padded across the hardwood floor, wending her way between books and a pile of newspapers to the edge of the mattress.

"Go away. Don't even think about it."

She stopped whatever she was doing in the dresser. "I beg your pardon."

"Mouse," he said. "I'm talking to Mouse."

Miss Mouse reached out a paw and gently tapped him on the cheek.

"Leave me alone. Go play in the traffic."

"Someone named Tanya called at the hospital this morning."

An image of Tanya dressed in desert camouflage, black knife in her hand, flashed through his mind. He groaned and rolled over and sat up, sheet gathered around his waist.

He held his head in his hands, elbows on knees. His mouth tasted of stale beer and elk sausage and—something else. Pickled beets, maybe? He couldn't remember if he'd gotten around to taking a shower . . . probably not.

"What day is it?" he asked.

"Wednesday. You don't know what *day* it is?"

Day before yesterday, he thought. Man, he'd never done that before. Not even after his last tour in Afghanistan.

"I can't believe you cut your braid off."

"I didn't." Miss Mouse crawled under the sheet and lay down next to his thigh. She started kneading his skin with her claws. "Ouch. Damn it, Mouse."

He reached under the sheet and with one hand grabbed her front paws and pulled her out. He scratched her belly, and then swung her off the bed, toward the doorway. She landed lightly, and sauntered toward the doorway, as if that's what she'd planned to do all along.

He looked up.

She was still wearing her nurse's uniform, soft blond hair in a new cut—a boy's cut. Her blue eyes watched him. She brushed a lock of hair away from her forehead, a tiny furrow between her eyes—the same little frown she got when she started to really get into the sex. Only right now she didn't look like she had sex on her mind. Just the opposite, as a matter of fact.

He cleared his throat again. "Who's Tanya?" he asked.

She held up what looked like a black wallet. His sheriff's badge set into thick leather glinted next to the laminated ID card. "She's the one who told me about this."

The feeling in his stomach melded perfectly with the sour taste in his mouth.

"I wanted to tell . . ." His voice trailed off. She was holding the baggie filled with his medals and badges and wings. Damn, he'd forgotten he'd put it in the dresser. He'd meant to give that stuff to his mother.

She dug into the baggie and held up a pair of wings.

"Are these what I think they are?"

"Jump wings. Yeah."

"But you wouldn't go skydiving with me?

"I was afraid—"

She held up a badge. "And this?"

"It's, uh, it's a special kind of dive badge—scuba diving. You have to die and your partner saves—"

She held up a medal.

He sighed. "Navy Cross."

"So you saw combat." It was a statement, not a question. "You killed people." Another statement.

She held up his Purple Heart.

"Stop it," he said.

She turned and dropped the baggie and the badge holder into the dresser drawer and gently shut the dresser drawer.

"A cop," she said to the dresser. "And my father was worried that maybe you were a drug dealer. And not only a cop, but a—"

"Marine," he said.

"A Marine," she repeated. She whirled around. *"A fucking Marine!"* she shouted. "What about non-violence and Native American spirituality and . . . and . . . talking about how you'd like to join the Earth Liberation Front, and—"

"Calm down," he said. "Calm down for a minute, will you? Let me explain, okay? It's got nothing to do with you—"

"Nothing to do with me!"

"I didn't mean it that—"

"Oh, go take a shower." Her eyes filled with tears, and she half-ran for the door. "You stink."

"—way," he said to the empty doorway. He stood and wrapped the sheet around his waist, forgetting for the moment how hung over he was.

"Shit," he muttered, and hurried to the door, "Shit. Shit. Shit." He stepped on a corner of the sheet, and nearly fell. He gathered the sheet around his waist and ran into the living room, through the open front door, onto the porch of the old farmhouse. Her new yellow convertible, a VW Bug, was pulling out of the yard, thumping across the metal cattle guard.

"Hey!" he shouted, running down the steps, one hand holding the sheet up. "Wait . . ."

He caught a glimpse of her blond hair, one arm straight up in the air, middle digit extended. He watched as the car turned onto the county road and quickly built speed, disappearing behind a cloud of dust—a tan and sandy fog that hovered over pasture and trees long after he could no longer hear the car.

Miss Mouse purred and rubbed against his leg.

He knotted the sheet around his waist and bent down and picked up the cat, and slowly walked back up the steps.

"You must be hungry," he said, scratching her neck and chin. "You don't look hungry. What've you been eating, anyway?"

TERRORISTS, BARNEY THOUGHT. *Al Qaeda assholes and assholettes. Abu Sayyaf, The Taliban. IRA, ELN, Al-Jihad. Aum Shinrikyo, Tupac Amaru, ETA. Tamil Tigers, Shining Path, Aryan Nation, ELF—the list went on and on, names added or deleted on a daily basis. Old names mutating into new names. New names claiming to be old names. Killers of all sorts and for all reasons. Domestic, foreign, it made no never mind. Their reasons for being become excuses. Their excuses become reasons. What it boiled down to is a whole lot of seriously bent people killing what they could because they can.*

He was sitting in an aluminum lawn chair that he'd found on sale at the hardware store, the orange and white plastic webbing new and clean and garish against the green of the front lawn and the yellow leaves of the maple tree. Beer cans crushed and bent littered the grass around the lawn chair.

Most of them watched too many videos, read too many of the wrong books, learned from the wrong people—hah! Listen to him, all high and mighty. Like him and Big and others like them hadn't listened to the fucking President of the United States and his—what did Big call them? Minions? That was it, minions. Low-life, no-talent, no sense of honor or duty or country minions. Damn good thing he hadn't applied for the Secret Service like some of his buds had. He felt sorry for those guys now. No fucking way he'd stop a bullet for any President, never mind for a minion . . .

In the distance, thunder rolled like an air strike. Heat lightning cracked, sounding like the vicious slap of a round outbound from an Abrams tank. The sky overhead was clear and blue, but across the valley a wall of darkness encroached on the sky, huge, white cumulous clouds growing out the top, boiling higher as he watched. *Well, this particular bunch of homegrown assholes don't know it but movie time is about over. He'd never seen Big this pissed off. Actually, he wasn't all that far behind hisownself. Cutting off Big's braid had been over the top; he'd felt it almost as if it had been his own.*

Yellow-gold leaves rustled above his head as a warm, dry wind swept through the trees. Empty beer cans skittered across the lawn, rattled against the fence. A skiff of autumn leaves blew out of the trees across the street.

Sitting in a metal lawn chair under a tree is probably not a good place to be in a thunderstorm.

He laughed out loud and reached inside the cooler next to the lawn chair for another beer.

A gust of wind blew leaves and bits of branches out of the tree and pushed the cooler up solid against the lawn chair. "Thunder and lightning," he muttered, the beer momentarily forgotten in his hand, as he stared up at the sky, fascinated by the fast-moving clouds, heedless of the wind and the debris swirling down the street and across the lawn.

The sound of the wind through the huge old maples was like the sound of a fast-moving river—a sound that reminded him of another time . . . of another storm and another river . . .

He'd been holed up at the top of a low ridge, in a pile of rocks somewhere on the Pakistan border—a set of coordinates on the GPS, was all. Dark clouds encroached on cloudless blue sky, the sound of thunder, the crack of lightning, the roar of the wind across the top of the ridge tuned to the rumble and crack of ordnance hitting the column of Taliban.

The Taliban column had been directly below his position on a road that meandered next to a white-water river rushing down the center of the rock-strewn valley. Hockey pucks—miniature smart bombs—and large dumb bombs impacted pickup trucks. Heavy metal sounds. BLANG BLANG BBBLANGG. *Silver and brown pieces of truck and meat-red pieces of people arced through dust and smoke and flame, some of the pieces splashing into the river, the splashes quickly lost in the white water.*

He smiled up at the fast-moving clouds.

The explosions had been eerie and wonderful at the same time, products more of the black storm that was enveloping the valley, than of anything unleashed by man. A natural event, rather than the manipulations of some Air Force pilot or a teenage kid with superior gaming skills sitting in a building in Florida or Saudi Arabia or on a ship in the Indian Ocean.

"Hey," Joe Big had called from the rocks above him. "Special Forces guy. You got someone coming to visit you—your eight, man, about ten meters. That small cave." And with his silenced pistol, Big had shot the snake in the head—a saw-scaled viper, the worst of the seven poisonous snakes with no known anti-venom in Afghanistan. Dark-edged whitish spots along its backbone. Yellowish underside. No doubt about it. A saw-scale. He didn't know it then, and not until he'd worked with Big for a while and they'd gotten to be friends, but it had really bothered Big to shoot that snake. He and his people had a special thing for snakes. He wasn't sure exactly what. They didn't talk about it much. Only that it went way back to some ancestor, a warrior wounded and hiding in a shallow cave from a revenge party of Crow. Apparently, the cave had been home to a den of rattlesnakes, and the Crow had believed that no human could hide in there without being bitten by the rattlesnakes.

Well, myth or not, it was a good story—one that explained why Big had felt bad shooting that snake.

'Course a saw-scale was not a rattlesnake, and Afghanistan sure as hell was not eastern Montana.

The wind buffeted his chair. He smelled rain. Raindrops splatted against his forehead and stomach and bare legs, and before he could sit up became gray sheets of water that hissed and pocked through the tree above him and bounced against the pavement. It was like lying in a cold shower. He popped the top on the beer and took a long drink.

Lightning cracked-smashed down the street, the flash only a second behind the sound. *Close*, he thought.

But not as close as mortar rounds searching for him and the rest of the team hidden in the rocks and scrubby bushes and trees, the rounds impacting only feet away, slivers of rock and metal whizzing through the air.

The rain was already letting up. Cars splashed past, drivers and passengers pale ovals looking through steamed windows at him lying in the lawn chair, the sound of thunder and the occasional crack of lightening moving off across the valley.

The mortar rounds had moved away, too, searching other likely spots where the team might be hidden. Below and on finger ridges he could see figures in baggy pants and loose jackets and old worn bits and pieces of uniforms, AKs and RPGs and a few long-barreled rifles of some sort. He could hear Joe Big talking. And just like that in a mix of flash and roar and heat most of the hillside below disappeared into smoke and dust. He could hear screams and panicked shouting beneath the ringing in his ears. The sound of the voices had reminded him of being underwater and listening to people talk on the dock above. More ordnance impacted below and to the sides. And then there was only the sound of Joe Big's sniper rifle firing—a three-or-four-second cadence. Fire. Eject the brass and jack a round into the chamber. Acquire target. Fire. Eject the brass and jack a round in the chamber . . .

Joe Big become a sniping machine.

The rain stopped completely, and for a moment there were no cars and it was quiet.

Drops of water fell from the maple tree onto the lawn and onto the chair and onto him.

No rain drops then. The sky had produced only dust and smoke and the stink of death. Adrenaline that tasted like that dead viper looked. More Taliban had appeared out of the smoke and dust and a handful had appeared on the ridge above and behind them and someone else, not Big, had called in a strike on the ridgeline and on the same area already hit once in front of them. But by then the rocks were infested with Taliban shooting at them and at each other, at anything that moved, and an RPG round had hit in the rocks near him, shrapnel—mostly rock shards—stitching his right leg from mid-calf to ass, and he'd seen a turbaned figure stand up on a rock and take aim at Big who was busy shooting people to his front, and he'd put half a clip into the figure, killing him before he could fire.

Barney looked down at the scars on his knee. His senior year, he'd been first-team All-State linebacker, and he'd had scholarship offers, but like Big, Nine-Eleven had pushed him into the military—the Army, not the Marines. He wasn't that dumb. Rangers, because his father had been a Ranger in Vietnam, his grandfather a Ranger at

Normandy. Rangers to Special Forces to sitting in a lawn chair in Montana. He laughed, and took a drink of beer.

It had been a mess, that fight. The first time he'd worked with Force Recon. They'd lost two men out of seven—he was the extra man on a six-man team—and everyone had been wounded, one guy with his entrails in the sand and across rocks. Entrails that looked a lot like that viper after Big had shot it. They'd had to ferret out every single one of the remaining Taliban, some of them not much more than boys—children, if you wanted to get technical about it, and if it had been America and not Afghanistan. The rocks and tiny caves and scrubby brush had made the fight feel oddly like fighting in an urban environment. They'd had plenty of fixed-wing and helicopter support, and the Marines hadn't been shy about using it, but for the most part it had been a long afternoon and evening and night of playing cat and mouse in the rocks. It got easier after dark because with their NVDs they owned the night. What he remembered most about it was being so damn thirsty.

He took a drink of beer.

None of his wounds had been major, and he'd been mobile enough to fight, but his wounds had seeped blood, and the blood had attracted flies and bugs, and that combined with the heat and dust and the stench of cordite and sweat and fear and dead bodies and pieces of dead bodies had made him thirsty in a way that would probably stay with him forever.

He drank again from the can of beer, a long thirsty drink this time.

He'd never admit it to Big, but those Force Recon Marines had been good, no doubt about it.

An approaching pickup, obviously with a defective exhaust, broke into his thoughts, and craning his neck around he could see the truck down the street, faded orange and white, front bumper skewed upward on the passenger side—a 1984 Chevrolet half-ton, Joe Big wearing a white baseball cap, leaning out the window and waving with both hands, as the truck went by.

" . . . beer!" he heard Big shout over the noise of the truck, as the truck continued down the block.

It looked and sounded like one of those Technicals that bad guys all over the Middle East used, Barney thought. Beat up pickup trucks with a machine gun mounted in the bed. All Big's truck lacked was the machine gun.

The truck made a U-turn and came back, a trail of blue smoke in its wake, and stopped at the curb in front of him.

Joe Big climbed out of the truck, and slammed the door shut.

"Grenade!" Barney shouted, and threw the empty can at the pickup.

Joe Big spun, and ran behind the truck.

Barney saw his head peek above the truck bed, and Joe Big vaulted into the bed and stood crouched, looking fierce, arms spread like a wrestler.

"Gadzooks!" he shouted. "Surrounded by Insurgents," and dropped to his knee, tearing at something in the bed of the truck, colored bits of cardboard arcing into the air. "Gooks, Ragheads, Politicians, Anyone Who Works For The IRS—you'll never get me!" And began lobbing full cans of beer at Barney. "Die, Crusader scum!"

Barney blinked as the first can arced through the air and smacked the aluminum support next to his elbow. Three or four more were already high in the air, arcing down toward the maple tree and him. "Hey," he yelled and tried to catch the cans. Full cans of beer fell out of the maple tree, slicing through the leaves, thudding into the ground around him, hitting the chair. "Ouch. God damnit, Big. You crazy fucker . . ."

"Mortars!" Big shouted, and Barney fell sideways, overturning the chair, and scuttled on all fours behind the trunk of the maple tree. "Allah Akhabar, infidel spawn!" Cans thunked off the other side of the tree, one of them popping open, hissing and spurting foam into the grass.

Joe Big leaped out of the truck bed and ran zigzag across the lawn and rolled onto his shoulder, and in one seamless motion scooped up a beer in mid-roll and came to his feet and popped the top. The can spurted beer and foam. He took a long, satisfying drink, beer running down his hand and arm and onto his T-shirt. He belched, as he walked over to Barney's tree.

"Man, you sure looked silly out here on that lawn chair in the rain," he said, leaning against the tree, looking down at Barney wet and bedraggled, grass stain on his forehead and cheek. "Lucky I came by."

Barney stood. He rubbed the top of his thigh where it had been hit by a can of beer. "Gadzooks?" he asked.

"Yeah, I heard it on the radio. You know: my radio that used to be a television? The one you put a nine-mil through? Now that it's a radio, it's only natural that I pay more attention to what gets said."

"Someone on television said Gadzooks?"

"Mouse likes the old movie channel."

"You're weird, you know that. Even for an Indian, you're really fucking weird."

"Well, it's nice of you to notice. But how weird would you say I was if I sat through a thunderstorm in a metal lawn chair under a tree?"

Barney blinked.

"Here," Big said, and handed him a beer. "In case lightning strikes twice."

Joe Big squinted toward the sunset. They were still out in the yard, Big sitting propped up against the maple tree, Barney lying in the lawn chair, the dark lenses of his wrap-around sunglasses refracting the bright reds and yellows of the setting sun. Overhead the sky was a deep azure blue.

"I need another beer," Barney said. Beer cans were strewn beneath the tree like so many metallic apples.

"The very first person I shot was a woman, I ever tell you that?" Joe Big said. "Shot her right through the head."

"I said I *need* another beer."

"There was a file of people and everyone had their faces covered because of the dust, and she was carrying an AK-47, and—"

"Earth to Big Snake Person. Barney needs a beer."

"—I squeezed the trigger, and moved on to the next person in line, and squeezed the trigger, and, well, you know the drill."

"If this is going to be a long story, I'll be needing a beer."

Joe Big took a drink of his beer. A trail of fat little clouds lit yellow and gold on the bottom were caught in the sunset. "The Voice tasked us to go down and check them out after we'd killed everyone. Someone unwrapped her headgear and there wasn't much left of her head. They told me later that she wasn't local; she was some Al Qaeda—"

Barney groaned and got up off the lawn chair. He walked toward a beer can tilted into the grass. "It looks like an Easter egg hunt out here," he said. He stooped and picked up the can and stood and shook it, as if shaking a can of paint, and walked over to Joe Big, and popped the top, spraying Joe Big with beer. "Gives the big bad warrior dreams, does it?"

Joe pulled up the bottom of his T-shirt and wiped beer spray off his face. "Well, that's the problem. It doesn't."

Barney walked back to the lawn chair and sat down. "And you think it should? Why should it? She would've been happy to light up your ass, that's for sure. And not just you but everyone you know. A woman like that, she was probably being groomed for big things."

"That's exactly what the Men in Black told me."

They were silent for a while, watching the horizon turn blood red, the little clouds became dark clots above black mountains.

"How do you suppose those assholes found out who we are?" Barney asked.

Joe Big snorted. "Oh, I don't hardly think they know who we are."

"You know what I mean."

"I'm just saying . . . whoever told them about us didn't tell them about us . . . if you know what I mean?"

"I wasn't looking at it that way, but you're right."

"Maybe someone set them up to bite off more than they can chew," Joe Big said.

"Which would mean . . ."

"Which would mean that someone is setting us up to do the chewing."

"Someone wants us to go off the Reservation, you mean?" Barney smirked. "Get it? Go off the—"

Joe Big picked up an empty can and threw it at him.

Barney let the can bounce off his shoulder, and shifted in the lawn chair. "I've got a bad feeling about this," he said.

"No shit."

They were silent, watching the sunset as it began to die.

"I read this book my old man had about the Vietnam War," Joe Big said. "Pretty good book, actually. Kind of like it was written more for today than back then. The guy who wrote it said the guys who fought in Vietnam were acting out a movie. And I thought, man, that can't be right. I mean, sometimes, maybe. But I've never seen, and I'm pretty sure the guys who fought the Vietnam War never saw a movie about the shits, or about sitting and waiting and watching for so long it seems like time is no longer part of the universe. You hear what I'm saying?"

"I hear it."

"I'm talking about Luke the Gook then, and Rashid Raghead now. Blowing the shit out of everything and everybody. And us returning the favor. Brains and blood and *really* fucked up bodies rotting in the sun. I'm talking about the smells. What it sounds like to hear a bullet hit someone you know."

"What's all that got to do—"

"But *we* sure have seen a lot of movies, haven't we? We grew up on movies and video games that were all about war. World War II. The Korean War. The Vietnam War. Man! We have seen a lot of movies!" He stood and started pacing back and forth under the tree and in front of Barney, gesturing with the can of beer. "Waxing the Evil Doers was supposed to be *fun*. No. That's not right. Killing Evil Doers was supposed to be fun and *noble*."

"Watch where you're waving that beer," Barney said.

"But it turns out most of the people we killed or otherwise fucked up had absolutely nothing to do with Nine Eleven. It turns out that "Evil Doers" is a matter of *perspective*—what do you mean, watch where I'm waving this? You just sprayed beer all over me, and you're worried I might accidentally get a drop or two on you?"

"Hey, it's all a matter of perspective."

"Yeah, well perspective this." Joe Big poured half the can of beer onto Barney's head, the beer running through Barney's buzz cut, onto his shoulders and back, dripping off the end of his nose.

"Oh, you are going to regret that."

Joe laughed, and reached out to pour the rest of the beer on Barney's head.

Barney held up his hand. "All right, all right. We're even." He wiped beer off the end of his nose. "It's time to get serious."

Joe Big slowly emptied the rest of the beer onto the lawn.

"They called Brittany at the hospital," he said. "Told her all about me."

"Who's Brittany? Oh, the blond nurse, right? The rich one."

"The point is, they know enough about me to call her."

Barney ran his hand across the top of his head, and then wiped his hand on his shirt. "They've got too much money," he said. "Too much lawyer. And that big dude has way too many connections."

"I don't give a shit about the computer chips or whoever it is they plan to sell them to," Joe Big said. "This is personal. They made it personal."

"That they did."

"That M16 had real bullets in it."

"I'm hearing that. I am definitely hearing that. But let's don't be forgetting that we were real sloppy and don't have much excuse for getting ourselves into such a predicament."

Joe Big began kicking the empty cans scattered around the lawn into a pile. "We fucked up, plain and simple," he said. "No excuses."

"Counted coup on us, though, didn't they?" Barney asked.

Joe Big grunted.

Barney stood and tossed his can into the pile. "Think you can keep a lid on that?"

Joe Big stopped, and looked at him. "Think *you* can?"

Barney laughed.

"Not a chance," he said.

4
Posthaste

Joe Big turned off the engine and let the truck coast. The worn tires slid on wet leaves and bumped to a stop against the curb in front of Barney's house. They still had no real plan of action, except to head up to Polson and Kalispell, where they'd first hooked up with Patrick The Big—Barney's new name for him—and his two "psycho-phants."

The idea was to trace their steps from when they'd first been briefed by Quinn. "Wander around. Poke a stick in the anthill," Barney had said. "See what happens. Who knows, maybe we'll even get to shoot someone."

Joe Big smiled. It wasn't so much the finding out that they were looking forward to as it was the doing something about it once they found out.

He opened the door and climbed out and stretched. The morning air was clear and crisp, smelling of mowed lawns and fallen leaves. It made him want to ignore all that had happened and go over to his uncle's place near Wild Horse Plains and hunt elk.

He squinted down the street. Cars moved furtively through an intersection five blocks down.

When he was a kid, sometimes he'd bring a friend, and late at night, they'd smear charcoal from the campfire on their faces, and creep back through the forest and try to sneak up on his father and uncle and count coup with willow sticks they'd cut down by the creek.

His father could sleep through a mortar attack—and probably had, more than once in Vietnam—but his uncle . . . well, sometimes his uncle wasn't human. No matter how hard they tried, no matter how quiet and sneaky they were, he and his friend would inevitably spend the rest of the night and most of the next day tied to each other and to a tree out in the forest.

He slammed the truck door shut, and turned and headed for the porch. No way those three assholes would've been able to handle his uncle the way they'd handled him and Barney. Ben Tails would have killed them.

Oh, man, he thought, as he walked up the steps, onto the covered porch. He hadn't thought about that. He hadn't thought about what his uncle was going to think about all this. Talk about denial. If his uncle ever found out his nephew had done something so dumb . . . so . . . so . . . *unaware.* And Ben Tails *would* find out. You could count on that. It wasn't a question of if or how; it was only a question of when.

He crossed to the far side of the porch and sat on the wooden love seat attached with chains at both ends to eyebolts sticking out of the porch ceiling. He pushed off with his feet.

What would his uncle do in a situation like this? None of it had been play with his uncle. Ever. You'd know he was awake and waiting because you could feel him. And you could feel him because he *wanted* you to feel him.

The Gunny had thought he was a natural, but the Gunny had not known about nights trying to count coup on his uncle. A Death Monster, his father had called his uncle. And he'd never forget the way the members of his father's small group of old Marine Corps buds had sagely nodded their heads.

He smiled at the memory. The overworked imaginations of young boys scared out of their minds because they'd convinced themselves that the monster in the forest was real? Old men who'd earned the right to call themselves warriors in Vietnam or Korea or even, a few of them, World War II, gathered together to make or to perpetuate Tribal Myth? Maybe. Probably. It would be interesting to see how he and Barney would fare against his uncle now.

He laughed out loud. Oh, the human ego could be an ugly thing, he thought. He wouldn't fare any better or any different today than he had as a kid. Ben Tails was not a myth. He was the real deal. His father could sleep through anything, it was true, but the only times he'd seen his father sleep well or long was when they'd slept out at his uncle's place.

He frowned.

Ben Tails had taught him well. And someone much like Ben Tails must have taught Barney equally well. Because both of them had known someone was in under the trees watching them. They'd been too arrogant and full of themselves to worry about it, that's all.

He sighed, the swing creaking back and forth. Joe Big Snake Person. Mr. Magic himself. Pretty slick when he had an eye in the sky and a voice in his ear to help him. So full of himself that he'd forgotten that men and women like his uncle would know you were coming before you even knew you were leaving. His uncle would have walked around that deck of logs and melted into the darkness under the trees and found her before she even knew he was there.

Joe Big Snake Person could have done that. He could have done it because his uncle had taught him how to do it. Mr. Magic could have done it. He could have done it because his experiences in the Marines had honed what his uncle had taught him.

But instead, he and Barney had let their egos, and the fact that this was Montana and not some misbegotten . . .

Well, fuck it. What was done was done. They'd made a mistake and that was that. It wouldn't happen again.

If they were smart, right now would be a real good time to take a time-out and go have a sweat with his uncle in his sweat lodge. Who knows. Maybe his uncle would even have a few words of wisdom.

He stood.

Fat chance. His uncle was real big on showing, not telling. There'd be no words of wisdom even if he had them to say. They'd sweat in silence, like always, his uncle as inscrutable as the stone Buddha he kept in a little shrine outside the sweat lodge.

And anyway, his uncle was in Japan or some such place working for an outfit no one would talk about—doing things no one *could* talk about.

He opened the screen door, and with his fist pounded on the ancient solid-wood door, peering through the small window at the dark interior.

"FRESH POT OF tea," Barney said. "Yunan Chi Tse Beeng Cha, or however you say it. You probably know, but don't tell me. Serious caffeine, so watch out." The house was an old wooden made-before-the-Second-World War house that Barney had remodeled himself. He'd made floor to ceiling bookcases and re-made the floors with hardwood slats scavenged from giant packing cases that parts and machines destined for the pulp mill and for various furniture outlets had come in. He'd cut the slats to size, had a local shop tongue and groove the boards, sanded and stained and sealed, and for less than the price of new flooring and boards he'd transformed the old house. New tile in the bathrooms, new appliances, new paint, carefully tended yard. Most people who had been to the house thought Barney had missed his calling. But Joe Big knew that in remodeling the house Barney was merely being Barney. He'd been intrigued with the idea of recycling hardwood packing case slats into finished floors and bookcases, and one thing had led to another, until the entire house had been transformed. Now that it was done, he had no intention of doing it again. Truth be told, he didn't much like doing woodwork. What he loved to do was to grow flowers, especially roses. Every year his mother sent him hundreds of dollars worth of flower bulbs from Louisiana.

"How'd it go with the nurse?" Barney asked, carefully pouring tea from a Japanese pot into teacups lined up on the counter.

"No sense beating a dead horse." Joe picked up one of the teacups.

"Like that, huh?"

"Yeah. Pretty much. Why's it so empty in here? What'd you do with the table and chairs?"

"Oh, the ex-old lady came by the other day and took most of the furniture."

"What happened to the plant that used to be in front of the window? Did she take that, too? That was *your* plant, man."

Midmorning sunlight filtered through the maples and through the window, blotches of sunlight and shadow like camouflage on the far wall and on Barney standing in front of the counter.

Barney took a delicate sip. "A divorce is what happened. The court gave her everything except my possessions. If I sell the house she gets a quarter of that, too."

"That's cold, man."

"She wanted a monthly payment, too."

"The high cost of infidelity."

"More like the high cost of giving her the clap," Barney said.

"But that wasn't your fault—this is good tea. Is this that cow-pie looking stuff that you got the other day? I don't understand why she can't understand that it wasn't your fault. We wouldn't have made the case against those Ukrainians if you hadn't gotten tight with that girl. Oh, hey. I meant to tell you: one of them already got knifed in prison. By the Indians, I think. Killed his ass dead."

"My heart soars."

"Yeah. Good riddance to bad trash, as my grandmother would've said."

Barney raised his teacup in a toast. "Your grandmother was an eminently practical person. I lament the fact that I only got to meet her once."

"Well, I don't know how eminent she was, but she was for sure practical."

"Hands of steel."

Joe Big smiled, remembering the expression on Barney's face when he'd shaken hands with his grandmother who'd been eighty-six at the time. "You knead bread dough every day of your life, and you'd have hands of steel, too."

"Barney the Baker."

"There you go. So what are you going to do if you sell this house? If you want to move in with me and Mouse, that's cool."

"What about the women you drag home? Most of them don't like me much."

"Yeah, you're a bad influence, what with your military experience, and all."

"*My* military experience. I can't believe the shit you get by with, you know that? I give my wife the clap—contacted while doing *a service for my country*—and the next thing I know even the kitchen table is gone. If it was you, you'd twist it so far out of shape she'd be bragging to her friends, like you bringing home a venereal disease was an honor or something. Her contribution to the War On Terror."

"Well, thanks to Tanya . . . you know Tanya who—"

"Yeah, yeah. Tanya. I hear she's telling people she scalped you."

"*Really*?"

Barney took a drink of his tea, watching Joe Big over the teacup.

Joe Big stared out the window, a vein prominent on the side of his forehead.

"How you feeling about that?" Barney asked. "Serious question."

"I'm feeling serene."

"Haven't seen you in a Marine Corps haircut for a while."

Joe Big turned back toward him, and held out his teacup for a refill. "Back to the future, I figure."

"What do you mean?"

"Well, we messed up so bad, I reckon we need to go back to the basics. Go back to when we weren't so full of ourselves."

Barney poured tea into Joe Big's teacup.

"That a good point, Big. A really good point. I'd appreciate it if you'd remember it."

Joe Big grinned. "Took you long enough to say something about my haircut."

"Just don't expect me to get one like it." Barney took a sip of tea. "So what's the deal with your nurse?"

"Well, as you know, she found my badge and a bag full of medals and jump wings and shit like that."

"And?"

Joe shrugged. "And I'm not the aspiring environmentalist and Native American poet that she thought I was."

"Depresses you, does it?"

"Nah. I don't know. I don't think so. Maybe. A little, yeah." He took a drink of tea. "This stuff really grows on you."

"Prices to be paid, bro. At least you're not married."

Joe Big looked at the patterns of light bobbing and weaving against the window.

"Felt like a piece of whale shit when I woke up this morning," he said.

Barney smiled. "You Marines and your nautical terms." His cell phone, on the counter next to the teapot, went off, the ringtone an old Jimmy Buffett song: Cheeseburger in Paradise.

"Guess who," Barney said.

Joe Big mimicked Quinn's voice. "Where are the computer chips do you still have the computer chips you better still have the computer chips I'll have your ass if you don't have the computer chips."

Barney picked up the cell phone and slid it open. "You have reached the Lambier residence. No humans are currently available. To leave a fax, please press . . . Oh, top of the mornin' to you, Miz Quinn, sir." He winked at Joe Big. "What? I did write a report. We have been around." He paused. "Out at Big's. Here. What, you want a complete itinerary now?" He shook his head, and squinted out the window. "Get our asses over there, what kind of language is that?" He grinned at Joe Big, his face almost elfin. "I am truly shocked at your language, sir—I mean, Miss—I mean—" He held the cell phone out in front of him. "She hung up on me. Can you believe that?" He closed the cell phone and put it in his pocket.

The phone rang again, Cheeseburger in Paradise coming from Barney's pocket.

"Yessss." Barney leaned back against the counter. "Oh . . . She said that, huh? No! I'm shocked that you would even repeat such an allegation. Big would never . . ." He eyed Joe Big. "I see . . . Wow, I didn't know he could be that inventive . . ."

Joe Big rocked back and forth on his heels, hands clasped behind his back, staring innocently out the back door.

"Well, sure," Barney said, glaring at Joe Big. "I can see why she might be unhappy. But they *are* consenting adu— That's not the point, ma'am. Ma'am, that not the point. She admits she consented, right?" He shook his head. "Well, all due respect, ma'am, I don't see a problem. It's a private matter, and none of our business."

Joe Big rapidly nodded his head up and down.

"Well, that's probably why she called, then. She's just trying to get Big in trouble. Yeah. Yeah. I know. You'll make sure the Sheriff has us shoveling shit at the stockyards. I got it the first time. There's no need to abuse your posi—" He held the phone at arms length, and they could hear, as Joe Big would later put it, "a very exercised female voice."

"You ought to make that your ring tone," Joe Big suggested.

Barney laughed, and put the phone to his ear. "No, ma'am, I am not laughing at you." He paused. "What? Kalispell? We had the same thought . . . Yes, occasionally we actually have thoughts. No need to . . . Yes, ma'am. Posthaste."

Joe Big opened the screen door and went out on the back porch. Barney could hear him laughing.

"Yes, ma'am. I understand that's an order. Hey, how about you kiss my . . ." He held the phone out in front of him again. "Damn," he said, and closed the phone and put it in his pocket.

"Get your ass in here, Big."

Joe Big opened the screen door and peeked in. "Problem?"

"You asshole. Is there something you neglected to tell me about Tanya? You know, Tanya: the sexy little thing with the M16 and the knife? *The very pissed off sexy little thing who would have gladly cut off your nuts instead of your hair if that big motherfucker had let her?*"

"Jeez, Barn . . ."

"Don't 'Jeez, Barn' me. You fucked her, didn't you?"

"You didn't know that?"

"That first night we met them—up at that bar outside Kalispell. You went out to the car with her."

"So what if I did? It's not so different than you and that Ukrainian girl—"

"Do. *Not.* Go. There."

"Sorry."

"The Ukrainians were talking about nukes and real bad bugs," Barney said.

"I know. I know. I shouldn't have said that."

"This is serious, Big. God damn it."

"I know it's serious." Joe Big rubbed his hand back and forth across the stubble on his head. "But it wasn't serious then."

"You were out in the parking lot, getting your rocks off when we were supposed to be working that big motherfucker. Maybe if you'd paid a little more attention to what you are being paid to pay attention to, we wouldn't have ended up . . . ah, fuck." He waved his hand in front of his face, as if to wave Joe Big away.

"She grabbed my package! What was I supposed to do? Just say no?"

Barney leaned against the counter, one arm across his chest, his other hand over his eyes. He shook his head.

"Our Leaderette has called a meeting. One hour," he said.

"You're just jealous."

"Jealous!" Barney's head snapped up. "I'm not jealous, you fucking idiot." His neck swelled. "But I damn sure would have been in serious fear when she had that M16 pointed at my balls if I'd known you'd—"

"Whoa! Whoa! Slow down. We were all drinking. You were just as tuned up as I was. We went outside, and it got . . . a little frenetic, and—"

"Frenetic! You've got to stop this shit, Big. You've got to get professional about what we're supposed to be doing, or else it's going to turn into some kind of death wish. You hear what I'm saying? You have got to stop this shit."

"You're right. You're absolutely right. A thousand percent right. It won't happen again."

"It's getting out of control with you and women. One of these days . . ." He considered Joe Big for a moment. "I probably shouldn't say this, but I'm pissed off and if I can't say it, who can?"

"Say what?"

"One of these days when you least expect it, and probably when you least want it, it's going to be someone you actually care about. And if you fuck that up, then you are really going to be in a world of hurt."

"What are you talking about now?"

"What I'm talking about is that you shot an enemy of this country. Who just happened to be a woman. She wasn't a civilian. And, since she was a woman, she wasn't Taliban. She was Al Quaeda. You did the world a favor, man." He held his hand up to stop Big from talking. "But that's not what I want to say. What I want to say is that all that happened in another place and time. And if you still have trouble dealing with it, *then don't fucking be there anymore, God damn it!* Because if you don't leave it alone, sure as God made roses, you are going to *fuck us up!*"

"Jeez, Barn . . ."

Barney glared at him.

"Okay, okay. I got it. Note to Joe Big. Stop fucking around."

Barney shook his head.

Joe Big grinned. "Additional addendum to Joe Big. Figure out how to keep your package from being grabbed by good-looking women with monster libidos."

Barney snorted. "You wouldn't know an addendum from a pudendum, a libido from a . . . Frito."

"I'll ask Quinn. She'll know. A *Frito*?"

Barney frowned. "Speaking of Quinn . . ."

"Yeah, what's this meeting about, anyway?"

"Who knows? She's probably going to use this as an excuse to give us her monthly talk-down-to-local-law-enforcement-lecture on how to do something we've been doing for years."

"Like how to buy dope, you mean?"

"That was last month. Today, it's probably going to be the Fed version of a pep talk-slash-ethics lecture."

"Like we lack motivation."

"Well, she doesn't know what happened. She doesn't know that for once we really *are* motivated. *Someone* in the bunch might know, but she doesn't."

"Why not?" Joe Big said. "She might know exactly what happened. She's perfectly capable of burning our asses if she thinks it's for the greater good."

"I don't think so. She's too pissed off—and maybe a little jealous."

"Don't start that again."

Barney shook his head. "You are a piece of work, you are."

"I *said* it won't happen again."

"Hey, maybe Tanya will call your mother, tell her how you accidentally fucked her on the hood of a car in the parking lot. How'd that be, huh? Too bad your grandmother isn't still alive."

"She wouldn't do that."

"Oh, yes, she would. Man, you ought to see the look in your eyes right now. Of course, she would. Especially if some little birdy—*me,* for example—put the idea in her pointy little head."

Joe's mouth opened slightly.

Barney nodded. "Uh-huh. That's right, asshole. If you don't get your act together, and get it together right now, this fucking second, I'll do it. You know I'll do it."

"Why you talkin' to me like this, man? We're bros. All the shit we've been through—"

"That's why I'm talking to you like this, *bro*. Are you hearing me? Am I getting through to you?"

"Yeah, yeah, I'm hearing you."

Barney stared at him for a moment.

"Okay," he said. "That's it. I've said my piece. Let's go outside. I need to let all this new information settle before we meet with Madame Fed."

He held the screen door open for Joe Big, and they went out onto the tiny deck that Barney had built in the back, and sat in the sun on the deck planks, their backs against the siding on the house. They were silent for several minutes.

"Now might not be a good time," Big said. "But I really hate to see what happened between you and your ex. She's good people."

"One of those things."

Right after he'd gotten out of the Special Forces, and without any Reserve commitment because of his wounds, at Big's urging he'd come out to Montana. He'd always wanted to see Montana, ever since he was a kid hunting in the bayou.

At the time, Big was still dicking around with Force Recon. So Barney'd moved to Hamilton to work for an outfitter, and that's where he'd met his wife-to-be. Ex wife-to-be. The outfitter's daughter. As capable in the back country as any man.

It had been a dream existence for him. But not for her. For her, outfitting was work, something she'd helped her family do since she was old enough to get on a horse by herself. She wanted a house in the city, and she wanted to go to graduate school, get a degree in Creative Writing—whatever the hell that was, he still hadn't got a handle on that. Be a soccer mom who could write poetry, he guessed.

"Middle-class America just sort of crept up on us," he said out loud. "She wanted to have kids, go to poetry readings, garage sales, concerts in the park." He laughed, and Joe could hear the whimsy in his laugh. "It was her dream, but it was like foot rot for me. You know what I'm saying."

"Not really."

Barney stood and walked over to the rose bushes at the corner of the house—his prize rose bushes.

"I think maybe she got confused by the roses," Joe Big said.

Barney bent down and smelled the bright yellow flowers. "You're probably right." He stood and walked back to the deck. "But don't let being right go to your head, because it's about the only thing you've ever been right about." He paused. "So are your feelings all hurt, or what?"

"Nope."

"Well, let's go, then."

"Posthaste," Joe said.

He stood and followed Barney into the house.

"This ought to be good," he said.

5
No Rules

"Hey, Mrs. W," Joe Big said. "Top 'o the mornin' to ya."

Mrs. Walker glanced over her shoulder at the two of them coming into the kitchen. She was tall and slim and elegant, as always. Pleated light-brown pants and dark-chocolate blazer. Short, kinky black hair peppered with gray.

Mrs. W was senior civil service, one of the few black women in the city. Quinn McBride's woman for all seasons. The glue that held the office together. In their opinion, she was totally wasted in her present position.

She shook coffee out of the coffee grinder into the hinged filter on the coffee maker, and closed the filter. She switched on the coffee maker, and turned toward them, arms across her chest.

Her eyes widened. "My goodness!" she said. "What in the world have you done, Joseph?"

Joe Big ran a hand over his buzz cut. He grinned.

Behind her the coffee maker began to spit and gurgle.

"Yeah, go ahead," Barney said. "Tell her what you've done, Jo-seph?"

Joe Big cleared his throat. He ran his hand back and forth over the top of his head. "I've decided to get back into triathlons," he announced. Barney laughed.

She frowned. It was amazing how much her eyes—dark and slightly hooded—reminded Joe Big of his grandmother's eyes.

"A new leaf," he said.

"Well, that's a good thing, then. A good thing. Though, I did admire your braid so."

She looked at Barney. Her eyes squinted and her lips pursed.

"Yes, ma'am," Barney said. "I think it's a good thing, too." He glanced at Joe Big, as if to say, what did I do?

"Uh-huh. Don't you be 'ma'am-ing' me, young man." Her gaze returned to Joe Big. "Nor you, Joseph Big. New leaf, my ass. If frogs had wings, they could fly. My husband's unit was full of men like you two." Her husband, a Marine grunt major, had been killed outside Baghdad in the early days of the war. She uncrossed her arms and wagged her finger at them. "Now I don't normally say anything, you know that. It's not my place. But this is getting out of hand, and someone needs to say something." She glared from one to the other. "Ever since you two got here, you been walking around like you two are too good to breathe the same air as the rest of us. Your attitude has caused that young lady in there more than a few sleepless nights. And I don't know what you've done this time, but in the twelve years that I've known her, I have never seen her this upset."

"Jeez, Mrs. W—" Joe Big started to say, but was silenced by the look she gave him.

"*And* when that young lady is upset, *I* am upset, Mr. Big. Mr. *New Leaf.* So both of you. You listen up. When you talk to her today, you be polite. You be respectful. You leave your sarcasm and your disrespect right here. Right here in this kitchen. Or you will be dealing with me." She looked from one to the other. "Am I making myself clear?"

"Yes, Ma'am," they chorused.

"That woman in there has paid dues that you two cannot imagine. Are you listening to me, Joe Big?"

"Yes, ma'am. I'm listening to you, I sure am."

"Then you best be wiping that smirk off your face."

"Sorry." *Exactly* like his grandmother, he thought.

"Mr. Lambier?"

"I hear you, Mrs. W."

"If my husband were alive, God rest his soul, he'd have you two standing tall."

"She needs a hug," Joe Big muttered out the side of his mouth to Barney.

"Yeah," Barney muttered back.

Before she could react, in unison they stepped over to her and, one to either side, put an arm around her.

"What . . .! What are you doing? You two get your hands off me right this instant . . ." She twisted out from between them, and waggled her finger at them. "There's going to be no sweet talking this time. No, sir. Not this time." She shoved Joe Big and then Barney toward the hallway. "You two go on up to the conference room and you wait there. And you be thinking about what I said. Go on. Git. I'm serious, now!"

"Sure could use a cup of that coffee," Joe Big said over his shoulder.

"There's a lot you could use, young man."

Barney laughed. "You got that right, Mrs. W."

"And you're no one to talk, Mr. Lambier."

"Yeah, you're no one to talk, *Mr.* Lambier," Joe Big said. He turned and stuck his head back around the kitchen wall. "Could I have that old white mug, Mrs. W. Please."

"You are really pushing your luck, young man, you are."

"Thanks," he said, and before she could reply, he turned and took the stairs two at a time behind Barney.

At the top of the steps the beautiful old hardwood floor had been carpeted with an anonymous brown and tan synthetic carpet—an industrial-strength, low-nap carpet designed for high-traffic office areas. The conference room was at the end of the hallway in what used to be the master bedroom suite. Two large windows against the west wall looked out over the roof of the house next door and the large maples turning fall colors in the neighboring yards. The windows were new and could not be opened, their frames made of plastic and aluminum, the windows themselves coated with some sort of high-tech film that was supposed to discourage electronic eavesdropping. Government-issue, they assumed. Useless because the bay window at the north end of the room was still the original single-pane, stained-glass window.

A massive corporate-sized conference table big enough to seat twenty but with only twelve chairs took up most of the room. Given the turn in the stairway, they figured it had probably been brought in through one of the windows when the windows were replaced. The carpet was the same anonymous brown and tan carpet as in the hallway. Two large flat screens were mounted side-by-side above beautiful old birch cabinets built into the wall at the end of the room. Cabinet doors had been removed and most of the drawers and shelves had been replaced with banks of electronic equipment—satellite receivers, video players, surveillance and security equipment. Next to the television screen and the banks of electronic equipment was the door to the bathroom.

Joe Big loved the bathroom. So far it had been spared a government remodel. The sink and claw-foot tub and the tile floor inlaid with two-inch square tiles were original. Even the spigots and handles were original, the hot and cold water handles real ivory, yellowed and cracked with age. The only new addition was a modern toilet commode and tank—no doubt added so that water usage would conform to California standards. As with the bathroom downstairs, real cloth towels and washcloths—yellow with green flowers today—were neatly placed on towel bars and stacked on a metal stand next to the sink. The small window behind the toilet was open and, as he relieved himself, he could hear the rustle of dry maple leaves, smell crisp fall air.

When he came out of the bathroom, his favorite white mug, a chipped relic of old railroad restaurants, was steaming on the table in front of the chair next to Barney. Barney was drinking from a shiny black mug decorated with the gold insignia of the U.S. Army.

"That was quick," Joe Big said. "I didn't even hear her come up."

"She didn't say a word. Gave me the evil eye. Put the coffee on the table, and left. I was afraid to say anything."

Joe Big sprawled in the chair. All the chairs were gray high-backed, generic office chairs with plastic wheels that refused to roll on the carpet.

"So who's going to be at this meeting?" He picked up the mug and took a drink.

"Dunno. I hope it's not the whole crew, though. That new ATF guy is a real pain in the ass."

"Well, I don't know about you, but I'm still a little confused about our role in all this."

Barney snorted. "No shit, Sherlock."

"I mean," Joe Big said. "With the exception of Quinn and that scary-ass dyke from the Department of Defense, or wherever she's from, these people might as well have flashing neon signs on their foreheads: Fed. Fed. Fed. Even Mrs. W."

"Yeah, but you got to admit some of them sure seem to know what they're doing. Half the stuff they talk about, I haven't a clue." Barney raised his arms over his head and stretched backwards. "Government-issue geeks," he said, and ended the stretch with his hands on top his head.

Joe Big took another sip of coffee. "Damn. This is good coffee."

"I heard she gets it from a friend in Africa."

"See. That's exactly what I'm saying," Joe Big said. "What are we doing with people who get their coffee from friends in Africa?" He shook his head. "I don't know, Barn. You got to ask yourself, what do we bring to the table?"

"I been thinkin' about that."

"Thinking about what?"

"Between the City Police Department and the Sheriff's Office, there must be at least ten other guys and a couple of women who are as good or better than us at being cops."

"Well, I don't know about that. We went through the drug community like Drāno through clogged shit in a toilet."

"Nice metaphor, Big." Barney picked up his coffee cup and took a drink. He set the cup back down. "I'm especially going to appreciate it when I wake up at night with it stuck in my mind."

Joe Big smiled.

"We're pretty good at the undercover narc thing, you're right." Barney said. "Mostly because we're just being ourselves. But we aren't in the same league as those guys we met from Vegas—not to mention that team of mostly women from Seattle."

"So why don't they have a couple of those people, instead of us?" Joe Big asked.

"Well, that's the question, isn't it?"

With his index finger, Joe Big nudged his coffee mug sideways on the tabletop. "I don't like where you're going with this."

"I don't much like it either. But ask yourself, what do we—or I should say, what *did* we do better than just about anybody?"

"Mmm," Joe Big said.

"How many times have you—have *we*—been recruited by some alphabet agency. Or by some civilian security contractor? Not two weeks go by I don't get a call from someone. That place in North Carolina even offered to make us instructors."

Joe Big stared at his coffee cup. He nudged it away from him. "These people," he said. "These 'government-issue geeks'. All their rules and regulations. All their technology. All their talk about ethics and standards and Affirmative Action. All their constant yipping and yapping about pay grade and preference points and who's back-stabbing who at The National Level." He poked his coffee cup again. "After awhile all that becomes background noise when you're around these people." He poked the cup hard. "And then, because of all the fucking background noise, when they say something important, we don't hear it."

"And yet, here we are."

Joe Big glanced at Barney. "How long you been thinking about this?"

"It hit me when we were walking up the steps, just now. I was thinking about what they've done to this old house, the windows and the carpet and all, and it hit me that we might be headed exactly where we said we'd never go again."

Joe Big was silent. He picked up his coffee mug and drained it. He put the mug on the table.

"What'd you say the other night?" he asked. "When we were talking about the War? Faceless men in faceless bureaucracies? Policy wonks. Strategists. Corporate managers. How'd you put it? A mind-boggling tangle of people and intrigue and psychosis that, to this day, we can't even begin to understand."

"All of that," Barney said. "But you said most of it, not me."

"All those people and their fucked-up reasons for existence reduced to the voice of a stranger in our ear," Joe Big said, "telling us to bring doom to people we didn't know and understand even less . . ."

"Word, brother. You know that."

"But this job . . . these people," Joe Big said. "I don't know, man. I been getting the vibe around here that all the rules and regulations and so on that are supposed to be part of the Fed thing . . ." He glanced at Barney. "I been getting the feeling that all that is antique thinking. You know what I'm saying?" He slid the coffee cup back and forth on the table between his palms. "This war on terrorism thing, they give a lot of lip service to civil rights, the legality of this or that, the Patriot Act, but when you come right down to it, what they are really saying with all their talk about rules, and—" He gestured toward the banks of electronic equipment below the television. "—all their geek technology, is that there are no rules. You know what I'm saying? No rules. Not even graveyard rules. But it's all messed up because these people have got rules and regulations branded on their soul. And when they try to fight with no rules against people who know how to fight with no rules . . ."

"Only bad things can happen," Barney said.

"That's what I'm saying."

"But we're not Feds."

"No, we're not."

"And all their bullshit about us knowing Montana communities and people, what about that?" Barney asked.

"I don't know, man. It doesn't make much sense to me. But since it's the Feds, I reckon it doesn't have to make much sense." He paused. "I guess we both been thinking about this in the back of our minds for a while now. Trouble is, when you take it out and look at it in the light of day, it seems pretty thin."

"You think?"

"Yeah. It's too complicated. I can't see any Fed giving up his or her mindset enough to make it work. At the end of the day, these people are bureaucrats. They want certainty. They want to know the future before they commit to anything. And we're loose cannons. Fuck-ups, by their standards. Compared to them, we never know what we're going to do, until we do it. So, yeah. Basically, I think we're over-thinking the situation, letting our paranoia get the best of us because some amateurs trampled our pride."

Barney sat upright. "Here they come."

"HEY! WE NEED MORE COFFEE," Joe Big shouted toward the doorway.

Quinn McBride walked through the doorway, a carafe of coffee in one hand, fat notebook binder in the other. "Shout a little louder, why don't you," she said. "They probably didn't hear you down at Starbucks." She put the carafe in front of Barney, and walked to the head of the table. She was wearing a crisp white blouse, cowgirl jeans and boots, skinny leather designer belt, her raven hair tied back in a ponytail. Both Barney and Joe Big eyed her ass as she walked away from them, around the table.

She pulled a chair out and sat, hitching the chair forward toward the table, and stared at them expressionless, as two other people came into the room: a large, muscular woman, early thirties, maybe, it was impossible to tell, tattoos and multiple piercings, black leather vest over loose white T-shirt, black half-finger gloves, ragged short-blond hair black at the roots, electric-blue eyes surrounded by coal-black eye shadow, spider-web tattoo on her right elbow. And a stocky middle-aged man with short graying hair and the two-tone tan on his forehead of a rancher who wears a cowboy hat all day, plaid shirt, sleeves rolled up to the elbow, large gnarled hands and Popeye forearms, jeans with ironed-in creases, scratched and dinged rodeo belt buckle, laugh lines at the corners of his eyes and mouth. His black eyes and hatchet nose told Joe Big the man was a tribal member. What tribe, he wasn't sure, but he looked familiar.

"Brianna McPherson, Paul Cyr," Quinn said. "Meet James Longstreet Lambier and Joseph Big Snake Person, aka Barney and Joe Big."

"We know Brianna," Barney said.

"Oh, that's right. I forgot. You met when you two first came aboard."

"Jimmy Street," the woman sneered, her voice raspy. "Joe Big Ego. How the hell are you? I hear you got your asses handed to you."

"Who told you that?" Joe Big asked.

"Wouldn't you like to know?"

Barney smiled at the man, and half stood and leaned forward across the table and extended his hand. "Barney."

The man stood and leaned across the table and shook Barney's hand. "Paul." His handshake was crushing.

Joe Big stood also.

Paul nodded. "Joe Big Snake Person," he said in Blackfeet. "I know your mother and father well."

No shit, Joe Big thought. Paul Cyr. Rodeo champ, successful rancher, member of the same loose-knit group of combat veterans that his father belonged to. A man well liked by almost everyone, despite being a Border Patrol cop. "I don't speak Blackfeet," he said. "I didn't grow up on the Rez."

Paul sat back down, and ran his hand through his thick graying hair, and the way he did it, Joe knew he was looking not to run his fingers through his hair but to push his hat up on the back of his head. "You understand enough, I think," Paul said in Blackfeet.

Joe sat, and made himself aware of Paul the way his grandmother had taught him, without looking directly at him. He could feel the lack of humor in Paul's smile.

In Blackfeet, Paul said, "Why is it that Joe Big Snake Person speaks the language of the Chinese, but refuses to speak the language of the *Niitsitapi*?"

"I belong to another, larger tribe now," Joe Big said in English. He looked directly at Paul. "The United States Marine Corps." He smiled. "You might say I'm an Apple to the Corps."

Paul laughed, a twinkle in his eyes, and said in Blackfeet. "You are your grandmother's grandchild, and your uncle's nephew, that is who you are, Joe Big, and I am very happy to meet you as a man at last."

"Paul comes to us from the Border Patrol," Quinn said. "He is in charge of a new unit that is patrolling the border on horseback and mules. He has been invaluable in helping to train Special Ops units, especially Navy SEALS, for back-country operations in the mountains of the Middle East and South Asia."

"Translation," Paul said to Barney. "I helped teach people who are half fish about the care and feeding and packing of mules." The lilt had disappeared from his English. "For some reason, their personalities fit well with my mules."

"SEALS," Barney said. "You got to love them. What *is* your problem?" he said to Brianna.

Brianna glowered. "Heap big tough men bonding, that's my problem. Hey, how'd you lose your braid, Joe Pretty Person. Got scalped by a woman, huh?"

Barney and Joe Big stared without expression at her.

Brianna leaned forward, her blue eyes cold. "Booga-booga," she said, and laughed, and slouched back in her chair. "Give me a break."

"That kind of talk is not necessary, Brianna," Quinn said. "We're all on the same team here."

Brianna snorted, her nose ring jiggling. "That'll be the day." She smiled and put her fist against her forehead and upside down waved her middle finger back and forth, like a windshield wiper in front of her face, at Barney and Joe Big.

"Brianna. *Enough.* Sorry," Quinn said to Paul Cyr. "We've got a little housecleaning to do before we get to the point of this meeting. I'm sorry you have to be here to hear it."

"No problem."

Quinn turned to Barney and Joe Big, and both could not help but notice she'd put on makeup: eyeliner, lipstick, turquoise earrings that complimented her green eyes.

Don't even think about it, Joe Big told himself. Do not even fucking think about it.

"I'm not going to ask you to re-write your report, nor am I going to ask you to tell us what really happened the other night. Thanks to Brianna's informant, and taking into account your appearance and your attitude when I last saw you, I think we can safely assume that you have put yourselves—and by extension, this office and this organization—in a . . . compromising position."

Barney and Joe Big looked at each other. Barney raised his right eyebrow.

Joe Big looked at her. "So fire us," he said.

Brianna grinned, and nodded, exaggerating the up and down movement of her head.

Quinn looked at Paul Cyr, and smiled, her smile wan, as if to say, see what I have to deal with.

She sighed. "If that's what you want, Joe. I can do that." Her voice stiffened. "But if I fire you, the Sheriff fires you. It's as simple as that."

Brianna bobbed her head up and down, her eyes wide and happy.

"Brianna," Quinn warned.

Brianna folded her hands on the table, and pretended to look contrite.

"Someday, somebody is going to make you eat that tattoo on your elbow," Barney said.

"I earned this tattoo, dickhead."

"Yeah," Joe Big said. "A skinny biker in Oakland wielding a potentially lethal crack pipe."

"I've never been to Oakland in my life, asshole."

"Knock it off," Quinn said. "The three of you."

"Who's your informant?" Barney asked.

Brianna smirked. "That's for me to know, and for you to never find out."

"I know who it is," Quinn said. "And the fact that I know details should tell you that it's someone reliable. You don't need to know the name."

Joe Big said, "Since Mr. Cyr and," he nodded at Brianna, "the Death Devo over there, are here, we can only assume that there is a good reason for us to sit here and listen to this bullshit—"

"Instead of having coffee with the Union rep," Barney finished.

"This is not a disciplinary hearing." Quinn sighed. "You two are perfectly capable of disciplining yourselves. Or not. It's up to you. As far as I'm concerned, what's done is done. We all make mistakes. Everyone here can learn from your mistake—everyone here *has* learned from your mistake. The reason why I'm bringing it up at this meeting—the *only* reason why I'm bringing it up—is so that we are all on the same page. Now, if you don't mind . . ." She looked from Joe Big and Barney to Brianna and back to Barney and Joe. "Can we get on with business?"

Joe Big stared expressionlessly at her.

"Go for it," Barney said.

Quinn looked at Paul and inclined her head. "Paul."

Paul cleared his throat. "We sometimes pack some pretty sophisticated equipment," he said. "Equipment that can sniff trace residue from materials used in NBC warfare applications."

Barney held up his hand.

"Joe and I are familiar with the kind of equipment you are talking about," he said. "Sorry to interrupt. But I thought it might help to know that."

Paul looked at Quinn.

"Probably not the state-of-the-art stuff," Barney said. "But we understand the basic equipment."

"And your point is?" Quinn asked Barney.

"Well . . . No offense," he said to Paul. "But you picked up some radiation or some chemical dust from an old mine. Found some bugs growing on a tree or in a pond. We went through all that in Iraq and Afghanistan and . . . other places."

Paul smiled, and nodded. "A lot of that, yes. You're right. And it's a real pain in the ass, if you want to know the truth. But a couple of weeks ago we found three dead mules. The cause of death has not been determined. The mules showed extreme physical distress that lasted for a very short duration. Minutes, at most. There were also patches of what appeared to be human vomit in the vicinity of the dead mules."

"What do you think it was?" Joe Big asked.

"Well, as you know, last summer was unusually hot. There have been a few cases of animals killed by algae blooms in lakes and ponds—even a few cases in some of the slower-moving rivers. Through my binoculars I could see what looked like a blue algae bloom in a large swampy area at one end of a nearby lake. But we never made it down to the lake to see for sure."

"What did your equipment say?" Barney asked.

"Well, that's the thing. The equipment is so sensitive that, like you said, we get readings on all kinds of shit—excuse the language, ma'am," he said to Quinn. "Radiation. Chemicals. Explosives. Arsenic, now and then. A lot of gold and silver mining has gone on over the years in that part of the State." He smiled at Barney. "This is Montana. The Treasure State. If you think you got a lot of false readings in someplace like Iraq, you can't believe what registers here. Most all the trails in the area, even the old CC trails, were at one time or another used to get from one old mine to another. The dead mules had no more and no less trace on them than did our own mules."

"But . . ." Barney said.

"But we found some white powder under the neck of one of the dead mules." He held up his hand to stop Barney's question. "No. It wasn't anthrax or Sarin or anything like that. It was uncut, 97.6% pure heroin. From the Golden Triangle, and probably from Burma specifically, according to the lab."

"You found heroin under the neck of one of the dead mules," Joe Big said. "A pile of it?"

"More like a little skiff, a swatch that covered an area about a foot and a half long by about five inches wide." With his gnarled hands, Paul indicated the approximate area on the tabletop. "It looked like someone had tried to sweep it up with their hands. But you are right, Joseph. It was convenient the way it was under the neck of the mule, protected from the elements."

"But no idea how the mules died?" Barney asked.

"No. The suddenness of it pretty much ruled out the usual suspects. No blue tongue or any other indication around the muzzle of algae ingestion. There was no sign that bears or coyotes had been at the carcasses—which in itself was sort of strange. Not even birds. We should have taken some swabs, maybe opened one up and taken a piece of the lung and liver and stomach, but we figured we'd come back with a vet the next day, and the vet could do all the dirty work."

"Should have?" Barney asked.

"A big fire blew up that night or early the next morning on the ridge right above where we found the mules. The Early Lakes Fire," he said to everyone at the table. "It's contained now, but still burning on the south end. So far it's burned about 37,000 acres."

"So that was what?" Barney said. "A month and a half ago?"

"About that."

"The fire ran right over the site?"

Paul nodded. "You know how dry the forests have been—still are. The wind pushed it straight down the ridge. The next day it looked as if a nuke had gone off, the smoke cloud was so huge."

"What started the fire?" Brianna asked.

"Don't know for sure," Paul said. "They think lightning."

"Convenient," Joe Big said.

"That's what I said," Paul said. "But then the circus showed up. And the incident commander treated it like it *was* a nuclear explosion. The field near the trailhead was tent city. Fire fighters everywhere. Planes and helicopters and dozers and semi-trucks. Meetings, meetings, and more meetings. By the time all that finally went away, there was about as much chance of finding any useful evidence as there was of finding an ice skating rink."

Barney looked at Quinn.

"What's all this got to do with us?" Quinn asked. "Well, Paul's report piqued the interest of someone back in Washington, that's what it's got to do with us. They want us to insert a team, undercover, into the area, see what might crawl out from under a rock."

"And 'the team' would be me and Big."

"And Brianna."

"Working alone," Brianna said. "Not with you two lame di—"

"Brianna!" Quinn's green eyes darkened.

"Just joking. Just joking. Sheesh."

"Where's the DEA in all this?" Barney asked.

"They'd have to bring in people who don't know Montana very well," Quinn said, "And, anyway, a little heroin on the ground under a dead mule isn't enough to get them excited. What is it, Joe? What are you thinking?"

"I'm thinking about what killed those mules."

Paul nodded his head.

Quinn pushed the fat binder to the side, and folded her hands on the table in front of her. "There's no way to know that. Not now. Right, Paul?

"No way."

Joe ran his hand across the stubble on his head. "Three dead mules and a sprinkling of heroin protected from wind and weather by the head and neck of one of the mules." He looked at Paul. "If that heroin had been anywhere else, there'd be no heroin to find."

Paul nodded. "Correct."

"And still there's no explanation why the mules died in the first place," Barney said.

"Can you address that please, Paul?" Quinn said.

"After we reported what we'd found, the whole area was saturated with, ah, I guess with what could euphemistically be called *surveillance.* It was pretty impressive, actually. They caught a couple of professional poachers, some tobacco smugglers, a bunch of kids smuggling backpacks full of pot, found and marked every old mine in an area that must be a hundred and fifty miles square." He looked at Joe. "They even had three or four teams of Force Recon Marines who were, quote, 'on a training exercise'." He smiled. "Some of your *Tribe* got a little bored and just for the hell of it scared the beejesus out of a group of archeologists and geologists from MSU."

"No!" Joe Big said. "The very idea."

"Wish it would have been me they pulled that shit on," Brianna said.

"So do we," Barney said.

"The Marines were a little more, ah, *focused,* than we are accustomed to," Paul said. "But even they could not find anything that indicated more than a drug smuggling operation gone bad."

Barney looked at Quinn. "Are the people we had our little set-to with involved in all this?"

"Maybe," Quinn said. "We're not sure. That's one of the things we want you two to find out."

"And how are we supposed to do that?" Joe Big asked.

"There's a homicide that might be related."

"A homicide? Connected to the dead mules?"

"Maybe."

"Dead how?" Barney asked.

"Gunshot wound to the head, made to look like a suicide."

"Whoa," Brianna said. "I'd like to see how that was done."

Everyone looked at her.

"I mean . . . You know . . . It's interesting, is all I'm saying."

"We have a witness," Quinn said.

Barney and Joe Big looked at her.

"Me," she said.

"You," they both said in unison.

She smiled. "I was bow hunting for elk a week ago." Her smile faded. "It happened right in front of me. I was hidden in the trees."

Barney looked at Joe Big. "She hunts," he said.

"So she does," Joe Big said.

6
Junkyard Dogs

"Tenuous link, my ass," Joe Big said, as they settled into the Subaru. "They called in the Marines. Not to mention satellite and probably drone surveillance. That must have taken an Act of God, at least. A very expensive Act of God."

Barney was silent, tapping the fingers of both hands on the steering wheel.

"Three dead mules," Joe Big said. "And even Paul Cyr doesn't have a clue as to what killed them. An Earth Liberation Front wannabe forced to blow his brains out at the end of a Forest Service road." He looked over at Barney. "A rich college kid from Connecticut pretending to be part of the Monkey Wrench Gang. Staying—when he's not in his dorm—with Patrick and the Psycho-pants."

"What's the Monkey Wrench Gang?"

"Ah, it's the name of a book from, I don't know, the 70s, I guess. You know, monkey wrenches to dismantle bulldozers. Sugar in gas tanks, spikes in trees, that kind of thing. We read it in high school English."

"It doesn't sound like the kind of thing you like to read."

"The monkey wrench guys drank beer, drove big cars, ate red meat, and got laid. They weren't anything like the rich, effete, metrosexual vegan pseudo-revolutionaries of today."

Barney laughed. "Effete? Metrosexual? You better watch out, Big. Some of these people are going to figure out you're not as dumb as you act."

"I could walk in with a copy of *Crime and Punishment*, and the only person who would notice would be Mrs. W. We are junkyard dogs, man. No pedigree whatsoever." He looked at Barney. "And I don't know about you, but I *like* being a junkyard dog."

Barney put the key in the ignition, but didn't start the car. He sat back. "If a group of guys like us—a monkey wrench gang made up of people like us—wanted to do some real damage, think we could do it?"

"No way."

"Why not?"

"Well, think about it. They called in the Marines for three dead mules and some readouts that are probably the result of residue left by generations of miners packing explosives and chemicals to and from old mines. If we did anything like you suggest, they'd call in the Marines or Army Rangers for real. We could do damage, I guess. Get creative. But soon as the Marines or the Rangers showed up, we'd be dead and it'd be over—and things would be worse than if we hadn't done anything at all."

"You're right. It wouldn't work."

"You thinking about starting a revolution or something?"

"No, I'm just saying."

"Saying what?"

Barney glanced at him. "I'm starting to think that someone out there, or some group of someones, think they've figured out how to turn people like us on and off."

"All it takes to turn us on is a nice ass in a tight pair of jeans."

Barney smiled. "Uh-huh. I thought so."

"What? Why are you looking at me like that? 'You thought so' what?"

"You know what."

"Oh, right. Like you didn't notice."

Barney looked straight ahead. He drummed his fingers on the steering wheel.

"Quinn makes me nervous," he said.

"And you think I—"

"I don't mean that way," Barney said. "I mean she's so smart she makes being smart look easy."

"She's supposed to be smart—and since she's a Fed, mean and cold and vindictive."

"So let's say you're Quinn and you've got two people working for you like us . . ."

Joe Big frowned.

"Why would she even want people like us, in the first place?" Barney asked.

"I don't know. Comic relief?"

"You've got this thing about perspective. So look at it from her perspective—or more exactly from the perspective of whoever pulls her strings. We aren't investigators—at least not as far as the Feds are concerned, we're not. Quinn can call on the resources of some of the best investigatory agencies on the planet. But she's calling on us?" He looked over at Joe. "I mean, what did she tell us to do? What kind of bullshit is that?"

"You think Quinn—"

"No, not Quinn. Well, yeah, Quinn. But she's caught in the middle of it, same as us, just at a higher pay grade, and with access to—"

"It? Man, you're blowing this up into some kind of movie or something. Let's go find those assholes, and fuck them up. Plant them in the ground, if that's what it takes. We don't need all this noise."

"It's like it was in Afghanistan, Big. We all thought we were part of a team cobbled together because of manpower shortages. But each of us brought something different to the table, and we learned to work together in an amazingly short time. Luck of the draw, like we assumed? I didn't buy it then, and I don't buy it now."

"What's that got to do with anything?"

"Just jack down a minute, okay? Stay with me here. I think better when I say it out loud."

Barney held up his right hand to stop Big from saying anything. "You're a GS-90, or whoever it is that is in charge of shit like this, and your job description says that you are tasked with fighting terrorists, foreign and domestic, within the borders of the U.S."

"Yeah? And?"

"Well, how are you going to do that without using the military? You're up against people who have been trained by the best from Russia, North Korea, China, and every other country that has ever had a hard-on for us. What're you going to do? Call the National Guard? The FBI? Local police and sheriff's departments? It doesn't matter how motivated such people are. It's going to take a lot more than a willing spirit to get the job done. Otherwise, the sky is going to fall on them, same as the sky fell on all those cops and firemen at Ground Zero."

Barney started the car. The sound of the modified Subaru flat-four was like a Harley Davidson motorcycle at idle. He stepped on the accelerator and the throaty thud smoothed into a deep-bass hum. He blipped the throttle, and then brought the tach up to a steady 6500, the deep-bass tone become a scream of power. He let off on the throttle, and at idle the sound again became a rough thud like that of a Harley motorcycle.

"Like that," he said. "Like the engine in this car. Rough until you put the pedal to the metal." He laughed. "The Death Devo. You asshole. I almost laughed out loud."

"Hey. If the shoe fits . . ."

"Well, that's my point, bro. The shoe *does* fit. She is a truly bent and obnoxious woman. No question. But answer me this: would you want her next to you in a fight? Bet your ass, you would."

Joe Big frowned. He rubbed the side of his face.

"And Quinn," Barney said. "She's from Boston, but she's bow hunting for elk in Montana? What's that all about? She's a viper, man. A heat-seeker. I kid you not. She's like that fucking saw-scale you shot that time."

He put the car in gear, and backed out of the driveway into the alley. Shifted into first. Blipped the throttle. Brought the tach up to 5500 rpm. Slipped the clutch and the Subaru launched, snapping Joe Big's head back against the headrest, only a tiny chirp from the tires. Barney grabbed second gear, and before they were halfway down the alley the car was at 65. He stood on the brakes, dust and gravel spewing off the tires, ABS chattering, and they were stopped at the end of the alley, calmly waiting for cars passing in both directions.

"Like that," he said again. "No smoking the tires. No drama. Zero to sixty in four seconds or less." He pulled out into traffic. "A team as modified as this car."

"Man, I got to get me one of these."

"I keep telling you . . ."

'Yeah, but . . . I got to get me one of these."

Barney smiled. "That's probably what they said."

"They?"

"Whoever put together this so-called team we're supposed to be working for. We're not all *that* unique, you know. There's got to be other teams scattered around the country."

"I don't follow?"

"I modified this car based on the experience of a whole lot of other guys who—through trial and error and the best advice of professional mechanics and engineers—had already done similar modifications to their cars. By the time I put it together it was pretty much by-the-numbers."

"And your point is?"

"How many terrorist events have there been in this country since Nine-Eleven? Not counting totally amateurish attempts that did almost no damage?"

"Got me."

"None. Nada. Zip. Zero. And you think that is luck? Coincidence?"

"Never really thought about it, I guess."

"Well, think about it, now. Think about us sitting there in that meeting, and Quinn is telling us that the connections are "tenuous," but that's okay, wander up to the Flathead and see what we see, do whatever we think we ought to do. Are you shitting me? She's telling *us*, the class fuck-up's, the guys who got their asses handed to them by three rodents, to go forth and exercise their—*our*—best judgment? Poor old Paul Cyr was sitting there wondering what language she was speaking."

"Nerve gas," Joe Big said.

"What?"

"We had a couple of weeks of Chemical Warfare integrated into our training—in case we ever did find some of Sadam's WMD. There's a family of nerve agents that start with the letter V. V for venomous."

"Yeah. VX. I had the same training. A tiny drop will do you. What about it? No one ever found any."

"VX is a liquid, not a gas. It's not like Sarin. It doesn't go away."

Barney looked at him.

"I think Paul was luckier than he'll ever know," Joe said.

"If you accidentally spilled some, how would you clean it up?" Barney asked.

"You'd burn it," Joe Big said. "You'd start a forest fire and burn it."

7
Surf's Up

"You drive," Barney said.

"What?" Joe Big looked at him over the top of the Subaru.

"You drive."

"You never let anyone drive this thing. You never even let your ex drive it."

Barney walked around to the passenger side of the Subaru. He was dressed in a retro-looking beige shirt with what at first looked like delta-winged butterflies on it, dark baggy slacks, and old school black-and-white high-top Converse Chuck Taylor All-Stars.

"Look at you," Joe Big said.

"Do not be dissing my clothes, man. You're the one said we need to change our image."

"Are those butterflies?"

"They are boomerangs. This is a genuine Boomerang shirt."

"Mrs. W helped you pick it out, didn't she?"

"So what if she did? Hey, you want to drive my car, you best stop laughing. And anyway, look at you."

Joe Big climbed into the driver's seat. "This is what I always wear. What are you talking about?" He was wearing green baggy cargo pants and running shoes, white tee under an unzipped gray hoody, light-green knit hat pulled low on his forehead.

"I'm a cool cat. A hip hipster." Barney lowered himself into the passenger seat. "But without your braid and soul patch that hat makes you look like a Vietnamese villain from Seattle."

"Yeah? Well, watch this." Joe Big produced a pair of gold wire-rim glasses from the pocket of his hoody, and put them on. He turned to face Barney.

"Damn. The hip hipster is seein' but he is not believin'." Barney frowned. "I didn't know you could do that. How come you never went DEA?"

"Right. As if I'm not fucked up enough already."

Barney sat back in the seat. "Hey, like I'm totally hearing that, Square Bear. Turn the key and let's, like, splitsville, daddy-o. Those glasses are, like, totally boss, dude."

Joe Big laughed, and shook his head. "You're mixing up your decades, you idiot."

He clipped in his seat belt and reached for the key. "Is there anything I need to know about this thing? The clutch, like that?"

"Indeed not, grasshopper. It pretty much drives itself."

Joe Big put in the clutch and turned the key and the engine caught immediately. He sawed the steering wheel back and forth. "I see what you mean. Once you start this thing, the car feels bigger."

Barney smiled to himself.

Joe Big revved the engine slightly and let the clutch slowly out and backed out of Barney's narrow driveway into the street. He shifted into first, and again eased the clutch out, and the car gently accelerated away. He shifted into second, the skin around his eyes and at his cheekbones already starting to relax. He grinned, and shifted into third.

"I'm going to get a ticket," he said.

"That's not going to happen."

"Why not? It's my ticket."

"Because we are going to be cool dudes, that's why. Trust Fund Babies who own property in the Flathead. Driving this thing twenty miles an hour over the speed limit gives you sweaty palms. Far as anyone else knows there are no real modifications to this car. It's de-badged and with some easy bolt-on's to make people think it's fast, that's all. Basically, it's a metaphor for us: all show and no go."

Joe Big glanced at Barney. "Not only does Mrs. W have you looking like Hunter S. Thompson, you are starting to talk like him, too."

"Who's Hunter Thompson?"

"You don't want to know. You're conflicted enough as it is."

"Well, whoever he is, he must understand what it means to be sartorially elegant."

"He's a was. Tell me again: why do we want to be a metaphor?"

"We want to be this particular metaphor because, *if*, as we both suspect, this little fishing expedition catches no fish, we'll make the rounds again on our way home—and I'll make some *major bucks* off all the people who think this is a bling-only rice rocket that has no chance against their American Muscle."

"Can I drive?"

"Not if we want to win."

Joe Big downshifted and turned left at the light, and gently stepped on the gas. The engine gave a slight hiccup, and then the car smoothly accelerated toward the bridge, drifting effortlessly in and out of sparse traffic. "I am definitely getting me one of these," he said.

He kept the revs up to make the next light, and then the one after that, and then they were down into the underpass, under the railroad tracks, the exhaust suddenly loud in their ears, up out of the underpass and headed for the Interstate on-ramp.

"Punch it when you get to the onramp," Barney said. "About three-quarters throttle."

Joe Big pushed down hard on the throttle and the car leaped forward, all four wheels chirping, and the tachometer needle went past redline and the injectors started to shut down, the engine bogging, as Joe Big shifted, wide-eyed and wired as tight as he'd ever been jumping out of a perfectly good airplane or helicopter, and they were under the Interstate, onto the long, curving, upward S of the onramp, the speedometer already winding past eighty."

"Stay on it," Barney shouted. "You can pass that semi on his right."

And they came up onto the Interstate at well over a hundred, Joe Big with no time to look at the tach or the speedometer, the engine sweet, living life the way it had been designed to live life. He shifted and floored the gas pedal and still in the on-ramp lane they shot past the tandem-trailer rig on their left, plenty of room to spare, not even close, the speedometer reading one thirty five, the tach once again in redline, when he looked down.

He shifted into fifth and let the car coast down to eighty.

Barney laughed.

Joe Big wiped his hands, first his right, then his left, on his pants. He held his right hand out for Barney to see. His hand was vibrating.

To their right, they could see the city spread below, most of the city a mass of gold and red and yellow maple leaves, a few tall buildings and church steeples rising above the trees. In the background Lolo Peak, 9,096 feet, big and massive and solid blue to the snowline, the top hidden by dark clouds, like clouds around the top of a volcano.

"Let's do it again," Joe Big said.

"I let you do that because I don't want you getting all morose."

Joe Big glanced over at him. "About what?"

"About your nurse."

Joe Big stepped on the gas and brought the speed up to ninety. He set the speed control, and took his foot off the gas, and relaxed back into the seat, one hand on the side of the steering wheel. "What it is," he said. "Is that I'm the best thing that never happened to her. Her father will be eternally grateful."

Barney stared at him for a long moment.

Joe Big raised his right eyebrow.

"Shotgun is on the backseat," Barney said. "Under the blanket. Everything else is in duffels."

FIVE OR SIX miles later, the blue Subaru wagon eased off the Interstate and up the exit lane onto Highway 93.

"I drive Highway 93," Barney said. "Pray For Me."

To the left, they could see a range of mountains stretching west toward Idaho, the largest nearly as tall as Lolo Peak, but with a sharp conical peak snow capped with the first high-country snow of the season.

"Maybe we ought to kiss this off and go elk hunting instead," Joe said.

"Stop at the truck stop. We need gas."

"Sneak up on the wily *wapiti*." Joe Big turned the Subaru into the truck stop. "Get our heads straight." Semis were scattered and lined up around the restaurant and gas station. A silver Mitsubishi EVO was parked at the gas pumps, black wheels nearly the same as on the Subaru, windows tinted darker than legal, larger-than-stock exhaust pipe, Washington plates.

"Get our heads straight," Barney said. "We could sell tickets to that. Pull in next to that EVO. I want to look at it."

"I need to take a leak."

"This car will do that to you."

"Word dat."

"Your hat says snowboarder, not gangbanger, you idjit."

"Whoa. My bad, dude. Totally not phat, dat."

Barney groaned. "I'll fill it up while you wee-wee. Grab some snacks and some Dew, will you?"

"Dew? I hate Dew."

"If you don't want to drive, get some beer, then. But get me some Dew."

"I'll get both—just in case." Joe Big guided the car up parallel with the EVO on the other side of the pumps. "That's a sick-looking ride, man." He snickered to himself.

Two men stood at the rear, one of them filling the tank, hand on the gas nozzle. Both men wore black wrap-around sunglasses, baggy green cargo pants, like the pants Joe Big had on, dark green sweat shirts. Buzz cuts, both of them. Their heads swiveled toward the sound of the Subaru idling on the other side of the pumps.

"Wigger twins," Joe Big muttered, and shut off the engine and opened the door. He climbed out and headed for the truck-stop store, ignoring the stare of the two men as he walked diagonally across an intervening island, and threaded his way between parked cars outside the store.

Barney leaned across the driver's seat, stretching his arm and hand toward the gas door release on the far-side floor, and flipped the release handle with his fingertips. He sat up and opened the door and climbed out. Both men on the other side of the island were looking at him, their eyes impossible to see behind the glasses.

Tweedle-dee and Tweedle-dum, he thought, some kind of college insignia on both their sweatshirts. Gonzaga frat boys, maybe.

He nodded at them. "Sick ride," he said, wishing Joe Big was there to hear him say that, and pulled the little gas door all the way open and unscrewed the gas cap.

"Nice shirt," one of the men said.

Barney glanced at him, and inserted his Visa card into the pump and quickly pulled it out. "Thanks," he said, and almost did a double-take when he saw what the insignia on the man's sweatshirt really was.

"A Boomerang, right?"

"What? Oh, yeah. Right." He inserted the nozzle and depressed the lever and locked it down. He glanced up at the man.

"Nice ride, too. Stealthy, I like that."

"Not in the same class as yours, though," Barney said. "This one is all show."

"It sounds like it has some go, to me. Hey, do I know you from somewhere?"

Barney smiled, the careless, condescending smile of someone who doesn't have a clue. "Not unless you'all are from Louisiana," he said, thickening his accent.

"Montana plate on your car," the other man said. He had come up on the other side of the pump.

"Montana plate? Oh, *Montana plate.* Yeah. This is the Montana car. The family has a place up by Whitefish, and we keep it there." He laughed, as if embarrassed to be rich. "My Montana mo-beel," he said. "Do everything, go anywhere in this baby. Especially in the winter."

"Must be nice," the second man said. His sweatshirt had the same emblem on it. A black and silver coat of arms, upright sword with crossed arrows over the sword, a banner unfurled around the lower half, Latin words in the banner. Both men were about 5'11", maybe 6', the first one. Same clothes, same sunglasses, same buzz cuts. The first man had a long, horsy face, dark tanned; the other was pale-skinned and red-haired. Another son of Ireland, Barney thought. Fucking Irish were everywhere, these days.

Both men seemed tense and focused. He'd seen their type plenty of times before. Had been one himself, once upon a time.

"You guys go to the same school, huh?"

"Same school?"

"Yeah, your sweatshirts. You've got the same school emblem."

The two men looked at each other, and laughed. The redhead leaned forward and reached toward the other man and they tapped fists.

The nozzle lever clanked off, and Barney removed the nozzle and put it back into the pump. He screwed the cap back on and shut the little door.

"So, you guys headed back to school, or what?" he asked.

"Nah," the horse-faced man said. "We're taking a little vacation. Breaking in a new engine and turbo. Kalispell. Glacier Park, like that."

His stare and not being able to see their eyes and the fact that they both thought he was a clueless idiot was starting to piss Barney off, even though they were reacting to him exactly the way he wanted them to.

"Way awesome," Barney said. "Y'all know people in this part of the State? Have a place to stay?"

"We know a few people."

"Oh, hey. I just noticed. Sorry about that." Barney hit himself on the forehead with the palm of his hand. "My bad. That's a military logo on your shirts, isn't it?"

"Uh-huh."

"You guys been in the military, huh?"

"How about you?" the redhead asked, his pasted-on smile more a rictus than a smile.

"Me?" Barney laughed self-consciously. "I always wanted to join, but I've got a heart condition—a murmur."

"I'll bet," the horse faced man said.

"No. Really. I had rheumatic fever when I was just beginning grade school. It's rare these days, but we were in Europe—in Italy, actually—and the doctors thought it was strep throat, and well, you know . . ." His voice trailed off.

"Fuck a duck," the redhead muttered. He turned and stepped down off the island behind the pumps. "Let's get out of here," he said to the other man, "before I throw up."

"Really," Barney said. "I always wanted to join the military." He brightened. "The guy I'm with was in the Marines for a while." He looked confused for a moment. "But he had to get out."

"How does someone like you put a car like this together?" the horse-faced man asked.

"What? Me put . . . Oh, no. I didn't put it together. A shop in Seattle did that." He laughed. "I wouldn't know a wrench from a wench."

The man stared at him as if he'd just encountered a rare, never-before-imagined life form.

An E-9, at least, Barney thought, with probably two or three tours in the Sandbox, hard to say where else. He looked vaguely familiar to him, too. Could be they'd crossed paths. Gear and grime and camo, there'd be no way to say for sure.

"Hey, maybe we'll see you up the road," he said. "I'd be honored to buy a couple of veterans a drink or three."

Without a word or sign, the man turned and stepped off the island and into the EVO. The engine started, and the throttle blipped, and Barney could tell by the sound that the car was far from stock. The silver car bolted forward, engine revving high as it darted for the highway.

Barney stared after it, listening to the sound of its exhaust as the driver took it through the gears.

Sweet car, he thought. Not so sweet people.

"MAN, WHO WERE those dudes?" Joe Big asked. "I got bad vibes just looking out the window at them." He put the sack of drinks and snacks in the passenger-side footwell. "You drive. I feel the need for a beer."

Barney got in behind the wheel. He leaned over and picked up the sack and put it on the center console. He peered inside. "What's this?" He pulled out a pair of black wrap-around sunglasses from the sack.

Joe Big climbed in. "I bought those for you. Make you look cool, like those two guys in the EVO."

Barney put them on.

"Perfect," Joe Big said. "A Cylon in a Boomerang shirt."

He took off his wire-rim glasses and replaced them with a pair of small, blue-tinted, octagonal wire-rim sunglasses. "How about these?"

"You look like a Chinese version of Ben Franklin."

"No, really."

"You look like one of those made-in-China, stuffed animals with dead eyes. Way too much edge for who we are supposed to be. The other ones make you look harmless."

Joe Big threw the sunglasses in the backseat and put the wire-rim glasses back on. "Nerdy is better than villain, I guess," he said. "I don't know why we bother with all this pretend—costumes and legends and shit. We always end up being who we are, anyway."

"I like these," Barney said, touching his fingers to the sunglasses. "They'll be good for fishing. They don't let any light in the sides." He started the car. "First impressions. Didn't your mother or your grandmother ever teach you about first impressions?"

"Yeah. I guess. You want a Dew?"

"With this shirt and these glasses? Give me a beer."

"You said I couldn't drive and drink beer."

"Yo, daddy-o. You got to be hip to the, ah, you got to be cool to the mule."

"Cool to the mule?"

"Leave me alone. It's the only thing I could think of that rhymes. You can't drive because you can't drive. It's got nothing to do with alcohol intake."

Joe Big handed him a beer.

"A Schmidt! God damn, Big!"

"Hey, I'm trying to keep you in character, is all. Schmidt is so cheap and awful that it's cool. You know what I mean? It goes with the shoes and the sunglasses."

Barney handed the beer back to him. "Give me a Dew." He started the car. "Sometimes . . ." He put the car in gear, and headed for the highway. "The World shudders to think what might happen if you ever did a spirit quest or whatever it is real Blackfeets do."

"I already did one." Big reached in the sack and pulled out a Moose Drool. "And here I am." He popped off the top, and took a drink. "Hey, this is pretty good. Too bad you're not a snowboarder computer-programmer dude."

Barney rolled his eyes. "Why me, Lord?"

"Surf's up," Joe Big said.

Barney glanced at him. "What does *that* mean?"

"Those two dudes, man. Surf's up. I can feel it."

8
Through the Wire

Never seen a sunset like this," Barney said forty-five minutes later. He was half-sitting, half-leaning against the closed metal gate of the new rest area, watching cars and trucks crest the hill and follow the highway down into the Mission Valley. Red light surrounded the World Rally Blue Subaru, making it seem as if it had been dipped in a dark, viscous fluid. Orange and red beams of light shot across the ridgeline behind them, disappearing into blood-red sky.

Across the valley, the Mission Mountains rose massively from the valley floor, the snow at the top chalk red. A train of cars swished past. A chip truck trundled over the top behind them, shifting gears as it headed down into the valley.

"So what are we supposed to do if we find the dudes who killed Quinn's informant?" Barney asked. "There's no evidence. And it's hard to imagine guys that cold confessing to anything."

"We don't need to give a damn about all that. It's her problem. Her informant. Either she was twisting him, in which case he wasn't clean. Or she was paying him, in which case he assumed the risk when he took the money. Or he was doing it out of some naïve, misguided sense of ideals, in which case she strung him along, and it's still right back on her. If it coincides with our problem, fine. We'll do what we can. But right now we need to take care of our own business."

Barney squinted down the fence line. Wire glinted red in the sunset. Big was right, he thought. When Quinn and Company were long gone, off on some other assignment or re-assigned to some other Federal task force, he and Big would still be here. Word would get out. It probably already had, thanks to the Death Devo, and thanks to Patrick and his crew. He smiled to himself: The Death Devo.

Two hundred meters down the fence two Bighorn sheep, both almost a full curl, lay side by side inside the fence, watching the two men.

"I'm really starting to dislike this working-for-the-Feds shit," Joe Big said. "We're getting a long way from serving and protecting our own, if you know what I mean." He looked toward the mountains, his eyes following the line of their march toward Flathead Lake and beyond to Glacier Park and Canada.

"Corporations," Barney said.

"What?"

"It's all about corporations these days," Barney said. "Government corporations. Private corporations. The mix of the two. It's not about 'by the people, for the people' any more."

Joe Big turned to look at him.

"There's a couple of Bighorn Sheep down there," Barney said. "See them?"

"I saw them when we pulled up. They know they're safe inside the fence."

"Yeah," Barney said. "But they really aren't. Anyone could stop and shoot them through the wire. Right? Which is why you never see elk over here any more. People were shooting the big bulls for their antlers. And now the Government keeps the elk away from the highway."

"Let me guess," Joe Big said. "Those sheep are another one of your metaphors? They're free, but they're not free, kind of thing. They think they're safe, but they're not really safe."

"Let's see how close we can get," Barney said.

They walked down the hill toward the two sheep. The side of the hill was in shadow, but even in shadow the air seemed permeated by the red light, filled with something undefined that made the backs of their necks tingle. The air reminded Joe Big of walking a trail in the mountains of Tajikistan.

The sheep stared steadily at them, their mouths no longer moving back and forth. A fragile breeze moved down the hill, stirring knee-high grass, raising goose bumps on Barney's bare arms.

He bent and picked up a rock.

"Don't throw it," Joe Big said. "This is a heavy thing going down here between these two big boys and us. This is some kind of Bighorn sheep mojo."

Barney dropped the rock. "You think?"

"Yeah. Can't you feel it?" The two rams abruptly stood and took a step toward the two men.

"Whoa," Barney said.

"These guys used to be big medicine to the Crow," Joe Big said.

The ram on the right took two powerful steps up the slope toward them, muscles rippling in his shoulders and haunches.

Barney stopped. "What's he doing?"

"Got me. Never seen anything like this. Maybe they know I'm part Blackfoot."

"Think they could come through that wire if they wanted to?"

"Probably. I saw a wild pig in Hawaii break the bottom strand on a barbed wire fence. Barbed wire is a lot stronger than what this fence is made out of."

Barney reached behind his right hip, and from under his shirt unsnapped and pulled his Glock.

Joe Big eyed him. "Man, you are way too hinky, these days, you know that?" He jumped up and down and waved his arms. "Booga, Booga," he shouted.

The two sheep stared. The one closest wheeled, and then the other wheeled, and the two of them ambled, unhurried, up the hillside, showing their backsides. They disappeared over a grassy ridge."

"Hinky," Barney said. "I wonder why." He raised the Glock with both hands, and bent his knees slightly, and fired at the nearest fence post, the shots stuttering in two-shots groups, like an out-of-timing automatic weapon.

Splinters flew from the fence post and it listed to the side, held up by the wire stretched tight to neighboring poles.

"Oops."

"What the fuck!" Joe Big said. "Why'd you do that? If someone heard that, we'll have half the reservation down on us."

Barney ejected the magazine and caught it with his left hand. "I thought you said these Indians are apples. The only reason they are even here is because your people wanted something to do in the early spring."

"My people . . . There is no *"my people."* What the fuck is wrong with you, anyway? Lot of good your target practice did, when—"

Barney slammed a fresh magazine into the butt of the pistol, and then re-holstered it, snapping the strap shut with one hand. "You got something to say, say it." He dropped the empty magazine in his pant pocket. "But you best—"

"Best what?"

Behind Barney, up the hill on the other side of the wire, Joe Big saw the heads of the two Bighorn sheep reappear, looking at them.

Joe Big stared at Barney. At Barney dressed in retro sports shirt and slacks and ridiculous Converse basketball shoes. At Barney angry and frustrated and recently divorced. All-American, student-athlete Barney, his childhood and his marriage truncated by the barren hills of Afghanistan. There was no mystery at all why he identified with two big Rams caught forever on the wrong side of the wire.

He shook his head. "Best we don't get to acting like this."

Barney glared at him.

"It wasn't your fault," Joe Big said. "I should have shot her, and then that big motherfucker. We could have blamed everything on that spineless shit, Harold."

"Yeah, you should have."

Joe Big nodded to where the two Bighorn were craning their heads and necks over the lip of the gully. "Those two Bighorn are enjoying this."

Barney turned to look, and Joe Big could see the tension go out of his shoulders and neck.

Barney smiled.

"They look like cartoons," he said.

"PROBABLY TOO MUCH listening to the Moody Blues and Dire Straits on my way to school," Barney said. "My old man's music. Every morning five days a week."

They were sitting on a large flat rock, a landscaping rock put there by whoever had built the rest stop, listening to Rhianna sing about shutting up and driving, while they drank the last of the Moose Drool.

"Last bottle," Barney said, offering it to Joe Big.

Joe Big took it from Barney, and then handed it back. "Yours," he said. "I'll drive, while you take a nap and dream of saving the world from evil doers."

Barney's eyes glittered. "Look. We don't owe a fucking thing to anybody but ourselves. We paid our dues, man—more than once. So fuck it." He paused, and considered the bottle. "Joe Big, Indian Extraordinaire, offering me the last bottle of stout. Can this be true?" He popped the top off, and dropped the cap in his shirt pocket. "I better drink it before you change your mind."

Joe Big laughed, and looked up at the ridgeline. Stars were beginning to show, the air already cold, biting through his open hoody. Barney seemed unfazed, but Joe knew it was only because his body was trying to burn the alcohol contained in the three beers he'd consumed in record time. Above the mountain the sky was a deep, ugly purple. Off to the right, one of the Bighorn was silhouetted, slowly picking its way up the ridgeline.

"So what's with the Crow and Bighorn?" Barney asked.

Joe squinted toward the Bighorn. "Oh, I dunno. Something about a Crow being saved by a Bighorn, and then assuming the powers of that Bighorn—strength, agility, sure-footedness, intelligence, all that good stuff. And then going home and telling the Crow that as long as the river that flowed out of their mountains was called the Bighorn River the Crow would live."

"That makes no sense."

"If not for the white man, the Blackfeet would have killed all the Crow, Bighorn River or no."

"Your people," Barney said.

Joe Big watched the Bighorn working it's way up the ridge.

"My people," he said, and pushed off from the rock. "Let's go."

9
Always There

Barney lay on the passenger seat, the seat all the way back and down, feeling the folded, nylon sleeping bag he was using as a pillow soft and fluffy against his face. Wind coming through the open rear windows eddied around his head, slid across his face. He smiled, caught somewhere between awake and half drunk. Out the window the sky was huge and star-filled, the universe tuned to the complex exertions of the car vibrating beneath him.

He turned his head and beyond the cluster of blue- and yellow-lit instruments, out the window beyond Joe Big, a tinge of pink colored the western sky.

It's out there, he thought.

He'd never seen it. But it was out there, all right. Kind of like one of those Dragons that Big had told him about—that the Chinese were always talking about. You can't see it. But you can sure feel it when it's there.

He squirmed his head against the nylon sleeping bag, and lifted his hand and wiggled his fingers in front of his face: pale worms wiggling in the dark.

He'd first met it when his father had died.

Eleven years old and I didn't understand, he thought.

He dropped his hand to his chest.

In Afghanistan and just about every other place he'd killed people, it was around all the time. Even when they weren't in a fight or bringing doom, it whispered around them, not quite seen, not quite heard. He'd look up from cleaning a weapon or reading a book, and nothing would be there. Everyone would be going about their business, no one paying attention to anything but what they were doing. But every once in awhile, he'd catch someone else with the same expression on his face as must have been on his own: head cocked to the side, like a dog will cock its head to the side when it hears a sound in a frequency that human beings cannot hear.

His hand balled into a fist.

Sometimes he could taste its breath on him—breath as dry and metallic as crushed, crusted blood.

You shot and sometimes stabbed and beat. But most of all, you watched, stunned by the sound, surrounded by pink mist part dust, part blood, part fecal stench. And when the tsunami of sound and heat and recoil was gone and you found yourself still alive, you looked around, and you felt as if you were the only person left on the planet.

But it was still there.

Still there in the blood covering the rocks, discoloring the ground.

In the corpses and body parts.

In the forever maimed.

A thrill that felt sick, like hitting his elbow on a sharp edge, swept smooth and cold and electric through his body.

Their death is my death, he thought.

He looked at the instruments through half-open eyes. And listening to the throaty sound of the car vibrating beneath him, felt his face and hands relax.

Sometimes. Sometimes, he thought. Sometimes I feel like I did when I was eleven years old.

I still don't understand.

And, as Joe Big pressed gently on the accelerator and the torque pushed his head down into the sleeping bag, and Vaya Con Dios sang about not crying for Louie, he fell asleep.

And on the horizon pink faded to gray.

10

Off The Reservation

A little over an hour later, Barney driving now, and one county north, they were in Whitefish. Ye Olde West, Joe Big thought. Quaint fronts on almost all of the downtown buildings made the downtown look more like a Hollywood set than a Montana town. Its restaurants and bars, coffee shops and jewelry stores, would be at home in Aspen or Vail or Tahoe. He was pretty sure there were more art galleries than bars.

"You sure we didn't cross into Canada?" he asked.

Barney gazed out the window. Beemer SUVs. A pair of Porsche Cayenne's. His and Hers, maybe? Cadillac Escalades so ubiquitous they were hardly even noticeable. "Maybe," he said. "But I only see one Hummer."

In a lisping falsetto, Joe Big said, "Hummer's are so yesterday."

Most of the people on the street were dressed as if they had been outfitted by REI or Patagonia. Coats or vests, tight jeans and expensive boots on the over-thirty women. Even tighter pants and tight, zip-up Patagonia tops for the younger women and the women who thought they could pass for younger. For the younger men, hiking boots and baggy cargo pants and layered shirts, the top shirt unbuttoned and worn like a jacket, sleeves rolled up to the elbow. The older men—those not interested in skiing or snowboarding—were mostly wearing jeans and cowboy boots, thick leather belts with fat belt buckles, shearling-lined leather jackets, their carefully tended hair a perfect gray at the temples. A Marlboro Man on nearly every block.

"Gee, there seems to be a dearth of tribal members," Barney said.

"These people are from a different tribe," Joe Big said. "The fuck-you-I-own-it-now-Tribe."

"Didn't you hook up with the daughter of some movie star the last time we were here?"

"That's how come I know what tribe these people are from."

"That bad, huh?"

"Stunning but slumming."

"Oh, I see," Barney said. "And the fact that she is the daughter of a movie star you can't stand meant no never mind?"

"Hey, I'm entitled."

"You're part of the flora and fauna, is all you are. And as everyone knows, God created flora and fauna to be exploited—or in your case, just plain fucked." He laughed.

"Hah. Hah. I hate it when you laugh at your own bad jokes."

In front of them, a group of five or six people, men and women both, walked out from between parked cars, into the middle of the street, forcing Barney to brake hard.

"Look at these idiots. What do they think they are doing?"

"I told you," Joe Big said. "They own this place. They can do anything they want"

One of the men, a middle-aged man, silver at the temples, big and burly and movie-star handsome and wearing some kind of expensive looking dark leather jacket and matching gloves, brought the edge of his fist down hard on the passenger side fender. "Watch it!" he shouted, his shout more a command than a warning. The other five people, three women and two men, all dressed Patagonia Perfect in scarves and jackets, glared at them, and then turned, shaking their heads and laughing, and walked down the middle of the street in front of the car.

"I hate to tell you this, but he dented the fender," Joe Big said.

"What?" Barney yanked up the emergency brake, flipped the gearshift into neutral, popped his seat belt and was out the door before Joe Big could say anything else.

The man in the leather jacket was striding away from the car, through the white glare from the headlights—a burly shepherd herding his flock down the middle of the street.

Barney hurried up behind him, light on his feet, and stuck out his right foot, gently hooking the outside of the man's right ankle, the hooked ankle catching the back of the other ankle, causing the man to trip over his own feet and fall awkwardly to his knees, outstretched hands smacking the pavement.

"Ouch," Joe Big said. "The Pit Maneuver."

The man picked himself up off the street, clearly confused as to how he'd managed to trip over his own feet, and Barney said something, and the man turned, and Barney grabbed him by the lapels of his expensive leather jacket, and bending at the knees, pivoted quick, and threw the man, legs cartwheeling, over his hip, slamming him flat on his back onto the street, careful to not let his head hit the pavement.

The other people continued to walk away, laughing and gesticulating, unaware that something not nice was happening behind them.

Joe Big climbed out of the car, and walked up next to where Barney had the man on the ground. The man was making weird woofing noises.

Barney hauled him to his feet, the leather coat bunched up around the man's face, sleeves pulled up nearly to his elbows. "SIR, WHAT HAPPENED?" Barney asked loudly. "YOU WERE WALKING ACROSS THE STREET AND YOU FELL DOWN." He released his right hand from the leather collar and using the man's body to block the view of the other five people—several of whom had finally turned around—hit him with a short, hard right to the solar plexus. "ARE YOU OKAY, SIR?"

Barney released him and the man fell to his knees and collapsed onto his side, wheezing and retching at the same time.

"SIR? SIR? ARE YOU OKAY?"

The man was making a worrisome *uh, uh* sound.

"Oh, my God, Ellis," one of the women said, and ran forward. The others stared, unwilling to accept what they were seeing: their friend curled into the fetal position and making awful sounds in the middle of the street.

"I don't know what happened, man," Barney said to the woman. "We were, like, totally stopped. And, Bam! This big dude here hit the fender. And then he walked over behind you cats, and fell down. Whoompf! Just like that. And then he started making sounds like a dawg with larry-gitis."

"Heart attack, maybe?" Joe Big volunteered, looking bemusedly down at the man. He prodded the man with his toe.

"Ellis, are you okay?" the woman asked. "Don't do that," she said to Joe Big. She looked up at Barney. "Don't just stand there. Do something."

Joe Big laughed, and walked back to the passenger side. "Come on," he said to Barney. "Let's go do something."

Barney climbed into the driver's seat and closed the door and released the emergency brake. He shifted into first, and they slowly motored around the five people standing in the middle of the street looking down at poor Ellis. One of the men watched them drive away, memorizing their license plate.

"Do you have your plates on?" Joe Big asked.

"Of course not. Mrs. W got a new stack the other day. They'll come back to an insurance company in Billings."

"Cool."

"Mrs. W. What can I say?"

Joe Big looked back. "He's up—sort of."

"Too bad."

"Where you going to park?" Joe Big asked. The street was lined with vehicles, all the parking places taken. "I have a feeling 'ol Ellis back there might take it out on the car if he sees it."

"I'll park in the City Police Department lot. Ask them to keep an eye on it."

"You've got anger management issues. I guess you know that."

"Hey, I'm just making sure the word gets out that we're here, is all."

"Yeah, right."

"Now we have an excuse to let the local cops know we're in town on a top-secret mission," Barney said.

"Uh-huh. And nimble-minded rocket scientist that you aren't, all that went through your head when you bailed and did a kung-fu on some old-guy stockbroker or lawyer who dented your fender."

"A lawyer! Damn. Let's go back and do it again."

"I've got a better idea, let's park this thing, and go get a beer. Maybe find some ladies. Listen to something besides Sitting on the Dock of the Bay."

"Tell me you don't like Otis."

"I like Otis. I really do. You were right. But I don't like *anyone* for an hour. Not even Otis."

"You've got anger management issues," Barney said. "Did anyone ever tell you that?"

Joe Big leaned his head back against the headrest and sighed and looked up at the ceiling. "You're not helping," he said to the ceiling.

"Helping what?" Barney asked.

"I'm not talking to you."

11
The Death Devo

I don't know about your shirt," Joe Big said, as they stood outside the door to a bar. "This place caters to snowboarders and skiers and wannabe cowboys."

"Don't worry. I'll manage."

A big woman, short blond hair with dark streaks, lots of metal in her face and ears, white T-shirt, black-leather vest, came out the door, and with both hands pushed Joe Big backwards into Barney.

"S'cuse me, Hiawatha," she said. "But get the fuck out of my way." She shouldered past them to the curb and stood, hands on hips, surveying the street. She swatted hair away from her eyes, a spider web tattooed on her right elbow."

"The Death Devo," Barney said.

"Larger than life, and twice as mean."

She glanced back at them, and turned and stepped out into the street, and both Barney and Joe Big closed their eyes as a cream-colored Cadillac Escalade chattered to a stop inches from her hip.

"YOU COCKSUCKING TOURIST MOTHERFUCKER!" She started for the driver's door, and the Escalade backed up fast.

"Come on," Joe Big said, and grabbed Barney's arm and pulled him through the door. "We've had enough violence for one night."

Heat and music and loud voices and shouts and, here and there, laughter assaulted them as they stepped inside.

The room was rectangular with a high ceiling. Old-fashioned light fixtures dangled from the ceiling, the light from the fixtures tinged yellow like the light in an old train station. Light sconces set at intervals along the walls and to the side of the massive old ornate bar complemented the overhead lights, the combination of the two light sources flattering the features of people who cared about such things—which, Joe Big mused, in this case was pretty much everyone in there. Clusters of tanned, perfectly groomed people trying to look hip and outdoorsy at the same time stood at the antique bar or sat in booths lining the wall opposite the bar. Here and there, scattered among the monotony of Patagonia and North Country and REI *apparel*, was a Stetson or a wool shirt or a sports jersey. The walls were covered with different sizes of signed, framed pictures of movie and sports stars—celebrities who over the years had frequented the bar. Many of the men sported ragged Billy-goat goatees or three-day growths—just enough facial hair to look like they might be called Mahmud or Ezekiel or Bruce. Long-sleeved shirts rolled up to the elbow over long-sleeved underwear on some of the men. Tight designer jeans and tight tops and short hair on the true snowboarders among the women. Expensive teeth were obviously *de rigueur*. And everywhere, Joe Big thought, enough people looking out the corners of their eyes to fill a Japanese subway train.

A crowd stood watching the play at two pool tables to their left as they threaded their way single file through clumps of people toward the bar. Dark wood paneling covered the lower portion of the wall behind the pool tables. Pool cues stacked parallel to the floor on racks fastened to the wall above the wainscoting reminded both of them of the practice Kendo swords displayed in the Aikido dojo that Barney worked out in sometimes.

The place was loud, but it was a refined loud, not a boisterous cowboy or university loud. The music was turned low—too low. It could have been rap or hip-hop or even country—the noise level in the room and the volume setting made it impossible to tell.

"Follow me," Barney said, and shouldered his way through a clump of the-young-and-the-haughty-looking, all of them pausing in mid-conversation or mid-drink or mid-pose to stare at his shirt. Some with curiosity, but most with an instant superciliousness that made Joe Big want to head-butt them.

"Nose up," his grandmother would have labeled them. But "nose up" would hardly do justice to most of the people in here, he thought.

At the bar, he eeled in next to Barney, trying with his body to nudge the person to his right over a step or two. "Excuse me," he said to what he abruptly realized was a very large immovable object. Judging from the skin color a very large immovable Mexican or Hawaiian object.

The man was wearing a white T-shirt under a long-sleeved dark gray-and-white checked shirt, only the top two buttons buttoned—buttoned the way Joe Big imagined an LA barrio villain would button a shirt. Okay, he thought. Mexican or Chicano, then.

He looked up. The man had a big square head, and a large handsome hatchet nose, no expression whatsoever on his face. Black eyes like buttons in a stuffed bear. Thick black hair pulled back tight in a single braid, the way he had worn his.

The man gazed without emotion down at him.

"Well, look at you." Joe Big grinned, and took off his wire-rim glasses. "You piece of movie-star shit."

The big Indian frowned, his eyes slowly coming to life, mouth broadening into a white-toothed grin.

Barney leaned across the bar. "Bobo Porter, if you've got it," he said to the blonde bartender. "Moose Drool if you don't." The bartender was too cute and too old and too athletic-looking to be anything but a skier or snowboarder working to support her snowboarding or skiing habit.

"You need one, too?" he asked the big man next to Joe Big. "Hey! Yo! Big Indian guy with a ridiculously expensive earring. You want a beer?"

The big man's head swiveled toward Barney.

Joe Big leaned forward elbows on the bar and covered his eyes with his hand.

"Don't mind him," Barney said over Joe Big's bowed head. "He's Chinese. Do you want a beer or not?"

The big Indian blinked, and looked down at Joe. "Huh?" he said, his voice deep and melodious. "Chinese?"

Joe Big swiveled his head toward Barney. He was laughing.

The big Indian started laughing, too, a deep, booming sound. Slowly at first and then harder, his chest and shoulders heaving.

The bartender looked worried.

With one of the biggest hands and forearms Barney had ever seen, the big Indian hugged Joe Big tight to his side. "Not-So-Big," he said, his voice resonant—the voice of someone narrating a program on the History or Discovery channels. "Where you been, man?" He released Joe, and stepped back, and with both hands held Joe Big by his shoulders. "Let me look at you, bro." With his left hand he pulled Joe's knit cap off, and with his right ran his hand back and forth over the stubble. "What happened to your hair, man? You used to love your hair."

Joe Big took back his hat. "I got scalped."

The big man stared at Joe for a moment. He frowned, and shook his head.

"You changed, Bro. Forget the hair, man. I see you without that hat and with those glasses, I don't know you." He paused, studying Joe Big intently "You okay, man? Everything going okay for you?"

Joe Big put his hat back on. "Older and slower, is all. Meet Roy White Owl," he said to Barney. "Cousin on my mother's side. My main man, Barney," he said to Roy White Owl.

The big Indian nodded to Barney. "How you doin', man?"

"Well, to tell you the truth, life can be a trial sometimes with Big around."

Roy chuckled, a rumbling sound from deep in his chest.

The bartender rolled her eyes, and went off to get another Moose Drool.

"Joe Big Snake Person," Roy said, lapsing into Reservation English. "Now I see you, I know I miss you. You big time warrior man now, hey? Your Moms be proud last time I see her. Your Pops give her that evil eye he used to give us when he think there's too much brag in our talk. But even your Pops can't hide the pride, hey."

"I heard you some big time movie star now, hey," Joe Big said.

Roy smiled. He spread his arms. "The camera likes me, what can I say?" he said, dropping the Reservation Speak—which wasn't really Reservation Speak, but was what he and Not-So had used around some of the Whites. "People like my voice."

"Sort of like finding out you inherited a gold mine or something," Barney said.

"That's it exactly, man. Exactly. All these movie stars, they work hard at being somebody they ain't. But I just be myself, and get paid for it."

"So what are you doing here?" Joe Big asked.

Roy White Owl looked over the heads of the people around them. "Oh, the whole crew is in here somewhere," he said. "We're shooting a stupid teenage horror flick over by Columbia Falls." He smiled at Barney. "I'm supposed to be the Indian version of something called a Windigo—an Indian boogy man."

"Must be a reality movie, huh?" Joe Big said.

Roy laughed, and slapped Joe Big on the back hard enough to make Barney wince. "Where you been, man? Where you *been?* I missed you."

An Indian version of Shrek, Barney thought.

Roy winked at him. "This is one crazy Indian boy."

"I am shocked and dismayed to hear that."

"But that's okay." Roy made a sweeping gesture that encompassed the entire room, his massive arm and hand somehow managing to miss the people around them. "Everyone in here is crazy, too. Right, bro?"

"Oh, not just in here," Joe Big said. "Outside, too."

SEVERAL BEERS LATER, Roy was telling tales of Hollywood and how he no longer felt at home on the Rez, everyone these days always after him for money or favors or to be in movies or television.

"Sometimes, I just want to go home and be me, you know what I'm saying?"

"You have no idea how much we know what you are saying," Joe Big said. He traded glances with Barney.

"You big oaf!" a woman's voice said, and a thin white arm and fist flashed out from behind Barney and smacked Roy in the kidney. "Where'd you go, when I needed you—Oh," she said, looking from Joe Big to Barney and back to Roy. "I'm sorry. I didn't know you were talking with someone. Excuse me," she said to Barney and Joe, and hit Roy again, this time in the stomach. "Don't you *ever* leave me alone like that again."

Six feet, at least, Joe Big thought. Thin and blond and Nordic-warrior beautiful. Roy's high school wet dream come to life.

But a whole lot more than that, he thought, looking more closely. No California bottle-blonde, this one. In fact, not California, at all. She was dressed like many of the women in there, blue jeans and vest and tight shirt, but her boots were well-worn cowboy boots, and her jeans were not designer jeans, and her vest had some miles on it, and it was from Cenex, not Patagonia. He smiled. And she'd hit Roy with serious punches. He'd bet she'd grown up on a ranch, and her dad had taught her to box right along with her brothers.

"Get me a beer, will you, Roy," she said, her voice tight. "Please."

"Sarah, why are you so pissed?" Roy asked.

"Those two assholes." She nodded toward the pool tables. And Barney and Joe Big and Roy White Owl followed her eyes. "That red-headed son-of-a-bitch."

Beyond the crush of people, Barney and Joe Big could see the two men they'd seen at the truck stop gas pumps—the two men in the silver EVO. They were both without their sunglasses and knit caps, and they had exchanged their sweatshirts for tight fitting black long-sleeved turtle necks, but there was no mistaking the fact that they were the same men they'd seen at the truck stop.

The redhead was bent forward over the far pool table into a circle of white light from a low-hung red and green plastic light suspended by chains from the ceiling. His buzz cut was a washed-out red under the bright light. The other man stood behind and to the side of the table, chalking a cue.

The redhead stroked his cue stick back and forth, and took the shot. They couldn't see if he'd made it or not, but from the way he stood and leaned hip against the table and sneered at everyone around him, they guessed that he had.

"What about them?" Roy asked. "You been beat before."

Joe Big looked at Barney. "Is that who I think it is?"

"Kind of like watching two mambas play." Barney said.

"Not by someone like that, I haven't," Sarah said. "He wants to tie me up and fuck me until I can't scream no more." There was no whine in her voice, only hard cold anger.

"Who he?" Roy asked.

"The red-headed one."

"Well, can't blame him for that," Roy said, but when he looked once more toward the pool tables, his eyes were black, a tiny spark in them that was more than the reflection of the light bouncing off the bottles behind the bar.

"Nice shirt," Sarah said to Barney, making an obvious attempt to break the mood she'd brought with her.

Barney smiled.

"No, really," she said. "It's a great shirt."

"Well, thank you, ma'am. It's nice to meet a woman who knows her haberdashery."

"He looks like he belongs in a 1950s bowling alley," Joe Big said.

She looked Joe Big up and down, her eyes doing all the talking. "Uh-huh," she said. "Who are you again?"

Roy laughed, and put his arm around Joe's shoulders. "This here is my cousin, Joe Big." He squeezed Joe's shoulders. "I told you about him, remember? We used to call him Not-So-Big."

Joe Big smiled at her.

She frowned, and looked to see if Roy was joking.

Roy gave Joe's shoulders a squeeze. "He looks like a pretty Chinese boy, but you don't never want to make that mistake with this one."

"Really?" She glanced from Joe to Roy. "You two are related? I don't believe it."

"More ways than one," Roy said, releasing Big. "My family moved off the Rez when I was in high school," he said to Barney. "I never would have made it through my senior year without Not-So writing papers for me."

She smiled. "Now I know you're kidding. You had really high SAT scores. I saw them. You showed them to me."

Roy grinned, a big homely grin as infectious as his laugh. He held up his massive fist and Joe Big, without taking his eyes or his smile off Sarah, tapped it hard with his.

Sarah frowned.

"This be my SAT score," Roy said.

"He took the test for you," Barney said.

"You knew that already, huh?" Roy chuckled. "It was just a test, man. Meant nothing. No way I was going to college. And Big here wanted the practice. Helped me with my math . . ." His voice trailed off, and he looked at Sarah with an expression approaching panic. "Ah . . . uh . . . . I . . ."

She stared at him, and then looked from him to Joe Big, and back to him again.

Her eyes narrowed.

Roy swallowed, his big forehead furrowed with worry.

Her eyes relaxed and she smiled. She raised up and kissed him on the cheek. "Lucky for you, I know your mind isn't your biggest attribute."

Joe Big and Barney laughed, both nearly as relieved as Roy.

"See what I have to put up with," Roy said, and pulled her toward him, his arm around her neck, forearm nearly as big around as her neck.

She slipped her arms around his waist and hugged him.

"I'm hungry," she said. "And those assholes over there have sort of ruined the ambiance of this place—present company excepted," she said to Joe and Barney. "*Really* hungry," she said to Roy, gazing up at him, her voice mock plaintive, making it clear that it wasn't food she was hungry for. She winked at Joe Big, and made a small gesture with her head toward the pool tables. And Joe realized that she wanted Roy out of there before he decided to do something about the two men at the pool tables.

Roy looked helplessly at Barney and Joe Big. "I guess I got to go," he said to Joe. "But you always my man, you know that. You come and see me—both of you. If you're hangin' with Not-So, then you're family, too," he said to Barney. "Your parents wouldn't tell me where you were," he said to Joe. He grinned. "And you know how well I write."

Joe tapped fists with him. "Won't be so long this time. Got a few ends to tie up, then we be seeing you most ricky-tick."

Roy's eyes glistened. "Man, I haven't heard that in a long time. Your uncle used to say it all the time. Don't just be saying it, though, bro. It's empty out there. I know you know what I mean."

"You got my word, man. We'll be there. Can't say when, but we'll be there."

"C'mon, Roy," Sarah said. "I'm hungry."

Roy grinned, and made a face as if to say, what can I do, and reached out and once again tapped fists with Joe Big, and then with Barney.

"Nice meeting, y'all," Barney said. "It's nice to know that Big actually has connections to the human race."

Roy laughed. "Later," he said, as Sarah mouthed, "Thank you," to both of them. And they turned and made their way through the crowd.

"Thank you for what?" Barney asked.

"For taking Roy's mind off those two guys."

"She's the one who told him about them."

"Yeah, but she knew she'd made a mistake. Roy's a piece of work, man. He killed a guy in a fight when we were in high school."

"Whoa."

"He was on his way to collect his mom, who was working at the hospital, and three guys—three grown men—jumped him outside a bar in downtown Missoula."

"What happened?"

Joe Big shrugged. "He was scared. They were grown men. He put one of the two other guys in the hospital; the third one ran away. He was a juvenile and there were plenty of witnesses. The County Attorney said it was self-defense." He shook his head. "Lot of hate, man. Letters to the editor. Threats. Far as I know, he's never been in a fight since. Hard to believe looking at him, but he's actually a gentle soul. Couldn't even shoot a rabbit, when we were kids. Couldn't stand to see an animal gutted out."

"So why worry about him now?"

"With him, you got to worry when he feels protective or afraid, not when he feels jealous. He's going to marry that woman—I guess you know that as well as I do. I haven't seen that look in his eyes since we were kids. I imagine that's the first time she's ever seen it."

He looked toward the pool tables. "She's plenty capable of fighting her own battles, I've got no doubt. But she was so pissed off she forgot for a minute who she was with."

"Or she was so pissed off she didn't care."

"There you go."

"You think he could handle the doom twins over there?"

Joe Big shook his head. "No. Not those two. Roy hasn't had much training. After he killed that guy, they wouldn't let him box or wrestle or play contact sports. She looks like she's been raised on a ranch—maybe even still lives on one—so she's no stranger to men and violence. I think once she got over her initial anger she knew that he couldn't handle those two."

"That's what the 'thanks' was for."

"Yeah."

Barney's eyes narrowed as he watched the two men. "Why don't we go get acquainted." He turned to Joe Big. "You go grab that booth over there. The people in it are getting ready to leave. I'll get some beers."

Joe Big edged his way over next to the booth, the last booth before the pool tables. Two young women were waiting patiently on the other side for the people to leave, but before they could sit down, he gently moved one of the women who was leaving out of the way, and slid into the booth behind her.

"Hey. We were here first."

The two women weren't as young as he'd first thought. Late twenties, early thirties. A blonde and a brunette, both slim, but not trim. Keeping the pounds off with a combination of nervous energy and too much coffee and tobacco. The blonde had a tightness around her eyes and mouth that told him she didn't much like men anymore. Divorced, or about to be divorced, he figured. Probably a kid or two, both of them, but especially the blonde.

"Sorry," he said. "But my friend has a disability."

"Yeah, right," the blonde said.

"We can share, if you want."

"We're waiting for someone."

He smiled up at them. "Sorry, then."

"You're an asshole," the blonde blurted.

He smiled. "But I'm the asshole with the table. So . . ." He made a shooing gesture with his hand.

The blonde made a strangled sound and, furious, took a step toward him. The brunette grabbed her arm. "C'mon, Lisa," she said. "He's not worth it." She dragged the blonde toward the crowd near the bar.

Barney placed two beers on the table and sat down across from him.

"It looks like somebody doesn't like you. That's got to be a personal record."

"The only way I could get rid of them was to be a little rude."

"Hard to imagine, isn't it?"

"What is?"

"You getting rid of a perfectly acceptable-looking woman."

"Were you interested?"

"Well . . ."

"The blonde, right? She's divorced and lives in a trailer house with her mother and two kids, one of whom is in kindergarten, and the other half-time at day care. Her mother, who is mean and bitter and hates men and smokes like a chimney, will hate you on sight—but she'll like your shirt. The kids will be calling you 'Daddy' by the third time you stop by the trailer to help mow the lawn and change the oil in the beat-to-shit cars parked in the yard." He grinned at Barney. "Still interested?"

"Once again, you've managed to ruin a perfectly good fantasy."

"You just got divorced, man. It's the least I could do." He reached for one of the bottles. "I haven't seen Roy for a long time. And I probably won't see him again for a long time. But he's family, man. I don't want any distractions." He took a drink.

"Well, okay. I hear that. I like Roy, too. I'm just a little horny, is all."

Joe Big set the bottle down and made wet circles with it on the tabletop. He looked toward the pool tables. "Those two sort of fit the description that Quinn gave us of the dudes who chased her down the mountain."

"That sounds suspiciously like an excuse."

Joe Big shook his head. "Not with everything that's been going down lately, it's not. Even without Roy and his lady, those two deserve our attention."

Barney made a face.

"Okay, then." Joe Big grinned. "It's an excuse."

"Thank you."

They both looked toward the pool tables. The view was unobstructed. Most of the crowd was on the other side, the bar side, of the tables. The redhead was strutting around the table, chalking his cue. He bent and quickly and efficiently took a bank shot and the ball went in the corner pocket. He strutted for the other side of the table, chalking his cue.

"Guy's a machine," Barney said.

"Got that look, don't he?"

"Here we go," Barney said, and raised his beer in greeting to the other man, the horse-faced man, who was leaning against the wall about thirty feet away, watching them. "Remember: we're Trust Fund Babies. You quit the Marines."

"To find enlightenment, no doubt."

The horse-faced man pushed off from the wall and walked over to them. "Blue Subaru. Right?"

"Hey," Barney said. "How you doin'? Have a seat." He scooted farther into the booth.

The man sat down on the edge of the seat, his pool cue held like a lance, butt end on the floor, and nodded to Joe Big.

Joe Big could feel an energy radiating from the man that he hadn't felt from another human being in a long time. The man was relaxed on the surface, but underneath he was all wire and sprung steel.

"Get you a beer?" Barney asked.

"No, thanks. I can't play worth a shit when I drink."

"Looks like your partner is doing all the playing," Joe Big said. "The man is a machine." He extended his hand. "Joe Wang."

The man reached across with his left hand and held the pool cue, and extended his right and shook Joe's limp hand. His grip was crushing. "Pick."

"Excuse me?"

"Pick. Everyone calls me, Pick. Short for Pickett."

"Oh, sorry."

"You're Chinese, huh? *Ni hao*?"

"Hen hao. Xie-xie, ni." Joe Big managed to look embarrassed. "But that's about all I speak. I'm third generation. Hawaii to Seattle to Washington D.C."

The man glanced at Barney, and then back to Joe Big. "Your partner mentioned that you were a Marine."

Joe Big put as much condescension into his smile as he could. "The Marine Corps and I march to the beat of a different drummer."

On the other side of the room stood a thick blond woman dressed in black pants and black vest and white T-shirt, black half-finger gloves holding a pool cue as she waited her turn at the table next to the one the redhead was playing on. Oh, shit, Joe Big thought.

Two women walked over next to her—the two women he'd aced out of the booth—the blonde talking earnestly and pointing in his direction. He almost laughed out loud. Well, that certainly explained the blonde's antipathy toward men. *"We're meeting someone."* Not that he minded. Different strokes for—the man across from him, Pick, was saying something.

"I'm sorry. I was looking at that tough-looking dyke over there."

Barney and Pick both craned around to look at Brianna talking to the two women. Barney glanced at him, and Joe Big nodded.

"You know her?" Pick asked.

"I aced the two women with her out of this booth. I have a feeling they want her to come over here and chastise me."

"*Chastise* you." Pick laughed, squint lines sharp as ironed pleats at the corners of his eyes. "That the kind of language they taught you in the Marines?"

"He went to Stanford," Barney said.

"Please don't tell me you were an officer."

"First lieutenant," Joe Big said, trying not to notice Barney roll his eyes. "Until I resigned my commission."

"Why'd you resign your commission?"

Joe Big shrugged. "Iraq."

"How about the War On Terror?"

"Not the same."

"And you know that, how?"

Joe Big shrugged. "Call it an opinion."

"You're allowed to have opinions in the Marines?"

Joe Big laughed. "Sure. As long as it's the same opinion as your commanding officer's."

"Once a Marine, always a Marine."

"Not if you resign your commission," Joe Big said.

"So how about you guys?" Barney said. "I guess you were in the military, huh?"

"You could say that."

"What'd you do?"

"If I told you that I'd have to kill you." Pick smiled, but his smile managed to convey the message that maybe he wasn't completely joking.

"Some of the guys I met who had been in Afghanistan and Iraq during the early days, I knew them before they went, and they were just normal guys," Joe Big said. "But after they came back it was like, I don't know, they learned to like killing, or something."

Barney rolled his eyes again.

"It happens," the man called Pick said. He nodded toward the pool tables. "But some people—like my partner there—they don't need to be taught how to kill. They only need practice. We call him the Leprechaun—with good reason."

"Whoa," Barney said.

Pick nodded. "War brings out the best in some men."

Barney laughed.

"You think that's funny?"

"Not at all. Sorry."

Pick squinted at him. "You sure I don't know you? You look damn familiar."

Barney shrugged. "Wang and I hang out around here in the summer and fall. But the rest of the year, I'm pretty much in Louisiana—the Big Easy, or what's left of it."

"And you've never been in the military?"

Joe Big smiled. "Dude, look at him. Look at that shirt."

Out of the corner of his eye, he could see Brianna starting to shoot pool against some snowboarder-looking guy about half her size. The guy was already intimidated.

The redhead was eyeing her. Pick was right. The redhead's eyes were feral.

"So you guys wouldn't know where we could get a little weed or some blow?" Pick asked.

"Do we look like the kind of people who know that sort of thing?" Barney asked.

"*You* do." Pick looked amused at Joe Big. "Him, I don't know."

"There's a lot of weed and blow around here," Barney said. "Just ask. Someone in here will sell you all you want."

"Well, I'm asking you because you look like maybe you might be interested to *buy* some weight." He looked from Barney to Joe Big, back to Barney. "We on the same page here?"

"Correct me if I'm wrong," Barney said. "But didn't you just ask—"

"Define weight," Joe Big said.

"There you go!" Pick said. "That's what I'm talkin' about."

Joe Big could see Brianna talking to the redhead. She had won her game, and he was about to win his. Brianna said something that made the back of the redhead's neck flush. She pushed past him and put a bill on the table. Then stood back, pool cue held butt end on the floor, and sneered at him with her patented Brianna sneer. Behind her, her two friends laughed.

Not good, he thought. Not good at all.

"What would you say to a key or two of ninety-three-point-seven percent pure, direct from the Golden Triangle?" Pick asked.

"A 'key or two'? I'd say you were a narc," Barney said.

"Free samples," Pick said.

"You served your country in war," Joe Big said. "And now you are selling pure product to the citizens of this country? You expect us to believe that?"

"I'm still serving my country."

"You sure got a weird way of doing it," Joe Big said.

"Well, what the fuck do you know about it? This country needs a wakeup call—a big-time wakeup call."

"And that's why—"

"Hey. What I think about the price of rice has got nothing to do with it. All you need to know is we got the product if you got the money."

"Well, we appreciate the offer," Joe Big said. "But you have surely got us mixed up with someone else."

Pick's smile was cynical. "Is that right?"

Joe Big glanced toward the pool table. Brianna was racking the balls.

He focused on the man sitting across from him. "What? You think we're rich spoiled dilettantes waltzing around the mountains, selling dope to all the ski bums and trailer trash? Is that what you think?"

"If you two are rich and spoiled, then I'm Bill Gates."

Joe Big glanced again toward the pool table. Brianna and the Redhead were lagging to see who would go first. Brianna said something that made the Redhead hit the ball too hard.

Pick looked at Barney. "I know who you two ain't the same way I know your car is a lot more than you say it is."

Joe Big heard the sharp, hard crack of pool balls: Brianna making the break. He looked toward the pool table. Balls ricocheted around the table.

"Really?" Barney said.

Joe Big could see that Brianna was already starting to run the table. And she was doing her best to be lewd about it. Shaking her ass and sticking her tongue out, wagging it up and down at the two women.

The redhead was watching her the way a cat watches a bird.

"Who's the guy you are with, again?" Joe Big said. "The Leprechaun? He looks like a Leprechaun."

"Why do you ask?"

"Because he's about to do something stupid. And I don't think we want to do business with stupid people."

Pick turned to see.

"Oh, man . . . He hates dykes."

"Well, that dyke is kicking his ass."

Brianna walked from one side of the table to the other, sizing up her next shot, taking her time. She glanced at the redhead, and made a jacking off gesture with her right hand around the pool cue. She leaned toward him, waggling her tongue, showing him the silver stud in it.

The red-haired man leaned back against the wall, smiling. Five-ten, Joe Big figured. Stocky-built, like Barney. Maybe 185. Heavy forearms and biceps that showed a lot of definition even under the black pullover. Pale. Freckled. Hair too short to grab.

Brianna bent far over the table to take her shot, one leg off the floor.

The redhead reached out with his pool cue, slowly inching it toward Brianna, the muscles in his forearm flexed with the strain of holding the cue steady. Brianna drew her cue back and forth several times. She shifted her foot and buttocks on the edge of the table, making sure of the shot. The pool cue inched toward her breast squashed down on the green felt, its hardwood surface shiny in the bright light over the table.

"You might want to watch this," Joe Big said.

Barney raised up so he could see over the back of the booth.

"God damn it," Pick said.

Brianna drew back her cue one final time, and as it snapped forward, the redhead's cue jabbed hard and deep into her breast, the end of his cue leaving a bright blue skid mark on her white T-shirt.

"Ahhh, *fuck!*" she screamed, as the tip of her cue bit into the felt, ripping it, the cue ball bouncing off the far side of the table. She dropped her cue and rolled off the table, cupping her breast with her other hand.

The redhead kept his arm extended, the end of the cue in the bright light over the table, like a snake poised to strike again. It flicked forward, striking between her fingers, into the softness of her breast.

"You mother-*fucker!*" she screamed.

The bar was abruptly quiet, people pausing in mid-sentence or mid-drink, faces turning toward the pool tables. The bartender already had a cell phone to her ear.

"Get him, Brianna," a female voice shouted. "Kick his ass."

Brianna crouched, arms held out in front of her. Her black vest hid the blue chalk marks. She reached over to the table with her left hand and picked the yellow ball off the table and flipped it to her right hand, and in one, seamless motion threw it sidearm at the redhead.

The redhead leaned backwards and sideways, and the ball blurred past his chest and impacted into the wall behind, disappearing into the drywall, a perfect hole in its wake.

The redhead grinned, and spread his arms, cue held in his right hand, as if to say, nice try. Try again.

Brianna turned and walked to the nearest table and grabbed a long-necked beer bottle by the neck, and walked back to the pool table.

Her arm flicked toward the table, the speed of her movement surprising even Joe Big, and broke the bottle against the edge of the pool table, beer and brown shards spewing across the green felt.

The redheaded man crouched slightly and grasped the pool cue with both hands.

"DON'T!" Pick yelled, dropping his pool cue to the floor and springing from the seat.

"Sit. Your. Ass. Down," Brianna said to him, her voice almost a hiss. The jagged edges of the bottle extended toward him.

And the redhead, stepping right foot forward, throwing his right arm and shoulder into it, hit her square in the mouth with the butt end of the pool cue, a dull chunking sound that snapped her head back as if someone had grabbed her hair from behind and jerked her head backwards.

Joe Big and Barney and Pick all thought the same thing: bayonet practice in boot camp. Parry. Thrust. And *chunk*: a mouth that already hurt to look at.

The redhead had hit her with speed, rather than with power, stopping the cue stick the instant it hit her mouth, instead of trying to hit all the way through. Glassy-eyed and trembling, she looked, if not for her mouth, as if she'd been hit with a taser instead of a pool cue.

Barney scrambled to get out of the booth.

Joe Big reached across the table and grabbed him by the arm and forced him to stop. "Not now."

Barney yanked his arm free, and Joe Big twisted out of the booth, and stood blocking Barney's way out from behind the table. "Not now," he said again, his voice low and intense.

He felt Barney subside.

He turned to look at Brianna.

Her mouth drooled blood and saliva. She spit out a piece of tooth, and still trembling edged forward, the broken bottle tightly clasped in her hand. The bar had gone silent, and in the silence they heard her moan, a deep, mewling sound more animal than human.

Her head shook from side to side, and a woman screamed, the lone scream releasing a cacophony of sound that washed over the two figures.

The redhead stepped forward and speared the butt end of the pool cue into her midsection. In almost the same movement, he jerked the cue stick back and raised the butt end high in the air, and Pick slammed into him, knocking him to the floor, the pool cue flying over the top of the pool table.

Women and men ran to Brianna. Her arms dropped to her sides, and the beer bottle splintered on the floor. Fighting to get air in through her wounded mouth and nose, she inhaled blood and coughed, the cough more a wheeze than a cough. Her eyes rolled up, the whites showing, and she sagged, but before she could collapse, the people around her lifted her to the table. A woman, a nurse or doctor probably, with a minimum of gesture and voice commands instructed people how to place her so that she would not choke on her blood. Reaching into Brianna's mouth with her fingers she cleared Brianna's mouth of a red gooey mass.

Pick had the redhead up off the floor, the redhead's right arm bent all the way up to the back of his head, and was hustling him toward the doorway, his other hand grasping the redhead by the belt and the back of the pants, already bulldozing through the portion of the crowd craning their necks to see what had happened.

A group of young men near the bar were laughing and applauding. A few couples were already moving toward the exit, their faces tense and white. Others milled aimlessly, excited and distressed at the same time. The blonde and the brunette stood on the far side of the tables with their arms wrapped around each other, crying.

Joe Big heard the faint sound of a siren.

The bartender was talking calmly into her cell phone, nodding her head. She was looking toward him and Barney.

The crush of people around the pool table had thickened and it was impossible to see Brianna.

"You okay?" he asked Barney.

"Fuck no, I'm not okay."

"I think they knew who she is."

"What?"

"I think they knew who she is," Joe Big said. "That's why Pick didn't stop it sooner."

"No way."

"Montana can be a small place. I just ran into a cousin I haven't seen since high school."

Barney crossed his arms and leaned back against the side of the booth. He frowned at Joe Big.

"She looks like she's in good hands," Joe Big said, watching the bartender watch them. "Let's get out of here before someone realizes we were with one of them."

Barney uncrossed his arms and pushed off from the side of the booth.

"Let's do better than that," he said. "Let's go find them."

12
Leaking Time

Joe Big was driving. "I know you'll find this hard to believe," he said. "But once upon a time, in small towns like this in Montana, bars were as much meeting and debating places as anything else."

They were on the mostly deserted five-lane, almost out of town, cruising past car dealerships and furniture stores that were far larger than normal for a community that size.

"Before movies and TV, people would gather in bars and debate the issues of the day. Not every bar and not in every town, I don't mean that. But in the old days, in small towns like this, it wasn't unusual for a bar to double as a community center."

Barney grunted.

"What I'm trying to say is maybe it hasn't changed all that much," Joe Big said, "Or maybe it has gone full circle."

"What *are* you talking about? Jesus," Barney muttered. "You and your fucking books."

"I'm talking about it really surprised me how many people were right there to help her. Some of them even knew what they were doing."

"What makes you think they knew what they were doing?"

Joe Big looked at him.

Barney shifted in his seat. "So some of them knew what they were doing. So what?"

"So maybe we haven't been giving people a chance. I mean, we walk around sneering at the world, happy to not be part of this fucked-up society, cracking each other up with the way we put citizens down. But then a little shit hits the fan, and all of a sudden, out of nowhere, some of the citizens we've been all cynical and sarcastic about stand up and damn if they don't handle it as well or better than we can." He rubbed the side of his face. "All our talk about yuppies and trust-fund babies, whole towns become playgrounds for the rich . . . I don't know, man. I'm just saying, maybe we are getting a little ahead of ourselves. I mean, never mind their looks—their Billy-goat goatees and their Patagonia-perfect clothes—maybe a whole lot of the people in that bar back there are the same people as used to populate it when it was much more to the community than merely a bar."

"What *are* you talking about? You're half Indian. I bet not many Indians were tolerated in bars like that. I bet most of the people were white and racist and totally ignorant of the world outside their little town."

"Well, you'd lose that bet. There were a lot of Indians around here. There were a fair number of Asians, too. There's even a Japanese graveyard in Kalispell. This place was a logging and railroad town, lots of people coming and going. There were a lot of mixed marriages, Indians and whites."

"Not among the mucky-mucks, I bet."

"I'm not talking about the mucky-mucks. I'm talking about the people in that bar back there."

"Prostitution, gambling, drinking, fighting, killing. Community centers, my ass."

Joe Big laughed. "You're probably right. But I don't know. This State has always been a refuge for people escaping what a war did to them—people who couldn't stand to live wherever they were from. Agnostics were the rule, not the exception. Most of the population could read. And as far as Indian blood was concerned, well, all I can say is that anyone who has been here more than four or five generations and has a French or a Scots name, there's probably an Indian in the woodpile somewhere."

"Man, I swear, you go off on some of the weirdest tangents at some of the strangest times."

Joe Big grinned. "Got you out of your funk, though, didn't I."

Barney shifted in the seat and sat up straighter. "That motherfucker might've killed her if that Pick dude hadn't tackled his ass. Maybe we ought to be talking about something besides 'community centers'."

"It woke me up a little, that's all, those people helping her like that. For a tiny moment in time there I felt like maybe we really do serve a function."

"We serve a function, all right. Same as the garbage man serves a function."

Joe Big allowed the car to coast down to sixty and set the cruise control. The blue light from the gauges mounted in the middle of the dash highlighted his face, making him appear more an apparition than a person.

"We can't expect people to be like us, Barn. And people can't expect us to be like them. But every once in a while something happens that bridges the gap. And that's what happened tonight with those people helping Brianna, that's all I'm saying."

Barney laughed—a short, sarcastic bark of sound. "What? You're saying these people have our back? Is that what you're saying?"

"Well, we have their back, right? Isn't that what we are doing with our badges and our experience? Isn't that what Brianna is doing? Even if they don't know it, or can't understand it, we've got their back. Why can't it be the other way around sometimes?"

"Nothing ever changes, Big, that's why. People kill and maim and generally fuck over each other the same today as they have always killed and maimed and generally fucked over each other. Those people back there, most of them, care about us—if they think about people like us at all—about the same way as they care about homeless animals. Actually, they probably care more about homeless animals."

"Well, there's no need to get all grim about it, man."

"Get grim about it? What is wrong with you, lately? You're usually the one who has to be talked out of some woe-is-us or another, not me. And now that we've got something to be really depressed about, you . . . We been beat on, and we don't know why or because of who. I just got divorced. You lost your hair and your girl. We're not getting any younger, and we don't know how to do anything but hurt or catch or kill people." He punched the dash hard. "And now some leprechaun motherfucker has put a serious hurt on one of us, and you're not exercised in the least—"

"Who says I'm not?"

"Well, you sure don't sound like it."

Joe Big laughed. "You know me, man. The worse it is, the calmer I get. It's a family thing. My mother and my uncle are the same way. It's like past a certain point there's no longer any need to maintain." He smiled at Barney. "You know: Be happy. Go kill."

Barney looked out the window, silent for several minutes. His mind was a riot of images. People. Places. His thoughts would not gel. Those guys at the bar applauding, while other people were helping Brianna. Tracers in the night. Laughing with his wife in the kitchen of their house. His mother and sisters and aunts and uncles and cousins and people he went to high school with and people who didn't even know him, all of them there at the airport, waiting to greet him for no reason other than he'd been to a war that should never have been fought in the first place . . .

"You know what our problem is?" Joe Big asked.

"I wish I knew."

"We're leaking time."

"Sometimes you are flat certifiable, you know that?"

"We're Rip Van Winkles. Really. Don't look at me like that. Think about it. One day we are in high school. You are playing football and wrestling and fucking any girl dumb enough to let you fuck her. And I am boxing and playing basketball and running cross-county and fucking any girl dumb enough to let me fuck her. And the next thing we know we are here. Right here. In this car. And because we are here, we aren't where we were when we were someplace that wasn't where we were in high school. You know what I mean? Rip Van Winkles, man."

Barney laughed. "I bet you can't even say all that again without losing your place."

"That's exactly what I mean! We're always losing our place. We're never completely here. We're always someplace else, too. And time goes by, and we aren't aware that time is going by because we're never quite anywhere. You know what I mean? And then something happens like what just happened to Brianna, and all of a sudden we are *here*. Really *here*. One-hundred percent *here*." He peered intently out at the night beyond the headlights. "And we don't know how we got here."

Barney ran his hand across the top of his head a couple of times. "I guess," he said. "For me it's mostly a jumble of images and sounds and feelings and . . . I can't seem to organize any of it."

"That's because you're leaking time, man."

"Well, we need to stop it."

"What we need to do is stop feeling sorry for ourselves. It's like seeing my cousin tonight—"

"That is one big Indian."

"He wanted to know what happened to me. But he didn't know how to ask. He's not sure he knows how to talk to the person I am now."

Barney grunted.

"And, I don't know," Joe Big said. "But maybe that is WORSE than the way our fathers were treated."

"Man, when you get a hair up your ass, you can talk, you know that? Most of the time you walk around like some Cigar-Store Indian or some Inscrutable Chinaman and make everybody believe that you've never read a book in your life. And then all of sudden, out of nowhere, you unload this kind of shit on people." He leaned forward, peering at Joe Big. "The War, I can handle. What I want to know is, *What the fuck did I do to deserve you?*"

Joe Big laughed. "Listen up, grasshopper. We are here. Right here. Right now we are here." He took one hand off the steering wheel and gestured toward the lights out in the valley. "You see all those lights."

Barney groaned and sat back.

"Those lights represent people who are here, too. But they aren't here the same as us." He looked over at Barney and laughed, and in his laugh Barney heard the bittersweet echo of his own laughter. "When you are in the shit, you be saying to yourself, 'Self. What the fuck am I doing here? I don't want to be here. I *hate* being here.' Your stomach feels like that redheaded Leprechaun motherfucker just put his cue stick into it. And you be starting to think about *prayin'*."

Barney smiled in spite of himself. He shook his head.

"But two days after you're out of the shit, you're cravin' it again, looking for ways." Joe Big abruptly jerked the steering wheel back and forth, the tires squalling in protest. "Like that," he said, "Only multiplied by a big-ass exponent. It's never enough. There's never an end to it. You want more and more of it. More and more intense."

He looked over at Barney. "*You*, Barney, my man. The latest in a long line of Southern whitebread stone killers for Mom and Apple Pie and the right of The Electorate to elect the wrong man for the job. In your dark little heart you want more of it. More and more intense. And, for a while there, you didn't give a shit if you were going to get *all* of it, become worm food, like all the others."

Barney laughed. "Man, you really know how to cheer a guy up."

"Hey, I'm no different. None of us are any different. We only think we're unique because it's us here and now. A hundred and fifty years ago, on the other side of those mountains over there, and we would have taken our weapons, and a couple of extra pairs of moccasins, and we would have walked all the way down to the Yellowstone, looking for Crow horses to steal. We wouldn't have ridden a horse, because we'd be stealing a horse to ride back. And if we got caught on foot out in the middle of the prairie by Crows on horses, then we were dead. How's that for a rush? And after we stole the horses, the Crow would follow for at least four days—and they wouldn't be pushing a herd of stolen horses, either."

"Sounds like fun to me."

"It do, don't it? That's why I'm feeling so mellow. Where are the cell phones?"

Barney patted the center console. "Here. The radios are in the back with everything else. Why?"

"Maybe we ought to give Quinn a call, let her know about Brianna."

"Why? She'll find out soon enough."

"Might be good to hear it from us."

Barney was silent for a long moment. He looked out the window. "Where are we headed?"

"Nowhere in particular. I just wanted to get out of Dodge."

"I think we should go off the grid completely. Not even turn on the phone or the radios until we really need them."

"We need some pictures of those dudes," Joe Big said. "We need to show them to Quinn."

"You mean because they might be the guys who killed her CI?"

"Yeah."

"Don't matter."

"Why not?"

"Because," Barney said. "We know who these guys are."

"We do?"

"They're us."

Joe Big laughed. "Cute."

They were silent for a moment.

"You mean," Joe Big said. "They're us, as in, there but for the grace of God go us?"

"Something like that."

"Well, I don't know about you," Joe Big said. "But there is no way I could do what she says they did to her CI."

"But you could do it to *someone,* if the circumstances were right."

Joe Big looked over at him.

"Maybe those guys thought the circumstances were right, is all I'm saying," Barney said.

Joe Big frowned.

"I mean," Barney said. "What did that Pick dude remind you of?"

"Who, you mean?"

"Yeah."

"He reminded me of every first sergeant I ever met in Force Recon."

"Or Rangers, or Special Forces," Barney said.

"Your point being?"

"Maybe he isn't so different from us."

Joe Big didn't say anything. He watched the lines on the road un ravel in the headlights.

"He's different," he finally said.

"I agree," Barney said. "The question is in what way is he different?"

"Money, maybe?"

"No way—not someone as squared away as he seems to be."

"Duty, honor, country."

"That's right," Barney said. "Duty, honor, country."

Joe Big was silent for a long moment. He drummed his fingers on the steering wheel.

"Man, you are a ray of sunshine, aren't you?" he said.

"The only thing that separates us from them, is—"

"Perspective," Joe Big said.

"That's right, *kemosabe.* Perspective. What your Gunny always talked about. And if we want to figure out where they are coming from, all we have to do is look at if from *our* perspective"

"*Our* perspective?"

"Yeah. Ain't that a kick in ass?"

"I still think we should call Quinn and let her know what's going on," Joe Big said. A full moon had come up over the mountains on the other side of the lake, bright enough to distinguish trees and individual bushes. He could see deer scattered among horses in a pasture up the hill from the highway.

"If we do, then she'll know where we're at."

"What's wrong with that?"

"I don't know. I guess it's okay," Barney said. "But if you're right and they knew who Brianna is, I kind of like staying incognito as much as possible."

"I meant that generically," Joe Big said. "Them knowing who Brianna is, I mean. The redhead reacted to her on a personal level. I doubt they would have had anything to do with her if they thought she was an undercover cop."

"Don't be too sure about that."

"If they knew she was a cop of some kind, I think they would've left."

"But you're not sure," Barney said.

"Well, they seemed mighty comfortable to me."

"The way he messed her up didn't that seem kind of premeditated to you?"

"Premeditated?" Joe Big asked.

"He pulled his punch, when he hit her in the mouth. Did you see that? After Pick jumped out and distracted her at exactly the right moment."

Joe Big thought about it, running the sequence in his mind.

"You're right," he said. "He distracted her, but he didn't really react until the redhead hit her in the mouth, and then he reacted big time."

"He was genuinely pissed," Barney said. "He really piled into him. And I can tell you this: he's played football before. Safety, would be my guess."

"But you think the redhead was supposed to instigate something?" Joe Big asked.

"Something, yeah? Just not anything that extreme."

"Why?"

"I don't know. It just feels that way."

Joe Big was silent, watching the road.

"So we won't call Quinn?"

Barney shrugged. "She probably knows about it by now, anyway. And the last thing we want is for her to get all conservative and tell us to back off."

"Someone's coming up fast," Joe Big said, leaning forward to see better out the passenger-side mirror."

"I see him."

"Full moon," Joe Big said.

"You better move over."

"I'm afraid to. He just moved into the right lane and he's really hauling."

They both tensed as a silver car blasted past in the right lane, red brake lights flashing on, flame shooting from the exhaust pipe, as the car decelerated about fifty meters in front of them.

"Speak of the devil," Barney said.

"You get the feeling they were looking for us?"

"Looks like we're going to find out." The car in front slowed to their speed, and the emergency flashers came on for a few seconds, then the right turn signal.

Joe Big flashed the brights twice to let them know he understood.

The turn signal went off, and the car accelerated to ten miles above the speed limit and held that speed. Joe Big moved into the right lane, and closed the gap, pacing the car in front of them.

"They're going to pull over in Painted Cliff," he said. "Probably lead us into the supermarket parking lot. It'll be closed this time of night."

"You want to take them down now?"

"For what? Brianna's the one who broke a bottle and went after him."

"Remember what we were saying about graveyard rules?" Barney asked.

"Yeah?"

"Well, Brianna might bark at the moon every now and then, but she's one of us—are we agreed on that?"

Joe Big glanced at Barney. "Why you got to ask that?"

"Because you the man with these dudes, that's why. You're the one going to get under their skin."

"Damn, Barn. Lighten up. You can't be throwing citizens on their ass in the middle of the street, and you can't be shooting people just because they need to be shot."

"We're talking our own kind here, Big. Makes it kind of hard to lighten up, don't you think?"

"She's the one broke the bottle."

"Like that matters."

"It matters," Joe Big said.

"You're the one said we should go shoot those assholes who kicked our ass up the Blackfoot."

"That's different."

"How is that different?"

"It just is," Joe Big said. "How the fuck do I know? Let's just handle the here and now, okay?"

"If they knew who she is, then why don't they know who we are?"

"You're saying the cat might already be out of the bag?" Joe Big asked.

"I think we have to operate on that assumption."

Joe Big was silent, staring at the taillights of the car in front of them.

"It's the same as it was up the Blackfoot," he said. "They might know *who* we are, but they don't know *what* we are."

"You don't know that. Not with these guys."

"You're right," Big said. "We don't know that. In fact, we don't know anything about these guys. We're getting way ahead of ourselves here. Mixing up what happened with those three assholes up the Blackfoot with Brianna getting the short end of the stick." He laughed. "Sorry about that."

"I don't believe you said that."

"Brings new meaning to the phrase, getting a woody," Joe Big said.

"Quit it."

"Putting—"

"—the wood to her. I got it the first time, you sick fuck."

"I'm just saying . . . "

"It doesn't matter if they know who we are or not," Barney said. He sat forward, squinting at the car in front of them. "No way these people are drug dealers."

"It rang true the part about the H, though" Joe Big said.

"You mean that they have it, or that they can get it?"

"I think they can get it. But I don't think they have it. And I don't think they are dealers."

"That doesn't make sense," Barney said.

"I know."

They were both silent, watching the car in front of them.

"We already know he doesn't believe our legend, because he told us so." Barney rubbed the side of his face. "Man, I don't know about you, but I am tired of this shit—feeling like everyone else except us knows what is going on. It's been like this since the Sheriff assigned us to this so-called Anti-Terrorism Task Force." He paused for a moment. "I say, short of gunfire, go for it if you get a chance."

"Rodger that, Obi-Wan."

The car ahead slowed, and they followed in train around a corner and down a long hill, headed into the small village of Painted Cliff. Street lights and the lights from a gas station and from a new condominium complex that looked more like a kinder, gentler prison trying to blend than a place where anyone would want to live made the village an oasis of light surrounded by the lake on one side, dark mountains on the other.

Barney opened the glove compartment and took out three loaded magazines, one filled with .40 caliber hollow points for his Glock, and two of 9mm for Joe Big's SIG. He handed the magazines to Big, and released his seat belt so he could lean sideways, and put a spare magazine in his rear pant pocket. He reached behind under the blanket on the backseat and retrieved the short-barreled twelve-gauge. He made sure the stock was folded, jacked a round into the chamber, and then made sure the safety was set. He wedged the shotgun lightly between the emergency brake and his seat, barrel pointed down into the footwell.

Joe Big put the spare magazines in the cargo pockets of his pants, one to each leg.

"Get away from the car if anything goes down," he said. "You go one way, and I'll go the other."

Barney laughed. "That's our plan? You go one way, and I'll go the other?"

The car in front turned off the highway, onto an unmarked paved road, and then fifty meters down the road turned into the empty parking lot of a small supermarket.

Joe Big drove to the center of the parking lot, and stopped the car and shut off the engine. He left both the headlights and the fog lights on. He put the gearshift in neutral and Barney picked up the shotgun. Joe Big pulled on the emergency brake, and they both climbed out of the car, Barney leaving the shotgun on the seat, both of them standing behind open doors.

The silver EVO made a half circle and came back toward them and stopped about fifteen meters away, the two cars nose to nose. A calico cat ran diagonally across the parking lot behind the EVO, and jumped up on the concrete base of the light pole in the middle of the parking lot. They could feel more than hear the heavy bass thump of the sound system in the EVO.

The lights went off, and the sound system died, and the driver shut off the engine. Pick climbed out the driver's door and the redhead climbed out the back on the passenger side. Another man—they couldn't see him clearly through the windshield—remained seated in the front passenger seat.

"Yo," Barney said. "Whassup, Pick, my man?"

"Too much Otis Redding," Joe Big muttered to himself.

"Hey," Pick said, walking toward them and stopping to the right of the headlights, "Recognized the car. Thought you might want to talk a little more about what we were talking about before we had to, ah, assume a lower profile." The redhead walked through the headlights, and stood a step behind his outside shoulder.

"That's one way of putting it," Joe Big said.

"How would *you* put it?" the redhead asked. They could hear the sneer in his voice.

"I wouldn't put it at all. I'd leave that to all the cops who are at this very minute looking for you."

"Hey, man. That fucking dyke started it. I didn't ask her to break a bottle and come after me."

"You should've stayed around and explained that to the cops," Joe Big said. "They'll especially like the part about why you speared her tit with a pool cue."

The redhead stepped out from behind the other man, and Pick reached out and held his arm. "Jack down," he said.

Joe Big turned toward Barney, and leaned across the top of the Subaru, and in a low voice said, "I'm going to hit this motherfucker."

"Go ahead," Barney said in a normal tone of voice. "So what can we do for you?" he asked the two men.

"Like we, uh, discussed. I thought you might be interested in some weight?" Pick said.

"Some weight?"

"H, man. I told you."

"Stepped on how many times?"

The horse-faced man smiled, and shook his head. "Pure H, man. Straight to you from your partner's little yellow relatives in Deepest, Darkest Gook Land."

"Not much call for Mister Harry around here," Barney said. "Good blow, good crystal for the ladies trying to keep the pounds off. Now and then a little Mexican tar, Big Island Weed, Oxycontin—anything that will make you mellow out or speed up. But not anything you need to shoot or worry about being too strong to breathe. That kind of shit, you need to go south to the Rez or west to the counties that aren't much more than ghettoes in the woods."

"Well, hey-howdy! You sure seem to know a lot about it for two guys that don't spend all that much time around here."

"We get around," Joe Big said.

"We get around," the redhead mimicked, his voice falsetto.

Pick put his hand on the redhead's arm. "We're all friends here," he said.

"No we're not," Joe Big said. "Let me disabuse you of that notion most ricky-tick. There is no way we are going to do business with some Red-in-the-head-like-a-dick-on-a-dog Irish psychopath who likes to hit women with sticks."

"Motherfucker!" the Redhead said, and shrugged off the other man's hand.

Joe Big stepped around the open door, and walked out in front of the Subaru. He held his arms and hands up in the air in a V "Come and get it, Doggy Dick," he said. He turned his back to the two men and stuck out his ass toward the redhead and, looking over his shoulder, with his forefinger tapped himself on the ass. "Pucker up, you faggot Green Beenie goatfucker."

Barney laughed.

Pick looked at him, and Barney could see that he was nearly as angry as the Redhead.

Barney shrugged. "What can I say?"

Joe Big had expected the Redhead to scream and shout, foam at the mouth before he did anything overt. But the redhead was staring at him, his mouth a thin, hard line, skin white and stretched tight across his forehead and cheekbones, freckles like dark raindrops on his pale skin.

"That cat over there got your tongue?" Joe Big asked. He shook his head in mock sympathy. "You one mongoose looking motherfucker, you know that?"

"Hold on my say," Pick said to the redhead. "Ranger," he said to Barney.

Barney frowned. "Range what?" he asked, pretending to not understand. Joe Big walked over to Barney's side of the car and stopped about ten feet in front of the redhead.

"This man is a United States Army Ranger," Pick said. "He has been trained by the best." His voice took on a military cadence. "He has been tested in fire. Your man does not know the kind of pain this man can bring. Ranger pain."

Joe Big laughed. "You sound like a bad movie. This man has been tested by fire," he mimicked. "He is an expert at using cue sticks to bring *Ranger pain* to United States Civilian Females Who Inhabit Montana Bars." He paused. "No cue sticks now," he said to the redhead. "Just little old defenseless gook-motherfucker me."

"Go," Pick said.

The Redhead snarled and gathered himself, but before he could do anything, Joe Big took two quick steps forward, into the Redhead's space, and kicked at his knee.

The Redhead jumped in the air, Joe Big's kick missing his knee by a foot, and as he was coming back down Joe Big hit him twice lightly in the face and once in the throat, and when the Redhead's hands went to his throat, hit him hard with a combination to the ribs and kidney on his right side. And then stepped back and kicked him for real on the outside of the knee, the knee collapsing inward.

Pick started forward, and Barney said, "Whoa, there," and Pick looked toward Barney and saw that Barney had stepped out from behind the door and had a short-barreled shotgun held at his side, barrel down.

He stopped, his face impassive. "You going to shoot me, rich boy?"

"You bet," Barney said. "And if whoever is in the car steps out of the car, I'm going to shoot him, too."

The passenger door on the EVO opened and Pick turned and shook his head no, gesturing with his hand for the man to stay in the car.

The Redhead was on the ground, one hand at his throat, the other grabbing at his knee. Joe Big stepped forward and punted him hard between the legs, and the Redhead folded like a knife closing, and screamed a thin, whistling scream, knee and throat apparently forgotten for the moment.

Joe Big thumped his chest with closed fist twice over his heart. "Gook-motherfucker pain," he said to Pick, and turned and walked toward the car. "Leprechaun, my ass," he muttered to Barney, and climbed into the passenger seat. Barney handed him the shotgun, and walked around the back of the car to the driver's side.

"No H," Barney said to Pick. "We've got our standards." He laughed and shook his head and climbed in. He started the engine, blipped the throttle, put the transmission in reverse and backed away from Pick staring at them in the headlights, the redhead vomiting at his feet. He shifted into first and revved the engine and slipped the clutch, and the doors slammed shut, as the Subaru launched past the other car.

Joe Big saw the cat on the light stanchion put its ears back and expose its fangs as they blasted past.

At the entrance to the parking lot, Barney feathered the clutch, and yanked up on the emergency brake and floored the accelerator, and they broadsided out onto the road. Barney released the brake and the Subaru shot forward to the Highway.

Ignoring the stop sign, he turned onto the highway, and the Subaru accelerated up the hill.

As soon as they were out of sight of the village lights, Barney stood on the brakes, the car slowing to thirty, and turned onto a dirt road. They followed the road through trees back up to the ridge they had just crossed on the highway.

He turned off the lights, and they coasted to a stop on the side of the road just below the ridge.

"Look at me," Joe Big said. He held out his hand. "I'm shaking."

"From *that?*" Barney asked.

"No, you asshole. *From your driving.* I almost peed my pants the way you went out of that parking lot."

13
Owls

Looks a little heated down there," Joe Big said. They were standing at the edge of a bald spot on the ridge a few meters off the gravel road. Through binoculars they could see into the lighted village about a half-mile below as the crow flies. The supermarket parking lot was deserted save for the silver EVO and three figures standing in front of it.

"He doesn't seem to be able to put much weight on that leg," Joe Big said. "I didn't think I kicked him that hard."

"You kicked him pretty hard."

They watched as the three men got in the car, one of them holding on to the edge of the roof. He backed into the rear seat, leg held straight out. The third man closed the rear door, and climbed in the front, and the headlights came on, and the car moved slowly out of the parking lot, down the road to the highway. It turned on to the highway in their direction, and accelerated rapidly up the hill, until the ridge blocked it from their view.

They walked to the other side of the ridge, and waited for the headlights to appear on the highway far below.

"Going somewhere," Barney said. "I'd sure like to know where."

"You believe them about the heroin?"

"Maybe. I don't know. What do you think?"

"Well, it's weird," Joe Big said. "They sure aren't the type. But my gut tells me they've got it or can get it."

Barney grunted.

"You think they are the ones Quinn says chased her down the mountain?" Joe Big asked.

"I doubt it. For one thing, there's three of them."

"She said there was three of them."

"Yeah, but she also said the three men she saw were hard to distinguish from each other. The Redhead is pretty hard to miss."

"It was just a thought."

"They might have something to do with the heroin Paul Cyr found on the ground, though," Barney said.

"That was way to hell and gone on the other side of the mountains."

"I don't think distance means much to these guys."

"We haven't seen the last of them," Joe Big said.

Barney yawned, and stretched. "So what do you want to do now? It's still early."

Joe Big looked toward the ridge road, a long winding stretch of pale through dark pines.

"Why don't we find a place to camp," he said. "Think about it for a while."

An hour later, they sat on tree rounds probably left behind by some woodcutter who had miscalculated how much wood his truck could hold. They'd carried the rounds down into a hollow, and built a fire that could not be seen from the road or from the valley below. The Subaru was parked behind a screen of trees next to an old gravel pit that looked in the headlights as if it was sometimes used as a backstop for target practice.

The fire popped and crackled, occasionally sending up a tiny shower of sparks, like fireflies, into the darkness above. Low clouds scudded overhead, the full moon a dull glow behind a layer of moving clouds. The night smelled of burning pine and of the bottle of Old Bushmills blended Irish whiskey they were passing back and forth.

"Feels like snow," Joe Big said.

"Tonight?"

"Tomorrow sometime. Rain at this elevation, snow maybe a thousand feet higher than where we are now."

"Is that your Injun blood talking?"

Joe Big smiled, mesmerized by the glowing, pulsating coals, the flames licking at the bigger pieces of wood. "It's my hip where I took shrapnel that time the Air Farce dropped dumb bombs practically on top of us."

"I thought they fixed that?"

"So they said. But I still feel weather change in the bone."

"I like the Injun-blood thing better."

Joe Big reached out with a long, crooked branch and poked the fire, sending a stream of sparks skyward.

"How come you told me to go ahead and hit him?" he asked.

"Well, number one, he deserved it. Number two, you were going to do it anyway. And number three, I figured it might confuse the issue."

"What do you mean?"

"Here you go." Barney passed him the bottle of Bushmills. "Give me another water, will you? I don't want to wake up all dehydrated."

Joe Big opened the plastic cooler next to the tree round he was sitting on, and retrieved a couple of small bottles of water. He leaned toward Barney and exchanged the bottle of whiskey for a bottle of water.

Barney put the water on the ground, and stood and picked up several large branches and placed them gently on the fire.

"Pick knew right away we weren't who we were saying we were," he said, sitting down. "And I think he was leaning toward law enforcement of some kind. Telling him we weren't interested in his heroin made him think we were being coy, is all. But when you put a hurt on the redhead, it erased all thought of us being cops."

Joe Big took a taste of the whiskey. He leaned over and passed the bottle to Barney.

"But now he wants to know who we are for sure," Joe Big said. "And if I'm right about them knowing who Brianna is . . ."

Barney held the bottle of whiskey up, looking at the fire through the amber liquid. "God knows what Brianna has been up to." He took a sip, and passed the bottle back to Joe Big. Something big and gray and dark flashed overhead at the periphery of the fire.

Barney ducked his head. "What was *that*?"

"Owl."

"That was a damn big owl!"

"What did you think it was?"

"I don't know what I thought it was."

"A ghost, maybe? That Windigo creature Roy White Owl is supposed to be playing?"

"Yeah, like that, maybe."

"Death," Joe Big said.

"Damn it, Big. Why do you have to go and say something like that? Here we are. Nice fire. Nice night. Nice bottle of whiskey—"

"Nice owl."

"See what I mean?"

"An owl is powerful medicine, my man. *Real* powerful medicine. You know what this one is telling us?"

"What?"

"This is heavy Indian mojo, dude. You sure you want me to tell you?"

"Just tell me."

"You sure?"

"I'm sure."

"It's telling us I forgot to put food out for Miss Mouse."

"You asshole."

"You kind of like her, don't you?" Joe Big asked.

"Mouse? Mouse is a cat. How much can you like a cat?"

"Not Mouse. Brianna. The Death Devo."

"Of course, I like her. She's one of us, isn't she?"

"She's a pain in the ass, and about as rude as it's possible for a woman to be," Joe Big said.

Barney chuckled. "That she is."

"Not exactly a dee-light to the eye, either."

"Man, I got to tell you . . . You seen my ex, right?"

"Of course, I've seen your ex."

"Beautiful, right? Capable of giving a man a hardon just watching her walk across the street?" He passed the bottle to Joe.

"How do I respond to something like *that*?"

"You don't, if you know what's good for you." Barney threw a small branch on the fire, and for a moment they both watched the flames lick at it. "I'm tired of beautiful women," he said to the fire. "Queen bees, every one." The pine needles on the branch burst into flame. "You've got to be on your game every second. And insecure? Man, beautiful women are the most insecure creatures on the planet." The bark hissed off the branch, shriveled by the flames licking at it. "Every day. Every single, solitary day, you have to tell them the same thing you told them the day before: you're okay, you're great, you're the most beautiful thing on the planet, you can do it, go for it, everyone will love you, you're beautiful, you're okay, you're great, you can do it, you're beautiful. And every day, no matter how many days in a row you've said all that, you have to say it all over again." With a long skinny branch Barney pushed the burning branch deep into the fire. "You have to argue and cajole and flatter, and it's always about them. And if you miss even one day—"

"Cajole? That's a pretty sophisticated word for you, dude."

Barney picked up a branch from the pile next to where he was sitting and threw it at Joe Big.

Joe Big laughed.

Barney went back to staring at the fire. "I'm tired of beautiful."

"Well, one thing for sure: Brianna isn't going to be pretty for a while."

"No she's not."

They both sat looking into the fire, both remembering the pool cue hit her in the mouth, the mewling sound she'd made. Out on her feet and not knowing it.

"Might probably lose some weight," Joe Big said.

"Always a silver lining."

"A new weight-loss program."

And even though it wasn't funny, they both laughed.

And laughed harder.

And then harder still, unable to stop laughing, Joe Big toppling off the round he was sitting on, laughing up at the sky and the night, Barney hunched over, shoulders shaking.

"Aw, damn," Joe Big said, sitting up. He wiped tears from his eye. "We are some kind of assholes, you know that?'

"Word, homey," Barney said, and they both started laughing again.

"This is not even funny," Barney said, and they were off again, laughing at nothing, laughing at everything.

Joe Big got up off the ground, and staggered off up the slope, out of sight over the lip.

Barney could hear him laughing in the darkness.

And then, abruptly, it was silent.

He frowned, and stirred the fire with the skinny stick.

He put the stick to the side, and threw on more branches. Building the fire until he could see nothing but darkness beyond the flames and the heat made the skin on his face feel glazed.

Joe Big materialized out of the night, and picked up the whiskey bottle propped up against the round he'd been sitting on, and sat down.

"We should probably go see her tomorrow," he said.

"In the afternoon," Barney said. "After Quinn has been and gone from the hospital."

Joe Big met Barney's stare.

"I was worried you were going to put your knife through his heart," Barney said.

Joe Big uncapped the bottle and took a sip. He passed the bottle to Barney. "I thought about it."

"We aren't them," Barney said.

"'I yam what I yam,' said Popeye the Sailor Man. That's what my uncle always used to say when we were kids."

"Once upon a time, Pick was the same as us."

"Might still be," Joe Big said.

"You think you could force a young college kid to shoot himself for no reason other than he was a tree hugger and he'd sabotaged a couple of Caterpillar tractors?"

"We don't know what the kid had done or not done. And we've got only Quinn's word for what those guys who chased her did or didn't do."

"Quinn," Barney said, staring at the fire.

They were silent.

"That was a big owl," Joe Big finally said. "And tonight I saw Roy White Owl for the first time since high school."

Barney looked at him.

"Heap big mojo," Joe Big said.

14
Swimming With the Fish

Barney opened his eyes. The inside of his mouth tasted like he'd eaten some of that goat cheese they'd chowed down on when they were in Afghanistan. A raven sat on the branch of a big bull pine not twenty feet away, staring at him with beady black eyes.

The morning sky was a ceiling of gray-streaked clouds. A stiff wind bent the tops of the surrounding trees. Tiny breezes filtering down into the depression stirred the embers of the fire, making the coals glow.

The double-sized sleeping bag, purchased when times were good with the ex, left plenty of space for his boots and socks at the bottom. He could turn over on his back without the bag getting all twisted.

The whiskey had hit like a wall of sandbags collapsing on him. He'd barely crawled in the sleeping bag before he was asleep, getting up only once to take a piss—and to see Joe Big sitting on a small rock outcropping, looking out over the valley and the lake far below. Joe Big looking more like a Buddhist monk than a Blackfeet warrior.

Both of them were drinking too much lately, he thought. He pulled the sleeping bag up to his chin, luxuriating in the fact that there were no weapons within reach, let alone attached to his body. He stretched his legs straight out, feeling the good stretch of thigh and calf muscles. Too bad they weren't hunting. It would be a good day to hunt elk: the wind and the flat gray sky, the promise of snow in the air.

It helped to drink too much sometimes, he thought. Made it easier to talk about things you wouldn't normally talk about. In the morning everything fell back into the same order it had been in before you started drinking, but at least talking allowed you to let off steam. They might be drinking too much lately, it was true, but anything that let off steam, especially that kind of steam, had to be a good thing.

Playing ring-around-the-mountain with an elk would be an even better thing. But that would have to wait. People to see, places to go, things to do.

Brianna was at the top of the list.

He lifted his arms out of the bag, and put his hands behind his head. What a strange woman. She radiated a weird, off-the-wall intelligence and sexuality that knew few bounds and even less gender. Without all the crap she put in her hair and around her eyes, he suspected she was decent looking. Not beautiful by any means, but not difficult to look at if she'd shed some of her camouflage. Well, not difficult to look at before last night, anyway. Big was right. He liked her a lot. But he liked her most of all because she was one of them.

He heard a small sound and looked to his left.

Joe Big was a lump inside a black sleeping bag, the bag zipped closed, only the top of his head visible. How does he do that, Barney thought. Anyone else would die of asphyxiation. Big, when he slept, was like a bear hibernating.

But if you disturbed him when he was sleeping, he would eel out of that bag faster than most people could get out of an unzipped bag. Big said it had something to do with his family's relationship with snakes, but Barney figured it had a lot more to do with Big's relationship with his uncle when he was growing up.

The Bushmills bottle and a pile of empty water bottles were grouped to the side of a rock. A chipmunk was darting and stopping, darting and stopping, trying to figure out if there was anything edible or worth taking from the pile.

He turned his head. The raven on the branch had been joined by two more ravens, each on its own branch, all of them staring at him. The ravens and the gray sky and the wind reminded him of the time he'd been showing one of their Afghani guides where they were on the map. He'd heard a strange sound, like a piece of wood hitting a tree, and he'd glanced up and the guide had taken a round in the temple. The guide had stared at him, his eyes slightly crossed, and then fell over backwards, dead when he hit the ground.

The ravens abruptly took flight. He heard a noise, and glanced back to his left. Joe Big was out of the sleeping bag, holstered 9mm in his hand.

"I hear a truck," he said. He pulled the handgun from the holster and dropped the holster to the ground, tucked the pistol into the waistband of his pants at the small of his back, and let his sweatshirt fall over the top of it. He pointed to the pine the ravens had been in, and turned and trotted, boots laces flopping, toward the low point of the depression, headed, Barney knew, around and up behind the rock he'd seen him on in the middle of the night. From there he would have a view of the road and the Subaru and the depression they'd camped in.

Barney unzipped the bag and threw it open and pulled on his hiking boots and, not bothering to tie them, grabbed the shotgun. He pumped a round into the chamber, as he trotted bent over to behind the tree.

Probably some kids or someone who lived up the road, he thought. But the way things had been going lately, it was better to play it safe. Pick was smart and experienced, and that was always an unpredictable combination. He could have figured out where they were, simply by asking himself where he would have driven if it had been him. Hard to believe that he'd be making enough noise to announce his arrival, though.

He crouched sideways to the pine, and made sure the safety was on.

Below, low hills spread toward the immense lake. On the other side of the lake the line of the Mission Mountains, snow-capped and rugged, marched sixty or seventy miles south down the valley.

The ceiling of gray clouds made the lake a flat gray expanse. The mountains were blue and without definition. Traffic moved along a ribbon of highway.

The wind had died. The air felt sullen.

The sound of a car or truck horn shattered the stillness—two drawn-out honks.

A car or truck door clunked shut.

He waited. A figure appeared at the edge of the depression. She stood hands on hips, surveying the remnants of their campfire—the blue and white plastic cooler and their sleeping bags.

"Barney! Joe Big! It's Quinn McBride. Come out, come out, wherever you are!"

Ah, fuck, Barney thought. Wouldn't you know it? He stood and ejected the shell from the shotgun, and fed it back into the tube, and then closed the action so that a round was not chambered. He dusted pine needles and dirt off his pants, and stepped out from behind the tree. It'd be a miracle if Big showed himself, he thought. He'd probably find him later, down at the coffee shop in the village.

He waved at the figure above, and Quinn started down the slope.

He picked his way over to the sleeping bag. When he looked up, Joe Big was about ten feet behind Quinn.

Quinn was dressed in jeans and hiking boots, a thin brown vest over a black and red checked flannel shirt. She looked bright-eyed and far too healthy for her own good. She stomped down through rocks and branches and yellow grass, unaware that Joe Big was behind her.

She stopped next to the blackened remains of the campfire. "Where's Joe?"

Joe Big reached out and stuck a pointed index finger into the middle of her back. "Right here."

She screamed and jumped, twisting away from Joe's finger, and launched a vicious backhand that forced Joe to stumble backwards up the slope and fall on his ass.

Barney shook his head. "The few, the proud, the Quinn and the Joe Big."

"Damn it, Joe Big," she said. "You scared the hell out of me." She stepped toward him and kicked him hard in the thigh.

"Ow! That hurts!"

Barney laughed.

"It's not funny!" she said, whirling toward Barney. Her eyes glittered with barely repressed tears.

He bent and placed the shotgun against a rock.

She turned toward Joe Big. Barney shook his head no behind her back.

"Sorry," Joe Big said. He dusted himself off. "No need to go postal."

Quinn turned back to Barney. "What are you two doing here?"

"Saving the U.S. Government the expense of a motel room." He threw the empty bottles into the cooler. "How'd you find us?" They knew, but she didn't need to know that they knew.

"The GPS locaters on your cell phones."

"ET, phone home," Joe Big said.

"Brianna is in a bad way."

"What happened to her?" Barney asked.

She looked from one to the other. "You don't know?"

Joe Big stared without expression at her.

Barney was silent.

"The bartender described two men who fit your description."

"What bartender?" Barney asked. "Where?"

"In Whitefish."

"What happened to Brianna?" Joe Big asked.

"She was beat up pretty bad—with a pool cue. She's got a concussion. The doctors had to drill her skull to relieve pressure. Her mouth is a mess, teeth knocked out or broken. And her spleen was bleeding. They managed to repair it, though."

Joe Big walked over to the cooler and opened it and took out a bottle of water. He handed the bottle to Quinn.

"You saw it," she said. It was a statement, not a question.

"There wasn't anything we could have done about it," Barney said. "It happened too fast."

"Do you know who did it?"

"We know," Joe Big said.

She turned toward Barney.

"You don't want to know," Joe Big said. He picked up his sleeping bag and holster and tucked them under his arm, and then picked up the cooler with his other hand. "I'll take these to the car," he said to Barney, and began walking up the hill toward where they had parked the Subaru.

"I don't want to know?" Quinn asked Barney. "What does he mean? What don't I want to know?"

Barney shook his head. "Trust us. You don't want to know." He knelt and rolled up his sleeping bag.

She watched him wrap elastic bands around the rolled-up bag.

He tossed the bag next to the shotgun, and sat on the ground to tie his boots. He was still wearing the slacks he'd worn the night before but his Converse All-Stars had been exchanged for boots, the Boomerang shirt for a gray sweatshirt.

He stood and went over to the fire and kicked dirt on the embers, stomping on the bigger pieces before kicking dirt over them. There was no chance the embers could spread or rekindle a fire, but he wanted to give her a chance to figure out that she shouldn't ask any questions.

She walked over to the lower lip of the little depression, and opened the bottle of water and took a drink. She gazed out at the valley.

She capped the bottle, and turned and toward him.

"Do you have a plan?"

"You don't want to know that either."

"I need you to tell me that you have a plan. You don't have to tell me what that plan is."

"We don't have a plan."

She stared at him. Her eyes were back to their normal green flinty self.

Big was right, Barney thought. You couldn't trust her as far as you could throw her. She was like a spider that ate anyone it mated with.

"We don't even know for sure who they are yet," Barney said. "We didn't want to run their license plates."

"I didn't hear that."

Barney shrugged. "Like I said."

She started to say something. Then started to say something else. She nodded, her smile and her eyes sardonic. "Joe Big already did something, didn't he?" She raised her hand. "No. Don't tell me."

Barney bent and picked up the shotgun and the sleeping bag, and gestured her ahead of him up the slope.

"You'd tell us if we were getting in over our head," he said. "Right?"

At the top of the slope, she paused and turned toward him.

"I've told you everything I know."

"You haven't told us shit. Don't be giving me that look. We are stumbling around in the dark here. And all I'm asking is that you at least let us know if we are getting in over our heads." He met her stare. "Brianna got in over her head."

She nodded. "I will. Of course, I will." And because she said it so earnestly, Barney knew it was another lie.

Wordless, he turned toward the Subaru and the burgundy Dodge Durango with Idaho plates parked behind it. The Durango was unwashed. Bumper stickers advertised membership in some kind of quarter horse association. It was one of the vehicles from the County Motor Pool.

Joe Big was on the far side of the Subaru, the passenger side, leaning against it with his arms on top the roof. He had on the black wrap-around sunglasses and his knit hat.

"Will they let us in to see Brianna?" Barney asked.

"If there's any problem call me, and I'll call the nurse's station. She'll probably be asleep, though. They wouldn't let her sleep until they were sure they had the concussion under control."

She opened the door, and climbed in and started the Durango. She put on her seat belt and then closed the door. Looking in the side mirror, she backed the Durango around in a half circle so that she was next to the Subaru.

She lowered the window.

"Keep me informed," she said.

They watched the Durango waddle over rocks and holes, around the screen of trees, heard it speed up when it hit the road.

Barney opened the hatch, and arranged his bag and Joe's bag to the side of the duffels containing their other gear. He closed the hatch, and opened the rear door on the driver's side, and put the cooler on the folded-down seat.

Joe Big looked at him over the top of the car. He raised his eyebrows.

Barney shook his head. "We are in so far over our heads," he said. "That even the fish don't know which way is up."

15
Sometimes Sam

You're not going to eat anything?" Barney asked. They were sitting next to the window in a coffee shop/deli in Painted Cliff, the only customers in the shop. The cheerful teenager who had been working the counter was in the back talking to someone.

"I want to go for a run," Joe Big said. "Blow it out a little."

Barney stared out the window.

"What're you thinking?" Joe Big asked.

Barney looked at him. "I'm thinking we're going about this wrong."

"What do you mean?"

A tall, slender, dark-haired woman who looked vaguely Oriental came out of the back, carrying a tray of cinnamon rolls. Joe Big felt his stomach rumble. He didn't know which was better looking, the tray of fresh-baked cinnamon rolls or the woman holding the tray. She was wearing a smudged white apron—a baker's apron.

"Damn," Barney said. "I've got to have me one of those."

The woman put the tray in the display case. She looked up over the top of the case and smiled at them, and inexplicably Joe Big felt as if the floor was suddenly pushing up on his chair—the way it sometimes felt when the airplane they were about to jump out of was pushed upward by an updraft, his knees and lower legs feeling squashed into the floor. The whiskey from the night before coming back at him, he thought. Caffeine and empty stomach and the alcohol still in his blood combining with the smell of fresh-baked cinnamon rolls to make him momentarily loose his center of gravity.

His grandmother had made cinnamon rolls at least once a week, and sometimes he'd help her knead the dough, his wrists and hands aching almost as soon as he started kneading, amazed that she could knead dough with no apparent effort for as long as it took.

A little boy came out of the back, white smudges of flour on his forehead, a faded picture of Cookie Monster emblazoned on his sweatshirt. Four or five years old. Green cargo pants too long. A handsome dark-haired boy with eyes too aware for someone so young.

The woman came over with a fresh pot of coffee, and filled their cups. Joe Big could smell flour and baking bread and a faint tinge of some kind of perfume that he'd never smelled before. Green, hooded eyes that looked familiar, he didn't know why.

"We have a breakfast menu, if you'd like to see one."

"I'll wash your car, rake your leaves, do your laundry—anything for a cinnamon roll," Barney said.

She chuckled. "I've got croissants coming out in a few minutes."

"I'm gaining weight just sitting here," Barney said.

"No breakfast then?"

Barney shook his head. "Just cinnamon rolls and coffee."

"How about you?" she asked Joe Big, her eyes and manner suddenly cool.

He could sense her waist and the swell of her hips next to him, and he knew—he could feel—that if he put his arm around her waist and hip and drew her to him, she would feel soft and strong and sensual all at the same—

Barney kicked him under the table. "Earth to Joe Big."

"Huh? Oh, ah—sorry. I'm going for a run," he blurted, his voice sounding like Foghorn J. Leghorn in the old Foghorn Leghorn cartoons he'd watched as a boy. He cleared his throat, stunned that he'd said something so inane.

Barney blinked, his mouth slightly open.

"Well, good for you." She smiled at Barney. "Be right back."

Joe Big watched her walk away. *"Ah, say. Ah, say,"* the voice of Foghorn J. Leghorn said in his mind.

The boy stared at him with knowing eyes. Joe Big felt himself blush.

"Hey, little man, what you doin' over there?" Barney said.

The woman looked up from behind the counter, and smiled. "He's really shy around strangers. I've been bringing him into work so he'll get more used to people. He won't bother you."

"No bother, a'tall," Barney said. He looked from Joe Big to the little boy to Joe Big, back to the little boy. Joe Big and the boy were locked into some kind of unspoken communication, information going back and forth at light speed—either that, he thought, or it was a case of a mouse being mesmerized by a rattlesnake.

"C'mon, Sam," the woman said. "Give me a hand in the back, will you?"

The little boy turned and followed her into the back, but before he went through the doorway, he looked back at Joe Big.

"Smile at the kid, man. I think he's afraid of you. Damn."

Joe Big shook his head, and picked up his coffee cup. "That kid is me when I was that age." He looked toward the doorway, and shook his head again. He lifted the cup to his mouth, but put it back on the table without taking a drink. "I look at a kid like that and I leak time."

"Leaking time again. Man, you need to take a real long run. Either that, or get some serious psychiatric help. His mother probably thinks you are some kind of prevert or something."

"You looked at yourself in the mirror this morning?"

Barney rubbed the stubble on the side of his face. "At least we don't look like cops."

The high-school girl came out of the back with a cinnamon roll on a plate, three or four pats of real butter next to it, and put the plate on the table in front of Barney. "Right out of the oven."

"I have died and gone to heaven."

The girl giggled, and went back into the rear.

Barney tore off a piece of cinnamon roll and put it in his mouth. He chewed a few times, and grinned—like a kid grinning around an ice cream cone, Joe Big thought.

"Oh, man," Barney said. "You have got to have one of these." He tore off another piece. "What's wrong with you? You look like your dog just ran off with your wife and your truck."

"I'm going for a run."

"So go for a run. Damn."

"Can I have your car when you are forced to buy a trailer to haul your fat ass around?"

"There's more to life than catching bad guys." Barney took a sip of coffee, and then a bite of cinnamon roll. He grinned his little boy grin. "Perfect," he said.

"You think Brianna can handle one of those?" Joe Big asked.

Barney stopped chewing. "Now, why'd you have to go and say something like that?" He sighed, and looked down at the table. He shook his head, and looked up at Joe Big. "Go for a run. Now."

Joe Big stood and walked to the door. He opened the door, and turned back toward Barney.

Barney tossed him the keys, and Joe Big caught them one-handed, and went out to the car.

Barney took a sip of coffee, watching Joe Big rummage in the back of the Subaru.

He turned toward the woman coming out of the back with another tray of pastries. Scones and croissants, this time.

"How far is it to the ski area?" he asked.

She looked at him and smiled. "About twelve miles. Most of it gravel."

"Perfect."

She looked at him quizzically.

"A perfect run for my friend," he explained.

"Twelve miles? It's all uphill once you hit the first turn." She nodded out the window. "And you can see the first turn from right here." She frowned. "Is he changing his clothes? People can see him from the highway."

Barney looked out the window. Joe Big was pulling a black long-sleeve Under Armor cold-weather shirt over his head, the long curving scar below his armpit and along his ribs vivid against his summer tan. The muscles of his back and side were clearly defined. Barney turned to see her reaction to the scar.

Her lips were pursed. She looked pissed off.

"You see people doing it all the time in the summer around the lake," he said.

She looked at him, embarrassed. "Oh, it's not that," she said. "He reminds me of someone, that's all."

"And who might that be? If you don't mind me asking?"

"I . . ." she began. She frowned at Joe Big coming toward the door. He was dressed in black training pants, a white, fluorescent stripe up the side of the pants, expensive running shoes, black Under Armor shirt.

"Well, that's strange," she said. "I guess I thought I knew, but I don't." She smiled at Barney. "Don't mind me. I spend too much time looking at the inside of an oven." She turned and went into the back.

Joe Big opened the door and stuck his head inside. "Do you have that hunter's orange knit cap in your bag? There are hunters out there."

"It's in the small blue duffel at the bottom of everything. It's twelve miles up to the ski area."

"Yeah, I know. Give me about an hour and a quarter and come and get me, will you? I'll run as far as I can. If the road to the lodge is closed at the top, I'll wait for you at the gate. Otherwise, I'll be at the lodge. That okay with you?"

"Go for it, man. I'm going to make a few calls. Maybe get the laptop out; they've got Wi-Fi in here. See if I can't find someone who knows those guys from the Army."

"Thanks, man."

Barney watched him sprint across the highway, and then slow to a jog on the other side. He watched until Joe Big disappeared around the first corner about half a mile up the road.

"More coffee," the girl asked.

"And another cinnamon roll, if you don't mind."

The little boy was standing next to the cash register, watching him with unblinking eyes.

"You want to hear the story about how my friend got his name?" Barney asked.

"What's his name?"

"Joe Big Snake Person."

The little boy walked across to the table and climbed up into the chair across from Barney. He squirmed around in the chair, getting comfortable, his arms and hands on the wooden armrests.

"You don't say much, do you?"

The boy smiled. "Sometimes."

"Well, Mr. Sometimes. Once upon a time—"

"My name is Sam."

"Well, Mr. Sam Sometimes . . . or is it Sometimes Sam?" Barney paused, looking at the boy.

The boy's face split into a grin. All right, Barney thought. A kid, after all.

"Once upon a time," he began, "a long time ago, in a land way over on the other side of those mountains across the lake out there, there lived a young Indian boy who looked an awful lot like Sam Sometimes. A little boy who sometimes called himself Sometimes Sam."

The boy giggled.

His mother reached around from behind Barney and poured fresh coffee into his cup. She walked to the other side of the table and with her free hand ruffled the boy's hair.

"Sometimes, Sam," she said to the boy, and winked at Barney. "Sometimes I don't know what to do with you, Sam."

The boy looked up at her.

"I'm leaving, I'm leaving," she said. "Don't let him bother you," she said to Barney.

"No bother at all. I like to tell stories."

"How about your friend?"

"Oh, he's pretty good at it, too." He looked at the boy, and winked. "Sometimes."

"I mean, is he really going to run all way up to the ski area?"

"He's going to try."

"Once upon a time . . ." the boy prompted. The woman rolled her eyes at Barney, and took the coffee pot back behind the counter and watched her son from there.

Barney looked Sam in the eye. "Once upon a time," he said, his voice low and intense. The boy's eyes widened. "On a day that looked very much like today, the sky all gray and threatening snow," he nodded to the boy's mother, and she turned away, smiling, "on a day when any sensible person would stay inside and drink a cup of coffee and eat a fresh cinnamon roll." He paused and took a loud sip of coffee, a big chomp of cinnamon roll, and waggled his eyebrows at the boy, as he chewed and swallowed.

The boy giggled.

"*But* . . . on a day that *wasn't* today, was instead a *long time ago*, when there were no cars and no bicycles, no tricycles or motorcycles. No electricity or running water or . . ." He paused, and leaned forward toward the boy, and whispered. "No toilet paper."

The boy grinned, and nodded, his eyes bright.

Barney leaned back, and waved his hand airily. "And certainly no coffee shops that served coffee and cinnamon rolls. And no one had ever even *seen* a white man. There lived a young Indian warrior called—"

"What's a warrior?"

16
Li'l Yellow Bird

I don't know.
But I been told.

Joe Big Snake Person heard the chanted cadence in his mind.

I don't know.
But I been told.
Eskimo pussy is mighty cold.

The first two or three miles had been hell, every step a chore, his breathing shallow, lungs not wanting to open, thigh and calf muscles too tight in his bad leg, a knot in his right shoulder and the back of his neck that wouldn't go away—probably from trashing that asshole last night. But he'd hit a level section of road that he'd forgotten about, just past the houses and just before the road turned to gravel, and his lungs had started to open and his muscles had finally felt oiled and he'd picked up the pace, and now, listening to the rhythmic crunch of his shoes in the loose gravel at the side of the road, he felt whole for the first time in weeks. Doing what he'd always done best. Running up a mountain.

The air was heavy and still, pregnant with the threat of rain and snow.

The grass in the creek-bottom meadow on his right was pastel yellow, clumps of birch and aspen skeletal in the drab light. A mule was standing next to a dilapidated barbwire fence, head up, ears out, a go-fuck-yourself look on its face.

"Mmmooo!" he said as he ran past, and the mule turned ass end toward him.

He laughed.

And spied a file of mule deer meandering slowly across the road about three hundred meters up ahead. One of them, the third one back, heard or noticed him coming, and they all stopped and turned to look, one after another, their ears sticking out like Disney cartoon ears. In unison they turned and hurried across the road, down the embankment, three of them pogo-sticking through bushes and grass, into the trees.

When he reached the spot where they'd gone down the embankment, there was no sign of them in the blue gloom of the forest. He could feel them watching, though.

Into the rhythm of the run now. The long straight stretch ending at a hairpin turn, the slope of the road becoming steeper. Around the turn—he loved running corners, loved listening to the gravel beneath his feet. Sweating. Lungs open. Muscles loose.

Feels good.
Sounds good.
Is good.

On his toes up through a steep winding section, out in the middle of the road, the gravel on the side of the road too deep to run in, following the road up over a finger ridge, into another long, straight uphill stretch, overgrown clear-cut to his left, almost a cliff on his right.

One. (Hit it.)
Two. (Kick it.)
Three. (Grab it.)
Four. (Kill it.)

He jabbed three times at the road ahead. Threw a right cross. Paused in the middle of the road. A left hook to the body, right hook to the head, his hands a blur. A flurry of punches and counter-punches, chin down, head tucked into his shoulder.

And took off running again, picking up the pace, feeling and hearing loose gravel squinch beneath his shoes, letting the sound of his feet on the gravel work him into a mechanical rhythm, an almost out-of-body thing, his body a machine timed to the snick of gravel beneath his shoes.

Li'l yellow birdie with a li'l yellow bill.
Landed on my window sill.
Oh, yeah.
Lured him in with a li'l piece of bread.
Oh-oh.
Then I crushed his little fucking head.
Me oh my I am such a klutz.
Say whaaat?
Missed his head and hit his nuts.
Sound off . . .

He smiled to himself. He'd crushed his nuts all right. A not-so-little redheaded birdie who was going to be chirping soprano for a long time.

Up ahead, a raven lifted off a tall pine, its deep *"grok-grok!"* letting the forest know he was coming, and banked off over the ridge. A few moments later, he heard the beat of its wings twenty or thirty meters behind him, as it made a low pass over the road, sizing him up. Probably wondering what sort of idiot thing he was doing, running up a road, when there was no apparent reason for doing so.

Feels good.
Sounds good.
Is good.

In bootcamp, he'd set the record for the obstacle course the first time he ran it—and from that moment on the drill instructors had never again let him finish the course, maliciously, malevolently creative in devising ways to make it impossible for him to finish until the entire platoon had finished ahead of him. Like making him walk on his hands across the top of the ladder bars—which he couldn't do. Or going again and again over the wall that slanted inward—again and again until he couldn't even crawl over the wall. Or going through the culvert without touching his arms or hands or back to the culvert walls. Or, Montoya's favorite, climb the rope all the way to the top without using his feet—which he also could not do. What he hated most about that one was the fall to the ground when his arms gave out.

Li'l yellow bird with a li'l yellow bill . . .

Gunnery Sergeant Montoya: mean, squatty-bodied, half Chicano, half Navajo—only he didn't know about the Navajo part then. The base hand-to-hand instructor. Forever goading and taunting him. "What's the matter with you, Small Dick Person? I thought you was supposed to be some bad-ass, last-of-the-Mohicans warrior." The venom and sarcasm in his voice truly spectacular. "Is that right, Mister? Are you the last of the Mohicans? You don't look like the last of the Mohicans to me. You look like a fucking Reservation Refugee who can't even climb a rope. Get off my rope, God damn it." And his voice suddenly a scream. *"Get. Off. My. Rope. God damn it!"*

And he would let go of the rope and drop to the thick layer of wood chips, the feeling in his stomach when he let go the same feeling as jumping off the high-dive at the swimming pool. *"Get up off my ground, God damn it!* Oh, you like that ground, do you?" the tone of his voice conversational. *"Then get back down on that ground you love so much and give me fifty."* And, as he started to do the pushups, dropping on all fours next to him, his face inches away, eyes boring into the side of his skull, "Kiss it. Kiss that ground you are trying to hump." And jumping to his feet: "That's enough, you fucking Indian pervert. *Stand up.* You're making me sick." And pacing back and forth in front of him, hands behind his back, black eyes full of disgust. "I seen your type all my life, Mister. The goin' gets tough, and you get goin'—right down to the liquor store. Ain't that right, Mister Last of the Mohicans?"

Oh, he'd been angry. Almost cross-eyed with anger. Trembling with anger.

Hit it.
Kick it.
Grab it.
Kill it.
Recon.

"You want to hit me, boy? I heard you some kind of puge-a-list. You want to hit me, Mister Last of the Mohicans *puke*-a-list?" Wonder in Montoya's voice, as if he'd just discovered the rarest thing on earth: a bootcamp recruit who wanted to hit him.

Joe Big smiled at the memory.

Grab it.

Kill it.
Recon.

The raven made its distinctive *grok!* high overhead, black wings spread against a gray sky. He could hear the sound of its wings.

No gray then. Pure Technicolor, his anger.

"Look at me," Montoya had said, menace in his voice, "Look at my eyes," and, he remembered being shocked, because you never, ever, looked a drill instructor in the eye.

"I said, look at me, God damn it. What the fuck is wrong with you?"

He'd looked into Montoya's eyes, and under the anger he'd seen a cold, hard resolve like he'd never seen before.

"It's just the two of us here," Montoya had said. And he'd stepped back a few paces, and taken off his Smokey Bear hat and put it on the log post of one of the obstacles.

He was taller, and had maybe three inches of reach on the Gunnery Sergeant, but Montoya was built squat, with almost no waist. He'd given a sit-up demonstration the first week of bootcamp, and had ripped off 500 sit-ups with no apparent strain. And then done twenty five one-armed pushups with each arm.

Joe Big grinned up at the raven riding an air current to keep pace with him. You like this story, brother? It's a good story. You can go home and tell this story.

Montoya had reached up and taken the insignia off the collar tips of his utilities, and put them in his pocket.

"Take your best shot, Tonto. You only get one."

He heard the sound of his feet in the loose gravel:

Yih.
Erh.
San.
Syh..

A fox sat next to a stump at the top of a twenty-foot cut in the road embankment, watching him. Joe Big pointed his finger at the fox, looking directly at it as he ran by. The fox yawned, a clown's yawn, exposing teeth and fangs and long lolling tongue. It closed its mouth and watched unblinking as he ran past.

Joe Big shook his head. Getting no respect from anyone these days, he thought.

He'd raised his hands and taken a step toward Montoya, and Montoya had kicked him so hard in the sternum that he'd fallen backwards on his ass into the thick wood chips of the obstacle course before he was even aware of what had happened. One moment he'd been sidling toward Montoya, and the next he was on his ass in the wood chips. It had felt like he'd been kicked by that mule with the attitude that he'd passed a few minutes ago.

He'd scrambled to his feet. Wiped his hands on his pants, and gone after Montoya, slow and careful this time, hands up, edging closer, no doubt in his mind that he was fast enough to counter Montoya's strength. And when Montoya had thrown another kick, he'd stepped inside the kick and hit Montoya twice, glancing blows to his neck and shoulder as, too late, he'd realized that the kick had been a trick to draw him in. With both hands, Montoya had grabbed him by the collar of his utility shirt and had used some kind of judo throw—like the throw Barney had used on that big guy in the leather coat—to throw him flat on his back, the wind knocked out of him, and then in a blur had hit him hard on the thigh and in the stomach and pulled the punch to his throat, leaning instead fist on his throat, choking him. In real life it would have been balls, solar plexus, throat, faster than you could say it.

Montoya had stepped up and back. "I don't give a *rat's ass* how special you think you used to be, Joe Big Snake Person. You are in my Marine Corps now. And if you want to stay in it, you best accept the fact that this is the only tribe you got."

He'd rolled over on all fours, and coughing, had forced himself to stand up.

"Walk it off," Montoya said, and began to put his collar insignia back on. "You fell off the rope, is that what I hear you saying happened?"

He'd nodded, pacing back and forth, hands on hips, struggling to get his breath back, trying to make his stomach relax, feeling more embarrassed and humiliated and angry by the second.

Montoya stood arms across his chest, looking at him critically.

"You want to be a Marine, Mister?" he'd asked in a normal tone of voice, the tone of voice as much a surprise as anything else that had happened.

He'd nodded.

"A real Marine?"

And he'd nodded again, and abruptly realized that for some inexplicable reason—that to this day he still didn't understand—he'd never wanted anything so much in his life.

"Then listen up. You will not be a squad leader. You will not be right guide. You will always be the last man. The rear guard. You will protect your platoon of Marines from all attacks from the rear. *Do you understand?"*

He'd shouted his understanding.

"You will help the members of your platoon, even if it causes pain and hardship to you personally. *Do. You. Understand?"*

Again he'd shouted his understanding.

"No matter what it is, you will help whoever in your platoon needs help. On a run. The obstacle course. Studying for a test. Squaring away gear. *Do. You. Understand?"*

"I understand, Gunnery Sergeant!"

"I can't hear you."

And once again, he'd shouted his understanding.

"And if it is too much to do alone, you will convince other members of your platoon to help. *Do you understand?"*

He'd looked at Montoya.

"Don't you be putting your eyes on me. Don't you ever be putting your eyes on me."

He'd shouted his understanding, but he hadn't really understood until the day he had graduated from boot camp, and Montoya had taken him aside and re-introduced himself using his Navajo name.

"You scored in the top ten on the PT tests, shot the highest score in not only the entire company, but the highest score of all recruits since I've been here, and scored in the top ten in the company on the written tests. You didn't make PFC, despite the fact that everyone in the platoon knows you are the leader of this platoon. What do you think about what I just said?"

"I think what everyone else thinks. I think it sucks."

Montoya had laughed. "Remember when I asked if you wanted to be a real Marine? Well, you now know what being a real Marine is going to be all about. Because, believe it, being a real Marine means there are going to be days when life truly sucks. Now quit feeling sorry for yourself, and come with me. I want you to meet someone."

And Montoya had taken him to see a hard-bitten, scarred, shaved-head, tough-as-an-old-leather-rope master sergeant.

"So you want to be in Force Recon," the master sergeant had growled.

"Force Recon?" He looked in surprise at Gunnery Sergeant Montoya. "Who said anything about Force Recon?"

Montoya smiled.

"I'm supposed to go to journalism school," he'd said to the Master Sergeant.

The Master Sergeant had taken a piece of paper off the desk and held it up. "You sign this paper, and you become a real Marine, not a sorry-ass journalist with a Marine Corps uniform. Your choice."

He'd signed the paper, and in so doing, of his own free will and with a total lack of common sense, nullified the contract for J-school that he'd signed before joining. Unknown to him at the time, Force Recon rarely recruited straight from boot camp. Most men who tried for Force Recon had at least three years in. Many had already been shot at. Many more had tried multiple times to get in.

"Wear these when you come back from leave," the Master Sergeant had said. And handed him a pair of Lance Corporal stripes.

Montoya had grinned and shook his hand, and, man, had a grin on Montoya's face ever looked unnatural. "Welcome to the tribe, Marine."

"Your uncle left you mighty big boots to fill," the master sergeant said.

"Master Sergeant, nobody can fill those boots."

The Master Sergeant and Gunny Montoya had laughed. "You'll do," the Master Sergeant had said. "If you know that, you'll do."

After bootcamp leave, he'd easily passed the indoc—the day of testing to see if he was fit enough to withstand Force Recon training. He'd completed the basic Recon course, and then gone immediately to scout/sniper school, and then to communications school, followed by Army Ranger school, advanced jump training, and then to a year of language school, a week here, two weeks there filled with specialized Recon training. By then he'd been in nearly three years. One of the reasons he'd joined the Marines was to avoid going to school, and all he'd done to that point in the Marines was go to school. He'd never studied so hard in his life. Language school had been unusual, but then, looking back on it, his whole career had been unusual. He looked Chinese, so . . .

Yih.
Erh.
San.
Syh.

In Force Recon he'd truly found a band of brothers. No more bringing up the rear. It was all he could do to keep up with everyone else. Force Recon was a hundred and fifty percent all the time—or at least it was with the bunch he'd ended up with. Five years was the tour of duty in Force Recon and then you had to re-cycle back to a regular unit. Unlike all the special ops guys in the other branches of the military, like Barney in SF, who could make Special Forces a career, a two-year extension was the most anyone ever got in Force Recon. He was into the first year of the two-year extension when he was hit seriously enough to know that his days in Force Recon, and probably the Marine Corps, were over. An Honorable discharge and a monthly disability check or a posting behind a desk were his choices.

Three years later, he and Barney were Sheriff's deputies. And the disability checks were still coming every month because the VA doctor didn't believe him when he said he was healed better than before he'd been hit.

Feels good.
Sounds good.
Feels good.
Is good.

The raven had left him, and the false top was only about a half mile ahead. He was feeling it now in his bad leg, but he was still good to go. He was going to make it, by God. The ski lodge was only another mile beyond the top.

Behind him, he heard the unmistakable sound of Barney's Subaru. Not hurrying. Puttering up the hill behind him.

The Subaru pulled even with him, and he saw the dark-haired boy from the coffee shop/bakery staring up at him from the passenger seat.

"Hey," Barney said. "I didn't think you'd be this far. How you doin'? How's the leg holding up?"

"Doin' good?"

"Yeah? You look like you got a little giddy-up in your gait, there."

"Who's your passenger?"

"That's Sometime Sam," Barney said. "Say, hello, Sam."

"Hello, Sam," the boy said, and grinned.

"Sassy, ain't he?" Joe Big said. "Sassy, ain't you?" he said to the boy.

The boy frowned.

"See you at the Lodge," Barney said.

The Subaru eased ahead, Barney careful not to raise dust.

The boy leaned his head and shoulders out the window, and twisted backwards to look at Joe Big.

Joe Big waved.

But the boy did not return his wave. And he was still looking back as the car disappeared over the top.

Joe Big suddenly felt alone, all by himself on a road at the top of the mountain, the solitude of the run broken, his memories consigned once again to the foot locker from whence they came—memories of a time when, despite his training, he was still naïve and full of himself, the Big Suck still months away.

He looked up. The raven was back.

"Hey, brother," Joe Big said. "Thanks for the company."

And he laughed, his laugh sounding bittersweet even to himself, knowing now that he'd taken a fork in the road when he'd signed that paper the Master Sergeant had handed him.

He hadn't thought about Gunny Montoya and bootcamp for years, but the memory had surfaced like an air bubble rising to the surface of the sea, released by the day and the run and the events of yesterday—a reminder to himself of who he'd been and the choices that he'd made to get to where he was now.

A jolt of adrenaline surged through his body. He could feel it fizzing in his blood. And, abruptly, his leg was no longer tired, and he felt strong and fleet of foot.

The raven *groked!*, and pirouetted far above, and spreading its wings swooped over the ridge, out of sight.

Ah, man, he thought. Whatever was coming, he could feel it the same as he could feel the change in air pressure, the stillness and dead humidity of a few minutes ago washed away by the first tendrils of wind slipping across the ridge, through the openings in the trees.

He looked for the raven. But the raven was gone.

And in the distance, little Sam Sometime was chasing Barney around the Subaru.

17
Fairy Tales

"Sam seems to have taken a shine to you," Barney said. They were headed to Kalispell to see Brianna and to meet with Paul Cyr. "Don't know about his mother, though."

Joe Big grunted.

"She was sure nice to let us use the bathroom and the shower," Barney said.

Joe Big swiveled his head toward Barney. "That kid has taken a *shine* to me because you filled his head with fairy tales about Indians. And as far as his mother is concerned . . ." He yawned. "I'll tell you right now—since you harbor lewd thoughts about her. She's got radar."

"Radar?"

"She knows who we are without us even saying anything."

Barney smiled. "You're good, Big. But you're not that good."

Joe Big looked out the side window, squinting against the light. The weather was changing. The sunlight had that washed-out effect, caught somewhere between fall and winter. Trees and bushes near the river were black line drawings on a field of yellow stubble. Even the houses and buildings seemed bleached by the light.

"She won't bite."

Joe Big again swiveled his head toward Barney. He didn't say anything.

Barney cleared his throat. "We're supposed to meet her and one of her girlfriends at the brew pub in Painted Cliff tonight."

Joe Big continued to look at him.

"What? I thought we could use a break before we drive off into the sunset to save the world, that's all."

"I thought we were going to pay Harold a visit."

"We'll do that tomorrow."

Joe Big turned his head to once again stare out the side window. They were silent, the car cruising effortlessly. Traffic was light on their side of the divided highway.

"You don't want me to tell stories to little Sam about how your family got its name. You don't want to talk to Paul Cyr. What is it with you lately?" Barney asked.

Joe Big pressed his forehead against the window.

Barney glanced at him.

Joe Big sighed, and made a production of sitting upright in his seat. He reached down with his right hand to find the seatback release.

"What is it with me and being Indian?" He leaned forward and then back, trying to find a better position for the seatback. "Is that what you want to know?"

"Well . . ."

The seatback clunked into position and Joe Big relaxed against the seat.

"Of course, I want to know," Barney said. "You've heard my stories about my people a thousand times. The Civil War Lambiers. The Revolutionary War Lambiers. My father jumping into Normandy and capturing a German general. Cajuns. Aristocrats. Football players and lowlife, white-trash, Bayou Bubba drunks. But since I've known you, you've hardly said anything about your people. All I know is what comes from your mother, and from a few people we run into here and there, like Roy White Owl."

"My people," Joe Big said. His laugh was a short harsh bark of sound. "You mean, *The* People. The *Niitsitapi*." He looked at Barney. "Made out of mud by *Naapi*, the creator." He sighed, and leaned his head back against the headrest, watching as they passed a tandem-trailer truck, the cargo covered with mud-streaked, dark-brown tarps.

"Or maybe you want to know about the other half of my blood. The half that no one talks much about because if you are on the rolls it doesn't matter if you are one thirty-second or if you are full blood or if you are anything in between. You are an Indian if you are on the rolls. Well, I'm not an Indian, even if I am on the rolls. I'm an American. How do you like them apples, Mr. Barney Lambier the Second—or third, or fourth, or ninety-second, or whatever you are."

"Apples. I get it. Cute, Big."

"*The People* had words for people like you, dickhead. If you were French, then The People called you The Original White Men. If you were Scots and English they called you The Real White Men." He sneered at Barney. "That's you. An Original White Man, if ever I saw one. A *Niitsaapiikoan*."

"So what does that make you?"

"I told you. I'm on the rolls. I'm one of *The People*. The fact that I also have the blood of Original White Men and Real White Men, doesn't matter. I'm one of The People, and that's fucking that."

"Except that everyone thinks you are Chinese."

"*Ni hao*. Can you believe he said that?"

"You've got a talent for languages."

"I've got a talent, all right." Joe Big turned his head toward the window.

"Oh, man. C'mon. Don't be getting all morose on me. We've got a date tonight."

"*You've* got a date tonight." He turned back toward Barney. "I'm probably going to be stuck with some Olive Oyl or another Maggie, my-ass-isn't-as-big-as-it-looks-it's—"

"*BIGGER!*" they shouted in unison. They laughed.

"Didn't stop you, though, did it?" Barney said.

"She had a sense of humor, what can I say? I value a woman who has a sense of humor. Watch out for that Suburban. It's a woman with a cell phone and no sense of humor." The Suburban was wandering back and forth, straddling the two lanes.

The Subaru surged forward, passing the Suburban on the right, the tires on Joe Big's side off onto the shoulder. Barney watched in the rearview mirror as the maroon Suburban jerked to the left to avoid gravel and dust thrown up by the Subaru.

"You want to know what I think about my people?" Joe Big asked. "*The* People."

"I do."

"It's complicated."

"What isn't?"

Joe Big looked straight ahead out the windshield, staring vacantly at the highway and the cars and the houses scattered across the valley floor and up on the hillsides.

"The People had guns before they had horses," he said. "They had guns because they got them from the Real White Men and the Original White Men—men like you who worked for the Hudson Bay Company and the Canadian trading companies. Guns made it possible for them to drive the Snakes back south and to steal horses from the Snakes and the Crow and the Flathead and anyone else who had horses."

He looked at Barney. "I told you, it's complicated."

"Not so far."

Joe Big pinched the bridge of his nose and closed his eyes for a moment. "Once they had guns—and beads and knives and metal arrowheads and pots and pans—their whole way of life changed. Thanks to the fur traders and their goods and guns, and thanks to the acquisition of horses, for something like one hundred and fifty years, the *Niitsitapi,* The People, became the mythical, mystical, badass Warriors of the Plains.

"One hundred and fifty years," he said. "That's it. From start to finish, that's it. About as long as it took Europe to fight the One Hundred Years War and the Thirty Years War. About *one-third* the time it took the Romans to create the Roman Empire. Two thousand three-hundred-and-fifty years less—*less!*—than the Egyptian Empire hung together. Never mind some of the civilizations put together by the ancestors of the people we fought in Afghanistan and Iraq and Iran."

"It only took Genghis Khan about twenty-five years to do his thing," Barney said. "A lot can happen in a hundred and fifty years."

Joe Big smiled. "You read that book I gave you, didn't you? Well, the Blackfeet weren't the Mongols. Not even close."

He ran his hand back and forth across the stubble on his head. "BH—Before Horses—when there was a fight, the warriors would line up far enough away from each other so that arrows and stones couldn't do much damage. They'd shout insults at each other. Lob a few arrows. Run out into the no-man's land between the two lines and piss in the direction of the enemy. Moon each other, that sort of thing. And then everyone would go home and brag about what great warriors they were. Before Horses and Before Guns, killing another human being was done only as a last resort. There were too many ways for a man to get killed as it was. Even BG and BH, there weren't enough men to go around."

"And you know all this how?"

"Books."

"Books!"

Joe Big laughed. "My uncle and my father used to argue about it. My uncle doesn't have much blood, but, well, you know. I've talked about him before."

"And this was his take on the history of your people?"

"No. This is *my* take on it. My father knows the history, or at least the Tribe's version of it, but my uncle doesn't care about the Tribe's version. Don't get me wrong. Ben Tales is about as spooky and spiritual as it gets. But he thinks most tribal histories have been distorted by a sort of Reservation Indian conventional wisdom. People are people, is his philosophy. The Blackfeet were no different from many other people at many times in many other parts of the world. I guess his view and my father's view and my grandmother's view . . . plus what I've read in books . . . all that has . . ." His voice trailed off.

Barney glanced at him. "Has what?"

"Huh? Oh. Sorry. I was thinking about my uncle." He rubbed his hand back and forth across the stubble on his head again. "Guns. Horses. Disease. Alcohol. The *Niitsitapi* went from what they were before they had guns and horses and disease and alcohol—and no one, not even anthropologists, knows for sure what that might have been . . ." He shifted in his seat.

"This is the part that gets me in trouble," he said.

"Like that would be a first."

"The *Niitsitapi* went from whatever they were Before Guns and Before Horses to a people who slaughtered other human beings for horses and for trading advantage with The Real White Men and The Original White Men. They slaughtered human beings for revenge or vendetta or for no fucking reason at all." He looked at Barney. "I have a great-something grandfather who killed more than forty Crow. He didn't know how many people from other tribes he had killed. A lot more than forty, was all he knew." He laughed without humor. "He didn't figure Real White Men or Original White Men were even worth killing, they were so pathetic."

"Sticks and stones, dude."

"No, man. I'm not insulting you. I'm just saying, these were badass warriors. It's how he really felt. According to family legend, he didn't fight white men because he felt killing a white man was beneath him. There was nothing to be gained—no war honors, nothing like that. Counting coup on a white man simply wasn't worth the effort."

"That's us," Barney said. "Vermin of the Plains."

Joe Big smiled. "You said it, not me."

"So what made them suddenly this way?"

"The buffalo, man, the food supply—this is the part that really gets me into trouble. You think it was just the white man who killed buffalo they didn't need? How else do you think The People could buy all those guns and goods and all that watered-down whiskey? Furs and beaver pelts in the beginning. But it was buffalo hides, man. The People basically helped to annihilate themselves in order to provide factory pulley belts and lap robes to city people in North America and Europe."

"Well, I hate to break it to you, but my people wouldn't have known a pulley belt from a snakeskin."

"I'm just saying, it was home on the range, where the buffalo roamed less and less, and the Indians, especially the Blackfeet, had as much to do with that as did the white man." He paused. "It's not politically correct to say anything that might even remotely imply that Indians might have been responsible for their own demise." He looked at Barney. "The reason why I don't like to talk about the *Niitsitapi* is because these days it's all bullshit about Indian Spirituality and The Warrior Ethic. You tell me how ethical or how spiritual it was to slaughter buffalo for only their hides or for only their tongues, and leave the rest to rot on the prairie. You tell me how a herd of buffalo is supposed to propagate if nearly all the cows and calves are gone, and only the bulls remain. You tell me how spiritual it was to indiscriminately slaughter other tribes for control of the buffalo, or just because it was fun and exciting.

"Think about it. I mean really think about it. For about one hundred years of that one hundred and fifty years, my Indian ancestors were bloody *all the time.* All the shit you and I have done, we haven't even scratched the surface compared to what was just life to them. If it wasn't killing and butchering animals, it was killing and butchering other human beings. And if they weren't killing each other, they were dying of disease."

He shook his head. "And then, all at once, in less than a generation, the proud, the mythical, the *spiritual,* became bums and Reservation Indians with few horses and no guns and even less hope. The buffalo disappeared and with them disappeared tribal life. In less than fifty years, the independence and freedom that made The People, *The* People, were gone. Gone as completely as the buffalo were gone.

"The *Niitsitapi,* the meanest, proudest, most badass warriors to ever inhabit North America, went out without even a whimper. They never fought the U.S. Army. When the buffalo disappeared, the warriors wandered off to die of broken hearts and enlarged livers. Their souls shriveled up and turned to dust.

"So you'll pardon me if I don't get all worked up about talking to Paul Cyr, and putting up with his sly guilt trips about not accepting my heritage."

Barney frowned at the road.

Joe Big smiled. "The Sacred Culture had a dark side, bro. Just like every culture has its dark side. The Mongols spread culture and learning and freedom of religion—they spread a mix of civilizations like no people did before or have done since. But if you didn't get with their program, they killed everyone, man, woman, and child, dismantled the city stone by stone, and then salted the earth."

"I smell another metaphor coming," Barney said.

Joe Big shook his head. "No metaphors. Not this time. The Buffalo *were* the *Niitsitapi* and when The People killed the Buffalo for robes and hides to buy guns and whiskey and pots and pans and beads, they killed themselves. Even if the white man and disease had not come along, sooner or later the tribes would have gotten big enough, and sooner or later they would have killed off enough of the calves and cows to make even the largest herd no longer able to sustain itself.

"And as soon as the herds began to disappear, warriors would have tried to kill off anyone from outside the tribe who threatened the food supply. Men, women, children, it made no never mind. First come, first die. Step right up. No waiting in line."

"You sure you're not talking about the Arabs and the Persians, Sunnis and Shiites, the Taliban?"

Joe Big looked at him. "Yeah," he said. "My uncle would put it that way, too. He'd say that if the Blackfeet and the Crow would've had car bombs they would have used them."

"I saw an article in the paper today about a movement to raise Federal money for monuments to great warriors and great battles."

"What I mean, man! Great battles . . ." Joe Big shook his head. "Like the one where three or four hundred Crow came north and slaughtered nearly every man, woman, and child of the Little Robes Tribe. A whole tribe wiped out in revenge for something a Blackfeet tribe, not even the Little Robes, had done to the Crow. First come, first killed, like I said." He shook his head again. "Monuments."

"I guess they don't teach that kind of history in school."

"No they don't."

They were silent for a while, both of them watching the road and the traffic.

"My uncle says it's all about myths," Joe Big said.

"Myths?"

"Yeah. Let me ask you something: How many times did we express what we were doing in terms of Indian Country? I don't know about the Army, but the Marine Corps practically has a fetish for using Indian names for operations and forward operating bases. And the operations are almost always into "Indian Country."

Barney eased the Subaru around a delivery truck that refused to get out of the fast lane, passing the truck on the right, and then once they were past the truck, slid the Subaru back into the inside lane.

"Indians, when they were at their best, operated in small units," Joe Big said. "Sort of like we did in Afghanistan."

"What do you mean?"

"It wasn't Big Army or Big Marine Corps that fought in Afghanistan. It was us in our small groups using tactics that American soldiers had learned from Indians ever since the French and Indian Wars. Only difference was we had a lot better training—"

"Not to mention laser designators and all the doom we wanted to bring from the sky," Barney said.

Joe Big laughed. "Yeah, you're right. I'm getting a little carried away."

"No, you've got a point. When you get right down to it, all generals do these days is try to keep people like us under control. They point us in a direction and they say, go do it. Go steal those horses. Go wipe out that tribe. And then they leave it to us to get it done. The only difference is that we're supposed to make friends with the indigenous people, while we're at it."

"Spoken like a true Special Forces A-Team Lieutenant."

Barney looked at him.

"No offense," Joe Big said. "But that's not the Marine Corps way."

"I'm trying to be serious here."

"So am I. The Marine Corps way is a lot closer to the way my Indian ancestors did things than the Army Special Forces way was . . . is."

"Sometimes you are so full of shit."

"Yeah? Marines are trained to go to the sound of bullets. Shoot at a Marine unit and it comes right at you. Army guys like you are trained to step back away from the sound of bullets, take cover, think about what you are going to do to stop the bullets."

"Seems reasonable to me."

"Yeah. To *you*. But not to me. It's one of the reasons we work so well together. We're the yin and yang of small-unit tactics."

"And you're saying that's what your ancestors did: they went to the sound of bullets?"

"A lot of them still do. That's what even Roy White Owl did. Most kids would've run away."

Barney was silent for a moment. They were coming into Kalispell, and the traffic was picking up. He frowned. "You know, for once you might actually have a point. That might be why they put a mixed group of Army Special Forces and Marine Recon together. I never thought of it that way before."

Joe Big snorted. "That's giving them a lot more credit than they deserve."

"I suppose."

They were silent again for a moment.

"I still don't get it," Barney said. "You don't want any part of what you call the mythical, mystical, spiritual side of your people, but yet you seem to admire them." He glanced at Joe Big. "In fact, you seem to have followed in their footsteps."

"It's not that. You don't understand. Those people, my ancestors, they're gone. The *Niitsitapi* of today bears no resemblance to those people. Even the language is a shadow of what it once was. Words that were huge long strings of sound have become sound bites in comparison. The Old People valued a good speaker more than they valued a stone warrior. The language was rich—more rich and colorful than any

European tongue. People liked to talk and to tell stories. Today, most of The People are shy and ill-spoken in any language—"

"Oh, give me a break, Big. Damn. How can you compare the Blackfeet language to the language of Shakespeare? You're smart, but you aren't that smart. You know, you get off on these tangents, and there's no telling where you might end up. Your mother isn't shy. And your father is quiet-spoken, is all. And from what you tell me about your grandmother, she wasn't shy about saying or doing anything—"

"But they all believe that Sacred Culture bullshit, Barn. That's why my grandmother moved off the Reservation. So she could be *more Piikani,* not less. And now my family and Paul Cyr and my father's group of old war veterans want to make me and others like me into a modern version of those mythical warriors."

"Well, what's wrong with that? It's not like you're a bad example."

"I'm an American, is what's wrong with it. I'm a mongrel, like nearly everyone else in this country. I'm not saying I don't believe in a lot of the old ways. I do. Some of it is in my blood. But there are a lot of other ways, from a lot of different kinds of people, that are also in my blood.

"Shit, man. We've both been around the world enough to know that I am nothing special or unique. There are people of every color and persuasion in every part of the world who have the same things in their blood that I have. That you have. You know what I'm saying?"

"I don't know, Big. Your people seems pretty special to me. I haven't met many people like your mother and father and your grandmother and Roy White Owl."

"I'm not saying they aren't great people. I love them, you know that. But they are not any more special than a whole lot of other people we've met."

"Well . . ."

Joe Big smiled at him. "You think there's any difference between you and me, just because I'm part Indian and you are French and whatever else you are? Didn't you tell me that every generation of Lambier has fought for America since one of your great-great's came over to fight alongside Lafayette? And didn't you say that your family can trace its military heritage back hundreds of years before that?"

"That's different."

"The fuck it is! Just because your family could speak French and eat snails doesn't mean they were any less bloody than mine."

Barney laughed.

"Thousands of years of your ancestors fighting wars versus a lousy one hundred and fifty years of my ancestors fighting other Indians. My Indian side was bloody for sure, but the carnage it produced sort of pales when stacked up against the carnage the other half of me produced, wouldn't you say?"

"Carnage? You mean like chili con carnage?"

"Yeah, like that. Fuck you. You know what I mean."

They were silent as Barney downshifted, slowing the car to fifty, cars and trucks in both lanes now. Large stores and automobile dealerships and small businesses lined both sides of the road. Take away the distant mountains, and it was the outskirts of any city in America.

"I guess I want you and your people to be all romantic and tribal because I want to believe that there is an alternative to the way people live today," Barney said.

"Ah," Joe Big said. He waved his left hand in front of his face. "I'm being way too one-sided about it. Plenty of elders tried to get the young ones to stop killing. Things got bent out of shape, that's all. One thing led to another. Just like one thing leads to another in a whole lot of the world today. I'll bet there are a lot of older, wiser people in Waziristan and Falujah and Palembang who know exactly what I'm talking about."

"No doubt."

"So, anyhow, now you know."

"Now I know. Now I know you are even more fucked up than I thought."

Joe Big smiled. "I like being a cop because sometimes being a cop lets me believe that what is in my blood is there for a reason, and not just because all the buffalo have died."

Barney glanced at him. "I really hate it when you make something that doesn't make any sense sound like it makes sense."

"So that we can protect our people from themselves. So that people—our people—won't commit suicide by killing off the food supply."

"Joe Big. The weight of the world on his back. Why am I not buying that?"

Joe Big shook his head. "No, man. I didn't mean it like that. It's no weight at all. It's us being who we are, is all. Most people, if they have a brain, run away. We go to the sound of gunfire."

"Speak for yourself."

"The People had special warrior societies that were made up of men who brought up the rear—who went toward the threat, whatever it was, so that the rest of the tribe could get away, and have time to defend itself." Joe Big gestured out the window. "And here we are. Two cops trolling for someone to shoot at us. If we are not who I say we are, then why are we here?"

"We're here because we don't know what else to do."

Joe Big laughed. "Well, there's that."

Barney stopped the car at a traffic light. The Subaru was dwarfed by pickup trucks in front and to the side and behind them.

"No need to get all heavy about it," he said.

"I'm not. You're the one who asked."

"Well, I asked because I don't want you getting all morose and introspective and—"

"Ruin your chances to get laid tonight."

"Yeah."

Joe Big smiled. "So why are we meeting Paul?"

"I want to hear about mules and heroin and all that, when it's just us and him around to talk about it."

Joe Big nodded. "Good idea."

"We've got to find a center to all this," Barney said. "Before we can figure out a way to give some of these people their just due."

"All this what?"

"All this exotic shit that seems to be happening all at once. We got our asses handed to us up the Blackfoot, and we still don't know what that was all about. Computer chips? Us being cops, and stepping on their trust? You screwing Tanya in the parking lot? I'm not buying it. Special Forces guys in an EVO, pretending to be drug dealers. Brianna. Dead mules and pure heroin. This task force that we're supposed to be part of, but that, after more than three months, we don't know why us and not other people better qualified. Quinn's CI murdered—"

"Allegedly."

"See? That's what I mean, right there. A couple of weeks ago, you wouldn't have said that. You would have taken what she had to say at face value."

"You don't believe it happened?"

"Oh, I believe it happened. I just don't believe that our Fearless Federette told us *everything* that happened."

"You think she's hiding something? Why would she do that?"

Barney shrugged. "I don't know. I just know that she's hiding something. Or isn't telling us the whole story, which is the same thing."

"Boy," Joe Big said. "And just when I was starting to like her."

18
War Wounds

That doesn't look good," Joe Big said. They were standing just inside the door of a private room at Kalispell Regional Hospital. Brianna was a pasty-white figure dressed in a hospital gown, sheet and blanket folded neatly at her waist, some kind of metal contraption holding her head and neck in place, tubes and wires in her arms and in her mouth and nose. Her head and lower face and jaw were heavily bandaged. A bank of portable monitors occupied most of the space to the right of her bed.

"It looks worse than it is," the nurse said. The nurse was a silver-haired matron with sad eyes and the build of an NFL linebacker gone to seed. "She has movement and feeling in her fingers and toes, and the swelling has gone down in her brain. The doctor thinks she'll have temporary paralysis of some muscles on the left side of her face, but in time that should go away."

Without makeup and without all the metal that she normally wore in her face and ears, and with her swollen, bandaged face, she was not recognizable. It was as if they'd entered the wrong room, and were looking at a stranger lying there on the bed, Joe Big thought.

"Notice anything unusual?" Barney asked.

"Is that a joke?"

"Check out her neck."

"No tattoo," Joe Big said.

The nurse smiled. "Most of her tattoos were washed off in the ER. I'm told they were just for show."

"Who told you that?" Joe Big asked.

"A black lady came in early this morning. My, such an elegant lady."

"Alone?"

"No, there were two men in suits with her."

"And were they elegant, too?" Joe Big asked.

The nurse chuckled. "Actually, they reminded me of my husband—God rest his tortured soul." She smiled at Barney. "My husband was a police officer in Seattle."

"Was?"

"Yes, he passed a few years ago—in his sleep. It was Vietnam and being a police officer that killed him, poor man."

"I'm sorry to hear that," Barney said, wondering why she was telling them all this. As far as she was concerned they were nothing more than two scruffy-assed friends of the woman lying in the bed.

"Is there anything she needs?" Joe Big asked.

"No. She's going to be out of it for a while. The oral surgeon is coming in again this afternoon to see what he can do, and how soon he can do it."

The three of them stood gazing at the figure on the bed, the nurse with professional fatalism, Barney and Joe Big with the feigned neutrality that cops and soldiers have when viewing or interrogating victims.

"Is it pretty bad?" Barney asked. "Her mouth."

"Well, it's not as bad as he first thought. Thank goodness. We see a lot worse from traffic and bicycle accidents. Her jaw was dislocated, not broken. The metal brace is for her neck. He'll save what he can of her teeth, replace the rest. I expect she'll have a bridge, maybe even dentures." She sighed. "Poor dear."

Barney looked at Joe Big, and Joe Big could see the cold fury in his eyes. It was strange, he thought. Barney became increasingly incensed the closer he came to doing something about whatever caused his anger. But he was just the opposite. At times like this, he felt detached from his surroundings. That forlorn figure on the bed made Barney angry, but for him it was an equation to be solved—a matter of target selection, more than anything else. And once the target was selected, it became a matter of logistics: ingress and egress, windage and elevation. Breath control.

"Can we go closer?" he asked the nurse.

"Certainly you can, sweetie. But don't wake her. The doctors kept her awake without pain medicine until the swelling in her brain went down. She needs to rest." She smiled her sad smile. "She doesn't look so tough now, but that is one very tough young lady lying there."

"Too tough, sometimes," Barney said.

He walked over to the figure on the bed. Joe Big walked to the window. A block or so away, on the other side of the parking lot, he could see traffic backed up at a stoplight. On the other side of the highway were houses and a motel. And beyond the houses and motel, across the valley, were hills dotted with houses. In the far distance snow-covered mountains stood dark blue and mute.

He turned toward the bed, arms folded across his chest. "At least she's got a good view."

Barney reached out and touched Brianna's forearm above the IV taped to the top of her hand. "Joe Big already put a hurt on him," he said.

The tube in Brianna's mouth made a sucking sound as a machine connected to the other end automatically pulled fluid from her mouth and throat.

Both Joe Big and Barney started.

"We're not doing any good here," Joe Big said. "Until she wakes up, we're just talking to ourselves."

"Yeah." Barney squeezed her forearm. "Get better, you hear?"

They turned and walked out of the room, Joe Big leading the way down the sterile buffed and polished hallway to the nurses' station.

"I'll give you our cell phone number, in case she needs anything," Barney said to the nurse.

The nurse smiled. "You're about ten on the list. But I'll put your number down; it'll make her feel good to know. She's allergic to chocolate so don't send chocolates."

"How about yellow roses?" Joe Big asked.

"Roses would be good," she said, her sad eyes somehow emphasizing her smile. "You young men go and catch whoever did this, that'll make her feel best of all."

Barney and Joe Big looked at each other. "We're not cops," Barney said.

"Right," she said. "And I'm not a nurse. That nice lady—the black lady—said to expect you two, and to tell you that she was taking care of everything. She said you should 'go do your thing'." She winked at Barney. "I'm sure I don't know what she meant by that."

Barney and Joe Big stared at her.

She smiled her kindly smile.

But this time her smile only made her eyes look more sad.

"WE'RE LOSING IT," Joe Big said, as they walked to the car.

"Lot of cops in and out of there today," Barney said. "And Mrs. W described us to her." He paused. "You know, I don't even know for sure who she works for. Brianna, I mean."

"Homeland Security, I guess."

They climbed in, and Barney started the car. "There's a coffee shop around here someplace, do you know where it's at?"

"Is that where we're going to meet my Indian brethren?"

"Yeah."

"Take a right. It's just a couple of blocks over there." Joe Big looked at him. "He's coming all the way over from Browning to talk to us?"

"Near as I know."

They pulled out into traffic, accelerating to keep pace with the cars in front. A string of expensive SUVs went by on their left, all of them either silver or black.

"Expensive cars around here," Barney said.

"Got that right."

"You get the feeling that as soon as we start poking at any of this, it's going to get interesting in a hurry?"

"That's why we get paid the big bucks."

Barney smiled. "Mr. Cool."

"Always."

"Uh-huh. That must be why your knee is bouncing up and down like you got it wired to a light socket or something."

"That was fucked up, man," Joe Big said. "It felt like—I don't know, déjà vu, or something. Her head wrapped up like that—like she got tagged by a sniper or shrapnel or something."

"War wounds."

Joe Big was silent.

"You okay?" Barney asked.

"No."

"Me, neither."

19
Biohazards

Paul Cyr, dressed in plaid wool shirt and jeans, the same two-tone tan on his forehead that he'd had the last time they'd seen him, was seated by himself at a table in the corner of the coffee shop. He smiled and raised his hand.

Most of the tables were empty. The coffee shop workers—three girls in matching tunics—were in a tight cluster behind the counter, giggling about something.

Joe Big started for the order counter.

"I think he already ordered for us," Barney said. Three tall containers of coffee were grouped together on Paul's table.

Paul extricated himself from behind the table, and walked toward them. For the first time both of them noticed how bandy-legged he was. What you get for riding horses around the backcountry most of your life, Joe Big thought.

"Mr. Lambier," Paul said, shaking Barney's hand. He nodded at Joe Big. "Joe Big."

"Paul."

"I thought maybe we'd have a little more privacy here."

"The coffee is better, that's for sure," Barney said.

"I took the liberty of ordering for you. I hope you don't mind. Order something to eat if you want—the Government is buying."

"Thanks, but we ate at a great little bakery in Painted Cliff."

"Oh, hell, I know that place. We should have met there. I don't know why I didn't think of it. Run by a Vietnamese woman, right?"

“Vietnamese?” Joe Big asked.

“Well, half-Vietnamese.”

“Did she tell you that?”

“She didn’t have to. Military Police. Saigon. Three tours. Turns out I might have known her daddy.”

“Well, this place still beats meeting at a cop shop,” Barney said.

“These days, the walls have a way of growing ears every time I go to the office,” Paul said. “If you know what I mean?”

“We do,” Barney said. “We most surely do.”

Paul gestured toward his table. “Might as well sit down, seeing as how Joe Big has already got the attention of the help.”

“Welcome to my life,” Barney said.

Joe Big looked confused. The only people in sight other than Barney and Paul Cyr was a bespectacled, white-haired man dressed in green hospital scrubs seated in an easy chair next to one of the big windows, and two matrons at another window across the room.

Barney and Paul Cyr laughed. Shaking their heads, they headed for the table.

“What?” Joe Big said. *“What?”*

“It’s not an act,” Barney said to Paul, as they pulled out chairs and sat. “He really doesn’t notice.”

“His grandmother was the same way.”

“Don’t just stand there like some kind of cigar store Chinaman.” Barney said to Joe Big. “Watch the girls behind the counter,” he said in a low voice to Paul.

The three girls behind the order counter, their heads turning in unison, like birds tracking a cat on the other side of a window, watched without expression as Joe Big threaded his way between tables to where Barney and Paul Cyr sat at the table with the three containers of coffee.

“Kiss my ass, both of you.”

He pulled out the third chair, and sat.

“Oh, did we offend you?” Barney asked.

“I don’t mind being the butt of a joke—as long as I understand the joke.”

“Trust us: it will never happen again.”

“Maybe you don’t notice, but you been doing it a lot lately.”

“No!”

"Mocha skinny latte," Paul said, laugh lines crinkling at the corners of his eyes. His chunky, scarred fingers pushed one of the containers toward Joe Big. "And a triple-shot, whole-milk, extra-foam for Mr. Lambier."

"How'd you know when we'd get here?" Barney asked.

"Old Indian trick," Paul said, and winked at Joe Big.

Joe Big's face darkened.

Paul chuckled, and shook his head. "Joe Big," he said, as if to say there was no accounting for Joe Big. "I saw you guys get in your car when I went past the hospital," he said to Barney. He nodded toward Joe Big. "He sure has a resistance to being an Indian, don't he?"

Barney considered Joe Big for a moment. "Well, the jury is still out about that." He shrugged. "But what does a Real White Man, a good old boy, such as myself, know about such things?" He cocked his head to the side, as if actually thinking about it. "Or is it 'Original White Man'? I cain't never keep the two straight."

Paul laughed.

"Mrs. W," Joe Big said.

"Say what?" Barney said.

"That's how Mr. Cyr here knew what we'd order in a place like this." Joe Big took a sip of his latte, watching Paul over the lip of the container. "Heap good drink," he said, putting the container down on the table. He crossed his arms across his chest.

Paul's eyes narrowed.

"It's Barney, not Mr. Lambier," Barney said to Paul.

Paul stared at Joe Big for a moment, and then nodded at Barney. He looked down, frowning at his container of coffee.

His right index finger tapped against the tabletop, and both Barney and Joe Big noticed how rough and gnarled were his hands and fingers. His index finger was bent at least ten degrees to the right, only a tiny yellowed remnant of fingernail left where the cuticle would normally be. Broken and dislocated, Joe Big thought, and probably more than once. Paul Cyr had been a nationally ranked bull rider at one time. He remembered his father talking about it. Paul was part of his father's group of old warriors, but it was news to him that Paul had been Military Police in Vietnam. He didn't look old enough.

In unison, both he and Barney lifted their containers of coffee and took a drink, watching Paul over the lids.

Paul's hands cupped his container of coffee, all but the top of the container lost between his pudgy, scarred fingers and oversized knuckles.

He looked up, and smiled. "Those mules weren't bringing something in. They were taking something out."

"The Early Lakes fire burned more than forty-thousand acres," Joe Big said. He lowered his container of coffee to the table. "How could you know they were taking something out?"

"The fire started at the top of the ridge a couple hundred yards above where we found the mules." Paul used his hands to describe a large triangular area on the tabletop. "It swept down into the valley in a big fan shape, with the apex of the fan at the top of the ridge." With his finger he traced a line across the top of the triangle-shaped area. "The ridge trail, which is what the mules were on, was intact from about a quarter mile down the trail from where we found their carcasses." He leaned back. "All the mule tracks I could find were going up the ridge, toward the border, not down toward the trailhead."

"How far did you backtrack?" Barney asked.

"Almost all the way to the trailhead—about twelve miles."

He looked at Joe Big. "The trailhead parking area was used by fire fighters. I lost the tracks in the clutter about a half-mile up."

"Barney is a better tracker than me," Joe Big said. "He worked for Old Tom. Honchoed his camp down the Bitterroot." He looked at Barney, and smiled. "Even married his daughter."

Barney winced, instantly irritated that he hadn't been able to control the wince—pissed off at the smugness with which Joe Big was taking a sip of his choco-fucking-latte. What kind of Marine drank chocolate lattes, anyway?

He looked at Paul, and for the first time could see the Indian in Paul, his face noncommittal, but his eyes with that special kind of curiosity that he'd noticed when he'd met Big's parents. Too polite to say it out loud, but asking anyway with his eyes.

"She wanted to be a city girl," he said. "Study poetry and shit."

"I've know her since she was knee-high," Paul said. "Hell of a woman."

Barney shrugged, still irritated at Big for mentioning it. "Sometimes you eat the bear. Sometimes the bear eats you."

Paul laughed. "Ain't that the truth, brother." He extended his hand toward Barney, and they shook, Barney's hand swallowed by Paul's. It was like shaking hands with a human vise, Barney thought.

"I've been through two wives," Paul said, leaning back in his seat, one arm draped over the seatback, his other hand reaching to push up a hat that wasn't there. He looked momentarily disconcerted. He ran his hand through the hair on the side of his head. "Good women, both of them. Can't say I blame them for not liking me gone all the time."

Joe Big rolled his eyes toward the ceiling.

Paul glanced at Joe Big, humor again crinkling the corners of his eyes.

"Yeah," Barney said. "I can hardly wait."

"His uncle was the same way," Paul said. "Then that Japanese gal came along, and damned if he didn't become almost human."

"Ain't it a bitch," Joe Big said. "You two being jealous, and all."

"Jealous!" Paul Cyr said, "Now there's a thought!"

Barney reached across the table to high-five him.

Joe Big picked up his coffee and took a drink, doing his best to ignore them.

"You ever meet his grandmother?" Paul asked.

Barney shook his head. "Not enough to know her."

"She was just like him, only with men, instead of women. Even in her seventies, she'd walk into a room and every man in that room would look at her."

Joe Big's face darkened again.

In a gentle voice, Paul said, "It's a good thing that you remind people of her, Joseph. It makes people who knew her think that maybe her spirit is still with us."

"Going *out* of the country," Barney said. Both men looked at him. "Why would anyone smuggle heroin *into* Canada?"

"Well, that's my question, exactly," Paul said. "We apprehend guys coming across from Canada with backpacks full of marijuana and hashish—sometimes with bags of that new kind of meth. But it's been a long time since we caught anyone with cocaine or heroin. And never, in over twenty-five years of patrolling the border, have I caught anyone taking drugs in quantity *into* Canada."

"Vancouver has all the Asian heroin it wants," Barney said. "It would be a lot more difficult and a lot more expensive to bring it in from the U.S. You'd have to import it into the States, get it to Montana, and then put it on mules and take it across the border. Why would anyone do that? Why would anyone bother with mules, when it would be easy to take it across in a truck or a car at a place where the border is not even manned?"

Joe Big sipped at his coffee, letting his mind wander. Barney always did this—and apparently so did Paul. Barney had to take apart even the obvious, break it down as far as it would go, every little piece. And then reassemble it in as many ways as he could make the pieces fit. Every possible scenario.

He took another sip, relishing the taste. His one weakness when it came to food was mocha lattes. It had been his uncle's friend, Manfred, of all people, who'd turned him on to them—at Manfred's bar in Wild Horse Plains, of all places. Rasty old Vietnam Special Forces veteran running a Yuppie-Guppie bar in Wild Horse Plains, jazz and blues, Cajun and blue grass next to Cold Play and Green Day and Lil Wayne and even AudioSlave on the old converted jukebox. Polished wood floor and ferns, instead of cancerous old linoleum and the smell of stale beer and stale bodies and country-western on an old beat-to-shit jukebox. Go figure. Far as he was concerned, none of these old guys were quite right in the head. His uncle. Manfred. Paul Cyr. Even his father. Crazy as loons, most of the time, all of them.

Not like him and Barney. He looked at Barney and Paul Cyr, barely listening to their voices. Not like him and Barney? He smiled to himself. Who was he kidding? Paul and Barney were like peas in a pod. Different generations, is all. Chewing on the problem until—

One of the girls had come out from behind the counter and was busy wiping an already-clean table on the other side of where Paul was sitting. She smiled at Joe Big, and he smiled back. She blushed and looked down at the tabletop.

Barney abruptly stood and walked toward the magazine and newspaper rack.

The girl waited for Barney to pass, and then, with a quick glance at Joe Big, walked back to her friends behind the counter. She was young and blond and even dressed in tunic and black slacks clearly had a nifty—

Paul Cyr's smile was wry.

"Ben Tails says hello," he said.

"You saw my uncle?"

"Had lunch with him the day before yesterday. He's the one suggested I come over here and talk with you two."

Joe Big turned to see where Barney had gone. Barney was standing in front of the far window, looking out. He was rubbing his hand across the top of his head. Joe Big had seen him do the same thing many times when they were in Afghanistan and Iraq—look out across a valley or a sea of barren mountains or a cityscape, and try to decide how far they could push it without getting themselves killed or creating an international incident.

"Your uncle is disappointed in you," Paul Cyr said.

Joe Big flushed. "You told him what happened?"

"He already knew. He said you owe him rent money."

"Mrs. W took care of it. I changed banks, and forgot to—he doesn't give a rat's ass about the rent, what're you talking about? He only charges me taxes and utilities, as it is."

"I think he is worried about you."

"Worried about *me?* Why would he be worried about *me?"*

"He didn't tell me that."

Barney sat back down. "Did you write up everything you just told us?" he asked Paul.

"Even took pictures, and a couple of small videos so you can see the trail in relation to the burned area."

"Did Quinn know about it before we had that last meeting?"

Paul nodded. "Both her and Mrs. Walker."

"How about Brianna?"

"No. Not before the meeting, anyway."

"Is there anything else that you know of that Quinn isn't telling us?" Joe Big asked.

Paul moved his container of coffee back and forth. "Those Marines they flew in weren't just testing for radiation," he said. "They had packs containing full Biohazard suits with them. Looked like space aliens, when they put them on."

"They walked up the trail in full Biohazard suits?" Joe Big asked. "That must've been a trick."

Paul smiled. "They put them on and tried them out back at the camp they had set up in the big meadow below the trailhead—near where they had their helicopter parked."

"They mention what they were looking for?" Joe Big asked.

"No. Not really. They were Marines. Friendly and full of grab-ass and questions about hunting and fly-fishing, when they weren't busy. But when they were busy they were all business. Most efficient, polite bunch I've ever seen in my life."

"My tribe," Joe Big said.

Paul Cyr's eyes narrowed. "Yes, Joe Big Snake Person. Your tribe. But your tribe doesn't need you anymore—if it ever did." His eyes glinted like black mica. "Your other tribe does."

"Do you remember what the leaves and grasses looked like around those dead mules?" Barney asked. "Did anything look like someone had poured oil on it?"

Paul frowned. "I don't think so. Maybe. Not around the dead mules, though. You worked for Old Tom so you know what it's like. You're riding along, not thinking about much. Mostly I react to movement or color. It gives me a headache if I try to eagle-eye everything. I didn't see the carcasses until my horse shied."

"Were they just laying there, or what?" Joe Big asked.

"Unh!" Paul grunted. He crossed himself. "They had died hard. Nothing should die that hard. Mule shit everywhere. Strings of mucous and blood on the rocks, on the ground, all over the bushes. Dried blood caked around the mouth and nostrils and eyes. It didn't take long, whatever it was. Birds and coyotes hadn't been at them."

"Smart," Joe Big said.

Paul nodded. "Sometimes they know."

"Have you ever seen someone choked to death?" Barney asked.

"Can't say I have."

"It's not a nice way to die."

"It's kind of hard to choke a mule to death."

"You've described some of the symptoms of a VX-type nerve agent," Joe Big said. "That's why Barney asked if you'd noticed anything oily on the leaves and rocks."

"Nerve agent?"

Barney nodded. "It's basically like you're being choked to death."

Paul looked from one to the other. "This is way out of my comfort zone."

"Yeah, and it doesn't help that it makes no sense, whatsoever," Barney said. "Packing pure Asian heroin and a nerve agent *out* of the country . . ."

"It makes sense if you are selling it to people who want to use it somewhere else in the world," Joe Big said. "Maybe to someone who wants to make it look as if it was there all along."

"You mean to Iraq or someplace like that?" Paul asked.

"It's a possibility," Joe Big said. "Kind of far-fetched, but possible."

"But the nerve gas would have to come from a Government installation, wouldn't it?" Paul asked. "It would be missed."

"We don't know that it was a nerve agent," Barney said. "Based on your description of the mules and how they died it could have been. That's all we're saying."

"Government-issue VX has a signature," Joe Big said. "It's got chemical markers in it so that it can be traced to wherever it was made. About the only way to get rid of it is to burn it."

"Even a tiny drop of it on your skin will kill you in minutes," Barney said. "All it would take is to touch bare skin to a branch or a leaf or a rock that has some on it."

"I thought chemical agents were fragile," Paul said. "Exposure to sunlight or heat or cold will kill them."

"Not VX. It'll stick around indefinitely. You're thinking of stuff like the Sarin gas used in the Japanese subway. Sarin is a lot easier to make, but the tradeoff is that it is very sensitive to the environment."

"VX is not a gas," Joe Big said. "It's a liquid that can be disseminated in aerosol form."

"Shit," Paul said. "Do you have any idea how paranoid I'm going to be now? Any shiny leaf or rock and my heart is going to go pitty-pat."

"Something killed those mules," Joe Big said.

"Do a lot of people use that trail?" Barney asked.

Paul snorted. "Hunters, campers, outfitters, backpackers—all sorts of people use it until the snow gets too deep. And then backcountry skiers and snowboarders use it. It's so well used that in places it's wide enough to drive a truck; in other places mules and horses have worn a waist-deep trench."

"Any rigs parked at the trailhead? I mean besides all the firefighters."

"Sure. Rigs parked there all the time. Outfitters and backcountry guides. A few local rancher wives who like to do marathon horseback rides. University people with their vans and SUVs. I thought of that. But there are too many to do you any good."

"Lot of mules, too, I suppose," Barney said.

"You have no idea. Mules are the 'in' thing, these days. Special trailers. Special, custom-built wagons for the mules to pull. Special tack. You should see some of the trailers. I saw one that the owner reckons cost about a hundred fifty grand. Living quarters in the front, the whole nine yards."

"Reckons?" Joe Big asked.

"He's so rich, he's not sure how much it cost."

"Did Quinn or Mrs. W or anyone else seem particularly surprised by any of this?" Barney asked.

Paul crossed his arms across his chest, and dropped his chin, eyes closed, thinking.

"Not really," he said to the table. He looked up. "Mrs. Walker took my report and said she would get it to the proper people. I'd done a good job, etcetera, etcetera. They'd take it from there."

"Don't call us, we'll call you, kind of thing," Barney said.

"Yeah. Like that."

"We get a lot of that, too," Barney said.

"Mrs. W took the report?" Joe Big asked. "Not Quinn?"

"Quinn didn't say much at all. Shook my hand, said she was glad to have people like me on 'the team.' Made me feel like I'd bought a car."

"So is anybody doing anything about it now?" Barney asked. "Are there any bulletins or warnings about nerve gas or radioactive materials crossing the border?"

"Nothing," Paul said. "One of my men reported he heard gunshots and explosions a couple of ridges over from where he was. Said he thought he heard helicopters. But he didn't actually see one. He's young, and kind of given to exaggerations mostly out of boredom, I think. There are a lot of days of riding, not seeing anyone but the people you are partnered with. It's easy to let your imagination wander. Plus, there's a lot of helicopter logging going on. And people are always shooting at something. I found a Tribal Member not too long ago shooting a modified Mini-14 full auto into a lake, trying to kill fish. The sound was echoing off rock walls on two sides of the lake. Sounded like a war."

"You ever see a silver Dodge four-by-four with big custom wheels and seriously gnarly tires?" Joe Big asked. "Yellow driving lights on the front, a bank of lights on the roof, half of them yellow, too? Confederate flag sticker on the rear bumper?"

Barney sat up in his chair.

"See it all the time. It belongs to a big white guy—I mean a really big white guy. Patrick Isaiah Huntington the Third. How's that for a handle? He's got a couple of big mules he likes to ride into some of the lakes to fish. Fancies himself a mountain man—never mind the truck and the mules and the fifty-thousand dollar trailer."

"Where's he come from?" Joe Big asked.

"You don't know the Huntingtons? The old man has one of the biggest ranches in Montana. Nearly one hundred thousand acres, maybe more, along the Rocky Mountain Front. Butts up against the Rez," he said to Joe Big. "He runs some expensive quarter horses, and his son, Patrick Isaiah, has his mules. Other than that, the place isn't much used. There's talk of a herd of buffalo, but he doesn't want fences."

"Lot of people in and out?" Barney asked.

Paul shrugged. "I couldn't say one way or the other. I don't get down that way much. We're mostly concerned with what's next to the border. Old man Huntington is filthy rich. A big contributor to both political parties. First Buddy, or something, to the last President. Pals with the Governor. I've heard that he lets some of the rich and famous hunt and fish on his land, but that's more a rumor than anything else."

"Do you know anyone who has been on his land?" Barney asked.

Paul thought for a moment. "Can't say I do," he said. "I heard something about he has his own security force. Ex-military types who patrol in four-by-fours and Humvees, shotguns mounted in the cab of the pickups. They're polite enough, from what I've heard. Like I said, I don't get down that way much. These days, rich people with big spreads are dime a dozen. And most of them have their own security."

"So you're saying there's nothing to set the Huntingtons apart from all the other rich assholes in the State," Joe Big said.

"Yep. That's pretty much what I'm saying."

Joe Big looked at Barney. "He has that ranch east of Missoula."

"Yeah. I got Rick at the S.O. to check it out. About twelve hundred acres. House and out buildings are insured for over three mil."

"Who're you talking about?" Paul asked.

"Patrick Isaiah Huntington the Third is one of the people we had the run-in with up the Blackfoot," Barney said.

"Ah . . ."

"But that was about computer chips," Joe Big said.

"Yeah," Barney said. "But computer chips to do what with? Guidance systems, maybe?"

The three men were silent for a long moment.

"It's too much," Joe Big said. "Too complicated. Too many people would have to be involved."

"Why?" Barney asked. "All it would take is someone who can run a good machine shop, and another person to program the computers. Maybe one person could do it all. Rocket science isn't rocket science any more. You could probably find blueprints on the Web."

"You'd still have to find some way to get your hands on some of that VX stuff," Paul said. "And once some of that turns up missing, the shit would really hit the fan."

"Paul's right," Joe Big said. "If any of this were possible, we'd be flooded with Homeland Security people. Quinn would be running around like the Energizer Bunny on steroids."

"You know what I think?" Paul said. "I think this is something dreamed up by a bunch of people who have nothing better to do than to find ways to ratchet up the fear factor. This whole thing of looking for terrorists in our midst has become a growth industry. There's over a hundred teams just like the team we are supposed to be part of. That translates to thousands of people who need results to justify their budgets. And some of those teams are less than honest about how they go about roping in crazies to do and say a lot more than the crazies would otherwise do or say."

"I've heard about some of the things they've done," Barney said. "But we haven't been involved in any of that. In fact, just the opposite. Half the time we sit around with our thumbs up our butts, trying to figure out what it is we are supposed to be doing."

Joe Big nodded. "And I have to say you are a natural at it."

"At what?"

"At sitting around with your thumb up your ass, what else?"

Paul Cyr smiled. "You two are worse than a couple of old women, you know that?" He hunched forward, both forearms on the table, hands clasped. "Look. Those mules are no laughing matter. They were real. And they were dead. And whatever killed them made the dying extremely painful." He looked from one man to the other. "Never mind ratcheting up the fear factor. That might be part of it, but for now put that aside. It took some hard men to do that to those mules. And it seems to me that if all it has to do with is making people afraid like they were afraid after Nine-Eleven, then simply saying that terrorists now have their hands on nerve gas and have the ability to manufacture unmanned delivery systems for that nerve gas—just saying that ought to be enough to make the public plenty afraid."

"There was an accident on that trail," Joe Big said. "What was done to those mules was *not* planned. The mules were *not* part of a plot to ratchet up the fear factor." He paused. "We have no way of knowing if it was a VX agent or not; only that it was something that kills like VX. It could have been Sarin. It could have been something new that we don't know about."

"What's your point?" Barney asked.

"My point is that it was an accident."

"What about the heroin?"

"The heroin for some reason could really be headed for Canada. I mean, if Patrick is involved, who knows what's going on in his head. The guy is bizarre. He even talks bizarre. And, as Paul pointed out, he's ridden that trail many times." He shook his head. "I don't know, man. Maybe it satisfies his mountain-man fantasies to do it by mule, rather than by truck or car."

"I could see that," Paul said. "He's a strange one, that's for sure."

Barney stood and walked to the window and looked out. He ran his hand over the top of his head.

"It's how he thinks," Joe Big said to Paul. "He did the same thing in Afghanistan—probably been doing it since he was a boy in Louisiana and his father died. Drove his ex nuts. She'd be talking to him, or they'd have friends over for dinner and everyone would be talking about something, and it would trigger something in his mind, and he'd get up and go over to the nearest window and look out and rub the top of his head. Then he'd come back and pick up the conversation like he hadn't left at all."

"He's a good man."

"He is for sure that. But that doesn't mean he doesn't know how easy it is to do bad if you make one wrong decision, one tiny miscalculation. These days it doesn't matter how good your intentions are. It doesn't matter how good your heart is. One little mistake and a lot of people die."

Paul Cyr nodded. "I understand."

"He's making a decision about Patrick Isaiah Huntington," Joe Big said.

"I understand that, too. What I don't understand is why he has to make these decisions by himself."

Joe Big laughed.

He shook his head, and looked around the room, at the empty tables, at the three girls staring inscrutably at him from behind the order counter.

His gaze came back to Barney looking out the window.

He focused on Paul, and Paul Cyr's eyes widened at what he saw in Joe Big's eyes.

"I made my decision a long time ago," Joe Big said. "I'm just waiting for him to catch up."

20
Spooky Little Girl

Stony Creek Brewpub," Joe Big said. "How quaint." The building was sided with a mix of wood siding and wavy, slightly rusted galvanized steel. Concrete curbs, concrete walks, paved parking area. Artfully arranged mounds covered with shrubs and wood chips. The landscaping reminded him of landscaping around a medical center or a bank. Heavy wood doors—of course.

Barney held the door open. *"Entrez s'il vous plait."*

"Uh-huh."

"C'mon, man. Cheer up. She said her friend is a lot of fun."

Joe Big stopped in the doorway. "Why don't I babysit Sam or something?"

"Too late for that."

Joe Big shook his head. "Here we go again . . ."

Inside, the place was much larger than he expected, the ceiling vaulted nearly three stories, rough-cut wood beams and steel girders holding it all together. A wide stairway to the left made of steel girders led up and over their heads to an area of tables and large windows on the second floor. An undulating path made to look pebbled meandered through the stressed-concrete floor. The far wall was all large windows and patio doors and a brick fireplace with a piece of steel girder set into the brick where the mantel would normally be. Average-sized tables and chairs—mostly empty—were grouped in front of the fireplace and in the area on the other side of the bar.

Extra tall tables against the wall to their left were filled with people dressed much like the people they'd seen the night before in the bar in

Whitefish: cargo pants, tight jeans, long-sleeved tees under shirts rolled up to the elbow. Billy goat goatees and soul patches and either very long hair or very short hair. One woman at the bar had on a bright banana-yellow knit hat that was as out of place as a dandelion in an arrangement of dried flowers.

The bar itself was a horseshoe of salmon-colored stressed concrete. Large, window-like openings in a brick wall separated the bar from a room filled with huge steel vats.

"Munich meets Yachats," Joe Big said.

"Vee can survey zee room from zee other side of zee bar," Barney said.

"Are you trying to sound German?"

"Das ist korrekt."

"Well, stop it. You sound like Ratatouille with a speech impediment."

"Je suis profondément offense."

"You should be."

The bartender, a wiry-looking middle-aged woman with a big smile, nodded at them as they walked around the bar. Barney pointed at a table, and she gestured to help themselves. The windows behind the table Barney had pointed to looked out on a dry creek bed lined with ancient willows.

ONE PINT LATER that wasn't really a pint but looked like a pint, Joe Big said, "I kind of like this place. It's got that industrial touch." He drained his glass of beer. "What did she call this stuff again?"

"Bear Grunt."

"See, that's all wrong. All this industrial motif, they ought to call it Lurp Slurp Stout or Pop-a-Smoke Piss, something like that."

"No one knows what any of that means."

"They could hang miniature smokejumper dolls with mini-parachutes from the rafters."

"Don't be getting weird on me, okay?"

"I'm just saying . . ." He glanced toward the bar.

Two women dressed in tight designer jeans and cowboy boots and flashy, satin-looking blouses—blood-red on one, soft-pink on the other—were at the end of the bar, talking to the bartender. Barney caught the bartender's eye, and pointed to their glasses, and she nodded, and the two women turned, coolly glancing their way, as if curious to see who the bartender had been nodding at, but both interested, Barney knew, to scope out Joe Big. They looked to be late thirties, but good looking in the fresh way that athletic college girls are good looking. He pegged them as part of the horsy set, their trim little booties and obvious good health the result of long horseback rides and advanced Pilates classes.

"Don't even think about it," he said to Joe Big.

"Man, you must really like those cinnamon rolls."

The bartender came over with two glasses of dark beer, and put them on the table. "On the house," she said, and scooped up the two empty glasses.

"Well, thank you, ma'am," Barney said.

"Domo arigato," Joe Big said.

"You did say you were meeting someone, didn't you?" she asked Barney.

"I did, and we are. One of them owns the bakery down the street."

"Spooky! You've got a date with Spooky?"

"Well, not a date, exactly. We're meeting her and—what did you call her? Spooky?"

"Yes. That's her nickname. She comes in here once in a while, but never with a date. Everyone knows her."

"Is that code for she doesn't like men?" Joe Big asked.

The bartender blushed. "Oh, no. No. Nothing like that. She's a neat lady. I shouldn't have said anything . . ."

"I bet that little boy of hers is the only man she's interested in right now," Barney said, looking pointedly at Joe Big.

"Oh, you've got that right. He's her little buddy, that's for sure." Her eyes darted toward Joe Big. "I better get back to work. Enjoy the beer."

"Thank you," Barney said, but she was already headed back to the bar.

They watched the two women lean forward to talk to her.

"You're supposed to be Chinese," he reminded Joe Big.

"Not tonight, I are not. Tonight I are going to be me."

"Yeah?"

Joe Big shrugged. "I don't know. Maybe. Why not? Something tells me our days working undercover are about over anyway."

Barney took a drink, watching Joe Big over the rim of the glass. He put the glass down, and with his forearm wiped foam from his upper lip.

"I won't know what to say if I have to talk about the real me," he said.

"You'll think of something."

Barney looked toward the door. "I hate it when women are late."

In the short time they'd been there, most of the tables had filled with groups or couples. There were only a few empty places left at the bar. The clientele had mutated into an eclectic mix of ages and styles and occupations. No suits, but a table full of men and women who were clearly real estate brokers and agents. Several joined-tables of loud women who obviously worked together. A handful of sleek-looking, middle-aged couples—rich, retired, horse or lake people, probably. But mostly young to middle-aged people of indeterminate means, conscious of themselves and their styles.

Most were not from Montana, Joe Big knew. But a few were. And unlike the people at the bar in Whitefish, those who weren't were doing their best to pretend that they were. It was the kind of crowd where if you asked someone where they were from, they'd say Montana, even if they'd only been here a couple of months.

"Something tells me you are not going to be disappointed," Barney said.

"In what?"

Joe Big turned in his chair to see what Barney was looking at.

Barney stood, and raised his arm to get the attention of the two women standing at the entrance. A tall woman with long dark hair—it took Joe Big a moment to realize it was Sam's mother—and a familiar-looking blond.

As the two women worked their way around the bar, stopping here and there to greet people, and to be cheered by the loud women at the joined-tables, he realized that Sam's mother was a tad exotic.

The blonde was saucy and bouncy, radiating energy even from across the room. Too short and solid looking to compete with Sam's mother in the looks department, but take-no-prisoners sexy, for sure. She was wearing out-of-style baggy, tiger-striped camouflage pants, and a pink, unzipped hoody over a white T-shirt. Even from where they were, the T-shirt moved in interesting ways. Blue eyes, he'd bet. A strong jaw and a bent nose stopped her from being cheerleader perfect.

Sam's mother stopped to talk with a dark-complected, fit-looking young man with shaved head and tattoos. Undaunted, the blonde continued to their table. Joe Big stood.

"Small world, huh?" she said to Barney. Her voice was husky. She extended her hand. "Michelle," she said, her grip strong as a man's. "But you can call me Mickey or Kodak. Mickey's my name, but snowboarding is my game." Joe Big could see that Barney was already smitten.

"Barney."

She offered her hand to Joe Big.

"Joe Wang," he said. "Kodak?"

She tossed her head back, her hair just long enough to flip away from her face. Her nose looked as if it had been broken more than once. "Some people think I show off too much when magazine photographers and video equipment are around."

"Kodak," Barney said. "I get it."

"Yeah?" She moved around the table, next to Barney. She crossed her arms across her chest, and cocked her head to the side and looked from one man to the other, cute little frown lines between her eyes. "You guys don't recognize me, do you?"

"Sure, we do," Joe Big said. "You were bartending at the bar in Whitefish last night." He had a flash of her staring at them from behind the bar as she talked on a cell phone. "How could we forget?"

"We weren't with those dudes," Barney said. "We met them at a gas station outside Missoula earlier in the day, is all."

"Nasty business," Joe Big said.

"She's in the hospital," she said, making it sound like an accusation.

"She'll be okay," Barney said. "They had to operate last night to relive pressure from a brain concussion. And she'll need oral surgery, but she's . . . tough . . ." His voice trailed off, as he looked at Joe Big, realizing that he had just admitted to far more concern than being mere bystanders to a bar fight would warrant. "She'll be good to go in a few weeks," he said, still looking at Joe Big. "We stopped by the hospital to see her this afternoon."

"Well . . . great, I guess. Did you—"

"Hello, again," a familiar voice said from behind Joe Big. "Sorry we're late. It's my fault. Sam wanted to come along, and it took some serious bribery to make him stay home."

Joe Big turned and found himself looking into sea-green eyes. Betty Davis eyes. The phrase popped into his mind—from where he had no idea. That explained why her eyes had looked familiar. Her hair was not black like he'd thought. Depending on the light and how she moved, it changed shades of brown. She reached up and with long, slim fingers swept hair away from her right eye and forehead. Up close like this he could see the Asian in her. Her nose was his Chinese nose, but her lips were full, her face more angular than oval. There was a tenseness around her eyes.

"We haven't met formally," she said. "You were running up the mountain, while your partner here was eating cinnamon rolls and regaling my son with stories about Indian warriors." She extended her hand. "I'm Mei. Me-i, not Ma-y."

"Big," he said, grasping her hand.

"I beg your pardon?"

He heard Barney laugh. "I mean, Joe Wang. Joe Big!"

Her eyes smiled, as she released his hand. "Pleased to meet you Joe Big Wang. My goodness. What a name. No wonder my son wouldn't tell me." She pulled out a chair and sat. She leaned toward Mickey. "Big Wang," she whispered theatrically.

"What would you ladies like to drink?" Barney asked. "Sit down Big Wang. You'll never get your other foot in your mouth, if you don't."

Joe Big ran his hand over his face, and lowered himself into the chair. The bartender and the two women at the bar were watching with wide eyes.

"I like the stout," Mei said.

Mickey nodded. "Me, too."

Barney pushed his chair back, and stood, "Coming right up," he said, and headed for the bar.

"You're friends with that giant Indian," Mickey said to Joe Big. "That movie star guy. I thought there was going to be a fight when you first came in. You should see that guy," she said to Mei. "He's huge. His girlfriend is at least six feet tall, but she's a shrimp next to him."

"We went to high school together," Joe Big said. "He's actually one of the most gentle people you could ever hope to meet." He could feel Mei's eyes on him. Sam's mother, he reminded himself. *And you do not hook up with mothers.* Ever.

"Yeah, I can see that," Mickey said. "They come in once in a while. She's really nice."

"So how do you two know each other?" he asked.

"We've know each other since kindergarten," Mei said.

"From where?"

"Oh, California. I don't know why, but I always expect people here to know that. San Rafael, which is near—"

"San Francisco. I know it. It's a nice place."

"How about you?" Mickey asked. "Where are you from?"

He smiled. "Where do you think I'm from?"

"I don't know." Mickey looked at Mei. "California, maybe?" Mei shrugged, as if to say, no telling with this one.

"Let me wait for Barney before I say anything."

"Oh! A mystery man. I like mystery men." Mickey's blue eyes flashed, and Joe Big could indeed imagine her ripping down a slope on her snowboard, jumping off cliffs, risking life and limb for the camera.

He glanced at Mei.

Mei was dressed in tight designer jeans and a dark T-shirt under a plain gray unzipped hoody. She was one of those lucky women who didn't have to worry about clothes. No matter what she wore, she would still be Mei, and she would still look good. He'd known sexier women. And he'd known women who were more beautiful, more model perfect, but none with her . . . her . . . He didn't know what to call it. Presence? Too bad she was a mom.

Barney set glasses of dark beer in front of both women. "The bartender says, hi," he said to Mei.

Mei turned toward the bar and waggled her fingers at the bartender. "Trish," she said. "She's from California, too." She smiled at Joe Big. "She used to work for me, but—two kids and a trailer house. She makes twice as much in tips alone working here."

"Times are tough," he said.

"And getting tougher. Unfortunately, the closest I can come to solving the world's problems is to make cinnamon rolls and pastries."

"There's always the Peace Corps," Joe Big said, and as soon as he said it, he knew he'd said something wrong.

Mickey's eyes darted toward Mei.

Mei's eyes glistened. "That's right," she said. "There's always the Peace Corps."

Joe Big looked at Barney, as if to say, what did I say now?

Barney raised his glass. "Here's to a few hours away from the problems of the world," he said. "Good people, good beer."

"I'll drink to that," Mickey said. She clinked glasses with Barney, and took a drink.

Mei laughed, her laugh a bit forced, but almost there. "You'd drink to anything," she said.

"Hey, watch your mouth, girl. These dudes might get the right impression."

"Oh, I don't think you have to worry about that," Mei said. "Not with these two."

"So tell us your big secret," Mickey said to Joe Big.

"I told them I'd wait for you to get back with the beer before I told them about us," Joe Big said to Barney.

"This ought to be interesting," Barney said.

Joe Big slid his beer in circles on the wood tabletop.

"My name is not Joe Big Wang," he said, looking up. He grinned. "Though some would say it could be."

Both women smiled dutifully.

Barney rolled his eyes.

"It's, ah. It's not even Joe Wang. It's Joe Big Snake Person. I'm half Blackfeet." He glanced at Mickey. "Roy White Owl is a cousin on my mother's side."

"Whoa," Mickey said.

Mei looked at Barney. "And you?"

"James Longstreet Lambier," he said, heavy on the Southern accent. "From the bayous of Louisiana. Barney's my nickname." He smiled at the two women. "No particular claim to fame. What ya'll see is what ya'll get."

"So that's the big secret?" Mei asked Joe Big. "You're part Indian, and Barney is named after a Civil War general?"

"No." Joe Big shook his head. He looked at Barney. "It's harder to say than I thought."

"I can see that."

"We're undercover Sheriff's deputies working for Homeland Security," Joe Big said.

"Sort of," Barney added.

Mickey looked from Joe Big to Barney. "I may be blond. But I rarely have blond moments. The last thing you two look like are cops."

Mei frowned.

"It's true," Barney said. He reached down to the lower cargo pocket on his left pant leg, and yanked open the Velcro flap, and pulled out a black leather badge and ID holder, and opened it. He leaned forward and placed it on the table between the two women, Sheriff's deputy star big and gold and bright.

"That looks real," Mei said.

"It's real all right," Joe Big said, thinking to himself, well, this was a mistake.

"May I?" she asked Barney.

"Help yourself."

She picked up the leather holder and ran her fingers across the star. She handed it to Mickey, who did the same thing.

Mickey handed it back to Barney. "Ociffer," she said, her eyes big and round and bright. "I-I-I j-just want you to know that I didn't do it."

Barney closed the holder and put it back in his pocket. "Didn't do what, ma'am?"

"Whatever it was that I shouldn't have done."

"That'd be a long list, for sure," Mei said.

"Girl . . ."

"We decided before you got here that for once we were going to be straight about who we are," Joe Big said to Mei. "It kind of goes against the grain, it's been so long, that's all."

"So usually you are Joe Wang, a Chinese guy?" Mei asked. "Is that it?"

"That's it."

She studied him for a moment. "You could be. I know the difference, but you could have fooled me."

"How about you?" Joe Big asked her. "You look like you might have a story, too."

She tipped her head forward, her hair falling to one side, and waved her hand in front of her head, as if to say there was nothing about her interesting enough to tell.

"It's a great story," Mickey said. "She was born in Vietnam. Her father put her and her mother and her brother on one of the last planes out. C'mon, Spook," she said to Mei. "Just this once? They're being open with us . . ."

Mei brushed hair away from her face. She sighed. "Mei-li O'Bannon," she said, raising her chin. "Spooky, to my family and friends. My father was a Marine guard at the Embassy in Saigon. Gunnery Sergeant Michael O'Bannon. Big Mike. My mother worked part-time at the embassy, full-time at a club—as a bookkeeper, not a bargirl. A couple of days before the fall of Saigon, my father—he was married to someone else back in the States at the time; my mother was basically his mistress—my father showed up with a big truck at the club—he'd told my mother to take us there and wait—and loaded my mother and my brother and me and everyone who was at the club that day into the truck, and drove us all to Tan Son Nhut, and somehow put us on a big military plane to the Philippines. From there we eventually made it to California."

"I didn't know all that." Mickey said.

Mei shrugged. "I was only three months old at the time. My parents asked us to not say anything. You know how things were when we were in grade school and high school. They were building a business, and trying to fit us into a place that didn't much like Vietnamese.

"My brother is really my half-brother," she said to Joe Big. "My mother's first husband was a Vietnamese Marine Colonel killed at Hue during the TET Offensive of 1968. That's how she got a job at the embassy in Saigon: some of the embassy staff knew him. As far as we know, he was killed in Hue at nearly the same moment my brother was born in Saigon."

"Tough math," Joe Big said.

She shrugged. "Depends on how you look at it."

"Her brother is so totally Broadway," Mickey said. "You wouldn't believe it. I had such a thing for him, when we were kids. Didn't I, Spook? He was Mister Everything in football and track, and that was cool, but on the snow he was completely *gang-star.* He'd try a new trick and it was, like, no matter how rad the trick, he had it in *lockdown.*"

"I have no idea what you just said," Barney said.

"Huh?"

"He's a twin planker," Joe Big said.

"Oh," she said, and pursed her lips, looking at Barney as if seeing him for the first time.

"Mei's brother is a fantastic snowboarder," Joe Big translated for Barney. "He makes it look so easy that merely by being on the snow with a snowboard he makes everyone else look bad. He'll do a trick for the first time and make it look as if he's been doing it forever."

"Yeah!" Mickey said. "Like that!"

"He's a super stud," Joe Big said.

"No, he's not!" Mei said. "He's a nice looking, very athletic guy, who took all his teenage angst and all his bad memories of Vietnam out on the snow. That's all. He still does."

"What does he do?" Joe Big asked.

She laughed. She was amazing when she laughed, he thought—when she really laughed. Her eyes flashed, and she wasn't afraid to open her mouth. He could see exactly what she must have looked like when she was a little girl. The apple of her father's eye, for sure. He bet it was her father gave her the nickname. She would be ninety and she'd laugh and she'd still look like his little girl. The tune, *Spooky Little Girl like you,* echoed through his mind.

"He's an accountant for the State of California," she said. "Two kids and a chubby, jolly, little Vietnamese wife who treats him like he's her oldest, most favorite son. He loves it, and I love her for it. He would get so dark and moody in high school. It would scare my parents. And then she came along, and it was like every time he was around her he was plugged into an electric socket or something."

"I think I'm going to cry," Barney said.

Mickey hit him hard in the bicep. "Ow," he said. "Damn, girl. You don't know your own strength."

"That's okay," Mei said. "It is a little over the top, even for me."

Barney raised his glass. "Here's to Mei's brother," he said. "May he live happily ever after in sunny Hobbit Land, or wherever it is that you live with chubby, jolly little Vietnamese women."

Mei laughed, and clinked her glass against Barney's. "I'll drink to that," she said, and took a long drink, nearly finishing the glass of beer.

"Whoa," Mickey said. "You go girl."

"Thirsty," Mei said, her grin a little goofy. And both Barney and Joe Big realized that she was so unaccustomed to drinking alcohol that even the one beer was making her a little tipsy. "For some reason, beer really tastes good tonight."

Barney signaled the bartender for another round.

"Excuse me," Joe Big said. "Nature calls." He shoved his chair back and stood. Mei looked up at him with her hooded Bette Davis eyes, and smiled. Her smile was open and without guile, and somehow he knew that it was a rare glimpse of her without whatever baggage it was that she was carrying around. He didn't know how to respond. Her smile turned into a crooked little grin.

She'd put him off his feed, and she knew it, he thought, as he wended his way between tables and people to the men's room. Spooky, wasn't the half of it. Scary was more like it. Sam's mother. He wondered who the father was. A real idiot whoever he was.

The restroom had a stressed-concrete sink with clever miniature spigots made to resemble old time spigots. More wavy galvanized steel for the stalls.

He looked at his image in the mirror. What did she see when she looked at him, he wondered. Had Barney told her that they had been in the military—that, like her father, he'd been a Marine? No. Barney wouldn't volunteer that kind of information unless he thought it was necessary to get close to someone they were working on.

Without warning, he felt the hair at the back of his neck bristle—a gray miasma that he hadn't felt for a long time filtering through his mind, the light brightening as his pupils dilated, the inside of the men's room abruptly seen as if in an old, washed-out tintype. He could smell the urinals, the faint odor of burgers and French fries, the musty smell of beer fermenting. He watched the hair rise on his forearm. In the mirror the skin was stretched tight and shiny across his cheekbones.

He swept his shirt to the side and reached behind his hip and pushed the thumb-break open and pulled the SIG from the holster. He jacked a round into the chamber, lowered the hammer, and put the semiautomatic back in the holster, safety off, thumb break open.

He removed the folding knife from his back pocket, and flicked it open and closed a few times with his thumb, debated what to do with it, and put it in his right front pocket.

He eased out of the men's room, keeping to one side of the small foyer that separated the main bar from the restrooms, his eyes scanning the room and the empty upper level, the steel stairway, the flat-black ugly I-beams, the chaos of people and color and motion melding with the feeling in his stomach.

Two men in dark clothes were at their table, backs to him. Barney was standing, facing them, his right hand behind his hip.

On the far side of the bar, at a table against the wall, three men were looking across the bar toward Barney and the two men standing at their table. All three were dressed in green cargo pants and black long-sleeved ribbed sweaters. To the casual observer they probably appeared relaxed, sipping at their beers and smiling, but he could read the body language, recognized it for what it was—recognized them for who they were. They weren't trying to fit in. They were being discreet, was all.

Harold was seated at the bar in front of and slightly to the right of the three men, dressed as usual like a wannabe Chicano Gangster.

There were maybe thirty people at tables or at the bar or wandering around between him and Harold and the three men.

A young woman came out of the women's room, brushing past him. As she headed across the room toward the bar, he fell into step behind her left shoulder, bending his head and holding out his hand as if looking at something in his hand. He split away from her as they approached the bar, and then it was four or five quick steps to the two men.

It was Pick and another, heavier, man, not the Redhead.

Barney kept his eyes on Pick, giving nothing away, but aware that Big had come out of the men's room and had crossed the floor and come up behind the two men.

"Mei," Joe Big said, getting her attention, and stopping whatever Pick had been saying in mid sentence. "You and Mickey go over and stand at the bar, please."

The other man with Pick started to turn around, and stopped when he felt the prick of Joe Big's knife.

"You turn around, or put your hand under your shirt, I am going to stick this knife in your kidney." Joe Big's voice was conversational. "Tell him, Pick."

"We're not armed," Pick said.

Mei and Mickey stood, eyes wide, and without a word turned and walked to the bar. All four men were impressed.

"The three guys over against the far wall," Joe Big said to Barney. "Can you see them?"

"They're not moving."

"Harold's at the bar."

"Who? Oh, yeah. Harold."

Joe Big reached with his left hand and pulled the Bluetooth ear bud from Pick's ear, and stepped back a couple of steps. He closed the knife with his thumb and put it in his pocket. He pressed the talk button, and held the mike to his mouth. "How you guys doing?" he said. "First one of you comes over here, this turns into a bad movie."

He dropped the ear bud to the floor and stepped on it, grinding it into the concrete.

"Oops," he said.

Barney's arm came out from behind his hip, Glock held straight down and against his thigh. He made sure that Pick and the other man could see it, and then moved it back behind his thigh so that it was hidden from the people at the next table.

Two blue and white fletched arrows were stuck into the tabletop, a cell phone that Joe Big had never seen before next to them.

"We came here to talk," Pick said. "That's all."

With his left hand, Joe Big took his cell phone from his pant pocket, and flipped it open, and punched 9-1-1.

"Really?" he said. "Yeah," he said into the phone. "We've got a situation at Stony Creek Brewery in Painted Cliff. There's five or six guys in here with guns." He paused, listening. "I don't know what kind. Big ones. Call the bar to confirm. I'm hanging up." He snapped the phone shut and put it back in his pant pocket.

He took another step back, as both men turned to look at him. Pick's smile was sardonic. The other man looked pissed off. He had had a three-day growth and a nest of white scars between his eyebrows where a riflescope had drawn blood. Even though he was a white guy, something about him reminded Joe Big of Gunnery Sergeant Montoya.

"You need to talk with us," Pick said.

"Like I told your guys over there, don't turn this into a bad movie. Just get the fuck out of here, and leave us alone."

"We owe you one," Pick said.

"Dick on a Dog, you mean?"

Pick smiled. "That would be correct."

"We see that weasel motherfucker again, we are going to put a permanent hurt on him," Joe Big said. He stared at the other man for a moment. "Where'd you get this one? Thugs-R-Us?"

"You're pretty slick," Pick said. "I'll give you that. But you aren't as slick as a couple of the men I've got in here tonight."

The other man smiled at Joe Big.

"What do you think?" Joe Big said to Barney.

"Your call. I wouldn't mind."

"You'd shoot unarmed men," the other man said, turning his head to look at Barney. "Riiight."

"Wouldn't be the first time," Barney said. "Wouldn't even be the third time."

"Let's go," Pick said. He nudged the other man toward the door. "He called the cops. We'll talk to them outside."

Joe Big stepped back.

"Ta-ta, for now, y'all," Barney said.

Pick shook his head. The two of them walked around the bar toward the door, shouldering people to the side. Pick made a circling motion over his head, and pointed at the door, and the three men stood and went out the door ahead of Pick and the other man. Harold scurried behind, looking worried over his shoulder at Joe Big and Barney.

Joe Big moved around the table next to Barney, keeping his eyes on the door.

"This just got out of hand," he said. "Way out of hand. We can't fight those guys."

"That's the understatement of the year."

"Why don't you go ask the bartender, Trish or whatever her name is, to call nine-one-one, and say all is cool, the bad guys have left the premises," Joe Big said.

"What are you going to do?"

"I'm going to go out the patio door here, and walk down the creek bed and make sure they are gone."

"Okay."

"You might also offer explanation to our two companions."

They both looked toward the two women—actually five women: Mei and Mickey and the bartender and the two women the bartender had been talking to before. All five were looking at them, as if he and Barney had just beamed down from another planet.

"Now I know how zoo animals feel," Barney said.

He turned his head toward Joe Big, but Joe Big was already out the patio door, headed toward the shadows under the big old willows that lined the creek.

"THEY LEFT," JOE Big said. Barney was standing at the bar, waiting for him. "Two new, white Suburbans. Too many antennas. Did you talk to that Sheriff's Deputy?"

"I badged him, gave him the they're-friends-of-dopers-we-arrested story. He didn't believe me. He said they were security for a high-tech company in Kalispell."

"Where are the ladies?"

"They're over at our table. Kind of thin ice with them, at the moment."

"I'll bet. Well, we told them we're cops. Did you give them the same story?"

"They're not buying it any more than the deputy did. Especially Mei. She didn't say anything, just pulled the arrows out of the table and tested the points with her thumb."

"Yeah, what's up with the arrows and phone?" Joe Big asked, looking around the room. No one looked out of place or interested in them. It was the usual—or what he took to be the usual—collection of people, doing what the usual collection of people usually did: drink, laugh, whine, argue, complain, try to get drunk or laid or both.

Barney shrugged. "You showed up. He never did say."

"So what do you want to do?" Joe Big asked

"I don't know. Talk to the ladies, I guess. I mean, what *can* we do? Did you get any plate numbers?"

"No plates. Stickers in the back windows."

"I think Pick was going to give us a bunch of crap about how we are in over our heads," Barney said.

"Well, we certainly seem to be that."

"I don't know about you," Barney said. "But I am sick of walking around in the fog. In fact, I am sick of this job. The Feds have no loyalty to us; they never have any loyalty to local law enforcement. I think we're being set up for something."

"So what do you want to do?"

"Fuck, man. I don't know. Harold was with those guys."

Joe Big looked between people standing at the bar, at the two women sitting at the table, heads close together. He could guess what they were talking about. The two blue-and-white fletched arrows were in the middle of the table.

"I don't want to walk away from these women," he said.

"What?"

"I said I don't want to walk away from these women. It's not going to do us any good to sit around and talk this to death. You know what I'm saying? Pick is a piece of work, but that guy with him is something special. He's been the same places we've been, probably done most of the things we've done."

Barney stared at him. Joe Big could see that Barney wanted to go blackside. Go fuck up the bad guys, no matter who the bad guys were.

"We owe these women an explanation," he said.

Barney looked toward the two women. Mickey raised a tentative hand in greeting.

"You're right," he said. "I don't think we should stay here, though."

"Let's go see what shakes out," Joe Big said.

"SORRY," BARNEY SAID, when they were again seated at the table.

Joe Big examined the arrows. He put them to the side, flat on the table, and picked up the cell phone. He opened the phone, and pushed a couple of buttons. The battery was dead, the LED screen blank.

"I should warn you. We have real good bullshit detectors," Mei said.

Joe Big looked at her.

Her smile was part challenge, part you've-been-warned.

He nodded. "Fair enough. But we shouldn't stay here. Maybe we could park the car behind your shop, climb in with you guys, go somewhere else?"

"Why don't we just go to my house? It's only a couple of miles, and the road is not marked." She looked at Mickey. "Is that all right with you, Mick?"

Mickey put her hand on Barney forearm. "She's got a really bitchin' place," she said. "In the winter, you can board all the way from the ski area to her back door."

"The house belongs to my family. It's not mine," Mei said. "There's a tiny guest house my mother likes to stay in. It's full of her stuff, but you guys are welcome to use if for the night, if you want."

"Is Sam home?" Joe Big asked.

"Are you okay with that?" she asked.

"With what?"

"With Sam being there."

Joe Big looked confused. "Why would I have a problem with Sam being there?" He looked to Barney for help.

Barney and Mickey were watching him blank-faced.

"I kind of wanted to say hello to him," he said. "That's all. He reminds me of me when I was that age."

Mickey smiled.

"So okay," Barney said. "First we need to take my car over behind the bakery and check it out."

"Check it out?" Mei asked. "Check what out?"

"Tracking devices," Barney said, as if everyone checked their cars now and then for tracking devices.

"Wow, you guys really are cops aren't you?" Mickey's eyes were bright with excitement.

"Look," Joe Big said. "We are being casual about those guys, but there is nothing casual about them. In a fair fight they would kick our ass. You need to be clear about that." He picked up one of the arrows. "This arrow has been used. The tip has been dinged up, and there is dried blood on the inside of the razors and along the shaft and here on the fletches. Something tells me that it is not animal blood."

He looked at Mei. "Think about it while we go over to your shop. If you don't want us at your place, we completely understand."

Mei looked at Mickey.

"You ready?" Joe Big said to Barney

"ACCORDING TO THIS nifty little toy that I liberated from Quinn's desk a week ago, there are two GPS tracking sticks and one bug," Barney said.

"Is that what she was screaming to Mrs. W about?" Joe Big asked.

"Yeah, she thought one of the ATF guys had taken it, and then lost it, and wouldn't own up to losing it."

The two women had gone inside the bakery to use the bathroom. Mei wanted to check on bread dough that she had left out to raise overnight.

The night was cold and crisp, smelling of lake and pines. An occasional car or a semi-truck went by on the highway. Joe Big stood in the shadows at the corner of the building. The paved parking area behind the building was large enough to comfortably hold six or seven cars or several large delivery trucks. A big white metal reefer with a touch pad on the door was set into a space at the back of the bakery, butted up against the wall of the shop next door.

A large blue dumpster stood alone on the lake side of the parking lot, the door secured with metal bars to prevent bears and other animals from digging through the trash.

"We've got a jammer that can be plugged into the cigarette lighter," Joe Big said. That'll take care of anything you missed. We can throw everything else in the lake."

"They were pretty half-assed about it," Barney said.

"Why not? There's only the highway going in and out of town, and a gravel road that goes over to a lake on the other side of the mountain."

"I'll put our cell phones in the bakery."

"No," Joe Big said. "We don't want to get Mei any more involved than she already is. Throw them in the lake, too. We've got those one-time phones in the duffel."

"Right. I forgot about them."

The two women came out of the building, the light from inside illuminating the blue Subaru and Barney on his back across the passenger seat, shining a small flashlight under the dash.

The bakery light went off, and the screen door slapped shut.

Barney extricated himself from the Subaru.

"Change your mind?" Joe Big asked them.

"Not on your life," Mickey said. "This is more excitement than we've had since Mei stole a car from her parent's car lot when we were in middle school, and the cops caught us on the freeway."

Barney laughed. "I wonder who instigated that."

"Whose car are we taking?" Joe Big asked.

"My jeep," Mei said.

"Okay, I'll go with you. Mickey can go with Barney, show him the way in case we get separated."

"It's only a couple of miles."

"He'll be driving without headlights or brake lights."

"Oh."

"After you, *mon cheri,"* Barney said to Mickey, and made a sweeping gesture toward the open passenger door.

Mickey giggled, and half ran, half bounced over to the Subaru, and slid inside, her athletic ability obvious.

"Don't scare her too bad," Joe Big said to Barney.

"I don't think that's possible," Barney said.

Mei laughed. "Smart man," she said.

JOE BIG WAS silent, scanning empty driveways, as they drove down a nameless paved street through the center of Painted Cliff, headed for the black, almost invisible bulk of the mountain behind the town. The old jeep smelled like the inside of a bakery.

"I don't see anyone behind us," Mei said.

"He's probably on a parallel street. He'll be along in a minute. That car is a monster. He'll wake her up, that's for sure. Half the time, he scares the sh—he scares me."

Mei chuckled. "Mick was being modest for once. She's been featured in some of those videos that show skiers and snowboarders doing totally insane things."

"He's been to all kinds of driving schools."

She glanced at him. "An irresistible force meets an immovable object."

"She's pretty whack, I hear you. But Barney is a whole different dimension of whack, is all I'm saying."

She chuckled. "We'll see."

The pavement ended, and they followed a gravel road filled with washboard bumps, as it wound up the side of the mountain, the old Jeep rattling and shaking past upscale houses with huge windows looking out over the town and the lake and the mountains beyond.

The jeep thrummed across a cattle guard, Mei wrestling with the steering wheel. A four-strand, barbed wire fence stretched away from both sides of the cattle guard. On the other side of the cattle guard, they turned on to a well-kept single-lane gravel road, a large, fluorescent red Private Property sign nailed to a tree on the right. Below the sign was another, smaller sign that said, Hunting By Permission Only. Trees on both sides of the road were banded with Hunter's Orange paint.

"You don't hunt?" he asked.

"I would if I had the time, but the bakery is busy during hunting season. Sam and I don't much care for beef. My brother keeps us well supplied with elk and deer. Sam gets real tense if I cook any of his precious elk sausage for guests. Even Mick is not allowed more than one sausage at a time."

She glanced at him. "My son can be a little precocious at times."

"He seems pretty normal to me."

The road turned into a series of long switchbacks that ended in a large parking area in front of a log house that looked to Joe Big like a log house advertised on the cover of a Real Estate magazine. The bot tom story was dark, but the top story was well lit, a warm golden light emanating from the windows in the vaulted center section. A large deck ran the length of the upper story. The entire front of the house was almost all windows and sliding glass doors. He knew from some of the houses that he had been in up near Whitefish that the light was golden because the windows were covered with a film that blocked heat and ultraviolet light.

Motion detectors turned on recessed lights set under the deck, exposing a concrete pad leading to a double car garage underneath the deck on the left side of the house. The garage door raised and lights came on inside the garage, exposing shelves filled with all sorts of sports and shop equipment. Two large upright freezers sat against the concrete wall at the far end. Sam stood in a doorway directly to his right, frowning as they pulled into the garage.

"Hey, Sam," Mei said, as they climbed out. "Leave the door open. Mick and Barney are coming behind us, and we want to put Barney's car in the garage."

In the distance, they heard the sound of an engine revving high, the exhaust popping as it decelerated.

"What's that?" she asked.

"That would be Barney," Joe Big said.

"I don't see any lights," she said, stepping out of the garage, onto the pad.

They could hear the engine rev high, then a quick shift, the engine winding up again, very loud now, and a dark shadow, dust billowing ghostly white against the trees at the end of the driveway, did a four-wheel drift into the light.

Sam ran to the garage doorway, as the blue Subaru drifted sideways all the way up to the concrete pad, and stopped. Dust rained down on the car, a cloud of it drifting toward dark, towering pines.

Sam turned and looked at his mother, a big grin on his face. He bounced up and down.

The engine revved, and the Subaru turned and sedately motored past Sam, into the garage, and shut off, the exhaust ticking loudly in the sudden silence.

Barney climbed out. "Sam, my man," he said. "It's been *sometime* since I last saw you."

Sam giggled, and ran to the front of the car and put his hands on the hood.

"What's she doing?" Joe Big asked.

Barney grinned. "I think Mickey may have had a little accident."

"Really?" Mei said.

21
Ten Acres of Oranges

"So besides being a cop, and a guy who likes to run up mountains, who are you?" Mei asked. They were sitting outside in weathered Adirondack chairs. The outside lights were off, only a light over the countertop in the kitchen left on to give a small glow bright enough to avoid furniture when they went inside. The stars were so bright they could see snow-covered valleys and ridges at the top of the mountains across the lake. Far below in the village an occasional toy-size car or pickup or chip truck moved silent along a well-lit strip of highway. Wind moaned off the ridge above the house bending and whipping the big pines at the end of the driveway, but sitting in the lee of the house, they felt only gentle eddies.

From beneath their feet, out an open window or sliding door, a female voice squealed. Barney shouted something unintelligible, and there was a dull thud. Mickey squealed again.

"Those two are made for each other," Joe Big said.

"It sounds like it, doesn't it? But maybe you should warn Barney that Mickey is a butterfly. Her attention span for anything but snowboarding is limited to whoever and whatever is right in front of her at the moment."

"Well, it's all good, then, because Barney is coming off a divorce, and we're in the middle of whatever it is we're in the middle of with those guys you met tonight. The last thing he needs right now is a serious relationship."

They were silent for a moment, listening to the commotion downstairs.

"You didn't answer my question," she said.

"I don't know how to answer it. I yam who I yam, said Popeye the Sailor Man. How's that?"

He caught a faint whiff of her perfume. He'd never smelled that kind of perfume before. He really liked it. She slouched down in the chair, fleece comforter wrapped around her shoulders, and stretched her legs straight out, puffy insulated slippers resting on the bottom deck rail. She had long legs, Sam's mother did. What a waste, he thought.

"I know you were in the military, and I know you were in the War," she said.

"How do you know that?"

She chuckled. "My father's friends still come around, even though he's been dead for ten years. I can spot a man who has been to war a mile away."

"I wasn't born to all this," Joe Big said. "It makes me a little uncomfortable—no insult intended."

"All this what? Oh, you mean this house and this land. Well, I've got news for you. Neither was I. My mother and brother and I lived in refugee camps until I was three. We got shuffled from camp to camp, and each time we got shuffled it made it more and more difficult for my father to find us. We finally ended up in Long Beach. My earliest memories are of sharing a mattress on the floor of an empty apartment with my mother and brother. We could hear the neighbors on both sides through the walls as if they were in the room with us." She turned her head toward the distant lake. "Most of the people in that apartment building were Hmong. They didn't like Vietnamese at all. The crazy Hmong man upstairs paced the floor for hours every night, arguing with people who weren't there. One night he died in his sleep. I guess that happened to a lot of the Hmong men."

"So how'd you get from there to here?"

"My mother. Her first husband had somehow squirreled gold away in a bank in France. Not a lot. Maybe a couple of hundred thousand dollars worth. But it was enough to give her a start in the restaurant business. By the time my father finally tracked us down, we were living above her first restaurant." He could feel her smile in the dark.

"Suddenly, out of nowhere, there was this very strong, very powerful white man, smelling of Old Spice and gun oil and fresh laundered uniform, holding me high in the air, hugging and kissing me. I had a rash on my face for a week." He could feel her smile again. "That night there was a lot of yelling and screaming. My brother was very agitated; it wasn't his father, after all—not yet, anyway. But it was my mother who was doing most of the yelling. My father mostly just sat there, arms folded across his chest, glaring at my mother as she hammered out an agreement with him." She laughed. "On paper, no less. You have to understand. My mother is Chinese from Cholon. She was not about to let her love for my father stand in the way of a business opportunity."

"You remember all that?"

She shook her head. "Only some of it. I remember this giant stranger holding me, the roughness of his cheek against mine. Tears running down his face. The story is mostly how my brother remembers it. My mother refused to live on a military base. She'd had it with soldiers and war. She wouldn't even let my father wear his uniform in the house. He had to change in the garage."

"Your father must have really loved her."

"He loved all of us, my brother like he was his own. And in her own way my mother loved him, too. Much more than her first husband, I suspect. But for her, family came—comes—first, and that meant her business and the education of her children first, everything else a distant third. She talked my father into buying a Nissan dealership, when it was still called Datsun. By the time I graduated from high school, they had a string of restaurants, three car dealerships, and five or six apartment buildings. We lived in a two-bedroom, one-bath house built in the 40s. The single-car garage was converted into a room for my father and his guns and uniforms. It had a table and chairs where his buddies would come over to play poker and smoke cigars and watch sports on TV." She paused. "I loved going into that garage." Joe Big could hear the waver in her voice. "I miss him so much."

She was silent for a moment. He heard her sniff.

"The house wasn't worth anything," she continued. "But the land was. The house was set in the middle of ten acres of oranges in Orange County. The driveway was dirt. The orchard equipment was old and forever breaking down. The house my mother built for the

Mexican family who took care of the orchard was better than the house we lived in ourselves."

Joe Big smiled at her dark form. "Am I hearing a little resentment there?"

"Not at all. I loved it. My brother loved it. All our friends loved our house and the orchard. One time, my brother's friend, Mike, found a rattlesnake in the shed. We watched that snake for a week—until my father found out about it, and trapped it and took it away. Things like that."

"When did they sell it? It must have been worth a fortune."

"It was. I was in middle school. My mother sold it to a development company that offered more than it was worth at the time. Next thing I knew, we were living in suburbia—the Steven Spielberg version. Five bedrooms, three baths, three-car garage, swimming pool in the backyard."

"An American success story."

"I guess. If you don't ask where my father and mother got the money to start their businesses. That house is long gone. She got rid of most of her properties before the real estate bubble burst. This is the only place she ever bought to keep. She bought it for me and for my brother, but especially for me." She laughed, and he could hear the affection in her laugh, and something else, too. Sadness? "She won't admit it, though. Every time she visits, she asks about local real estate values."

Somewhere off to the west, over the mountain behind the house, Joe Big could hear the quiet drone of an airplane. He searched the sky over the ridge, but couldn't find any navigation lights. Sound carries funny in the mountains, he thought. The plane could be on the other side of the mountain, or even out over the lake somewhere. There was a thud from directly below his feet. Barney shouted.

"I hope none of that is keeping Sam up."

"Sam is like me. He can sleep through anything."

They were silent for a while, looking out over the shifting pines at the village and the lake and the mountains beyond, comfortable with each other.

"Sam doesn't know what to make of you."

"I don't know what to make of him."

He could feel a tension in her that hadn't been there a moment ago. She was making her mind up about something.

"You haven't asked about Sam's father."

Uh-oh, he thought. "Not my business."

"It is if you want to be Sam's friend."

They were silent again, Mei giving him time to digest the fact that it was about Sam and not about her. Yet another first, he thought.

"Gadzooks!" Barney shouted.

They both laughed.

"Gadzooks?" Mei asked.

"It's a long story."

"Sam's father died in the Peace Corps in Africa—in a traffic accident," she said. "I didn't even know I was pregnant at the time."

"The Peace Corps?"

"Yes, people die in the Peace Corps, too."

She wiped her eyes with the palm of her hand.

"I want to say something," he said, "but anything I say will be a cliché."

"No need." She forced a laugh. "I told you for Sam—and also in the spirit of full disclosure."

He was silent, considering the concept—alien to his and Barney existence at the moment—of full disclosure.

"Marine," he said.

"What?"

"I'm a Marine—a former Marine."

"I know *that*. I even made a bet with Mick. What kind of Marine?"

"The only kind there is. You know. Your father was one."

"There are Marines and then there are Marines, Mr. Big."

"Force Recon."

"And your job—your MOS?"

"I have more than one, but sniper first, I guess."

She was silent, unmoving, wrapped in her comforter. As impassive as a Buddhist monk, he thought.

"Kind of wish you hadn't asked, huh?"

"My father died seven years after he retired," she said. "He hated being a civilian. But he was an honorable man, and retiring at twenty-five years was part of the deal he made with my mother."

She pulled the fleece comforter tighter around her. "He and his friends talked about Vietnam like it was yesterday."

"Barney and I are not like that. For one thing, we were in only a little over six years, total."

"So who are you, Joe Big?"

He laughed. “That question again. Why do I think there’s more than a little of your mother in you?”

In the distance he could still hear the drone of the airplane. Kind of late to be flying around the mountains, he thought. The sound of the airplane engine was familiar.

“Do you want to sleep with me?” she asked.

“Shit!” he said, and jumped up out of the chair. “Let’s go inside.”

“Well, jeez. I appreciate enthusiasm, but—”

He reached down and grasped her arm inside the comforter and pulled her awkwardly to her feet, one foot catching on the railing. He let go of her arm and wadded the comforter in a big ball under his arm. He pulled her stumbling across the deck, through the sliding door, into the living room. He slid the door shut.

“Joe? What—”

“Stay here. Don’t go outside. I’ll be right back.” He hurried over to the stairway, and ran down the stairs to the lower level. The carpeted hallway was lit with nightlights about eight inches off the floor. The hallway reminded him of a movie theatre. Noises were coming from the middle door of five doors.

He pounded his fist on the door. “Barney. Yo! Barney!”

“Go away.”

“Yeah, go away,” a female voice echoed.

“There’s a drone flying around over the ridge where we camped last night.”

“A what?”

“A surveillance drone. I can hear it.”

“So go moon it, or something.”

He heard laughter.

Joe Big opened his mouth to reply. He stared at the door, feeling like an idiot. Barney was right. Even if it was a drone, and not a product of his overworked imagination, there was nothing they could do about it.

He slapped his hand lightly twice on the door, and turned and walked back upstairs.

Mei was folding the comforter. She put it on the back of a couch. The light from the kitchen made her T-shirt diaphanous. He could see a hint of how long and lean she was, the fullness of her breasts

“There’s a surveillance drone flying around where Barney and I camped last night,” he said. “I recognize the sound.”

“Are you sure?”

“No.”

She smiled. “I have to get up early.”

“Oh, sorry. I keep forgetting you’re a baker.”

She walked over close to him, her hooded, slightly almond-shaped green eyes warm and predatory at the same time. He swallowed.

“You didn’t answer my question,” she said.

“No,” he blurted. “I mean . . . well . . .”

She leaned back, evaluating him.

“Are you afraid of me, Joe Big? You seem like the kind of man who is not afraid of much—certainly not of women.”

“I have this rule of never hooking up with mothers . . .”

“Why?”

“Well . . . you know.”

Her eyes became even more hooded. He hadn’t realized how full her lips were. Swollen almost. He felt a rush of heat in his face and the back of his neck.

“You sleep in my bed,” she said. “I’m too tired to make up the bed in the guest house. I’ll sleep with Sam.”

“I can’t ”

“Yes, you can. I do it all the time—sleep with Sam, I mean. Sam will be happy that I’m sleeping with him and not with someone else—not that I have ever slept with someone else in this house,” she said, as she turned and walked toward a dark hallway off the kitchen.

“It’s the first door on the left,” she said. “It’s got it’s own bathroom. Help yourself to towels and whatever.” She disappeared into the darkness of the hallway.

He heard a door open, and then some whispering. The door closed with a quiet click. And then it was silent and he was standing there alone in the middle of the living room, feeling like he’d done something really stupid, even though, near as he could tell, he hadn’t. She was something, that was for sure. But his rule was a good rule. It had grown out of a promise he’d made to his grandmother. Single mothers are easy to take advantage of, his grandmother had explained—before he’d been old enough to know what she was talking about. And then the single-mother girlfriend of one of the SEALs at Dive School, after she’d caught the guy with another woman, had taken her life and the life of her infant son, and his grandmother’s words had come back at him.

Not that Mei was hurting for attention from men. He'd bet most of the men who knew her had either hit on her, or had at least dreamed about it.

But as his grandmother had explained, it was as much for his own good, as it was for the good of the woman and her child.

Of course, there was nothing that said grandmothers couldn't be as full of shit as anyone else. His grandmother would've been the first to admit that.

The door to her room was open. The glow from a nightlight illuminated the door to the bathroom and the edge of a very large brass bed. Next to the bed a large square wooden nightstand—more a table than a nightstand—was littered with lamp and books and magazines, a small egg-shaped alarm clock on top a stack of books. Large stuffed animals—moose and bears and floppy-eared rabbits—occupied one side of the unmade bed.

He found the switch, and turned on the long-necked lamp. There was a sliding glass door on the other side of the bed that opened onto a back balcony. Oriental-looking pleated blinds covered the top half of the windows. Japanese and Chinese and, he assumed, Vietnamese tapestries adorned the walls. A large bookcase made out of plastic—the kind sold at hardware stores, and meant for storage rooms and garages—took up most of one wall, piles of folded clothes on the top shelves, shoes of all sorts piled haphazard on the bottom. Next to the bathroom was a large walk-in closet. It looked as if the bathroom had both a Jacuzzi tub and a glass-enclosed shower.

The bed had been slept in, the covers and sheet thrown to the side, the pillow still dented.

He sat on the bed, and took off his shoes and socks, and then turned off the light and lay back. He was tired. Real tired. The mattress was extra firm—the way he liked it—and her pillow was more solid than soft—the way he liked it. He could smell her on it. He felt his limbs relax, his face hot against the cool pillow.

He sat up and took off his pants and shirt and eased under the sheet, not horny for her in the slightest, the smell of her on the pillow and bedding inexplicably more intimate than he'd ever been with a woman.

Strange, he thought, I better not be having a malaria attack, and fell asleep before he could separate the two thoughts.

22
In The Company Of Snakes

He was floating on a thermal high above a rift in the vast expanse of green rolling hills. The rift looked like the skeletal remains of a snake vertebrae, the rocks and small cliffs that made up its leading edge pieces of bone exposed by the elements.

Monstrous clouds dark gray at the top, ink black at the base, formed a wall perpendicular to the rift. The wall of clouds stretched from horizon to horizon, a towering malignance encroaching on clean blue sky.

He could smell earth and sun-baked rocks, new grass and prairie flowers, a hint of pine.

Far below, a lone horseman, black hair streaming, rode a horse the same color as his hair at full gallop across the hills.

As he swooped closer he could see that the man, an Indian, was riding a pad saddle with short stirrups, a single very long leather rope—a war bridle—bunched in his left hand. The horse's withers were shiny with sweat.

The horseman and the horse pounded down a gentle grass-covered slope, the horse grunting with effort as it charged up the opposing slope, hooves throwing clods of dirt and grass.

The man and the horse disappeared over the hill and it was quiet, the echo of horse hooves a memory, the only evidence of their passage a line in the grass down one slope and up the next.

His vision wavered, shook, as he turned over in her bed, and then he was alongside the man on the horse, close enough to hear the hollow grunts made by the horse, the sharp clicks the man was making to urge the horse on. The horse was painted for war, pictographs depicting past coups in red and yellow and white paint on its shoulders and flanks and haunches—which was sort of strange because the man wore no war paint.

The man had managed to coil the bridle—maybe twenty feet of it—and wedge the coiled rope inside the leather strap that held up his leggings. The bridle itself was nothing more than a very long rope with a permanent loop at one end. Two half hitches had been tied around the lower half of the horse's jaw, and then the long portion of the rope passed though the loop. But the man was not using the bridle to control the horse. The horse had free rein, its nostrils flared, shoulders and chest slick with sweat and foam.

A hank of very long greased hair was knotted around a leather strap at the man's waist. A wad of hair and scalp slapped wetly against his legging.

Skin the color of old oak. Black raptor's eyes. Wide face. Prominent cheekbones. The classic hatchet nose of a Blackfeet warrior. A big man. Six-five or so. Broad shoulders, barrel chest, lean muscles sinuous in his forearms and biceps, neck and shoulders. His long legs made the horse appear smaller than it was, the leather at the upper end of his leggings wrapped so as to help shield his privates. Red stripes circled the leggings from mid calf to knee. A large knife with antler handle was sheathed at his waist.

Bright red arterial blood covered the right side of his neck and chest and the legging on his right leg. There was dried blood on the top of his hands; his moccasins were wet with it. A blanket roll was held tight to his back by a rawhide strap across his bare chest, a small leather pouch that looked almost like a leather can tied to the outside of the blanket roll. There was pemmican or dried meat in the leather pouch, he knew.

His view rotated again and even though he was there with that blood-stained horseman and his horse, pounding up and down grassy hills and steep coulees—even though he was there, he knew it was a dream and not real.

The man's hair was like a living thing in the wind, a black shiny banner.

He frowned: there was something familiar about the man.

And thinking that there was something familiar about the man, he vaulted far up in the sky, at the edge of the immense wall of storm clouds. He could see roiling streaks of gray and black within the clouds, feel the wind buffet him.

A mile or so behind the horseman, clear blue sky at their back, five riders streamed down a distant hill, riding hard, but not so hard as the lone horseman.

One of the figures pointed a long lance in the direction of the fleeing man, and all five pressed their knees tighter to their horses, turning to follow a long, grassy ridge, their yips and yells barely heard, lances and one flintlock held low and out to the side. The lone horseman had long hair, but these men had even longer hair, their hair worn in elaborate braids, war medicine feathers attached to the braids, two with impressive pompadours.

Their faces and their horses were painted for war.

He felt himself wheel in the sky, pirouetting next to the monstrous wall of clouds. He swooped, gliding down next to the figure on the black horse.

And without warning, and with such force that he grunted out loud, throwing the covers to the side, he was inside the mind of the man on the horse, his mind rent by a single-minded intensity, a fierceness almost beyond his ken.

He smelled horse and prairie and the oncoming storm with a clarity and with a complexity that he had never before experienced. It was almost as if he could see with his sense of smell alone. He felt the horse in a way that made it difficult to say where the horse began and he ended. Bending forward slightly, and pressing his knees harder into the horse, he felt the response in the great muscles as an extension of his own muscles. Mane whipped and snapped in his face. All that melding into his being until there was no delineation between what he smelled and what he felt and what he thought: he was in the mind of a man who lived in the present in a way and to an extent he had never before imagined.

And understanding all that, the inherent fatalism in it, he lost the thread of who he was . . .

Naapi. The Old Man. The Creator. Naapi the Trickster was playing with him. He'd slid down the steep hillside into a gully filled with trees and bushes, following a deer trail, still wearing the wolf skin that he had donned to scout the Crow village and the large horse herd beyond the village, and there, standing partially hidden by the tall grass and bushes, was a short, stocky, muscular Crow in war paint and feathers, his greased hair worn free to below his buttocks. The Crow was standing with his back to him, next to a black horse painted for war.

The horse backed into the bushes, ears pointed toward him, nostrils flaring, pulling on the rope in the Crow's hand.

The Crow had not seen him, and he grinned to himself, for he knew this Crow, had seen him before, at dusk, a Piikani scalp held high above his head, his war song and his taunts echoing across the deceptively placid waters of the mighty river.

That Crow, this very Crow, had laughed and shaken the scalp of a man he had known since childhood. And then the other Crow had exposed their buttocks toward the enraged Piikani massed on the far bank.

He threw off the wolf skin and rushed the Crow, ignoring the grab and slap of bushes and tree branches, and as he did pulled the knife from its sheath and, holding it blade protruding from his fist, brought his arm and hand back across his chest and, as the Crow whirled toward him, stabbed hard into the far side of the Crow's stomach and ripped the blade with all his strength through the middle of the Crow's body, feeling muscles and organs and bone rip and sever. The knife came free and he raised his hand high and plunged the knife into the Crow's neck and pulled the knife forward and out. Blood spurted into the bushes and onto him, as the Crow's insides spilled out onto the ground and onto his right foot.

He laughed, and grabbing a handful of the Crow's hair, pulled the Crow face first onto the ground, the body hitting the ground with the sound of a deer carcass tossed onto the ground for his wives to butcher. Straddling the Crow from behind he pulled hard on his hair, and with the beavertail blade made a larger than normal half-moon slice into the scalp, pulling and ripping the scalp back as he sliced, a round, ragged piece of scalp and a mass of very long hair and feathers coming free in his hand.

He tied the long hair to the rawhide cord around his waist and slid the knife into the sheath. He wiped his bloody hand on the Crow.

The horse threw its head back. Air whistled from its nostrils. He took hold of the war bridle and jerked on it hard and looked into the horse's eyes, and saw immediately that it was an exceptional horse, intelligent and not afraid of the smell of blood. A buffalo horse. A war horse.

The horse quieted immediately, and he led it out of the bushes and scattered trees into the short grass at the upper end of the gully. The Crow saddle was a fine, comfortable pad saddle made out of well-tanned antelope hide and stuffed with grass. Designs made with porcupine quills decorated the corners of the saddle. He vaulted up onto the horse, hearing, as he did so, shouts behind him. *"Sh, sh,"* he said, and gently kneed the horse forward, guiding it silent up out of the gully and over the crest of the hill. He pressed his knees into its sides, and the horse responded immediately, galloping along the ridge, away from the Crow, headed toward the old war lodge they had rebuilt the day before. He was pleased with the power and agility of the horse. A fine horse. It would make a good present for the old man who had given him his war medicine—his war song and his face paint and the rattlesnake skin.

Far to his right, following a distant ridge he saw at least fifty Crow headed in the direction of the war lodge, and knowing he could never get there first to warn his partner and the other men and the two boys they had brought along to do camp chores, he turned the horse north, off the ridge and out of sight of the Crow. Maybe The Small Weasel, the other scout, would be able to warn them.

Huh! he thought. He had told The Bull Running that it was bad medicine to use the same war lodge they had used the last time they had taken horses from this particular band of Crow. And then The Owl Medicine had a bad dream. The Bull Running had told The Owl Medicine to go home, and The Owl Medicine had silently left—much to everyone's relief.

But even then The Bull Running had not moved the war lodge.

The Bull Running had led many successful horse-stealing raids, but if he survived this one, no one would ever follow him again.

This band of Crow always had the best horses and the most beautiful women. But they were unusually stubborn and belligerent even for Crow. They would not easily give up pursuit.

He bared his teeth, shouted at the wind. If not for the fine horses, his people would have long ago destroyed these Crow. Maybe the time had come. Equally fine horses could be found among the Snakes.

He smiled, feeling the scalp slap wet against his bare leg above the legging.

Oh, the Old Man was playing his tricks today. He would make many people laugh for many years when he told the story of the look on the Crow's face when his insides spilled onto the ground, and the knife ripped his throat from his body. He shouted again, feeling the dried blood of the Crow on his hands and face, and began to sing his war medicine song, singing it to the storm clouds and to the blue sky and to the horse.

The Bull Running might have bad medicine, but his own medicine was good. He would return with a beautiful strong horse, and the scalp of an old hated enemy.

To his right, the entire horizon was a great wall of dark clouds, black and sinister-looking at the base. To his left, the sky was a great blue bowl, light at the edges, deep blue at the center.

The tall grass on the hillsides and ridges had begun to toss and flatten in the direction of the oncoming storm.

High above, a raven swooped and pirouetted.

He frowned. A good sign? The Raven was not his spirit animal. He didn't like Ravens. They were sly. Their beady eyes knew too much.

He rose in the short stirrups and turned to look behind. The Raven might be someone else's spirit animal.

His eyes caught movement far behind. A straggle of tiny, mounted figures crested a hill, headed directly toward him.

He turned forward and kneed the horse to a faster gallop, flattening himself against its neck and mane.

He felt blood hurry through his body. A new feeling. He was the hunted; he had never before been the hunted. *Naapi* again. The Old Man had given him the Crow and the horse and now the laugh was on him. The Crow were wolves. But unlike wolves, they would play with their prey before they killed it—especially since he had already killed one of their most famous and admired. He laughed out loud. The great trickster was not *Naapi*. The great trickster was himself. He had chosen to kill that Crow, tricking himself into believing that he could get by with it.

Hiyah! It was a good feeling, the horse and the day and the blood spilled onto mother earth. They were wolves, but he was not a buffalo calf. His eyes were not white with fear.

He did not like this new feeling, though. It made him feel small. He had his war medicine and it had already proved that it was powerful medicine. If the Crow did not kill him, he would avenge himself against the Crow for making him feel this way. He would kill every Crow he encountered, man, woman, child, until the stain of this new feeling went away.

Veils of lightning spidered the darkness at the base of the vast wall of clouds. With his knee, he turned the horse in the direction that the sun enters the world, straight toward the darkness that was eating the earth. The wind was at his back now, his hair streaming forward on both sides of his face.

He rose again off the saddle, and turned. The distance had increased between him and the Crow. He turned forward and, sitting upright, held both fists in the air, and shouted his defiance. But then, in his mind, he saw four horsemen streaming down a small rocky hill, where before there had been five. He turned again, and this time saw that one of the Crow had broken away from the others and had begun to close the gap.

What kind of horse that must be, he thought, to be faster and stronger than the one he was riding. There was no doubt in his mind that no matter how special that horse was, the Crow behind him would ride it to death, if that is what it would take to catch him. The Crow were like that.

He stared at the black wall before him. Behind, the way he had come, the sky was shrinking. The grass had flattened toward the storm. If the fast-horse Crow separated far enough from the others, he would stop and kill him and take his horse, too.

And imagining himself arriving home alone with two such horses, and two scalps, and with the story of this chase to go along with the story of the first Crow, the black horse stepped into a badger hole invisible in grass flattened by the wind, and he felt himself flying through the air. He tucked his head and shoulders and rolled as he hit the ground, the long war bridle unraveling from the strap at his waist.

He came to his feet, facing back toward the horse, hair streaming behind him, his legs shaky. The horse struggled upright, trembling and snorting. Yellow-white bone protruded through skin darkened by blood on its right shin.

He bent and grabbed the end of the war bridle, and then dropped it and turned and began running, slowly and painfully at first, and then, his head clearing, legs and lungs gaining strength, picked up the pace. His blanket roll with his war medicine and extra moccasins inside was still intact and held onto his back by the leather strap across his chest. With his left hand he felt for his knife and found it half out of the sheath. He pushed it back in.

He was a big man, big even for the Piikani, but he was a good runner, one of the best. He knew that given enough time, and if he had enough of a head start, he could outrun a horse—across flat land.

Running up and down hills he had no chance against a horse as powerful as the one coming behind him. The Crow was going to catch him, and the Crow had a lance and a bow and a quiver full of arrows. He had only his knife and his war medicine.

He ran hard, knowing from experience how far he could push his body before his legs cramped. Cramps could fell him as surely as an arrow or a lance. He ran a slight diagonal up hills and reversed the diagonal on the way down the other side, running hard for the blackness and the veil of dancing light that was eating the earth, his hair whipping and snapping in front of him, the wind at his back like a huge, soft hand pushing him up and over hills, dying as he ran down the other side, hair in his eyes and mouth and nose.

Behind, as he ran up a hill, he heard the not-so-distant war cry of the Crow.

As he crested the hill, the wind reversed, slamming him so hard in the face and chest that he almost came to a stop, his hair suddenly streaming straight behind, pulling at his scalp.

His eyes narrowed and he leaned into the wind, the effort to run downhill nearly what it had been to run uphill.

The Old Man was angry. This was not a trick. There was no humor in this. This was like nothing he had ever experienced before, the power of the wind only a hint of what lay at the bottom of the immense cloud that now blotted out the sun and the sky, the air around him become murky, the wind an angry moan. A bright flash lit the murk, leaving in its passing a pulse of yellow light that lingered for a few breaths before being replaced by yet more flashes of white light, each flash dying to a yellow glow. He tensed for the terrifying clap of sound that always accompanied the lightning, but the only sound was the shriek and moan of the wind.

He wanted to turn and run back the way he had come, to find a hole or a rock or a fallen tree to shelter beneath. But to turn back would be to die at the hands of the Crow.

He ran faster, muscles no longer aching, the certainty that the storm was a manifestation of *Naapi's* ill temper making him run harder than he had ever run before, his breathing become ragged sobs, part fear of *Naapi's* fickle temper, part lungs unable to keep up with his body's demand for oxygen. White balls of ice and shards of ice and blobs of rain and slush smacked his head and chest, cutting and bruising his scalp and the edge of his eye. A pink haze obscured the vision in his left eye, his other eye equally blurred by wind and wet.

He screamed defiance, death no longer a factor, as he ran almost blind into the heart of the storm. Abruptly, shockingly, he was weightless, his arms and legs flailing, as he ran off a thirty-foot drop-off, fifteen feet straight out into wind and rain and hail and pulses of light, and dropped straight down onto rocks and bushes and fissures in the clay, some of the fissures already become rivulets of water.

He fell hard, twisting both ankles badly, hearing a snap as his forearm hit a rock, a numbing hollow crack as his skull hit another.

The hail had turned to a sheet of water cold enough to keep him semi-conscious. Dimly he heard the blast and crack of lightning hitting rocks at the edge of the drop-off. Ozone stink filtered through the rain.

He crawled out of the rocks, barely aware of what he was doing, sliding across hard-packed clay made greasy by the water, along the base of the drop-off to rocks splotched gray and black with lichen. His vision fogged by blood and rain and the wound to his head, he crawled toward a vague, thin darkness beneath a slab of rock, sand piled at its edge.

The fingers of his good hand clawed sand, pulling him toward the cave. Slivers of pain shot up the back of his legs into his lower back, as he pushed feebly with his knees and feet. He wedged himself into the long, narrow opening, sand cascading down into the cave, blanket roll scraping the rock above.

He tasted blood trickling into his throat, felt the scrape of his exposed penis across gravel and sand and rock. Another immense crack of light and sound hit and he felt rock shards pepper his side and shoulder. The reek of ozone made him want to vomit. There was a smell he had never smelled before inside the cave—a musty, fetid smell a little like the smell of green squash cut open—and he wondered if he was crawling into a coyote den. No. It was not the smell of dogs or coyotes.

The cave was much larger than him. Inside the sand was dry. He blinked his right eye clear of blood and rain and sweat and saw that *Naapi* had the head and neck of a rattlesnake too big to be anything but The Old Man himself.

Naapi came closer, eyes glittering like the black rock that his partner, The Bear Child, had found at the bottom of a stream.

The Old Man leaned closer, tongue vibrating. He felt a warmth spread through his body. His vision misted, and the throbbing in his arm and ankles faded, as a moving, sliding, coiling darkness on his back and legs pressed him gently into cool dry sand.

A good way to die, he thought. Cheating the Crow of their revenge. Part of his mind laughed. They would not even find his body . . .

HE WOKE TO the taste of sand in his mouth and to the musty melon smell that in his mind connoted death. At first, he thought he had been blinded, but lifting his head the darkness behind his eyelids changed. One eyelid and then the other cracked open. Flakes of dried blood blurred his vision.

A vague form, long and dark, rippled past his face, its skin rasping against the sand.

His body felt swollen, muscles numb and unresponsive, as if they had been too long dormant and no longer knew what to do.

He heard distant, muted voices, human voices, and the light at the cave opening flickered as feet and shins clad in moccasins and leather leggings moved across the opening. Crow voices. Crow leggings. He could understand the laughter, but he could not understand the words.

The dark shadow again moved across his vision, blotting out a portion of the light as it slid with muscular purpose out the narrow cave opening.

"Aiii!?" he heard. And the dark shape slid faster, disappearing into the light. Other smaller, similar shapes followed. He heard a babble of shouts and exclamations, growing more distant . . .

A dream, Joe Big thought, and closed his eyes and let the darkness claim him once again, feeling the sand replaced by pillow and sheets cool against his skin, the smell of Naapi replaced by her smell. He smiled . . .

And found himself sitting in the shade of a tree, next to a large flat rock. A small pool of rain water in a bowl-like depression at the other end of the rock reflected blue sky and puffy white clouds.

His bedroll was open next to him. But for the snake, he was naked, his ankles wrapped with strips of leather cut from his leggings, his broken forearm bound with birch bark packed with dry moss, leather straps tight around the bark.

He felt the snake coiled around his ribs and chest relax as he bent at the waist and with his good hand put on the spare set of moccasins, tying them awkwardly with both hands.

He sat back against the rock, and felt the snake again tighten against his broken ribs. His fever was gone. He had been able to eat the pemmican in the pouch on his bedroll, and he'd drunk as much as his ribs would allow from the pool of rainwater left over from the storm—the storm that had almost killed him.

He would begin the trek home tonight by the light of a full moon. His ankles would take most of the moon to heal; the going would be slow. But the other snake, the great snake, as it had done last night, would hunt for both of them, and in the morning he would find what it had killed while he slept.

With his free hand he reached up and touched the dent in his head, the wound still soft and springy in the center.

Maybe his mind was gone, he thought. Probably it was. Like the minds of men who had been kicked by a horse or been hit in the head with a war club—men with faces slack and useless on one side.

He gazed up at the infinite blue sky, the full moon white and nearly transparent on the horizon, and *felt a weight move beneath the covers behind him. A dry calloused hand slid across the ridged scar on his side, and constricted against his ribs, the same as the snake had constricted against him . . .*

Joe Big opened his eyes and it was dark and there was no blue sky and no transparent moon on the horizon. He could feel her length pressed against his, feel her breath soft at the back of his neck.

She pulled away, and he felt her sit up in bed.

"You were having a dream," she said. "I could hear you from the other room."

"Yes," he said, their voices and the language they were using unfamiliar to his ears.

"Are you okay?"

He turned around, his hand sliding to the inside of her thigh. It surprised him how easy and natural it felt to put his hand there.

Her hand stilled his, kept it pinned against her thigh.

They were silent, staring at each other in the darkness.

She released the pressure on his hand, and he pulled it back onto the sheet between them. She was wearing pajama shorts and a tank top. Her bare arm around his chest and the feel of her bare leg against his had made him think she was naked.

He felt more than saw her cross her arms and grasp the bottom of the tank top and pull it over her head.

She lay back onto the bed and arched her stomach and buttocks upward and pulled off her shorts. She pulled the covers over herself. He could feel her heat, smell a hint of her perfume. His mouth was dry. He felt off balance, the dream still with him. Part of him, the most important part, wanted to be back in the company of snakes, walking up a coulee in the moonlight.

He was incredibly attracted to her. And it was more than her looks or her sensuality that attracted him. But merely putting his hand on her inner thigh had been enough. It had established an intimacy that was all he could handle at the moment.

She turned on her side and propped her head up with her arm.

"Are you okay?" she asked.

"I'm okay."

"You sound a little out of it."

"My mind is full of rattlesnakes."

"What?"

"My dream."

"You're not married or engaged or something like that are you?"

"No. I'm gay."

"What?"

He smiled. "Not really."

She was silent.

"Really," he said. "I'm not gay."

She was silent.

"It was a joke," he said.

"Let's see," she said. Her hand snaked beneath the covers and found him, and he was surprised by how hard he was. "Hmm," she said. "Not exactly the legendary Big Wang, but adequate, I suppose."

She pulled him toward her, and he felt the smooth fit of her body as they came together. But as she lay back on the pillow, he saw *Naapi's* eyes cold and hard and black peering hypnotic into his mind, and his entire body flushed with heat. His erection wilted in her hand.

She released him and her hand went to the side of his head where his skull had been caved in when he landed on the rocks. She sat up abruptly, covers falling to her waist, breasts heavy in the darkness, and put her hand on his forehead.

"You're burning up," she said. "You've got a fever."

"You do that to me," he said.

"It's not funny," she said. "You've really got a fever. And it's not a little one, either." She paused. "You didn't have one a minute ago . . ."

"I have malaria," he said. "It comes and goes. You never get completely rid of it. It's no big deal. Sometimes, I wake up in the middle of the night and my T-shirt is soaking wet. I change my shirt and go back to bed, and it's okay. You'll see. It will go away in a few minutes."

Her hand felt the side of his face, then back to his forehead again. It was the way she checked Sam for childhood fevers, he thought.

His body felt hot. Leaden. The way it had felt when he'd woken up inside the cave in his dream.

"It's probably why I was dreaming so hard," he said.

"Does it happen during the day, too?"

"No. Just in my sleep."

She turned and lay back on the bed and pulled the covers to her chin. "I told you my father was a Marine."

"You did."

"He was very competent. He had medals. I can remember him being asked to be an officer. He was a very competent businessman, too."

"I wish I could have met him."

"That's not what I'm getting at. He was a good man. A good husband and a good father. He had a great sense of humor. He always knew where my brother and I were going before we got there. Do you know what I mean?"

"I had a grandmother like that."

"Most of his friends were Marines or former Marines. They would come to our house a lot. The garage, even when we moved to the upscale neighborhood, was always sort of a clubhouse for all those guys. Most of them were like uncles." She paused. "But a few of them were hard men."

He felt sweat trickle down his ribs and down the sides of his face. His legs behind his knees were damp and clammy on the sheet.

"My father and most of his friends were tough, but they weren't hard men. Do you understand what I mean?"

"I understand exactly what you mean."

"Those men tonight in the brew pub, they are hard men."

"Yes, they are."

"Are you and Barney like them?"

"Yes, we are."

"I don't want you to be like them."

"You want me to be like your father?"

She laughed. "Oh, God, no. I don't mean that. The world couldn't handle another one like him. I couldn't, that's for sure."

"I was a Marine," he reminded her.

Her head turned toward him

"My mother and my brother will have trouble with you." She pulled the covers to her chin. "Shoot," she said. "I have to get up in a few hours."

"The life of a baker," he said.

Her head turned away from him, and she stared up at the ceiling. "I like being a baker. I like making things with my hands. I love looking out the back window at the lake at first light, a fresh cup of coffee in my hand, the smell of the bakery around me."

"Sounds good to me."

She chuckled. "No, it doesn't. It sounds stifling to you. Pure claustrophobia. You'd like the smells and the coffee and the view of the lake, but the bakery, the responsibility associated with living that moment almost every day of your life, would make you—well, you just couldn't do it, that's all."

"Could your father?"

"I think he could have if he hadn't been a Marine. And if he hadn't done the things that he had done in Vietnam. If all that hadn't happened, then, yes, I think he would have been very happy doing what I'm doing. But as it was, I think he kept busy and surrounded himself with friends so that he wouldn't have quiet moments to himself—moments like I have every morning at the bakery."

"You're pretty smart, you know that?'

Her head swiveled toward him. "My mother is the one who is smart about these things. She has outlived two husbands who were professional soldiers."

"And thus she won't like me?"

"Probably not."

"What about her? What's she like?"

She laughed, a laugh full of affection for her mother. "She's the Eveready Bunny. Her mind and her body never stop moving. Everybody loves her, but she drives everyone crazy. We're trying to get her to stop driving. She drives like a maniac. Even down to the corner store, it's pedal to the metal the whole way."

"Kind of hard if she owns car dealerships."

"A couple more tickets and she won't have a say in it because she won't have a license. God pity whoever has to drive her around, though."

"I really like you," he said.

"I know. Most men do."

"Even Trish the bartender, I suspect."

"What? Are you imply—" She grabbed the pillow from behind her head and hit him full in the face with it.

"Oh, I'm sorry! I forgot . . ." Her hand again found his forehead. "My, God. You're all wet."

"Lots of people tell me that."

"You're dripping wet. The sheet is all wet."

"My bad."

She put the pillow behind her head and lay back on the bed, silent. Her head turned toward him, and he could feel her evaluating him. Her father had been a Marine, he thought. In California. He wouldn't be surprised if Montoya and the crusty old Master Sergeant who had gotten him into Force Recon had known him, maybe even been friends. A small world, sometimes, the Marine Corps. Her mother had worked at the Embassy in Saigon and at a Saigon night club. Her mother's first husband had been killed in battle. She had come to America with her two children. Figured out America enough to turn herself into a successful American businesswoman. Spooky Little Girl, the apple of her parents' eye, had absorbed who her parents were and what they knew about people and about the world. Almost every man who went in the bakery must have either hit on her at one time or another, or at least thought about hitting on her. She was a widow. Had a son named Sam . . .

And she was in bed with him. And what was he doing about it? He was sweating his ass off, ruining her sheets with his sweat, that's what he was doing. It would be funny, if it wasn't so pathetic.

He felt clammy, and realized that the attack had passed.

"Do you mind if I take a quick shower?" he asked. "The fever is gone."

She felt his forehead, wiped her hand on the sheet.

"There are clean towels in the basket next to the closet," she said. "I didn't have time to put them away."

IN THE SHOWER, he quickly washed his head and body with a body wash that smelled of green apples. Barney would make a joke, he thought. Not only was he, Joe Big, an apple, now he smelled like one, too. He rinsed off the soap, and turned the shower to cold, the sudden blast of cold water taking his breath away, making him gasp. The well must go deep, he thought, tapped into some kind of underground stream or small river coming out of the mountains.

The water abruptly turned colder, and he found himself making deep huh's of sound, his lungs unable to relax enough to take in air.

"Are you all right in there?"

He shut off the water, his skin tingling, his breathing restored to normal. Damn, he thought. At his place, you had to wait until winter to get a cold drink of water. "Fine," he called. "No problem."

He stepped out of the shower and grabbed the towel. A big fluffy white towel—of course. And rubbed his hair hard and fast to get it as dry as possible, forgetting for a moment that he didn't have much hair any more. "Well, that was weird," he muttered.

The light next to the bed was on and the sheets and pillowcases were in a pile next to the doorway. A clean sheet and pillows with clean pillowcases were on the bed and she was spreading the top sheet across the bed. It took him a moment to realize that she was still naked, the small light and the shadows emphasizing how lean she was, a small softness at her stomach accentuating her sensuality.

She paused, looking at him. Her eyes conveyed nothing.

"Feel better?"

"A new man," he said.

She lifted a corner of the sheet and slid into bed, the sheet serving only to outline her form, nipples poking against the sheet.

He walked awkwardly to the bed, aware that she was looking critically at the evidence of his erection beneath the towel. Another first, he thought. Never before had he felt awkward about his body around a woman.

He reached out and turned off the light.

"You can keep the light on, if you want."

"That's okay. I don't like to fall asleep with it on."

He climbed into bed, the towel still around his waist, feeling a fool, but unable to let it drop to the floor.

"Are you always this shy?" she asked.

"I don't know. This is my first time. Please be gentle with me."

She chuckled.

"Well, it's my first time with you."

Her hand grasping the towel at his waist paused.

"No games," she said. "That's all I ask. Okay?"

He pulled the towel from his waist and tossed it out into the room. Somewhere in the house, he heard a door slam, and the drum of running feet. A sliding door banged open, and from out in the yard somewhere he heard a scream. Barney shouted something. Distant laughter.

"Special Forces meets Snow Slut," he said. "We'll call their offspring Yeti."

"Um-huh," she said, and her arms were around him, their bodies sliding against each other, twining and untwining in a sinuous dance, her breath smelling of sex, groaning, as she rubbed him against her, her lips pressed so tight against his that he was afraid he might be bruising her. And then he was inside and above her, looking down, unable to see her eyes in the dark, but feeling them, as, for the rest of the night, until first light, they lost themselves in each other, and finally, when she slid out of bed to take a shower and hurry off to the bakery, he fell asleep to the sound of the shower.

For the first time in more than a decade, he slept a dreamless sleep, a black comfortable nothingness.

He opened his eyes, and rolled over, the sheet twined around his lower body and legs. Sam was sitting cross-legged at the foot of the bed, watching him.

"Hey, Sam. What's up, man?"

"Who are you?" Sam asked.

"I'm Joe Big. We've met."

"My grandmother wants to know."

"What do you mean?"

"You have a super bad scar."

"I do, indeed."

"My grandma says my mother doesn't know who you really are."

"You talked to your grandmother?"

Sam nodded. "She calls every day."

"Is that a good thing?"

He shrugged. "Sure. She's fun."

"Well, I don't know what to tell you. I am who I am."

Sam frowned. "I told her you were a warrior, because that's what Mr. Barney said you were."

Joe laughed. "Mr. Barney, huh? And what did Grandma say to that?"

"She said, Oh, My God, and then she said something in Vietnamese. I don't understand Vietnamese. I don't think it was good, though."

Joe Big sat up and swung his legs over the side of the bed, scrubbing his face with his hands. He looked at Sam. "The truth is, I don't know who I am."

Sam cocked his head to the side.

"Can you live with that, Sam?"

Sam climbed off the bed. At the door he turned and looked back. "Mom said to come down to the bakery and have breakfast when you woked up."

"How about Barney and Mickey?"

"They left in Mr. Barney's car. Mickey said you could drive hers."

"Hey, Sam."

"Yeah?"

"Who are you?"

Sam frowned. "I'm Sam."

"Lucky you, huh?"

Sam stared at him for a moment. He grinned.

"Yeah," he said.

23
Head 'em up, Move 'em out

"Well, that was certainly domestic," Barney said.

"She slept in Sam's room last night."

They were standing at the shoreline behind the bakery. Seagulls clustered noisy around the dumpster.

Barney glanced at Joe Big. "All night?"

Joe Big was silent.

"Uh-huh. That's what I thought."

"We're supposed to hook up with them again tonight," Joe Big said.

"Is there a problem with that?"

"Well . . . yeah. Those guys are mercs, man. They might as well have neon signs advertising that fact on their foreheads. They're former Green Beret or Army Ranger or Navy SEAL . . . Well, it doesn't matter what they used to be. It only matters that they have an interest in us. And if they have an interest in us, then they have an interest in anyone around us. As far as Mei and Sam and Mickey are concerned, we are toxic right now."

"Don't you think that horse is already out the gate?"

"I don't think so. If we leave right now, then it was only a one-night stand. There's no reason not to give them a pass."

"Is that all it was?'

"All what was?"

"A one-night stand?"

Joe Big gave him a look.

Barney grinned. "I guess you wouldn't be talking like this if that's all it was, huh?"

"Let's stick to business for once, okay?"

"Absolutely."

"What were you two doing, anyway? Running around outside, yelling and screaming."

"She bet me I couldn't find her in the forest in the dark. She said she'd met former Green Beenies before, and all that Special Forces stuff is—quote—horse pucky. So while she was hiding in the trees, I went to the garage and dug out that nifty little night-vision scope you got when you were in Tajikistan. It was funny as hell. She'd squeal like a piglet every time I'd grab her in the dark."

"Did she ever figure it out?"

"No way. She thinks I'm superman or something. You ought to try it sometime. It's kind of kinky, when she doesn't know you're there, and you can see everything she's doing, even when—"

"Thank you. That's probably more information than I need." Joe Big looked at him. "I hope you're not getting all—"

"Serious about her? No chance, man. She lives life the way I imagine she snowboards. And she's been known to jump off cliffs when she snowboards. Plus, she's as neurotic as it gets. She took a dump and had to tell me what a great dump it was. A single turd the size of a submarine—"

"Jeezus, Barney! Do you mind?"

"Sorry, man. You brought it up. She's fun. I'm not on the rebound, if that's what you're worried about."

Joe Big stared pensive at the snow-capped mountains on the other side of the lake.

"We don't know why Pick let the Redhead beat on Brianna," he said. "But I think we both agree that that is exactly what he did—what Pick did, I mean. We know they are lying about being drug dealers. The Sheriff's deputy said they are security for a high-tech company in Kalispell. We don't know if their interest in us is tied to me beating on the Redhead, or if it has to do with them knowing we are cops, or if it is both, or if it has to do with something else that we don't know about. Does that pretty much sum it up?"

"Don't forget Harold."

"Harold is too much of a coincidence to be a coincidence. Nevertheless, he still feels like a coincidence."

"Well, break it down some more, then," Barney said. "Harold was there to ID us. There is no other reason I can think of for him being there. Pick already knew us—"

"But he didn't know us in the context of the computer chips," Joe Big said.

"That's right. The car is what connected us to Harold."

"The car?"

"My guess is that they were talking about you trashing the Redhead, and they had decided to do something about it, and about the time they were ready to head out, Harold heard them talking about the car—because they were going to find us by finding the car—and he said, 'Hey, I think I know those guys,' and they loaded him in the car, and brought him along. That's the coincidence part you were talking about."

Joe Big thought about it for a moment. "I could see Harold hanging around them, that's for sure. All their talk about guns and tactics, shit like that."

"Well, you know Harold better than I do. I spent most of the time with that big motherfucker."

"That was because you are a Bible-Belt, Church-Going Whitey, and I am a Heathen Indian."

Barney shrugged. "Whatever works, man. You saved our bacon with those Latino guys in Spokane."

"I'm kidding," Joe Big said. "Patrick and I didn't like each other from the get-go. Race and religion were excuses, that's all."

"So you think maybe Harold is a way in?"

"Maybe. He's some kind of computer genius. According to his file, the company he works for is in Columbia Falls, not Kalispell, but they are probably one and the same. They make real-time control units for surveillance and weapons drones, that kind of stuff."

Barney frowned. "You're saying Harold works for a company that supplies hardware and software to the U.S. Military? How did I miss that?"

"You weren't at the briefing. You were down in Wyoming working that big meth deal that you put together before the Sheriff sent us to the Feds. My bad, man. I assumed you got the same brief I got."

"All I got was a 'happy to have you with us' from Quinn, and a cup of coffee from Mrs. W. The rest I picked up from you when we were plotting how to 'accidentally' meet Patrick and Company."

"Well, Harold is basically a thirty-something wannabe gang villain who, in real life, is a computer nerd. In his free time, he likes to talk about guns and women and obscure Marvel comic book characters. Actually, he's kind of a fun guy. Smart and funny, when he forgets to pose."

"Does he have any politics?"

"I don't think so. He's one of those people who are super-smart at one thing, and weird and out of sync about everything else. He's not a bad guy. I mean, he could be, he's that different. But like I said, he's kind of fun to be around. He doesn't seem to have much trouble finding women."

"Well, he sure seemed to get off on what they did to us," Barney said.

"It was one of his comic books come to life. He doesn't understand what's at stake."

Barney was silent.

"Don't get me wrong," Joe Big said. "If they ended up killing someone, he would probably get off on it. That's one of the reasons why he's into the L.A. Chicano Villain thing." He shook his head. "The man has a whole closet full of Zoot suits. Real expensive retro stuff. But he doesn't have the *cojones* to wear any of it in public. That's Harold, man."

"It's time to pay Harold a visit," Barney said.

He bent and picked up a rock from the edge of the beach, and threw it at the seagulls gathered around the dumpster. The rock clanged against the dumpster and the gulls took wing in a cacophony of screeching, most going only twenty or thirty yards out into the grass, and then waddling back toward the dumpsters. "Do we know where he lives?"

"Columbia Falls. I've got the address in the car."

"So . . . what?" Barney said. "We just get in the car and drive away?"

"It would help if they were a little pissed off, don't you think? In case anyone talks to them. Mei is smart enough and been around enough to put two and two together. Once she thinks about it, she'll know we're up to something."

"I don't know, man. That's asking a lot."

"Either way, it's for their own good."

Barney yawned, and stretched, hands behind his head, rotating the trunk of his body from side to side. He dropped his hands to his sides and turned and began walking toward the car. "Head 'em up, move 'em out, then," he said. "You drive. I need a nap, if we're going to go save the world."

Joe Big took a last look around, at the lake and the mountains, the stand of aspens and the gaggle of seagulls. There was a little sign over the door to the Bakery that said simply, 'Spooky's'.

He shook his head, and headed for the car.

Another one of those choices, he thought. The ultimate trickster was man himself. And he was about to prove it. *Naapi* was laughing his ass off.

He climbed into the driver's seat, and put on his seat belt.

"Spookaay," Barney sang, as they came around the building and onto the highway. "Spooky little girl like you . . ."

"Go to sleep," Joe Big said.

24
No Rules, Part Deux

The neighborhood was a blue-collar neighborhood, most of the houses built shortly after World War Two. The original houses had been small wood-frame structures with single-car garages built to house young veterans with new families. But those people were long gone, most of their children migrated to places that offered better jobs. Over the years, many of the houses had been renovated or added on to or simply torn down to build larger homes.

The town had never gotten around to sidewalks, at least not in this section, and lawns grew to the street. Huge old spruce and pine dominated some of the yards.

Lilac bushes enclosed Harold's house at the front and on the west. The lilacs were at least ten feet high, fat and untrimmed. The house to the east had a neatly trimmed lilac hedge tall enough to block the view of Harold's house. To the west, on the other side of Harold's lilacs, an empty weed-infested corner lot contained a rusty bicycle and a mound of black, torn-open lawn bags, leaves spilling from the bags. The mound of bags was about ten meters from the edge of Harold's property.

The house itself was a small post-war house with new porch, new shingles, new windows, new cream-colored siding. The garage had been painted but still had the original wood garage door with single-pane windows. New asphalt driveway. Large concrete pad between garage and house and driveway. No cars in evidence.

Joe Big backed the Subaru onto the concrete pad, out of sight behind the lilac bushes. He shut the engine off, and they climbed out. Barney pointed to the security alarm decals on the windows.

"I'll go to the front," Joe Big said.

"Okay."

Joe Big walked up the steps, onto the small covered porch. He pulled open the screen door, and with his fist banged on the door. "Sheriff's Department," he said in a loud voice. "Open up, Dickhead."

At the rear of the house a large deck made with planks of recycled plastic ran the entire width of the house, an expensive-looking stainless steel barbecue grill at the far end. Five redwood chairs with floral-cloth cushions and a matching table with folded umbrella sat in the middle of the deck.

Barney picked up one of the chairs, and when Joe Big shouted, "Is anyone home?" Barney yelled, "Come in," and threw the chair through the French doors that opened onto the patio.

He waited for Joe Big to come running around the corner, and then stepped through the shattered doors, his Glock holstered. Inside, the old kitchen had been remodeled, real tile on the floor, stainless steel appliances, counters cluttered with boxes and books and papers. The floor was clean, the sink empty of dishes. Harold stood in the entrance to the hallway, baggy pants and extra-large light-blue shirt that looked a little like the shirt Barney had worn in Whitefish. A 50s bowling shirt, Barney thought. Not bad. The man had style. He shouldered past Harold. Harold was fumbling with a semi-automatic pistol of some sort.

"Here. Let me help you with that," Joe Big said, and took the pistol from his trembling hands. "It's got an ambidextrous safety." He held the pistol in front of Harold's wide-eyed, ashen face. "See. Here and here. All you have to do is hold the grips like this, and reach up with your thumb and click the safety off. Of course, you should first check to see that a round has been chambered." With his left hand he worked the slide. "Jeez, Harold. You didn't even have a round in it."

He pressed the barrel into Harold's forehead, pinning his head against the hallway wall. "You understand how it works now, bro?"

Harold's mouth open and closed. His eyes strained cross-eyed to see the end of the barrel pressed into his forehead. The acid reek of urine filled the hallway.

Joe Big safed the pistol, and stuck it in his belt at the small of his back. He shook his head in mock consternation. "Harold, Harold, Harold."

"Check this out," Barney called from the living room.

"Anyone else here with you, Harold?" Joe Big asked.

Harold shook his head.

"Let's go say hi to Barney, then." He shoved Harold toward the living room.

Dark brown, floor-length curtains covered the living room windows. The room was lit by large widescreen computer screens on three large and two smaller tables arranged in a horseshoe that took up nearly the entire living room. The smaller tables made forty-five degree angles at the corners. There were at least eight screens and all were running either pictures or programs. A large comfortable-looking captain's chair sat in the middle of the polished oak floor, swiveled toward them. It was one of those chairs with a sound system built into it. A white leather couch was placed behind the opening in the horseshoe, a glass coffee table piled with books and manuals in front of it.

The small dining room to the left of the front door was cluttered with expensive-looking bicycles and bicycle parts—mountain bikes and racing bikes both. Silver surround-sound speakers inhabited the upper corners of the living room.

"Whoa. What's this?" Barney said.

One of the large screens, a thin LCD or plasma, was split into eight images: the front of the house; the back of the house; both sides of the house; the alley as seen from the house; the street in front as seen from the house; the room they were in, Barney standing in front of the computers; and the kitchen, the deck chair lying on its side in the middle of the floor, the French doors blown open. Barney waved. The image on the screen waved back.

He looked up at a surround-sound speaker in the corner. A small, molded, black plastic mount with a tiny lens, about the diameter of a 9mm shell, was on top the speaker.

"What's this flashing icon mean?" he asked Harold.

"It's, uh, it's a feed that goes to the security office at the company I work for."

"You sent an alarm?"

"When you threw a chair through the doors, the computer automatically sent it."

Barney wrinkled his nose, and sniffed. "Harold, did you piss your pants?"

Harold's face turned beet-red. His eyes darted to the camera.

Barney looked up at the lens. "Hey, there, whoever you are. Harold pissed his pants."

He walked around the tables to the corner, and reached up, and with both hands pulled the speaker off the wall and dropped it to the floor. With his heel he kicked the molded plastic holder and camera off the top of the speaker, and stomped on it. The plastic shattered, but the camera itself showed no inclination to even dent.

He dug inside his pant pocket and pulled out a small knife and thumbed it open, and bent down and cut the wires at the back of the camera.

The image of pieces of black plastic and Barney's foot on polished oak floor went black.

"Got it," Joe Big said.

"Who was watching us?" Barney asked Harold.

Joe Big pulled Harold's pistol from his belt, and held it up for Harold to see.

"Why are you doing this? What do you want?"

"We want to know who was watching us," Barney said.

Joe Big smacked Harold across the side of the head with the barrel of the pistol.

Harold reached his hand to the side of his head. He looked at the blood on his fingers. "I'm bleed—"

Joe Big hit him again.

"Okay, okay! Stop it! The feed goes to Company security."

"Not the Sheriff's Office or the Police Department?"

Harold shook his head. "I programmed the system myself."

"Who responds?" Joe Big asked.

"Company security."

"What's normal response time?" Barney asked.

Harold brightened. He smiled. "Fifteen minutes max, unless someone is already nearby. Most of the sensitive people are required to live within a ten-mile radius of the Company campus. You're fucked, dude."

"Campus?" Joe Big asked. "What campus?"

"Time to go," Barney said.

Joe Big again put Harold's gun in his belt at the small of his back, and shoved Harold face first against the wall. He pulled Harold's wrist behind his back.

Barney handed him a set of handcuffs, and Joe Big handcuffed Harold. He grabbed him by the ear and pulled him stumbling down the hall, through the kitchen, their feet crunching through broken glass, and guided him out the broken doors.

Barney passed them and went ahead to open the back of the Subaru. He rummaged in one of the duffels, and produced a long white plastic tie.

"Get in," Joe Big said. He pushed Harold's head down below the opening, and shoved him forward, face down on the duffel bags and packs and sleeping bags. Harold squirmed, unable to go further into the car with his hands behind his back.

Barney opened the rear passenger door, and leaned inside and grabbed Harold under the armpits, and pulled. Joe Big lifted Harold by the back of his belt and his pants behind one knee and threw him the rest of the way inside.

"Oww," Harold said. "Where are you taking me? You can't do this!"

"Shut up," Barney said.

Joe Big wrapped the white tie around Harold's ankles and pulled it closed, the tie making a sound like a zipper closing.

Harold screamed—a piercing girlish scream.

Barney hit him three times in the side of the mouth and nose, short, chopping punches, not hard enough to do damage, but hard enough to make him stop screaming.

"If you make another sound, one fucking word, I'm going to wrap your head with duct tape. You got that?'

"Ye—"

Barney hit him again. "You made a sound. Do not make another sound. Nod if you understand?"

Harold nodded, his eyes wide, white showing around his pupils.

Joe Big unfolded a small blue tarp, and pushed one end toward Barney.

Barney pulled the tarp inside, covering Harold, and tucked it in behind the front seats.

Joe Big picked up Harold's legs and wedged the remainder of the tarp under his feet. He forced Harold's legs to bend at the knee, and then slammed the hatch shut, and went to the passenger side and climbed in.

Barney started the car.

"Where do you want to kill him?" Joe Big asked.

"I dunno," Barney said. "Take him into the mountains I guess. Make the grizzlies happy."

"No," Harold said. His voice was muffled by the tarp. "I didn't do anything. It wasn't my—"

Joe Big reached back and slapped the bulge that was Harold's head under the tarp.

"Time to die, Homey. Don't be a baby; you knew we'd be around."

Barney looked at him, one eyebrow raised.

"Blade Runner," Joe Big said. "I love that movie."

Barney shook his head, and put the car in gear.

"Do you know that movie, Harold?" Joe Big asked, as they motored slowly down the street. "Blade Runner."

"One of m-my favorite movies," Harold said.

"Remember the part where that big blond motherfucker—the Replicant leader—sticks his thumbs into his creator's eyeballs and crushes his skull?"

They could hear Harold mumbling to himself.

"I always wanted to stick my thumbs into someone's eyeballs," Joe Big said. "Soon as I saw that scene, I said to myself, Self, you got to do that someday."

"*Hel-lo*," Barney said, as a dark-gray Chrysler 300 did a high-speed drift around the corner, blue law enforcement lights strobing in the grill, two men in black in the front and two in the back. Behind the Chrysler was the silver EVO.

Barney jerked the Subaru to the side to get out of the way. "How rude."

Joe Big waved at Pick and the Redhead, as they tore past in the EVO.

"Damn, Harold," Barney said, as he stepped on the gas, headed for the highway three blocks ahead. "You must be some important dude to warrant that kind of response."

"Y-y-you shouldn't have killed James," Harold said.

Joe Big and Barney looked at each other.

"How did we kill James?" Barney asked.

"Y-y-you know."

"Refresh our memory," Joe Big said.

"An arrow. Y-y-you shot an arrow all the way through his body."

"The arrows," Joe Big said. "I forgot about the fucking arrows."

"We didn't kill anyone," Barney said. "And if we had it sure wouldn't have been with an arrow."

"Th-they think one of you did. P-probably Big."

"You Injuns and your bow and arrows," Barney said to Joe Big. "What's wrong with you, anyway?"

"Is this when they chased me down the mountain?" Joe Big asked.

"I th-think so."

They looked at each other.

"Bamboozled again," Barney said.

"I told you, man. You guys just don't get it, when it comes to her."

"Do now," Barney said. "Haar they come, pilgrim." He checked to see that Joe Big had his seat belt on.

"We are duly sworn Sheriff's deputies, and we have just made an arrest," Joe Big said.

"F-for what? I d-didn't do anything?"

Joe Big laughed. "Assaulting two undercover police officers in pursuit of their duties, trafficking in stolen computer chips that are supposed to include secret technology—I doubt one page will hold all the charges you face, Homey."

Harold was silent.

"But lucky for you," Joe Big said. "We are prepared to spare the taxpayers the needless expense of prosecuting and incarcerating you."

"W-what do you mean?"

"We want to know everything . . . What is he doing?" he asked Barney.

The EVO had come up behind them, and then dropped back nearly half a block.

The dark-gray Chrysler 300 passed the EVO, and came storming up on their bumper.

'Oh," Joe Big said.

"The front passenger has an M16 or an M4," Barney said.

"I see that."

A siren went off behind them, an obnoxious whoop-whoop-whoop, and Barney jerked the Subaru to the side to prevent the Chrysler from coming up next to them.

"Long barrel out the back window," Joe Big said. "These guys aren't fucking around."

"Better call for backup," Barney said. "If they've got a radio or a scanner it'll pick up the officers-need-help, when dispatch puts it out."

"Doing it. Don't let them pass."

"No shit," Barney said, swerving the Subaru back and forth in front of the Chrysler.

"He's going to ram you."

"No, he's not." Barney downshifted and the Subaru easily accelerated away from the dark-gray car. He hit the brakes, and the Chrysler decelerated back away from them, the EVO dodging out into oncoming traffic to avoid it.

Barney snickered.

"Yeah. Hello," Joe Big said. "I am a Montana Sheriff's deputy taking part in an undercover drug operation in Columbia Falls. Just listen, please. We have arrested a key suspect, and are now being pursued by members of his crew. We are on Highway 2, headed east out of C-Falls. We will be turning toward Bigfork. Request that you roll units in our direction. The bad guys have automatic weapons."

He was silent for a moment, watching in the side mirror as the dark-gray car again came up behind, this time holding a distance of about twenty meters. The siren had shut off, but the grill lights were still on.

"She says no units on this side of the county," he said. "Big accident on the other side of Kalispell, and a possible hostage situation near Kila. What? Okay." He glanced at Barney. "Highway Patrol rolling from West Glacier, a Sheriff's Deputy coming from near Finley Point. What? Say again. Yeah. Yeah. That's us in the little blue wagon. No the guys behind us are *not* law enforcement officers . . ." He was silent, listening. "Look, lady. I don't give a fuck what they say. I don't care if they have been deputized by your Sheriff's Department. They have machine guns and they want to shoot us and we are not under any circumstances going to stop for them. What? Of course, we are armed." He shook his head, and made a circling motion with his finger next to his ear. Barney was watching the mirrors more than the road in front of them, jinking the car back and forth, accelerating hard to keep the Chrysler from rear ending them, and then slowing back down. He could see the passenger talking into a cell phone.

"Let me speak to the supervisor," Joe Big said. "You are the supervisor. And your name is?"

He turned to Barney. "We're on our own," he said. "What? Listen, lady. You best be rolling units to help the people behind us, then. Because we are going to start shooting if they don't *back the fuck off*." He squinted at the side mirror. "Next time you move over to block the Chrysler, the EVO is going to try to take us on the side." He snapped the cell phone shut. "Hang on Harold."

"Traffic coming," Barney said. "Here we go."

He downshifted into second, brought the rpm's up, waited for the oncoming traffic to draw even—a string of five cars—and floored it, the revs going past redline in a matter of seconds. Without lifting his foot from the gas, he shifted into third, the revs a little slower this time, the speedometer winding past one hundred. At redline, he shifted into fourth, holding the speed steady at one-twenty-five, houses and barns, trees and fences blurring past on both sides of the highway. The shoulders were almost non-existent, the highway barely wide enough to accommodate one lane of traffic in both directions.

He downshifted, using compression to slow, as they approached a string of cars in their lane.

He touched the gas, and pulled two cars, dodging into the gap between the two cars he'd passed and the next car, standing on the brakes, as a chip truck blasted past the other way, headlights flashing, the driver giving them the finger. He floored the accelerator and the Subaru jumped around the cars in front, Joe Big smacking his head against the passenger door glass.

"Ouch. Shit."

Harold was silent.

A brown pickup truck flashed past on the left, horn barely heard.

Barney shifted, and again held the speed at one twenty five.

Joe Big looked in the side mirror. "Objects may look smaller," he said, as the traffic behind them receded at an alarming rate. He turned to look behind.

"The Chrysler is down in the barrow pit," he said. "Dust and shit everywhere. I don't see the EVO. Whoops! The Chrysler is back up on the highway. It's all over the place. Almost hit a pickup. The EVO has dropped back to get out of the way." He shifted in his seat to better see out the rear window. "How you doin', Homey? Okay, they are back in front of traffic." He turned forward. They were approaching a long sweeping S-curve. "These guys want us bad enough to risk losing their badges—if they really have badges," he said to Barney.

Barney's lips were compressed tight. A muscle jumped on the side of his jaw. "Or they want Harold." He let off the gas slightly, and then halfway into the first curve put his foot in it, the centrifugal force gluing them to the road. He let off as they came out of the first turn, and then again stepped on it as they went into the apex of the second curve, the g-forces again pressing Joe Big into the seat.

"My stomach doesn't like this," he said.

Harold was thrashing around, the tarp making a crinkling sound.

"Hey, Homey," Joe Big said. "Have you ever wondered what a bug feels like when it hits the windshield?"

Harold quit moving.

"If we crash, you're going to find out." Joe Big laughed.

Barney shifted into fifth, the speedometer needle momentarily going past the 140 mph limit on the speedometer. He braked hard, and down shifted, and pulled out into the other lane as they approached a logging truck pulling a tandem trailer piled too high with logs. As they glided even with the truck cab, he again floored the accelerator, the Subaru squirting ahead. Plenty of room, as he guided the Subaru smoothly back into the right-hand lane, a series of seven cars and pickup trucks arriving and departing in the other lane. Now you see them, now you don't, Joe Big thought. He figured the closing speed was about two hundred miles per hour. They wouldn't even find pieces, he thought. They'd explode on impact.

"My stomach really doesn't like this," he said.

"Take a Tums." Barney slowed to one twenty. The road ahead was long and straight but with gentle hills and swales. The Subaru hit a swale invisible in the gray-black ribbon of highway, and they were airborne for what to Joe Big seemed a seriously disconcerting length of time—a freeze frame that left his stomach hollow.

Harold was praying out loud. Hail Mary's, it sounded like.

The car came back to earth with only the smallest of jars, and Barney smiled, and the car hit another swale and they were airborne again, this time longer, and when they came back to earth the car squashed hard onto the pavement, exhaust scraping and throwing sparks out the back end.

"Sonofa*bitch!*" Joe Big yelled.

Barney braked, and downshifted, and they slowed to eighty-five, a series of three swales coming up, the car going up and down, up and down, up and down, as if it were on rails. Joe Big felt his stomach go light every time they came off the up, the seat belt tight against his waist.

Barney again floored the accelerator, and they went up a small hill, onto a long, flat stretch leading to the junction of another highway. They could see miniature cars moving perpendicular to the road they were on.

Joe Big looked behind. The Chrysler and the EVO were not in sight—stuck behind the logging truck they had passed.

There was a large gas station and convenience store on the right side of the T intersection, a golf course on the left, a stop sign just past the gas station, empty fields on the other side of the T.

Barney stood on the brakes, the ABS chattering, and downshifted from fifth to second, and turned into the gas station, the Subaru drifting sideways, correcting the drift in time to blast at about forty-five miles per hour through the pumps. He made a hard right as they cleared the pumps and drove around behind the building. He backed into a space between two large dump trucks, the two trucks effectively hiding them from passing traffic on both highways.

He put the gearshift in neutral, and yanked up on the emergency brake, and they both jumped out.

Joe Big opened the back hatch, and pulled the tarp off Harold, and they both grabbed him by the legs and pulled him backwards, and then grabbed him by the arms and legs and picked him up and dropped him face down in the dirt and gravel.

Joe Big rolled him over. There was dried blood on the side of Harold's face from where he had hit him with the gun barrel. Harold's mouth was opening and closing like a fish landed on the shore, eyes big and white and not really seeing him. There was barf all over his expensive retro shirt, a big wet spot at his crotch, where he'd wet his pants when they were at the house.

"Damn, Harold," Joe Big said.

Barney knelt next to Harold and with his left hand grabbed him by the throat and pulled him upward. Harold choked, his eyes bulging even wider.

"Listen to us, asshole," Barney said, his voice calm and reasonable. He shook Harold's head. Harold's face was turning an ugly shade of red. "You only get one chance."

"Don't choke him out," Joe Big said.

"I'm not."

Harold arched his back, his knees pistoning up and down.

Barney released his hold on Harold's throat.

Harold gagged and coughed, trying to suck air into his lungs.

"Where are they?" Joe Big asked Barney. He peered underneath the dump truck at the highway.

"Maybe someone called them off," Barney said.

"Which way do you think they'll go?" Joe Big asked.

"Doesn't matter. We'll go the other way."

"What if they split up?"

Color was returning to Harold's face. He groaned.

"We can handle one car," Barney said.

"Why did Patrick want the computer modules?" Joe Big asked Harold.

Harold shook his head. "Not sure." His voice was a throaty rasp.

Barney reached out and put his hand on the side of one of the dump trucks for balance, and put his foot on Harold's throat.

"Something to do with his father," Harold rasped.

Barney removed his foot. He leaned over, staring down at Harold.

"I don't know," Harold said. "I really don't know. Patrick is on the Board of Directors of the Company I work for. His father owns it. We don't hang out much. If it wasn't for Tanya, I wouldn't see him at all."

"What about his father?"

"His father has a huge ranch on the other side of the mountains. Some of the suits hunt deer and elk over there. One of them said there is a big lab and machine shop and a testing range on the ranch."

"A testing range for what?"

Harold coughed and shook his head. "I don't know."

Barney put his foot on his throat.

"I really don't know." His voice was frantic. "The modules are used in smart bombs."

"Nukes?"

"No. No nukes. HITs mostly."

Joe Big turned toward Barney.

"High Impulse Thermobaric," Barney said. "Fuel-air explosives. What do you know about such things?" he asked Harold.

"I designed AI systems for drones at the last place I worked."

"Here they come," Joe Big said.

"If you are anywhere in Montana when we finish this, we are going to find you and fuck you up." Barney pressed down with his foot. "Do you believe me?"

Harold tried to nod. His eyes bulged.

Barney removed his foot from Harold's throat.

"Tell them we didn't have time to question you. Say it."

"Tell them you didn't question me."

Barney squatted down so he could see under the dump truck. The dark-gray Chrysler, silver EVO in tow, flashed past on the highway. Both cars braked hard, cutting the corner through the gas station, the same as Barney had done, reappearing in tandem behind and to their right on the highway to Kalispell.

"They think we're running for the Sheriff's Department or the Police Department in Kalispell," Barney said.

"That EVO sure sounds sweet," Joe Big said.

"Let's go," Barney said.

"What do you want to do with him?"

"Leave him. We'll call it in."

Joe Big slammed the hatch shut, and they got in. "I left the tarp," he said. "It's got barf all over it."

"We've got another."

Barney shifted into first, and released the emergency brake, and they accelerated out from between the dump trucks, around the other side of the building, and back out onto the highway.

At the Stop sign, he turned left, headed for Bigfork and the lake, accelerating the Subaru to eighty-five. A string of traffic was up ahead, four cars and a chip truck, another two cars in front of the chip truck.

A mile ahead a line of cars was coming toward them.

Barney accelerated to one hundred and passed the four cars and the chip truck, but instead of passing the entire string, he downshifted and eased in front of the chip truck, slowing to the speed of the cars in front.

"What are you doing?" Joe Big asked.

"They'll be monitoring Dispatch to hear if anyone is driving like a maniac on Highway 35. Lot of traffic between here and Bigfork. If I pass, I'll have to pass on the shoulder, and if I do that it'll only be a matter of time before someone calls nine-one-one and they know where we are."

"They're probably already turned around and headed back this way, anyway."

"Probably. But I don't want to push our luck any more than I have to. I've never driven this car that fast before."

Joe Big looked behind at the stuff in the back. He put his window down. "Harold threw up all over one of the duffels."

Barney pushed the buttons for the back windows, and air filled the inside of the car. Joe Big put his window back up. He flipped his cell phone open, and dialed 9-1-1.

"Yeah. It's me again. The cop who isn't a cop. We let a guy out at the junction of Thirty-five and the highway that goes to C-Falls. Behind the big gas station at the T. You know where I mean? Yeah. That's it. You better call and have someone from the store go out back and help him before somebody runs over him." He was silent for a moment. "Well, he's handcuffed and his ankles are tied, that's why. What the fuck is wrong with you people? Just make the call, okay?" He snapped the phone closed. "Man! They make it sound like it's them who have to get off their fat asses and do something."

Barney smiled.

They were silent for a while, watching the traffic in front of them. All Joe Big could see in the side mirror was the front of the chip truck behind them. The driver was talking on his cell phone.

"I think that truck driver is talking about us."

"No doubt," Barney said. "All the chip trucks talk to each other. That guy who flipped us off seemed seriously exercised."

"And people wonder what's wrong with the world these days" Joe Big said.

"Assuming we've shaken those guys, what's next on the agenda?"

Joe Big was silent for a moment. "Talking to Quinn isn't going to do us much good. She was probably covering her ass, more than anything else. I reckon in the world she inhabits it might be a little hard to explain how she came to kill someone with an arrow."

"Maybe we should have kept Harold with us for awhile?"

“No need,” Joe Big said. “I vote we go find Patrick and ask him in person.”

“What about the woman?”

“Tanya?”

“Yeah.”

Joe Big snorted.

“Don’t underestimate her,” Barney said. “You never know when a woman like that might know something she’s not supposed to know. Just because she’s bark-at-the-moon political, doesn’t mean she’s stupid.”

The line of traffic they were in went in train around a long, gentle curve to the right, and Joe Big could see a mile or so back behind the last car in line. “They’re baaack,” he said. “About a mile, and closing fast. I bet they’re monitoring the truck drivers.”

“Well, shit,” Barney said, and downshifted, and steered the Subaru onto the wide, paved shoulder, and accelerated around the cars in front, a cloud of dust and road debris billowing behind, both cars honking and the air horn on the truck bleating as they slid back into the driving lane.

“Speaking of losing badges,” Joe Big said.

Barney glanced at him. “I don’t know about you, but I’ve about had it with badges.”

“Badges? *Badges?* We don’t need no stinking badges!”

Barney smiled. “These guys aren’t terrorists,” he said, shifting into fifth. There’s no way people that proud to have been in the American military could be terrorists. If we hadn’t become cops, we might be doing exactly what they are doing—working for a private security company that pays a hell of a lot more than what we are being paid.”

“Speak for yourself, dude. There is no way, no how, I could be a fucking merc. Everyone hated those guys. *All* the Iraqis and Afghanis hated them. *We* hated them. They cause way more problems than they ever solve. And I don’t mean only the Americans. Fucking Brits by the thousands. Ex-SAS and SBS and Paras with their noses so far in the air you couldn’t talk to them without getting a nosebleed. Poles and Romanians and Colombians and those really mean bastards from Chile—”

“I’m just saying, it might be time to turn our badges in for another line of work,” Barney said. “Watch for deer, will you.”

There was no one in front of them, and he accelerated the car to one-thirty, and held it there for the next seven or eight miles, slowing to fifty and going through a red light at a junction with another highway, Joe Big silent because he didn't want to upset Barney's concentration.

There was another chip truck and a line of six or seven cars going through the tight little defile that led into the outskirts of Bigfork.

"They're coming," Joe Big said. "That Chrysler must have a serious engine in it."

"It's one of the big Hemi's. I can't get around these people for a half-mile or so. There's a suicide turn lane up ahead. I'll pull as much traffic as I can, then."

The chip truck and the cars slowed to thirty-five as they came through the rocky defile. On the right was a VFW Club perched on a hillside, cars and pickups and Harleys parked to one side, and then it was like coming into the outskirts of any small town in Montana, businesses lining both sides of the highway.

Barney downshifted to second and as soon as the road widened pulled into the suicide lane and began passing traffic.

A car edged into the middle ahead of them, its turn signal on, and Barney squeezed the Subaru between it and the car in the driving lane. Joe Big thought he heard a tick as they passed behind the car that was turning.

The chip truck driver was not happy, but once past the chip truck, they accelerated down the long hill toward the lake. It was a spectacular view, the lake stretching more than twenty miles to the south, the Mission mountains along the east side.

A rustic-looking mall and a Dairy Queen went by on the left. Ahead was a stoplight, cars and trucks stopped, traffic crossing in front of them. Barney stood on the brakes, the ABS again chattering, and slowed to thirty, picking his way through the intersection, cars swerving around them, or braking to a halt.

"The Chrysler is right behind us," Joe Big said. "I see at least two long barrels. Someone made a decision, man. We just entered another universe." He put Harold's pistol, a 9mm Berretta, in the glove box, and pulled his SIG from the pancake holster on his hip.

Barney floored the Subaru, going through the gears, as they flashed down a gently curving hill, across a small bridge, and up the hill on the other side. Something pinged into the back end. The side mirror on Barney's side shattered.

"Hang on," Barney said, and cranked the steering wheel hard left and at the same time pulled up hard on the emergency brake handle.

Joe Big felt his shoulder bounce off the side window. The Subaru drifted sideways. Barney released the brake, and they rocketed up an empty highway that joined the highway they had been on at another T intersection. He had a vague impression of a white car nearly broadsiding them.

"They missed the corner," he said. "The EVO is coming."

"Wouldn't want it any other way," Barney muttered, keeping the revs up as they took corners at nearly four times the speed the corners were designed for.

On the left was a tight valley. The Swan River, a white-water river, coursed through it, dumping into the lake at the bridge they had crossed just before the T. The steep mountainside on their right was heavy with yellow and gold leaves.

"We need to get away from civilians," Joe Big said. "There's a road coming up on the right. We were on it that time we were supposed to be making a buy from those rednecks, but went grouse hunting instead."

"I remember it." Barney downshifted, using the emergency brake to slow so the brake lights wouldn't come on, the car decelerating to about thirty-five, and, as the valley opened into a much larger valley, turned onto an unmarked gravel road, the Swan Mountains rugged and snowcapped on the other side of the valley.

Heavy washboards and potholes made both of them clench their teeth. Barney ignored the road surface and accelerated the Subaru. Behind was a huge, billowing cloud of dust. Rocks pinged off the undercarriage. The exhaust pipe and muffler made a heavy knocking noise beneath the car—no doubt loosened when they'd bottomed out on the highway, Joe Big thought.

On the right, the mountain was thick with gold and red and yellow bushes, tall pines beyond the bushes. The tight valley with the Swan River in the middle had marked the tail end of the Mission Mountains. They were now driving up the backside of the lowest portion of the Missions, the Swan Valley and Swan Lake on their left.

They glimpsed a scattering of houses set back from the road, SUVs and 4×4s parked out front, the plume of dust no doubt pissing off a lot of people.

The front tires hit hard into the leading edge of a cattleguard, throwing both of them against their seat belts.

"God *damn!*" Joe Big said.

"I hope we didn't break a tire or a wheel," Barney said.

They were silent for a long moment. "Feels okay," Barney said.

"Why are you slowing, then?"

"No way they can follow close in the dust that we are putting up. There's not much wind to blow it away, either. It'll be like driving in thick fog for the EVO. The Chrysler will have to drop way back."

The road turned steeper, a sign telling them to watch out for logging trucks.

"Switchbacks coming up," Barney said. He downshifted, bringing the revs up high, using the torque to drift around the first corner, the wheels clawing at the dirt and gravel, dust boiling off all four wheels, gravel pinging hard against the undercarriage and inside the wheel wells. The tires found purchase and the Subaru rocketed uphill, airborne for a few feet.

"Ohh, man," Joe Big said. "My stomach does not like this."

"Plastic bag on the floor behind my seat," Barney said. "From the stuff you bought at the truck stop."

Joe Big leaned over and reached behind the seat, his face smacking into the side of the seat, as Barney cranked the steering wheel hard to the left, drifting the car around the next switchback. His hand found plastic and he sat upright and opened the bag in front of his face and vomited.

"It sucks to be the passenger," Barney said.

What seemed to Joe Big like an interminable number of switchbacks later, the road came up onto a ridge, and he threw the plastic bag out the window into the road behind them.

Barney slowed for a corner. Immediately on the other side of the corner was an overgrown old logging road. He stopped the car and reversed onto the old road, running over small firs and bushes growing in the road.

He shut the car off, the exhaust ticking and popping loud in the sudden silence.

"They shot at us," he said.

"And unless they have a serious dislike for the side mirrors on a Subaru, they were trying their best to kill us," Joe Big said.

He felt pale and washed out, seasick. He pinched his nostrils shut and blew out hard through his nose, forcing his ears to pop.

"You okay?" Barney asked.

"Good to go."

"Well, if they are stupid enough to follow us up this mountain, let's go kill these motherfuckers."

"They think we are cops, and I was a Marine officer, is all."

"I hope you're right," Barney said, as they climbed out of the car. Joe Big opened the back hatch and pulled out a duffel and unzipped it.

"Do we really have to do this?" he asked.

"They're shooting at us, and they don't care where they are at when they shoot at us. And we're about out of places to run to that aren't full of civilians."

Barney came around the front of the car and Joe Big handed him an M4 with a standard military gunsight (ACOG) attached, and three twenty-round magazines.

"This is about as clean as it's going to get," Barney said. "It's just us and them up here."

Joe Big pulled out an M14, with a scope mounted, and three twenty-round magazines of 7.62 ammunition for himself.

He stuffed two of the magazines into the thigh pockets on his pants, and inserted the third into the rifle. He tossed the duffel in the back and closed the door, and began running for the other side of the road. He stopped in the middle of the road and, looking back the way they had come, turned toward Barney standing next to the car, and pointed down the road toward the hillside, and held up five fingers and shouted, "Fifty meters."

He turned and ran to the far end of the corner, and scrambled up over the berm, and slid under the tight little stand of young fir at the top.

Underneath the trees, the ground was bare of all but small rocks and pine needles. He chambered a round, and set the safety, and then, on his stomach, squirmed his way under the trees to the top of the berm.

He had an unrestricted field of fire for about two hundred meters straight down the road.

Barney came over the ridge, and Joe Big watched as he worked his way diagonally down a slope relatively clear of bushes and deadfall to a stand of very large larch that had been left by loggers. Barney took a knee behind one of the trees. He cocked the M4, and then looked toward him.

Barney stared at him for a long moment, and then gave a thumbs up, meaning that he couldn't see him under the trees.

A slight breeze coming over the ridge had dissipated the dust they had kicked up, pushing it into the trees below the road, making it look as if smoke from a ground fire was filtering through the tops of the trees.

He heard the distant sound of a high-revving engine fading in and out, as the EVO negotiated the switchbacks, the sound growing louder.

He put the stock into his shoulder, the sling wrapped around his left arm, pulling his arm tight and solid under the rifle, the magazine snug against his arm. He looked through the scope and with his knees and toes squirmed a little to the side so that the crosshairs could be moved easily the width of the road. With his trigger finger he pushed the safety off.

The engine noise grew louder, and then died as the EVO slowed before coming around the corner, wary of what might be on the other side. Still moving too fast, he thought, as the silver EVO came slow around the corner and then accelerated hard up the long open stretch of road.

He put the crosshairs on the driver. Took a breath and let half of it out. Waited for the EVO to come within fifty meters or so of where Barney was standing next to the larch. And fired three rounds into the driver and then three rounds into where the passenger should be, and then, as Barney put a magazine into the windows, another four rounds evenly spaced across the windshield.

The silver car drove up the embankment, continuing up the hillside until the front end on the passenger side impacted one of the big old larch, folding the hood up, the engine revving to a shrill pitch.

Barney ran crouched sidehill to the car, the M4 held to his face, and put most of another clip into the two figures in the front seats, and then turned and ran to the top of the little ridge and knelt next to a stand of fir and looked toward where Joe Big was hidden.

The engine began making a clanking, rattling sound, smoke sifting out from under the front end and out the wheel well, and abruptly quit.

It was silent save for the ringing in his ears. He could feel the smack of the stock against his shoulder and cheek. It had been a long time.

The M14 was a great old weapon, he thought.

He waited, his body completely still, blending as much as possible into the trees and the berm, keeping his head angled down as much as possible so that light would not reflect off his skin. The Chrysler shouldn't be too far behind, he thought. At least not in terms of time.

Barney pointed down toward the far corner, and eased into the stand of fir, his weapon pointed downhill.

The front end of the Chrysler edged around the corner, and Joe Big put two rounds through the windshield, knowing that the angle would probably keep the rounds away from anyone seated in the front, and then put the eight remaining rounds into the radiator and right front wheel, shredding the tire.

He ejected the magazine, hearing the measured cadence of Barney's M4 putting three round bursts into the area that the Chrysler had quickly retreated. He picked up the spare magazine lying on the berm and inserted it into the rifle, released the cocking lever, and then methodically fired the entire twenty rounds into the bushes at the edge of the road where he had last seen the Chrysler.

He picked up the first magazine and scrambled to his feet and forced his way through the firs, and ran down the berm, across the road to the Subaru. He opened the back hatch and threw his rifle in the back, and Barney threw his M4 in next to it. Barney took a road flare from a small wooden box under a duffel, and handed it to Joe Big.

"Throw this over next to the EVO—anyplace with good fuel."

Joe Big grabbed the road flare, and ran back along the ridge, and down to the EVO. He lit the flare with the striker, and sidearmed the flare under the front end of the EVO.

Running back to the Subaru, he heard the soft whump of gasoline exploding.

Barney had the Subaru rolling out onto the main road. Joe Big ran up beside the open passenger door and jumped inside. Barney slowly accelerated up the road, trying to raise as little dust as possible.

"We got any water?" Joe Big asked. They heard an explosion, and Barney stopped the car, and they turned to see a small dark cloud boil into the air over the ridge.

"I smelled gas so I threw it under the front end of the car," Joe Big said.

"Good thinking." Barney let out the clutch out and they slowly motored away, up through an alley in the forest, thick, impenetrable bushes on both sides of the road, most of the bushes bare of leaves at this altitude.

"There should be water in the cooler," Barney said. "Open me one, too, will you?"

Joe Big reached back and pulled a duffel away from the cooler wedged against the far passenger door, and flipped the top off the cooler, and reached inside and pulled out two bottles of Mountain Dew.

He unscrewed the lids from both bottles, and handed one to Barney.

Barney tipped the bottle up, and at the same time braked the car to a stop in the middle of the road.

Joe Big took a swig, and washed it around inside his mouth, tilted his head back and gargled. He leaned out the window and spit into the dust at the side of the road.

Barney finished the bottle, and belched and reached back to put the empty bottle on the floor behind his seat. He let out the clutch.

Joe Big took a long drink, and then put his head back against the headrest. Both of them looked drawn and worn out, their eyes hollow, the skin tight and oily on their foreheads and across their cheekbones.

"War," Joe Big muttered. "War all the fucking time. We can't seem to get away from it."

"Truer words you will never speak, my man."

"Even in my dreams," Joe Big said, and leaned forward and took another drink. "You want the rest of this?" he asked. "I'm thirsty, but not so thirsty I can handle a whole bottle of Dew."

Barney reached out his hand, and Joe Big handed him the bottle.

Barney tilted the bottle up and drained it, belched, and put it behind the seat along with the other bottle.

"I doubt we hit anyone in that Chrysler," he said. "Maybe nicked someone, if we're lucky. I bet they're already at the EVO."

"Well, we put their car out of commission, anyway."

"They're calling for reinforcements and a cleanup crew, as we speak," Barney said.

He increased the speed, but this branch of the road was much rougher, filled with old ruts and large potholes. "Which way?" he asked as they approached an intersection.

"I don't know. Follow the one that looks most traveled, I guess. There was a closed gate down at the bottom, about a quarter-mile after we turned off the highway. I bet this comes out there. The main road follows the top of the mountains all the way over to the Rez, and comes out somewhere on Highway 35, but it's probably gated, maybe in multiple places. They'll expect us to follow that road. Probably have someone waiting."

"Want to bet they've got a helicopter somewhere?" Barney asked.

"Nothing we can do about it now. We had to get away from civilians, the way they were shooting at us."

"Mercs, for sure," Barney said. "Used to doing any fucking thing they want."

"You think that's it?"

"Well, yeah. Don't you? I mean, what the fuck. A high-speed chase down a highway full of civilians? Shooting at us with automatic weapons? What did we do to deserve that?"

"Too many movies, maybe?"

"No way. These guys are the real deal," Barney said.

"Well, they were pretty stupid to charge up the road like that. Pick and the other guy, I mean."

"It was the redhead."

"I thought so when we first saw them, but then later on the highway, it didn't look like him," Joe Big said.

"It was him all right."

"Naapi," Joe Big said.

"What?"

"The *Niitsitapi* thought that men are the biggest tricksters of all."

"I don't get it."

"*Naapi* likes it most when men fool themselves. The last laugh is on you, kind of thing."

"How does all that apply to what we are doing?"

"Pick and the Redhead . . . I'm just guessing here, okay? I don't think they understood they were chasing two guys with our experience and training."

"You think they thought they were chasing two cops who had gotten in over their heads and were running for cover?"

"Well, how else to explain them blasting up the road like that. They slowed a little before they came around the corner, but not like they would have if they knew there might be a sniper waiting for them."

Barney was silent, thinking about it. "The bullets that took out the mirror and put holes in the back didn't come from the EVO."

"The EVO was behind the other car; it couldn't fire," Joe Big said. "But those guys in the Chrysler didn't try to light us up unless Pick said it was okay."

"So you're thinking maybe these guys spent too much time in The Suck, blasting down roads shooting at anyone or anything that looked even remotely suspicious. No worry about Iraqi law or American law or even the UCMJ. No rules, basically." He paused. "It's got to be more than that. These guys are pros, man. It doesn't matter how long they spent in the sand. This is America. There's no way they'd lose their cool like that. Would you?"

"What could it be then? We kidnapped Harold? For all they knew, we still had him. A couple of those rounds that went through the rear door would have hit him for sure if he'd still been in the back. You're missing the driver's side tail light, by the way, and there's a serious knick in the left rear tire."

"No wonder the people over there hate us," Barney said. "Can you imagine this shit happening on a daily basis?"

"I can now."

"Here's another idea," Barney said. "Harold thought it was you who put an arrow through one of the security guys."

Joe Big was silent for a moment. "I forgot about that. He did say that, though, didn't he? Payback time, is that what you're thinking?"

"Yeah. Damn, this road is really rough. I think you're right: we're headed down toward where we came in."

"Locked gate at the end, remember."

"We'll drive this thing through the forest, if we have to."

"Might be able to go cross country to one of the houses, go out a driveway. There were some fields and meadows on the valley side of the road."

"I expected a helicopter by now," Barney said.

"It's only been twenty minutes or so."

"Seems like half a day."

"Doesn't it always?"

The view to their right was of a long, thin lake, the steep slopes of the Swan Mountains beginning on the far side of the lake, tiny cars seen on the highway that wrapped around the far side.

Behind and to his right, Joe Big could see the valley stretching south for seventy miles or so, rugged snow-capped peaks on both sides of the valley. Far above, out over the lake, a tiny dot rode the wind—an osprey or an eagle.

"Really in the shit now," he said to the tiny dot.

"Patrick and the Psycho-phants was one thing," he said to Barney. "But this . . . I don't know what this is?"

The front end banged into a pothole, the skid plate that protected the oil pan scraping and gouging the road. "Don't do that!" Barney shouted.

"Not much farther," Joe Big said. "We're almost off the mountain."

They motored down a long smooth stretch bordered by tall larch and spruce and immature stands of cedar, the air damp and humid, the sides of the road thick with bushes growing out over the road. Branches scrapped and scratched and whipped against the side of the car.

Joe Big powered his window up, and Barney closed the back windows.

The bushes thinned and the road blended into a well-maintained gravel road, the forest on both sides recently logged. The mountainside receded to their left, and on both sides of the road it was open and park-like, dotted with trees that had not been logged.

To their left, Joe Big glimpsed a house and outbuildings.

"House to the left," he said.

"Let's see what the gate looks like before we drive through someone's yard," Barney said. "If we can get past the gate and onto the highway, we can drive over to the other side of the lake and find a place to hide until dark."

"Every cop on the planet is going to be watching for this car."

"Maybe. Maybe not."

"Should I call for help?"

"Call who?"

"I don't know. Quinn? The Sheriff? The Colonial Space Marines?"

"Better not," Barney said. "And anyway, we already tossed the cell phones, right?"

"All but the one-time phones, and I think one of them took a round."

"It's out in the open now," Barney said. "They'll know who we really are in a matter of hours, if not minutes. We were lucky. If Pick had taken the time to find out, it would have been different. We wouldn't have had a chance."

"One thing at a time until we can talk to Quinn," Joe Big said.

"Talk to her! Fuck that! Let's go shoot her. Then tell these assholes it's all her fault. Maybe then they'll leave us alone." Barney slowed the car, and stopped. "We're getting close," he said. "Why don't you get out and run ahead, in case someone is waiting at the gate?"

Joe Big climbed out and opened the back hatch, and took the M4 off the pile of duffels and equipment, and rummaged in a duffel for more loaded magazines. He put a magazine in each of his thigh pockets, and one in his left back pocket, and slapped a fresh magazine in the receiver.

He put the rifle on the roof, and bent back inside and removed the shotgun from the duffel. Barney handed back two boxes of shells from the glove compartment, and he loaded alternating slugs and double-ought into the shotgun, racked a round in the chamber, set the safety, and put in one more double-ought round.

He closed the back door, and put the shotgun, barrel down into the passenger-side footwell, and pushed the butt end toward Barney. Barney wedged it between the emergency brake and the passenger seat.

Joe Big closed the door, and took the M4 from the roof, chambered a round, made sure the safety was set, and then ran across the road, and into the forest. About fifty yards in, he turned and ran parallel to the road, toward the gate. The floor of the forest had been cleared by loggers, but there were still a lot of small mounds and bushes and shallow holes too wide to jump. He ran as best he could, trying to keep trees between him and where he thought the gate might be.

A half mile later he could see the highway embankment through spaces in the trees. He crouched and slowed to a walk, the M4 held to his cheek, swinging the rifle toward whatever he was looking at. Something flickered, and he pushed the safety off and looked through the scope. A whitetail ear. A deer was watching him. At least three or four more took shape near the one he'd spotted.

He lowered the rifle, and took a step toward them. They scattered in the direction of the gate, white flags bouncing through the forest.

He relaxed. They wouldn't run toward men.

He trotted toward where the gate should be, and halted at the top of a small embankment. The gate was a single solid metal pipe about eight inches in diameter, a sign announcing the road closure attached to the other side. The locked end was set into a heavy iron barrel assembly that made it difficult to get at the lock. The road was bermed on the other side of the gate, making it impossible to drive around the gate.

He ran down the road toward the blue Subaru coming toward him. He stopped and waited where the berm petered out, and with arm signals directed Barney off the road into the forest. The low-sprung Subaru scraped bottom, pushing through and over low-lying bushes and tiny new fir trees, engine revving as Barney forced it through small mounds of dirt overgrown with bushes.

Joe Big walked ahead, pulling up moss-covered rocks and old branches and throwing them to the side. Barney got out to help him move a fallen snag. Bark sloughing off stained their clothes orange.

Joe Big held up his hand. He could hear vehicles going by fast on the road they had come in on.

He motioned Barney to get in the car and head back toward the road.

Barney angled the Subaru down what was left of the embankment, onto the road. They were about fifty meters past the gate, and about another fifty meters from the main road.

Barney stopped the car, and climbed out and went around to the passenger side. He reached in the wheel well and tore the black plastic wheel well liner loose and threw it into the forest. The front bumper was cracked and broken in places, but was still hanging together. He shimmied on his back as far as he could under the car next to the driver's side front wheel, and pulled bushes and pieces of branches out of the suspension.

Joe Big did the same on the other side, and then climbed in, the M4 held barrel up between his legs.

Barney wiped his hands on the front of his sweatshirt. "Here goes nothing," he said, and put the car in gear, and quickly accelerated down the road, shifting into third as they hit the main road. He stopped at the highway to check for oncoming traffic, and then they were on the highway, Barney going through the gears, a visible vibration in the steering wheel, as they cruised at 70 through a 45 zone, past houses, roads intersecting the highway every quarter mile or so, past a convenience store in an opening in the thick forest, to another T intersection. He turned south onto the Swan Highway.

A few miles later, they were on the twisting, winding portion of the highway that ran along the lake—the portion that Joe Big had seen from the mountain—driving past lake houses and businesses on both sides of the highway. Most of the intersecting roads led to houses or to small neighborhoods or were marked with National Forest road signs.

"I'm looking for an unmarked road," Barney said. "A logging road, maybe, that goes into private forest owned by Plum Creek or BLM."

"Right there," Joe Big said.

Barney downshifted and turned left off the highway, up a graded road, over a lip, onto a forested plateau. Ahead the road wound through cleared forest and small meadows.

He turned again on the first road they came to, barely a track through the trees, headed back toward the highway. He stopped the car, and Joe Big climbed out. "Go ahead," he said. "I'll walk the rest of the way in."

The Subaru motored off through the forest, tiny puffs of chocolate dust at the wheels, a veil of dust behind the car.

Joe Big pulled branches off one side of a young fir.

He walked back to the road and with the branches brushed away the tracks that turned into the side road, the soft, sooty dust making it easy to obliterate evidence of the Subaru's passage. He swept the tracks for another hundred meters, and then threw the branches to the side, and began jogging toward wherever Barney had hidden the car.

The air was heavy with the smell of dust and pine, deep blue sky between the trees. Flies and other flying bugs flew through shafts of light and dust.

As usual, he had no coherent thought of what they had done, only a mélange of images and snippets of action: a trucker flipping them off, Harold with barf all over his nifty shirt, the Subaru sideways to oncoming traffic, whitetail bounding through the forest, tails up. Freeze frames of action, the frames changing too fast to comprehend if he tried to wrap his mind around one of them. He knew from experience that the best thing to do was to not think about it—to be in the present totally and completely, like the ancestor in his dream had been.

Barney had the Subaru parked around the side of a huge moss-covered rock outcropping. The outcropping overhung the Subaru on one side. Close-knit fir on the other side of the car made a wall that enclosed the Subaru as if in a garage.

"That's handy," Joe Big said.

Barney smiled. "We get to be lucky once in awhile." He handed Joe Big a bottle of water. "Think you can stay awake? I'm whipped."

Joe Big opened the bottle and took a big pull. "Ahh, damn," he said. "It's even cold. No problem."

"If you climb up on this rock, you can see the road we turned off the highway on, and you can see the highway itself for about a mile in both directions.

Joe Big offered the bottle of water.

"No, it's yours. I've got another bottle of Dew. There's camouflage stuff in the duffel on the right side, pants and shirts and fleece jackets. A couple of hats. Also, some grease. If anyone shows up, other than the bad guys, we can pass for bow hunters."

"Where you going to bed down?"

"In the trees on the other side of the car there. I'll take the M4, and you can take the Fourteen, okay?"

"Okay." Joe Big drained the bottle of water.

"What do you think?" he asked. "Wait until after bar closing to head out? Four in the morning, or so?"

"Sounds like a wiener to me."

"Go ahead," Joe Big said, "You look like you're about to tip over."

25
Follow the Rabbit

Joe Big held his hand up into the star field, his fingers black shadows obliterating part of the Milky Way. He imagined his hand that dark intelligence, not human, not alien, that followed his uncle around. A monster, like Barney's Death Monster, consuming whole galaxies.

A sudden breeze rustled the trees, whispered across his face. He was lying on his back in a mossy trough at the top of the rock, feet crossed, the hood of the fleece jacket pulled over his head, M14 next to him on the upper side of the mossy indentation.

Hours before, a mud-encrusted heavy-duty Ford four-by-four with a steel tool box and an oiler in the bed had come out of the forest on the road they'd taken when they'd left the highway, and had pulled out onto the highway, headed south, only one man in it that he could see. The truck had for sure obliterated any tracks the Subaru might have left.

Two helicopters had flown around the top of the mountains across the lake for a couple of hours, but there was no sign of smoke from the fire that the burning car must have started. He assumed that the four guys in the Chrysler had been there fast enough to put it out.

Other than that, it had been a fight to stay awake, the rock warm and comfortable from the afternoon sun, traffic on the highway light—logging trucks and pickups, for the most part. No cars full of bad guys. Early on, a black and white Sheriff's SUV had swept past, top lights on, but no siren. Rotsa ruck, he'd thought. 9-1-1 had no doubt been busy. He still couldn't believe the guys in the Chrysler had actually fired automatic weapons at them—on a busy highway, in the middle of the day, no less. A little more elevation and at least one of them would have been hit. As it was a line of bullets had gone through the hatch and impacted inside the duffels. Good thing they'd dropped Harold off.

He held both hands up into the star field. *Spooky,* echoed in his mind. *"Spooky little girl like you."* She made him, Joe Big Snake Person, feel like a teenager.

The magazines on her bed stand had been fashion and home decorating magazines, a catalogue for Victoria's Secret. But on the other side of the room was a built-in bookcase filled with hardcover and paperback novels. A lot of authors he didn't recognize. A few of the obligatory, whiny, we-grew-up-so-tough-in-Montana female writers that, to her credit, didn't look as if they'd been read. One shelf seemed to be dedicated to history. Books about Montana and—surprise, surprise—even a few books about the Blackfeet. Ewers and Jackson and Dempsey mixed with books about Southeast Asia and Vietnam: Fall and Herr and Anderson, McAfee and Haing Ngor—authors that, thanks to his father and uncle, he knew well. Vietnamese-English, and Vietnamese-French dictionaries. Man's Fate by Malraux—in French. An entire section of French translations of American authors. Two shelves of books in Vietnamese . . .

He wiped out more galaxies with his fingers. *Spookayyy.*

Below, in the trees on the other side of the parked Subaru, he heard rustling, the zip of a sleeping bag zipper, the clunk of something hitting a tree trunk.

"You up there, Big?"

He sat up, legs straight out in front. "No. And I'm never coming back."

"I hear that. How's it look?"

"It's been me and the stars and your snoring. No critters at all. A vehicle on the highway every twenty minutes or so."

"Cops?"

"Only one, and that one shortly after we got here. Headed back the way we came."

Joe Big stood and surveyed the surroundings. There was no moon, but the star field was so bright he could easily make out individual trees in the forest, see the dotted line on the pale ribbon of highway.

He picked up the M14, and walked down the rock to the low edge, and sat down and slid the last four or five feet to the ground. Barney was standing in the shadow.

"You should've got me up. It's almost four."

"I can sleep while you drive."

"Only the one cop. I don't like the sound of that. I thought I heard a helicopter."

"There were two of them flying around for a couple of hours."

"I *really* don't like the sound of that."

Joe Big shrugged. "They're mercs. No telling what kind of equipment the company they work for has."

"I feel like we followed the rabbit in Alice and Wonderland down the hole and the little bastard turned off the lights."

Joe Big smiled.

"If I can find him," Barney said. "I'm going to put a knife in his heart, make rabbit stew."

"And in the meantime?"

"In the meantime, we need to get rid of the car. That's a priority. Then, I guess, go talk to Quinn, find out what's going on."

"You think she knows?"

"Yeah. I think she knows. Maybe she didn't know what was going on when she put an arrow into one of the them, but by now I bet she has a pretty good idea."

"I think you're right."

They were silent for a moment, both of them standing in the gloom next to the rock, unconsciously facing away from each other, their eyes constantly moving, searching for movement.

"She might even be the rabbit," Joe Big said.

His forehead hit the window and he opened his eyes to the sight of twin beams of bright light illuminating the highway. Tall trees were like dark canyon walls on both sides of the road.

Barney cursed and the car slowed and the shudder subsided. They swept around a series of S curves, trees and large rocks briefly lit by the projector-beam headlights.

Joe Big cleared his throat and sat up. He rubbed the top of his head and the sides of his face. His skin felt greasy, his eyes puffy.

He laid his head back against the headrest and looked out the window. They were going past a small lake, the water a black blot between the trees. Beyond the trees, under the star field, he could see the backside of the snow-capped Missions. He cleared his throat, and turned toward Barney.

"How's it going?"

"Ah, the front end is all fucked up. I can't drive over seventy or it rattles and shakes so bad I'm afraid we won't have any tires left by the time we get to your place."

"We decided to go to my place?"

"I got to thinking that no one at the office has ever been there. All your mail gets sent to a Post Office box or to your parents. And the place is in your uncle's name."

"A lot of people from the City and the S.O. have been there."

"It's the people we work with now that I'm worried about. Quinn, especially. Besides, your uncle has a couple of trucks in the barn. I figured we could sort of borrow one."

Joe Big put the window down, and spit into the night, and put the window back up.

"We could borrow the newer one, I guess. But not the old International. Anything happened to that thing and he'd have both our asses. Where are we?"

"Clearwater Junction. Go back to sleep."

Joe Big reached down and pulled up on the seat release, putting the seat all the way back against the duffels piled in the back.

"Okay," he said, asleep again almost before he said the word.

26
Something Else

The Subaru crept slowly, lights off, down the dirt road. The road was a pale line winding through dark fields. It rattled across the cattleguard, and stopped in the large cleared area in front of the house and the old barn, both of them squeezed against the doors, one hand on the door release, ready to bail if necessary. The huge old firs between the house and the barn loomed like cowled monks.

Joe Big could see Miss Mouse sitting on her haunches at the top of the steps. A ghost cat. Her gray hair lighter than the shadows behind her.

The car coasted to a stop in front of the barn door. Barney reached up and made sure the interior light was switched off.

Joe Big got out, and walked to the two large wooden doors held closed by a two-by-six plank set in metal hangars on each door. He lifted the board off the hangars and set it upright against the wall, and then opened the doors wide.

Barney drove the Subaru inside, and waited for Joe Big to close the doors and turn the lights on over the workbench.

The fluorescent lights stuttered on, and Barney parked the Subaru behind an old faded green International 4×4. He shut off the engine and climbed out.

"Did you dust off the International?" he asked.

"When have I had a chance to do that?"

"Well, somebody did. Don't you think we ought to check out the place before we turn on lights?"

"No need. Mouse was sitting on the front steps. If anyone was here, she would be hiding."

Joe Big walked to a dusty, chocolate-brown, ten-year-old Chevy 4×4 with a black shell over the bed parked in the gloom at the far end of the barn. He opened the driver's side door, and reached in and toggled the hood release, and then walked around to the front and opened the hood.

"Grab one of those batteries on the workbench, and a flashlight from the top drawer of the big tool chest, will you?"

Fifteen minutes later, they had the battery in the truck, and the bed filled with all their gear from the Subaru, and were sitting in the house in the dark at the kitchen table. Miss Mouse purred loudly on Joe's lap. He scratched her chin and ran his hand along her back. Her teeth nipped at his hand.

"I feel weird sitting here in the dark," Barney said.

"Yeah. Me, too. But the logic of them not knowing this place doesn't seem nearly as compelling now that we're here."

The phone in the living room abruptly started playing a tinny version of "Light My Fire" by the Doors.

Joe Big stood, dumping Mouse unceremoniously on the floor, and drew the 9mm from behind his hip. He flicked off the safety. "That's not the ring tone I programmed into the phone."

Barney picked up the .45 Colt that he had exchanged for his Glock, and quietly cycled the slide with his left hand. He moved to the far side of the refrigerator.

They strained to hear sounds other than the phone—a creak or a sigh in the old house under the tinny music. The phone stopped, the sudden silence filled with the rush of adrenaline in their ears, the thud of their hearts. They both knew that their survival depended on the bad guys not knowing where they were.

Miss Mouse jumped up on the table and meowed and tried to reach her head out far enough to rub against Joe Big.

"You filled the cooler, right?" Joe Big asked.

"Yeah."

"The house is empty or Mouse wouldn't be so friendly; she'd be investigating. But someone has been here. No way would I program The Doors into my phone."

"I like that song."

"You would." Joe Big handed him an old camouflage butt pack filled with loaded M16/M4 magazines, and several boxes of 7.62 match rounds for the M14. "Pick up the other end of this cooler, and let's get out of here before the three bears come back."

Barney safed the .45, and stuck it in the pancake holster on his belt. He opened the back door, and grabbed the other handle on the plastic cooler, and they went out the door, pausing only to let Joe Big pull the door closed behind them.

Inside the barn, Barney opened the tailgate and they slid in the cooler and closed the tailgate.

"No one is here but us," Joe Big said.

"How do you know?"

"I can feel it."

"I trust you, when you get a feeling. You know I do. But this time *I'm* feeling something, and whatever it is makes me *really* want to beat feet out of here."

"What you're feeling, is it kind of heavy and claustrophobic?" Joe Big asked. "Seriously. I'm not joking. Are you feeling like something massive and dark is sniffing you out?"

"Stop creeping me out. Let's go."

"It's okay. It's my uncle. My uncle changed the ringtone, and he dusted the International. It's his way of telling me he was here."

"He called to tell us to leave?"

"Yeah."

"How do you know it was him? How does he even know we're here?"

"He doesn't know we are here. He thought we might be here. That feeling you have, that's the feeling we always had trying to sneak up on him when we were kids. I'm serious, man. Don't look at me like that. I know how it sounds. When he is around, sometimes *something else* is around, too."

"Something else? What the fuck are you talking about? What something else?"

"What you are feeling, that something else. Your Death Monster something else. There are no English names for it. There are Blackfeet names, but the elders who know them won't tell me, unless I join their group."

"This is another one of your Indian jokes, like the owl mojo."

"No joke. My uncle was here and he left a piece of whatever-it-is behind."

"God damn it, Big!"

Joe Big laughed. "Okay. Okay. I'm joking. Lighten up, dude. We're back in the shit. And you are all weirded out because a piece of what happened today is here with us, where it's not supposed to be, ever, and everything that is normal and trusted is suddenly a potential threat. The Boogeyman is real, that's all."

"That's *all*!"

"No, that's not all. What the fuck is the matter with you, man? Of course, that's not all. Throw the shotgun and the M4 in the front with us, and let's get out of here. The hair is standing up on the back of my neck and on my arms."

"Big . . . I'm warning you . . ."

"I'll drive," Joe Big said. "Since you aren't used to big rigs."

He backed the truck out, and Barney shut the barn doors, and secured them with the crosspiece.

Joe Big kept the lights off until they were on the county road headed for town.

In the east, a deep bruised purple outlined the mountains.

Barney rolled the window down, and sat forward to look back. The old house and barn stood mute and dark. He had the uncomfortable, irrational feeling that the house was tracking him, filing him away for future reference.

He rolled the window up, and sat back.

"You weren't joking," he said.

"Nope."

"What have you got me into this time, Big?"

Joe Big laughed. "It's not me."

"Who is it, then?"

"It's that rabbit, man. And it's your fault for following him."

Barney stared at him.

Joe Big glanced at him. "Everyone thinks the rabbit is doddering and eccentric," he said in the Rod Serling voice that Barney liked to use. "Disney cute. But Longstreet and Big are beginning to understand that it is not. The rabbit is sinister. Real fucking sinister."

"You are so weird, you know that?"

Joe Big smiled at the road ahead. "We'll see," he said.

27
Night Vision

"Where are you going?" Barney asked. "Town is the other way."

"I thought we were going to have a chat with Patrick the Third and his concubine."

"Don't you want to go by the office first?"

Joe Big swung the pickup onto the Interstate onramp. The sky had lightened to gray, and streetlights were beginning to shut off. Early morning traffic had picked up as the first wave of workers streamed into the city.

"If we go into the office, we'll get stuck answering questions. By now, Quinn and Company are running in circles, screaming and shouting—in a repressed, Federal way, of course."

"Or not," Barney said.

"Or not. That's true. But I don't think we want to take the chance, do you? These guys, whoever they are, have resources that law enforcement doesn't. And they don't give a rat's ass about putting citizens in danger. If they were willing to shoot at us before they knew for sure we were the ones that put an arrow into one of them, imagine what they are going to be like now."

"How about Paul?"

"What do you mean?"

"Maybe Paul has heard something that can help us."

"Paul represents the Border Patrol and the Tribe. We don't want to get him and his people crossways to the guys who were shooting at us. I mean, screw it, man. Let's go grab this motherfucker and see what he has to say. What have we got to lose?"

"He's going to have some real people with him."

"Why? They'll expect us to either run or to show up at the office. They'll be watching your place, and they'll be watching the Rez, thinking there is a chance we might be headed to my parents."

"Maybe we *should* get out of the country."

"These guys are just like us, Barn. If we don't do something about it now, we'll be looking over our shoulders for the rest of our lives."

"I really hate it when you're right."

"By now, they have our military records. We are no longer two County Mounties working undercover for the Feds. And that's not a bad thing. They are going to give us a little space before they come at us again. As long as we stay one step ahead, we should be okay."

"Nice theory, Big. But it's a theory. For all we know they might shoot on sight. Damn. I'm feeling exactly the way I felt that time those Taliban had Chechnyan snipers with them."

"We're off the leash, man. Let's keep it that way, is what I'm saying. We go into the office now, and we lose all that."

Barney sighed, and slouched down in the seat.

Joe Big squinted at Hellgate Canyon coming toward them in the gray morning light. A hundred and fifty years ago, Hellgate Canyon was one of the bloodiest places in North America. A traditional place for Indians to ambush Indians. It didn't seem like this kind of shit should happen here, in America. Not today. But why not? Because it was America and not Iraq or Afghanistan or the PI or Indonesia or Ecuador or Columbia or Burma or anywhere else in the world? It was America when Indians were still ambushing Indians in Hellgate Canyon. Being America didn't stop anyone then, why should it stop anyone now?

"So what do you want to do?" Barney asked. "Storm the house, like we did with Harold?"

"We need to slow down a little. I don't know about you, but I'm having trouble wrapping my mind around all this. I know a place up the Blackfoot where I used to hunt when I was a kid. We can build a fire. Eat something. Take a snooze. My uncle keeps everything we need in that box behind the cab. Anyone who sees us will think we are hunters."

"Please tell me not MREs."

Joe Big smiled. "He's old school. He loves MREs."

"HUNTING SEASON WILL be over before we even have a chance to go hunting," Barney said, kicking dirt over the already drowned embers of the campfire.

They'd found a spot at the end of a grassy road, where the truck could be backed in beneath a stand of old-growth cedars. The ancient cedars were as big around as the cab of the truck, the area beneath clear of vegetation. Across the road, a reasonably large stream meandered through a grassy meadow. The box of supplies had yielded a tiny, one-burner stove and a package of butane cylinders, a coffee pot with packages of coffee stuffed inside the pot, and boxes of self-heating meals—not MREs—in an old, padded cooler. The meals came with packets of salt water that when added to the heating pad inside the box heated the food.

"There's a rice cooker and some rice in here, too," Joe Big said, digging through the large wooden box. "Looks like we can plug it into the cigarette lighter. Some kind of Japanese noodles. Nasty-looking dried mushrooms. Tea, if you don't want coffee."

"I want to try one of these Heater Meals."

After they'd eaten, "Better than MREs, anyway," Barney said, they had taken sleeping pads and bags from the truck and slept for most of the day, Barney in the back of the truck, Joe Big up the hill in a hollow behind a giant larch shedding its needles, the M14 next to him.

He'd wakened once to see Barney fishing down at the stream with a rod and reel that looked like a kid's toy. The next time he'd wakened, Barney's feet were sticking out onto the tailgate, the rest of him lost in the duffels. They'd had fried Cutthroat trout with a pot of rice. It had been a long time since he'd tasted anything as good.

Barney packed up the small stove and the coffee pot and skillet and took them back to the pickup.

"Most excellent," Joe Big said.

"I thought your uncle was some kind of mountain man, or something. This was better than staying in a hotel with a good restaurant."

"He likes his creature comforts, just like anyone else. When we were kids, he would bake sourdough rolls in a little oven that his grandfather had invented. You should see it. It collapses down to a box smaller than a suitcase of beer." Joe Big threw the rolled-up pads and sleeping bags into the pickup bed. "But he can live off the land for months if he has to, and at the end of that time be healthier than when he started."

"Unlike you and me."

"You got that right."

"Sun will be down soon."

"The thing about my uncle is that he functions best on his own. He's pretty unusual in that respect."

"What do you mean?"

"Most of us who have the ability to be loners don't much like it. We are most comfortable when we work in teams made up of members of our tribe—Special Forces, Force Recon, SEALS, whatever. Blackfeet warriors were nearly always in groups. No one went raiding or horse stealing alone. Maybe hunting, but that was about all."

"How about the scouts? They must have had scouts?"

"The scouts were called wolves. They even used wolf skins to disguise themselves. The point is, they identified with wolves."

"A murder of wolves."

"A murder of ravens. Wolves go in packs."

"But murder fits wolves better than it does ravens."

"A murder of wolves." Joe Big tried the words out to see how they felt. "That's what we are all right."

"So is your uncle a Tribal member?"

"He's an honorary member of my father's group of combat veterans—which is a pretty big deal among those who know. But he doesn't want anything to do with being a Tribal member."

"So he's not a product of tribal thinking," Barney said. "He's not part of a pack."

Joe Big laughed. "You and me, man. *We're* products of tribal thinking. Indians today aren't tribal—at least not most of them, and for sure not in the traditional sense. They're a loose collection of individuals and families organized into a political unit invented by the white man. Even the word, sacred, is a white man's word. My uncle started out with a tribal mindset, same as you and me, but I think it was the War—something that happened in Vietnam—that made him a loner. My theory is that he did something that put him outside his tribe. Something that only he knows about."

"He sounds like a real piece of work."

"You have no idea."

"That's what I felt at your place last night? Your uncle?"

"Nah. What you felt is something else. Something that my father says follows my uncle around."

"Uh-huh. Something that follows your uncle around. I trust you, when you start talking like that, about as far as I can throw this truck."

"That's harsh, man."

"What would your uncle suggest we do now?"

"What we should do now would not be an issue with him. He would have killed them all, by now."

"See what I mean . . ."

Joe Big closed the tailgate, and fastened the handle on the topper.

"You sure you want to do this?" he asked.

"Are you?"

"Fuck no."

Barney grinned. "You're thinking of little Sam Sometime and his mother, aren't you?"

"So what if I am?"

"Well, we sort of passed the point of no return, when we lit up Pick and the Redhead."

"I suppose."

"It is what it is, Big. We are who we are. Chewing on it isn't going to change anything."

Joe Big was silent, staring pensively at the copse of ancient cedars. Light from the setting sun slanted in great smoky beams between the giant tree trunks. In the distance, they heard the faint scream of a bull elk in rut, and almost immediately from their right, on the other side of the stream, an answering scream of defiance from a larger, throatier bull.

"Shit. He's right over there," Joe Big said.

"They crossed the creek about forty meters above where I was fishing. Totally ignored me. He's a big sucker, seven on one side."

"I heard them, but I thought it was a bunch of whitetail."

"Still want to do a snatch?" Barney asked.

"Well, we can give it a try. But there's no guarantee they are going to come down that road—or if someone comes down the road that it will be them."

"We'll just have to hope that whoever it is they think the truck belongs to bow hunters."

"You're making it sound easy," Joe Big said.

"Yeah, about as easy as someone catching you and me when we don't want to get caught."

Joe Big frowned.

"Hey," Barney said. "It's like we talked about. Patrick and the other two messed us up. Those mercs tried to make us dead. If they catch us now, they *will* make us dead. We did not do anything to provoke those kinds of responses. We're on our own here, Big. If we tell Quinn, she'll put us on ice."

"And nothing will get done or solved," Joe Big said.

"That's right."

"Except that some very bad-news people will want to get even with us for killing a couple of their own."

"Exactly."

"So why are you standing around talking about it?"

Barney shook his head. "Mei has no idea what an asshole you can be sometimes."

Joe Big grinned. "Sam does, though."

Surprised, Barney stared at him for a moment. "Well, damn. That's about the smartest thing I've heard you say in a long time."

"Part of the charm."

Barney rolled his eyes, and turned and climbed in the passenger side.

Joe Big looked across the meadow. The bull elk was silent, as if it was listening to him and Barney, and not the other way around.

He didn't know if that was a good sign, or not.

It felt like it could go either way.

THE LONG SHADOWS had disappeared from the highway. Most of the oncoming traffic had headlights on.

"Check this out," Barney said. "Is this who I think it is?"

A silver Dodge 4×4, chrome deer catcher and tires that stuck out past the fenders, a bank of lights mounted above the cab, roared past going the other way, headlights on bright.

"In the flesh," Joe Big said. "Tanya, too."

Joe Big slowed the truck.

"No, keep going," Barney said. "Pull off when you can. Let's think about this."

A mile or so later, Joe Big turned left across the highway, into a State Park next to the Blackfoot River. The park was deserted, kayakers and rafters gone for the day. He stopped the truck next to a picnic table, shut off the engine, and rolled down the window. They could hear the distant rush of water.

"What's today?" Barney asked.

"Sunday, I think. Yeah, Sunday."

"No night life tonight."

"Not much."

"Could be headed up to the Flathead."

"They'd go the other way," Joe Big said. "Up the Swan."

Barney was silent, thinking.

"They went into Missoula for dinner. Maybe a movie," Joe Big said. "She likes movies."

"That's what I think, too."

Joe Big started the truck, and turned the headlights on.

At the entrance to the park, he turned left, in the direction they had been headed before the silver Dodge passed going the other way.

"I swear we're like an old married couple sometimes," Barney said.

"Do you remember the road?" Joe Big asked.

"Probably not as well as you."

"I seem to remember a flat spot with a big rock to the side. It's on the other side of a cattle guard. They'll slow for the cattle guard. We can put the truck by the rock. Put a note on the windshield in case anyone comes by."

"What if someone tries to break into the truck?"

"We'll cuff them and put them in their rig and drive it into the forest, deal with them later."

"The way our luck is going, we'll have a forest full of tied up people and vehicles before they decide to come back."

"Oh, ye of little faith."

Barney snorted. "And a lot of experience."

But three hours later, only one vehicle had stopped. A new Ford SUV with every option known to man had pulled up behind the truck, lights on bright. A fat teenager with a baseball cap on sideways had gotten out and taken the note from under the wiper blade, read it, and then put it back, and walked to the back of the truck and peered inside, both hands at the side of his face, nose pressed against the back window. He stood undecided. Looked around. Got back in the Ford and drove away.

Joe Big had watched from next to the rock. Barney was thirty meters down the road in some bushes.

Cold, damp air had rolled in from the direction of the river. Both men had their hands clasped in their armpits, watch caps pulled low over forehead and ears. Barney wiped his nose on the arm of his fleece jacket. This time of year back home . . .

He heard a vehicle coming fast up the road. Lights bounced through the trees.

The vehicle ignored the cattle guard—it had to be them—one solid BLANG, as the big off-road tires hit the metal bars in the cattle guard.

The surrounding forest was lit white and washed out by the headlights and driving lights and the bank of lights on top the cab. The truck locked up its brakes. Dust and debris rolled off the tires as it slid past Barney. It came to a stop about ten meters from their truck. Their truck looked as if it was broken down, the note clearly seen in the lights.

The truck idled, modified exhaust sounding more like a boat than a truck.

Barney crouched, no longer cold, and put the M4 to his shoulder, aiming at the back tire.

The truck suddenly bellowed, as the driver threw it into reverse and stepped on the gas. The big tires clawed at the road, spitting rocks.

Barney fired a burst of three rounds, the bullets impacting the rear tire. He shifted his aim to the front tire, and fired another burst. Joe Big stepped out from behind the big rock, into the light, and with the shotgun put a round of double ought and another round, a slug, into the radiator and engine, the dual booms of the shotgun loud over the sound of the truck engine.

The truck shot backwards. Across the cattle guard. And did a wobbly drunken one-eighty in the cleared area on the other side of the cattle guard. They could hear the flattened tires smacking against the inside of the fenders.

Barney and Joe Big ran for the pickup. Joe Big had it started and moving as Barney jumped in the passenger side.

"That is one crazy motherfucker," Joe Big said.

"They won't get far. He's already on the rims. And I think you cracked the block with that slug. Better take it easy, though. He's bound to be armed."

Joe Big stopped the truck, and turned the lights off. "Hand me my eyes, will you?"

"Good idea," Barney said. He reached behind the driver's seat and retrieved a small duffel already unzipped, and handed Joe Big a set of night-vision goggles.

Joe Big fiddled with the goggles. "Might as well go active," he said. "Unless he's got NVDs with him, he won't see the infrared."

Barney adjusted the straps, and switched on.

Joe Big put the truck in gear, and they slowly rolled down the road. "Can't do anything about the brake lights."

"That's okay. I doubt he's going to stick around, armed or not. He'll be headed up the mountainside to the ridge. It's only a mile or so back down to the road on the other side. Another two miles or so to his ranch."

"There it is," Joe Big said.

In the green light, they could see the back end of the Dodge sticking out of a clump of fir. The doors were open.

Joe Big pulled off the road, into the trees. He turned the engine off, and they got out.

"I'll head up to the ridge," Joe Big said. "You see if you can pick up their trail. The ridges around here are soft and open; we shouldn't have any trouble hooking up. If you catch the woman, cuff her around a tree and stuff something in her mouth. We can talk to her later."

"You got it, Bwana."

Joe Big turned and began to half run, half walk through the forest, everything seen in crisp green detail through the Night Vision Device. His depth perception was slightly off. It always took a few minutes to get used to an NVD.

The valley floor quickly gave way to steep forested hillside. The ground was clear beneath the trees, only a few large rocks and falldown here and there to impede his progress. He began to run up the hillside, the toes of his boots digging into a carpet of pine needles and soft dirt, thighs and calves tight, breathing labored. He'd be okay in a few minutes, he knew, once his heart and lungs woke to the fact that serious exercise was at hand.

They were off to his right somewhere, probably on a diagonal up to the ridge. Even if they were smart enough to angle toward the low end of the ridge, he wouldn't run into them for a while. They'd be moving as fast as they could, but Patrick was way too big to last long running uphill. And the woman would be scared shitless, her breathing all over the place, heart rate through the roof. He wouldn't be surprised if Patrick left her behind.

Something moved to his left, and he stopped, his hand going to the pistol holstered high on his hip. At first he couldn't figure out what it was—an animal of some kind—and then it picked up its head, and he saw that it was a medium size black bear turning over rocks—looking for bugs and whatever else might be edible. The bear sat back and looked in his direction. The wind was moving left to right so it hadn't winded, only heard him, its vision too poor to actually see him.

He turned uphill—short, choppy steps, toes digging in, the slope too steep to run up for another hundred meters. The bear looked like a cartoon bear sitting on its ass.

He picked up a rock and threw it toward the bear. The rock hit the bear in the foot—a lucky throw—and the bear was instantly running full tilt up the hill, crashing through bushes.

Fastest critter in the world for about fifty yards, he thought, watching the bear stop and turn back toward him, snout up, swaying from side to side, as it tried to scent him. He knew that it would head uphill, across his path, and then loop back down the hillside on the other side of the draw to get his scent. Nothing like a curious bear to get in the way, he thought. He smiled to himself. In a few minutes, that bear was going to wonder where all the people had come from. Once it realized the hill was swarming with people, it would probably run all the way down the hill, across the road, and out into the valley somewhere.

Sure enough, as the angle of the slope decreased, and he started to run again, he saw far up the slope the bear hurry across his path and disappear into a heavily treed gully off to his right. The top of the ridge was only another five or six hundred meters. He had his legs and lungs now.

WELL, DAMN, BARNEY thought. The trail that he'd stepped up on to was wide and well traveled—mostly by horses, it looked like. That's why the big man had abandoned the truck where he had: this must be an old Forest Service or CC trail that local volunteers and horseback riding clubs kept clear. It probably went all the way to the top of the mountain and tied in with a road network at the top. For sure, it went up to the ridge, and then probably followed the ridge, either on the ridge itself or just off the ridge so the horses wouldn't be in the wind.

He looked uphill, and caught movement far above—either an animal of some kind or someone on one of the upper switchbacks.

He could see the next switchback about forty meters above. He slung the rifle across his back, and left the trail and began hiking straight up the hill. He'd cut the switchbacks until his legs were too tight, and then he'd walk a switchback until he had his legs back, and then cut switchbacks again. He'd have to hurry. It wasn't that far to the ridge, and once to the ridge, they would abandon the trail and head straight down the other side to the ranch road. The other side was a south-facing slope, which meant it would be relatively open, and they could run downhill if they wanted to, even in the dark.

He and Big had driven the road far enough to get the lay of the land. Big's instincts in the mountains were unerring. The guy couldn't get lost if he tried. If Patrick and the woman managed to get over the ridge, Big would run them down long before they got to the ranch.

The worry was that one of them had a cell phone and was calling for help.

Damn. His breathing was already raspy, his thighs tight. Maybe he should have gone for a run with Big, instead of chowing down on cinnamon rolls. Nah. He'd gotten at least as good a workout chasing Mickey around all night. Good damn thing it wasn't her up ahead. They'd never catch her. That woman ran on batteries. And her batteries never ran down. She just switched off. Wide awake and full of energy one moment, dead asleep and snoring the next. He'd never seen anything like it. And neurotic? Man . . .

He liked her, though. Liked her a lot. He had a feeling that once they got control of the sex thing, they'd be friends. Lovers now, and that was great, but it was obvious she was a creature of the moment. And he wasn't much for sharing.

He stopped, one hand and both knees on the upslope, panting, thighs leaden and aching. A battery-powered female buddy. He wished he had her batteries right now.

Big wouldn't understand. But why not be friends with someone like Mickey? Life couldn't get any stranger than it had gotten the last couple of weeks—especially the last couple of days. What was it Big had said? War all the time? Only this was like no war they had trained for. He didn't know what this was. All he knew is that if they didn't keep the initiative, then like Big said, they were dead.

He gritted his teeth, and forced himself up the slope. He found the next switchback and turned onto it and started jogging, accustomed now to the NVD on his face, the world green and ghostly and a little claustrophobic.

She was up ahead, sitting on the uphill side of the trail, head in her hands. He stopped, and carefully scanned the trail and the surrounding forest. The big man was nowhere to be seen. He stood watching her, waiting for his breathing to quiet.

She was crying—sucking in large gulps of air and crying at the same time. Hiccupping as she talked to herself. He could almost feel sorry for her if not for the memory of her firing an M16 over their heads, and then booting him face down into the dirt. And, oh, yeah. Cutting off Big's braid and then slapping him across the face with it. Telling people she'd scalped him.

He walked up to her. She was unarmed.

"Boo."

She screamed.

He grabbed a handful of her hair and twisted his hand in it and pulled her upright, forcing her head back at an awkward angle.

"Shut up," he said. He could smell urine sharp in the mountain air. Why was it people were always pissing themselves? First Harold. Now her. Even Mickey when they drove up the hill to Mei's place—well, to be fair, he'd almost pissed his own pants a couple of times on that trip. "Be quiet," he said, and lightly yanked on her hair.

He felt her try to nod.

"Where's Patrick?"

"I-I don't know. H-he left me. Don't kill me, please."

"I'm not going to kill you." He felt her sag in relief.

He jerked her upright by the hair. "Oh, wait. I changed my mind. I am going to kill you." Pulling her by the hair, he walked her off the trail to a lone fir, most of its branches on the side facing the valley.

"Sit. Put your legs on both sides of the tree." He released her hair, and pulled the Velcro flap open on his back pocket and took out the handcuffs.

"Arms around the tree. Toward me." He had to give her credit for at least doing what he was telling her to do. Terrified to the max, but who wouldn't be? He reached into the branches and handcuffed her wrists, making sure the cuffs were ratcheted snug.

"Do I need to gag you?"

She shook her head, her hair catching on some of the lower branches.

"If you make noise, and I have to come back, I'm not going to be happy."

She nodded.

Something moved through the bushes and trees in a shallow dent in the hillside about seventy meters downhill, and he saw a green bear run up onto the lip of a depression and stop and taste the wind, facing away from them.

"There's a bear down there," he said in a low voice. "Be quiet and it'll leave you alone."

Her face jerked toward him, eyes wide, mouth opening and closing. He stood and looked uphill. No Patrick anywhere. He walked back to the trail, and began jogging.

He ran to the end of the switchback, and continued straight off the turn on a diagonal across the hillside, headed for the ridge. The big man was moving better than they had expected. He hoped Joe Big wouldn't have to shoot him before they got a chance to talk to him.

Joe Big heard the big man before he saw him, the big man's boots digging into the soft, rocky hillside, small rocks and pebbles cascading downhill with every step, as he worked his way across the steep slope, coming into view about fifty meters below where Joe Big was standing next to an ancient bull pine.

The slope below was a bit steeper than it had been on the other side of the ridge, but except for large old trees, like the one he stood next to, was mostly covered with dried grass and here and there bare patches of scree. The starlight was so bright he probably didn't need the NVD. He was tempted to take it off, but it would take too long for his eyes to transition to natural light. The big man didn't look that tired. He was moving well, his strides powerful and confident. No doubt he'd hiked or ridden his mules on this mountain before. He had a Western-style six-shooter wedged into his belt at the small of his back. Probably a Ruger .44 magnum, knowing him.

The big man abruptly halted, and looked back the way he had come. His eyes scanned the ridgeline, pausing a moment where Joe Big stood next to the tree.

Impressive, Joe Big thought. The big man had felt someone or something watching him.

The man stood stock still, listening. Joe Big waited for him to convince himself that no one was there, that it was all his imagination.

He'd be confident that he knew the mountain better than whoever might be chasing him. He would not be expecting night vision devices. And he didn't know Barney and himself well enough to know that he had no chance of outrunning them in the mountains, not even at night, and not even if they didn't have NVDs.

The big man turned to continue downhill and, as he took a step, Joe Big took a step out from next to the tree, timing his steps in unison with the big man, so that the sound the big man was making would mask the sound of the footsteps behind him.

Joe Big closed the gap to thirty meters as the slope flattened and there were more trees and bushes and the footing was less noisy. The steep slope became a series of gentle hillocks and shallow gullies.

Two hundred meters downhill in front of the big man, a group of whitetail bounced through the trees, the big man unaware of them. He was heavy on his feet now. Joe Big could hear him grunting. His legs looked rubbery.

The big man stopped and Joe Big stopped, caught in the open. It didn't matter. Even if the big man looked directly at him all he would see was something that grew vertical and dark against the backdrop of trees and bushes. The big man leaned forward, hands on his knees, and spit. He was dressed in jeans and one of those long-sleeve, Cowboy-style shirts with snaps instead of buttons. Lace-up boots instead of cowboy boots. He'd probably had the boots in the truck, and had the presence of mind to grab them, when they'd exited the truck. No doubt there was a pair of cowboy boots littering the ground somewhere on the other side of the ridge.

Below, between two hillocks, Joe Big could see a pale green ribbon of road.

He could take him right now. Run up behind him and hit him over the head, trip him down the slope or something. No. Too risky. The man was simply too big and strong, and from the way he had hit him when they were up the Blackfoot, he probably knew how to box, maybe even knew some sort of martial art. It was better to let the big man tire himself as much as possible, take him when he was on the road.

The big man pulled the front of his shirt out of his pants and wiped his face.

He took a deep breath, and not bothering to tuck the shirt in again turned and once again began moving as fast as he could down the hill, Joe Big behind him.

The big man caught his foot on a half-buried rock and sprawled face down, hands in front of him. He climbed to his feet and rubbed his palms against his pants and, limping, started downhill again. The limp disappeared after a hundred meters or so.

Guy is an animal, Joe Big thought.

The big man stopped when he reached the road embankment, hands on his knees, wheezing.

Joe Big looked uphill. He thought he saw pinpricks of light on the ridge. Barney's NVD. He wagged his head back and forth, hoping Barney would see the infrared signature of his own NVD.

The big man straightened. It was amazing he'd lasted this long. He had to weigh close to three hundred pounds and, muscle or not, that was a lot of weight to drag up a steep ridge and down the other side in such a short time. He really hoped he wouldn't have to shoot or knife him, but more and more it was looking like the guy was going to be difficult to put down.

The big man slid on his ass down the road embankment. Joe Big watched from the gloom of the trees at the top of the embankment, while he stood bent over in the middle of the road, hands on his knees, still trying to catch his breath.

The big man straightened, and began to walk down the road.

Joe Big removed the NVD and put it in the thigh pocket. He fastened the Velcro flap, and then ran down the embankment, headed for the big man now jogging down the road. The big man had a serious hitch in his gait. He must have hurt a knee or an ankle when he took the spill, Joe Big thought.

The road snaked around a finger ridge and, as it did, in the far distance the ranch lights came into view. Joe Big ran up behind the big man.

Patrick was practically staggering. He could have driven up behind him in a truck and he wouldn't have known he was there.

Ahead was a metal stock gate closed to keep in cattle and horses. The big man would have to stop and open the gate. He was running toward it like he'd forgotten it was there.

Joe Big jerked the pistol from the big man's belt, and threw the pistol out into the field, and dropped back a step, and shoved the big man as hard as he could in the small of the back, propelling him forward, arms windmilling, tired legs unable to stop him from smashing head first into the metal gate.

The small chain holding the gate closed snapped, and the gate clanged open. The big man was face down in the road, arms splayed to the side.

Joe Big peered at the figure in the road, worried that he had broken his neck.

The figure groaned, and rolled onto its right side, and struggled to all fours.

Joe Big ran forward and kicked him hard in the ribs. It was like kicking a wet sack of sand. The big man grunted and his torso rose slightly and that was all. His head turned toward Joe Big, and Joe Big could tell that the man was not hurt at all.

He reached back and unsnapped the 9mm and drew it from the holster and pushed off the safety. The big man planted one foot flat on the ground, and slowly and laboriously stood upright. The Thing come to life, Joe Big thought. "Okay," the figure rumbled, and turned toward Joe Big.

Joe Big shot him in the left knee, the larger-than-life figure upright one second, toppled to the ground as if it had been kicked by a horse, the next.

"Oh, fuuuck," Patrick groaned. He rolled over and sat up, both hands holding his knee.

Blood pooled dark against the pale road surface. Shit, Joe Big thought. The bullet must have hit something majorly important.

"You're bleeding to death," he said. "I suggest you take off your belt and use it as a tourniquet."

The figure on the ground looked up at him. Joe Big could feel the malevolence. There was no way he was getting close to those hands. It didn't matter that the big man was knee-capped and on his ass in the middle of the road. There was no way he was getting within reach of those hands.

The big man undid his belt and jerked it free of his pants, and put it around his leg above the knee. But instead of threading it through the buckle, he looped the two ends of the belt together, and pulled the two ends tight, as if it was a leather string he was tying instead of a thick belt.

Joe Big holstered the SIG, and walked over next to the gate and pulled a thin wooden survey stake out of the ground. He broke the stake in half over his knee and threw half to the man on the ground.

The big man loosened the belt, and tied it in a knot, and then slipped the stake through the knot and rotated the stake so that it screwed the belt tight around his leg. He hooked the end of the stake in the belt so that it could not unwind, and leaned back, both hands flat on the ground behind him, elbows locked.

"I knew you were going to be trouble," he said.

"Who told you about us?"

"You mean that you are cops?" The big man sat upright, and reached into his pant pocket.

"Careful." Joe Big drew his pistol again.

"It's my cell phone. See." With one hand he flipped open the cell phone, his thumb hitting a button.

Joe Big shot it out of his hand, the 9mm hollow point splintering the cell phone and sending plastic into the big man's palm and fingers.

The big man bent forward, cradling his hand in his armpit. His bald pate was a pale orb in the darkness, rocking back and forth.

"A hunter poaching a deer in the middle of the night during hunting season," Joe Big said. He looked toward the distant ranch house. "No lights coming on that I can see."

Gravel and rocks slid down the embankment behind them. He turned toward the sound.

"It's me," Barney said.

Joe Big holstered his weapon, and sat down in the road, legs folded and crossed Indian style. He leaned forward and picked egg-sized rocks from the center of the road and laid them in a small pile next to his thigh.

"Howdy, y'all," Barney said.

"Howdy, yourself," Joe Big said. "Did you find her?"

"She's being her tree-hugging self. You had to shoot him, huh?"

"It was either shoot him or run back up the hill to get away from him. I shoved him head first into the gate—you can see where it's all dented in. But it didn't seem to bother him much." He raised his voice. "He's going to lose his leg from the knee down if he doesn't get help soon."

The big man was silent.

"What was the other shot?" Barney asked.

"His cell phone."

"Uh-oh."

"Yeah. I should have thought of it."

"You probably called someone from up on the ridge, huh?" Barney asked the big man.

"Actually, I don't think he did," Joe Big said. "I think he wanted to handle this all by his lonesome." He raised his voice. "But I also think he was able to push a pre-programmed button on his cell before I shot it."

"You two . . . are on . . . the wrong side." They could hear the stress in the big man's voice. From personal experience, they both knew that the nerve endings in his knee were coming back to life.

The big man made a sound deep in his chest, part groan, part grunt.

"I bet that hurts," Barney said.

"And what side would you be on?" Joe Big asked.

"The side of . . . the righteous." He sat forward, and with his good hand, his left hand, twisted the tourniquet tighter.

"And what are the righteous up to these days that they have to shoot at us in the middle of the day on a busy highway?" Joe Big asked.

"What are you talking about?"

Joe Big picked up one of the egg-sized rocks. He threw it hard at the big man's knee.

"Ahh." The big man swayed. He leaned to the side and vomited onto the road.

"Isn't that just the worst feeling?" Joe Big said. "Sort of a sick feeling from the bone out."

"Makes you want to puke and pass out all at the same time," Barney said.

"It was a mistake," the big man said. "Some of the men are recently returned from doing the Lord's work . . . They have not yet made the transition back to a Godless legal system."

"Damn," Joe Big said. "Would you just listen to yourself?"

"Two men are dead," Barney said.

"Yes. Two good men. Devout Catholic men. Crusaders for Christ and country, both of them." He groaned deep in his chest, his groan reminding Joe Big of the bear he'd seen on the other side of the ridge. "Killed by heathens such as the two or you."

"Did you have any idea he was like this?" Barney asked Joe Big.

Joe Big shook his head. "I knew he was weird, but this is *way* beyond mere weird."

"The deaths of those two men are on you," Barney said to the big man.

"We don't give a shit about your bent philosophy or your fucked up ideas about religion," Joe Big said. "Tell us what is going on, and maybe we'll get out of the way."

"The Lord's Will, will be done," the big man said.

"Who told you about us?" Barney asked.

The big man was silent. Joe Big picked up another rock.

"Someone who is at heart a good Christian person." They could hear in his voice that he had the pain under control.

"Quinn?" Barney asked. "*Quinn* is a good Christian person?"

The big man chuckled. "A harlot from Boston. An unrepentant bitch."

"I guess he means it's not Quinn," Joe Big said.

"What did you want with the modules?" Barney asked. "The computer chips we were supposed to sell you? Your company makes them."

The big man's pale pate rocked back and forth. "We are patriots, even as you two, with your misguided ways and ideals, are also patriots."

"Those men weren't patriots," Barney said. "They were mercenaries. No matter what kind of spin, religious or political or otherwise, you put on it, they were mercenaries who were breaking the law and putting civilian lives in mortal danger."

"Whoa," Joe Big said. "Barney, my man!"

"The men you killed represent the best of what this country is capable of producing," the big man said. "They were as patriotic as any man serving in uniform—"

"And if Custer had had a brain he would have taken his Gatling gun with him," Joe Big said.

Barney looked at him.

Joe Big shrugged. "I'll work on it."

"You're not telling us anything," Barney said to the big man.

"Nor shall I."

"So what is it?" Joe Big asked. "You *patriots* are going to put this country back on track. You're going to free us from the clutches of Non-Christians With Liberal Tendencies? I can't fucking keep it straight with you people, who has the right to live and who has the right to die."

"Doesn't matter with people like him," Barney said. "Politics and religion are excuses, is all."

Joe Big stood, and threw a rock at the big man, the rock winging past his head out into the field. "Less taxes, more taxes, wrong war, right war, one nation under God, or one nation of, by, and for the people. The right to bear arms, or the right to be safe from people who bear arms. A country controlled by religious elites. Or a country controlled by economic elites. Or a country controlled by both or neither. Man, *you motherfucking people!* All of you. Right wing, left wing, Martian, it doesn't fucking matter!" He leaned toward the figure on the ground. "You make me think that maybe homicide is not such a bad thing sometimes."

Barney started laughing.

"Laugh," the big man said. "Mock me. The Lord is sure to wreak his vengeance."

Barney and Joe Big stared at him for a moment.

"Wreak," Joe Big said.

"He sounds like a priest on acid, even when he's hurt bad," Barney said. "I guess you noticed the way he assumes we know everything is connected."

"Now that you mention it."

"You cannot hide from the people who will be looking for you," the big man said.

"What do you know about dead mules on a trail leading to Canada?" Joe Big asked.

The big man looked up, his teeth a pale white band in the darkness.

Joe Big threw a rock at his knee.

"Unhh."

A helicopter thudded low over a ridge farther down the valley, flying nap of the earth toward the ranch house.

"Calvary is here," Barney said.

"Any more words of wisdom before we shoot you?" Joe Big asked.

The big man chuckled, his teeth again seen in the dark.

The Cheshire Cat, Joe Big thought.

"You would be wise to see that I get to a hospital," the big man said.

"Hey, there's a concept," Barney said. "Us with wisdom." He took the monocular night vision scope from his pant pocket, and looked toward the distant ranch house. The scope was also a four-power telescope.

Bright lights had come on near the ranch house, illuminating what was apparently a helicopter landing pad behind the barn. The helicopter, European sleek, its long nose broken by air-to-ground surveillance equipment, was landing in the middle of the light. Tiny, black-clad figures in full SWAT gear, five or six, at least, streamed from the helicopter. The figures exited in a crouch, and moved fast toward the shadows, rifles up and pointed to the sides and front.

The helicopter lifted, and peeled away, headed for the other end of the valley.

"We're out of here," Joe Big said, standing. Barney put the monocular in his pocket, and they turned in unison, and began running down the road away from the ranch, Barney with his right hand holding the sling so that the M4 would not slap against his back.

"You want me to carry that?" Joe Big asked.

"I'm good."

"Soon as we get around the next curve, find a low spot where they can't see our tracks going up the embankment, and head straight for the ridge. Did that chopper have FLIR?"

"Yeah."

Both of them ran easy, their boots creating a cadence.

"They'll expect us to stick to the road and try to make it out before they can locate us," Joe Big said.

"Doesn't matter. They have to use the helicopter for a medevac. We'll be out of here before they get back."

"Good thing I shot him."

Barney laughed. "Oh, yeah," he said. "We probably know some of the people who are going to come looking to shoot *us*."

He jumped the low embankment, into sparse yellow grass and rock and pine needle covered hillside.

TEN MINUTES LATER, they stood on a rocky outcropping, breathing hard. The tree they were standing under was bare of branches to well above their heads. They watched the helicopter fly low down their side of the valley. It flared, and turned toward where they had left the big man. Two powerful landing lights came on, bright even from where they stood, and the helicopter disappeared from sight behind the low hills at the base of the ridge.

They put on their NVDs, and turned and headed down the other side of the ridge, into a phantasmagorical world of green.

They ran the trail, until Barney spotted the lone pine off the end of the switchback, and then they ran sidehill to the figure slumped arms around the base of the tree, on her before she was aware they were there.

Joe Big put his hand over her mouth. "It's us," he said in a low voice. "Keep quiet. Nod if you understand." He felt her head nod frantically. He took his hand from her mouth. Barney unlocked the cuffs and took them from around her wrists, and put them in his pocket.

He stood and unslung the M4 from across his back, checked the safety, and then checked to make sure the end of the barrel was clear.

"Barney is going to run the trail ahead of us," Joe Big said to the woman. "We are going to move fast. If there is any firing, you hit the ground and don't move. Got it?"

"Y-yes."

Barney ran back to the trail. Joe Big watched the green figure until Barney was out of sight.

"Let's go," he said. "Don't talk. If you fall, don't scream."

He grabbed her hand, and led her stumbling to the trail.

"Can you see the trail?"

"I c-can see it."

"Follow me."

"W-what i-if I d-don't?"

"Listen to me. If you pull any bullshit, I'll knock you out and carry you on my shoulders." Actually, he would just leave her there to fend for herself, but she didn't need to know that. Maybe not a bad idea, anyway. He could move a lot faster without her. But she was a loose end, and even though he doubted it, she might know something she didn't know she knew.

He turned and began moving down the trail, pausing to see that she was following him. She was.

Her politics were seriously deranged, but you had to hand it to her, he thought. Most people would have been a wreck by now. But she was keeping it together enough to follow him down the mountain.

Barney was waiting next to a tree.

"It's just us," he said. "But that not going to last for long. How you doin'?" he asked the woman.

Both of them abruptly realized that she was crying, her shoulders slumped, arms across her stomach. She nodded, hiccuping.

They each grabbed an arm and hustled her across the relatively open flat to the truck parked between trees at the side of the road.

"Get in the middle," Barney told her, as Joe Big got in the driver's side and took his NVD off and put it on the dash in front of the steering wheel.

He started the truck, and without turning on the lights, they bumped and swayed across the broken ground, onto the road. He switched on the lights and accelerated, both he and Barney tense, expecting to run into a roadblock of some kind any second, relieved to reach the highway without meeting any traffic.

Joe Big turned the truck onto the highway. A mile or so later, he relaxed back into the seat, steering with one hand. His whole body felt shaky and tired. He wanted nothing more than to stop the truck and get out and fall asleep on the side of the road.

"What are you going to do with me?" Tanya asked, her voice small.

"Good question," Barney said.

28
Vaya Con Dios

Early morning, not yet light outside, and Barney stood guard at the women's bathroom. He used his badge to repel the few early arrivals who wanted to use the bathroom, directing them to the facilities at the other end of the airport.

They'd driven into town, to a Starbucks off the Interstate open early for hunters, and one at a time he and Joe Big had used the restroom to wash the camouflage off their faces and to swap camouflage clothing for the ubiquitous combination of cargo pants and T-shirt and long-sleeved shirt worn open. The usual lattes for them, an extra-large hot chocolate for the woman.

Comforted by the hot chocolate and the city, she had regained her politics and her foul mouth, spouting radical Earth Liberation Front dogma about nature and society and the military-industrial-one-world-conspiracy to rape the planet and all who lived on it. Or something like that, Barney thought. They'd let her rant, get it out of her system.

Near as he could tell, she was a spoiled rich girl from Seattle. Her father was a dot-com multi-millionaire who'd cashed in his shares in his dot-com company at exactly the right moment and now owned, in addition to "safe" investments, pieces of Microsoft and Google and Pixar. She'd graduated from Connecticut College, an exclusive school that catered to "people like her," whoever people like her were. He didn't much care. It sounded more than a little elitist to him. While at university, she had been radicalized by some of the people she'd met, all of them rich, pampered, and sure they had a handle on what was wrong with the world. ELF people, Animal Rights people, Anti-War people, Anarchists, you name it. Listening to her, he lost track. Sex and drugs, Emo's and Goths, coffee-shop intellectuals, artists and poets and horseback riding in Central Park, kayaking and rock climbing and study abroad in Italy and Austria.

It made him wonder if they lived on the same planet.

She'd come out to Montana with a young man, an ELF she'd met at a loft in Manhattan. The loft belonged to a rich former rock star who fancied himself some kind of guru, but who was in reality just another dirty old man with gross fingernails and toenails and way too much nose hair—decadent and dissipated and functionally incoherent from decades of drugs and alcohol and kinky sex and music turned too loud to carry on a conversation. The young man had shared her contempt and her purity of thought and purpose (Joe Big had been forced to get out of the truck and walk around outside, he'd been laughing so hard). She was subsidized, of course, by her parents, and by her trust fund—which could not be fully accessed until she was thirty-two years old.

Once started, she'd rattled on and on, until her voice was merely ambient sound. Joe Big had opened the door and taken her face in his hands and stared into her eyes until she subsided, and started to silently cry again. Barney had seen him do the same thing with a lightly wounded Taliban they'd captured in deepest, darkest Waziristan, the man full of religious fervor—willingness to die for Allah, fight for Jihad, earn a thousand virgins, and all that. Big had taken his bearded face in his hands and stared into the man's eyes, no one saying a word, the entire team and the other prisoners staring at the two men. You could almost literally see the man crumble. One of the team—Mike the Troll, who was himself walking, talking proof that once upon a time there had been more than one branch of the human race—had a theory that Joe Big had the ability to reduce the relationship—the communication or whatever it was—to a time when humanity still had tails and webbed feet and speech was not necessary.

The Taliban had looked around the room, at the Force Recon Marines, their eyes feral in blackened faces, and he'd asked to go outside and talk with the CIA guy who'd been doing the interrogations. The CIA guy had come back into the room all smug, like it had been his doing. The Taliban had agreed to trade everything he knew for a new life in Europe somewhere.

He said that looking into Big's eyes had been like looking into the eyes of a poisonous snake.

According to Tanya, she'd hooked up with Patrick more for the size of his dick, and the fact that he was "like, totally charismatic when it came to politics and religion," than for any other reasons. To tell the truth, she was more attracted to Harold who was, "like, a totally smart guy, an honest-to-God Brainiac when it came to computers. Harold was "cute and funny and forever horny," her own private pet, near as Barney could tell.

"Tell us about the mercenaries and what they might be up to," Joe Big had said.

"First of all," she said, primly. "Most of them are, like, really nice guys, despite their obvious Fascist failings. They aren't mercenaries. They are civilian contractors. There is a big difference, you know. They do what they do not for money, but, like, out of patriotism and a super-developed sense of morals and ethics."

"Your sarcasm is pissing us off," Joe Big said.

"I'm not being sarcastic. At first I hated them. They represent everything that is wrong with the world. But once I got to know some of them, I saw that they really believe what they say. They are not tricksters."

"*Tricksters,*" Joe Big said. "I don't believe you just used that word."

"You two are a lot like them," she said. "Well, you are," she said to Barney. She wouldn't meet Joe Big's eyes.

The helicopter was in and out of the ranch a lot, she said. Suits arriving and leaving. She didn't know who the suits were, didn't recognize anyone, never talked to them. Patrick made her go out to the guesthouse, or go hiking or horseback riding when the suits were there. Sometimes the suits had their own security. Their security looked liked the Secret Service guys you see on the news around the President or Vice President. There didn't seem to be much difference between them and the mobile security teams, especially when the security teams did their drills, or whatever you called it, dressed in suits or in everyday clothes.

"Rehearsals?" Barney asked.

"Yeah. *Yeah!* Like that."

Joe Big shook his head.

Sometimes Patrick left for days at a time, and she was free to come and go as she pleased. One time, when there was going to be a big meeting at the ranch, he paid for her to spend a week with Harold in L.A. That was when Harold had started acting like he was from "like, some fucking barrio, or something." Harold had really connected with the language and the music and the style, she couldn't understand why. The "indigenous people" had connected with him, too. "It was amazing. It was, like, you know, Harold was going to die any minute, or at least get jacked up serious bad by these Latino thugs. Tats and eyes like garter snakes. All of them with really evil smiles. But, nooo. Not Harold. No way. They really dug on Harold. They would explain shit to him. What they were saying and all. You know, they would, like, *translate*. And Harold would explain stuff right back. Surveillance systems and computers. Shit like that. He'd tell it in a way they could *understand*.

"I mean," she said, "I couldn't understand a fucking word he was saying half the time, but these ignorant little beaner gangbangers, some of them were right with him. It was *surreal!*"

"Surreal," Joe Big said. "*This* is surreal."

"I know!" she said. "Exactly."

"Is that how you learned to use an M16?" Barney asked. "Those "security" guys taught you?"

"No way. I learned when I was a teenager and my family spent a couple of months in Hawaii. They have big shooting ranges there for all the Asian tourists, especially the Japanese. And, anyway," she said, "the security teams don't use M16s much. They use German weapons, mostly."

"How about protective gear?" Barney asked. "You know. Space-suit-looking stuff."

She shook her head. "No. But Pat was watching a video of a bunch of guys that looked like Men on the Moon or something. The video was taken, like, at another ranch his family has somewhere on the east side."

"Have you ever been to that ranch?" Joe Big asked.

"I haven't, but Harold has. He said it was, like, a lot bigger. Miles and miles of nothing but grass and hills."

"Any special buildings?" Barney asked.

"He said something about "the laboratory," once. But I didn't know what he was talking about." She frowned. "He had that look you get when you, like, say something that you shouldn't say or don't mean to say." She glanced at Barney.

"Harold always looks like he's guilty of something," Barney said.

"Oh, I know. Isn't that the truth? He can be such a mouse sometimes."

"Hey," Joe Big said.

She looked at him, her eyes big.

Joe Big opened the door, and climbed out.

"Get out of the truck," he said, his voice bleak.

She shook her head no.

Joe Big reached in and gently grasped her by the bicep. "You knew this was coming," he said.

Barney raised his eyebrows from behind her.

Joe Big pulled her gently out onto the ground next to the truck. He moved her to the side so that her back was against the pickup bed and the topper.

He put his fingers under her chin and raised her head so she would look at him. Tears were silently streaming down the sides of her face. Her eyes were an ugly combination of fear and pleading.

"Where is it?" he asked.

Her mouth opened.

"My hair," he said. "What did you do with my hair?"

"I'm sorry," she said, her face crumpling. "I'm so sorry." Her head dropped so that he was looking at the top of her head, hair falling on both sides of her face, shoulders soundlessly working.

With his right hand he grabbed the hair on the top of her head and yanked her head back, the back of his hand banging against the aluminum topper. He stared into her eyes. "Where. Is. My. Hair?"

"I put it in a box, and buried it up near the ridge behind the house."

"Why there?"

"It's my secret place. There's a spring, and a little grass-covered area between the spring and a big rock. I-I buried it at the base of a giant pine."

"Why?"

Her mouth opened, and she stared at him, too terrified to say anything.

"Why?"

"It s-seemed like the right thing to do."

"What kind of box?"

"A-an extra-big cigar box. He gave it to me for my rock collection."

"Your rock collection. How old are you?"

"Twenty-nine."

Joe Big released her hair and stepped back.

"I'm so sorry," she said. "I am so sorry."

"You cut off my hair." His knife appeared in his hand. He held it in front of her face, and moved it back and forth slowly, her wide eyes tracking it. "The Blackfeet—I'm part Blackfeet, did you know that?"

"Y-yes. Piegan."

The knife paused. "You know the difference?"

Her eyes remained locked on the blade. She nodded.

"How?"

"I met an old woman—a-a Blackfoot woman from Canada."

"Did she tell you how a Blackfeet man would sometimes cut the nose off his wife if the wife was unfaithful."

Her eyes widened even more.

He touched the tip of the knife to the end of her nose, and pushed the tip hard enough to produce a drop of blood.

"Your nose for my hair. Does that sound fair? Ah, fuck it," he said to himself. The knife disappeared back in his pocket.

"We don't want to see you again. Ever," he said. "Do you understand?"

She nodded.

"This State is not for you."

She nodded again, more enthusiastic this time.

"You will go home and apologize to your parents. You will do something real with you life."

"Oh, yes."

"No, you won't. In a month you'll be just as fucked up as you are right now. Get in the truck."

Tanya came out of the bathroom, and Barney pushed off from the wall, and put his badge case in his back pocket. She looked pale and wan, dark half-moons under her eyes.

Joe Big walked up to them, boarding pass in hand. He handed it to her. "One way to Seattle, compliments of the United States Government. Let's go."

Using their Federal ID and their badges, they escorted her through security and up the steps to the gate she'd be leaving from. The first flight of the day.

Barney and Joe Big walked to one of the windows, keeping an eye on her sitting alone.

"We're getting soft," Barney said.

"Think so?"

Barney thought about it for a moment. "No. Not really, I guess. She was pissed off that you fucked her in order to twist her to your nefarious ends, that's all."

"Nefarious ends?"

Barney smiled. "Yeah."

"It wasn't easy being mean to her."

"I could tell."

"I'm serious. She's not the enemy. I only did it because I thought if I scared her bad enough—if she saw for even a few seconds how real it can get—maybe she'd go home and get a life."

"Well, you never know," Barney said, looking at her. "Stranger things have happened."

A young man in a dark windbreaker with the airline logo on the left breast, sound suppressors around his neck, came through the door leading to a tunnel, and stood behind a small podium and announced that the flight would board.

Tanya looked at them. They both nodded.

She got up and, glancing at them several times, as if she couldn't believe they were really going to let her leave, walked to the young man and handed him her boarding pass. At the doorway she looked back once, and then hurried through the door and down the tunnel.

"Maybe it ought to be us getting on that plane," Barney said.

"Where would we go?"

"Good point."

They moved to the window, and looking down at the propeller-driven plane, watched as she climbed the stairs close behind a couple of suits, crowding them to get on the plane faster.

"Vaya con dios," Barney said.

"Or not," Joe Big said.

29
Exposure

Zero-dark-thirty, black sky above orange streetlights, frost on parked cars and on the hood of the truck. The only people out and about were paperboys and people headed into or away from night jobs—nurses, all-night convenience store workers, burglars. A City Police cruiser silently crossed the street two blocks down.

"I guess you know there's no going back to being a deputy," Barney said.

Joe Big snorted.

"When you think about it, it's amazing we've lasted this long," Barney said.

A small, chubby dog hurried down the sidewalk on the other side of the street.

"Where do you suppose he's going?" Barney asked.

"He's going home. He's had a tough night dicking someone's prize poodle."

"Look at him. Tongue hanging out."

"Remind you of anyone?" Joe Big asked.

"Hey!"

They watched the dog turn off the sidewalk and disappear in the shadows between houses.

"I think we are caught in the middle of something," Barney said. "Those guys might have been pissed off enough to come looking for us, but they are too professional to do it without some kind of sanction."

"There's a word I haven't heard in awhile."

"I don't know how else to put it."

Joe Big yawned.

"We've been here two hours," Barney said. "No lights. No movement. We killed two men. Brianna is in the hospital. We are in the wind somewhere . . . I guarantee you that ranch is lit up like a Christmas tree. Men who know what they are doing are on that ridge. Patrick is in surgery, or just getting out. Men who know what they are doing are at the hospital with him. But this place is dead. No good guys. No bad guys. Not even a City car nosing around."

"No sentries," Joe Big said. "No surveillance."

"At least none we can see," Barney said. "There could be someone watching the house all the time—from cameras hidden in the trees or in surrounding buildings, for all we know."

"And you think Quinn has figured out what is going on?"

"Why not? We figured it out, and we're not exactly Mensa candidates. She might even be using it."

"Using it for what?"

"Only she knows that."

Joe Big looked at him. "Then we are—"

"Dude, we are like that dog that just walked by. We have managed to put our noses and our dicks where we were not supposed to put them. And now we are expected to waddle on home to be neutered by the veterinarian."

"And you accuse me of lame metaphors."

"Somebody set us up, when we met Patrick and Harold and Tanya up the Blackfoot."

"Well, I been thinking about that," Joe Big said. "I think Patrick thought he was dealing with a couple of local Miami Mice. His out, if it turned out he needed an out, was to say that he was dealing with a potential National Security threat."

"Little did he know we would go off the reservation."

"Just had to say it, didn't you?"

"Somebody had to."

Joe Big stared at the dark house two blocks down. "Maybe we ought to go ON the reservation."

"What do you mean?"

"Lay low on the Rez until this blows over. Plenty of people would hide us, no problem."

"You think Quinn, or Patrick and his merry band of mercs, would let us do that?"

"If we can remove ourselves from the equation for long enough, maybe it will go right past us," Joe Big said. He rubbed the side of his face, and sat up and checked behind the truck.

"Fuck this," he said. "This is just mental masturbation. Let's drive over to those four-plexes below the Interstate. It's a hike back to the office, but at least we won't have to worry about someone spotting this truck. We can cut over to the railroad tracks, follow the tracks, and then come down the alley to the office. Walk in like we own the place. You can call Quinn and tell her to meet us. Tell her we're an hour out, or something."

"And then?"

"And then, we'll see what she has to say."

"You plan to shoot her in the knee, too?"

"It will take a lot more than a bullet in the knee to make that woman talk."

"I'm glad you realize that."

"We've got the arrows," Joe Big said. "And we've got that cell phone. She has a charger on her desk, and spare batteries in a drawer."

"How do you know that?"

"I needed a pen."

"Of course, you did."

Joe Big started the truck.

"That's a camera phone," he said. "And I bet there's an elk on it."

THEY WERE SILENT, as they walked the railroad tracks, and then up the embankment, between houses, to the alley. They paused in the alley across from the cracked and heaved concrete parking space behind the office.

"We're being watched," Joe Big said. "But not from the house."

They crossed the alley, and walked up the steps. Barney opened the door with a key. Inside, he crossed quickly to a kitchen cabinet, opened the cabinet door, and punched off the alarm.

Joe Big ghosted into the bathroom. He sat on the toilet seat to wait.

Barney turned on the kitchen light, and then shut and locked the door. He made a production of making coffee, banging around so that if anyone were in the house they would come to the kitchen.

Once he had the coffee maker doing its thing, he went to Quinn's office and rummaged through the drawers that weren't locked. In a bottom drawer he found spare cell phone batteries, and put one into the cell phone. He turned on the cell phone.

He walked through the office to the bathroom and silently held the phone out for Joe Big to see. The screen showed Quinn's list of speed-dial numbers, including their own. He pushed buttons, and a picture appeared of an elk on the ground next to a wallow, arrows in its ribs and shoulder.

He cycled back to the list of numbers, and selected "home."

"That was quick," he said into the phone. "You must've been up." He paused. "It's Special Anti-Terrorist Agent Lambier."

He turned and walked into the kitchen. "Well, that's a mystery, isn't it? Why your caller ID is showing this call coming from your very own cell phone." He found two cups in the cupboard, USMC on both mugs in red and gold letters, and poured coffee into both.

"We're on our way into the office. We're about an hour out." He listened. "At a rest stop near Drummond." He took one cup over to the bathroom and handed it to Joe Big. "He's using the facilities." He walked back to his cup sitting on the counter. "In my car." He picked up the cup of coffee. "Is there some reason why we shouldn't be in my car?" He took a sip. "You don't say? People are looking for us? Flathead County has an APB on a car fitting the description of my car . . . Two guys fitting our description . . ." He took a drink, smiling around the cup. He put the cup carefully down on the counter. "Look, ma'am. This is a courtesy call. If you want to talk to us, we'll be at the office in about an hour. Be there or be square." He snapped the phone shut, and put it in his pocket, and then went around and turned out all the lights he'd turned on. He hiked himself up on the kitchen counter between the coffee maker and his cup, and picked up the cup and took a drink.

Five minutes later, a black Suburban pulled up across the street and three men in dark clothes and with long rifles or shotguns got out. One of them knelt on one knee next to a maple tree. The other two walked across the street, one to the back of the house, the other to the front.

Barney walked to the front of the house and looked out through the stained-glass window in the top of the solid old antique door, careful to keep his face back far enough to not be seen as a pale blur from outside. The figure that had gone to the front was talking to another figure—in full combat kit, it looked like—that had come out of the neighboring yard.

He walked back to the kitchen and looked out the window over the sink. Two figures, one in full combat kit, were conversing in the middle of the driveway. They broke apart, one to shadows between the garage and the house, the one in combat kit in under the hedge of blue spruce. He and Big must have walked right by him when they came in.

A Police cruiser pulled up next to the Suburban parked across the street, and the man next to the tree walked over and talked to the cop. The cruiser moved away, its headlights and brake lights switched off, and turned into the alley behind the house, and motored down the alley. Another Police cruiser went by on the street.

Barney walked to the bathroom and showed Joe Big five fingers, and then made a circling motion to indicate the house was surrounded.

Joe Big gave him a thumbs-up.

Car lights bounced against the counters in the kitchen, as a car or a truck pulled into the parking area. Barney put his cup on the counter and went to stand behind the door. A car door closed outside, and he heard murmured conversation, and then footsteps at the back door.

A key turned in the lock, and the door swung open toward him, and Quinn came through the door. She went to the cupboard and punched off the alarm.

She closed the back door, startled to find Barney standing there, even though she must have known they were in the house. He hit her hard in the solar plexus and threw her face down on the floor, a knee in her back. He forced her arms one at a time back behind her back, and snapped the cuffs on her wrists, making sure they were snug. She was making soft grunts of sound, trying to draw her knees to her chest.

He stood and stepped to the side, checking the back window and the side window. No one was visible.

She started coughing, and managed to get to her knees.

He walked to the counter and retrieved his cup and topped it off at the coffee maker. He leaned back against the counter, and took a sip of coffee, watching as she struggled to regain her breathing.

He set the cup on the counter, and retrieved the phone from his pocket. He opened it, and cycled to a picture of the elk. He showed her the picture.

She sat back on her heels, and stared at it for a moment.

"Where'd you get that phone?" she asked, her voice tight, anger barely repressed. He was glad he'd cuffed her.

"One of the guys who was there when Brianna got beat with a pool cue gave it to us."

She was silent. He could feel her fighting for control.

"Where's Joe?"

"Joseph is unavailable at the moment."

"What do you think you are doing?"

"People are dead or fucked up because you lied to us."

"I haven't lied to you."

"Not telling us everything is the same as a lie."

"What haven't I told you?"

"You tell me."

"If I don't tell the men outside that I'm okay in here, they are going to come through this door and shoot you."

He laughed. "You better hope not."

"Fuck you, *Deputy* Lambier. I don't have to justify my actions to you."

"That's the spirit."

"What are you going to do? Shoot me?"

"No, ma'am. I don't believe so. I believe I will simply break your neck with my bare hands."

"Oh, spare me the drama. What do you want?"

"No offense, but those are Feds out there. If it was the bad guys, I'd be worried."

"Who are the bad guys?"

"Cute."

She was silent.

The screen door opened, and there was a knock on the back door—a rifle barrel against the wood. "Ma'am? Is everything all right in there?"

"I stand corrected," Barney said. "Tell that Marine you are in the bathroom."

"Fuck you. Tell him yourself."

"It's on your head," Barney said.

"Goddamn it," she said. "I'm fine," she yelled. "I'm in the bathroom."

The figure at the door muttered something, and the screen door shut.

"What do you want to know?" she asked, staring past him into the hallway.

"He wants to know what side he should be on," a familiar voice said from the hallway. "Stay where you are, Mr. Lambier. This is a .45 in my hand, and well do I know how to use it."

"Mrs. W?"

Quinn struggled to her feet. "You motherfucker . . ."

"Quinn!" Mrs. W said. "Control yourself. This young man has a right to be angry. We can't blame him for—" Her voice caught in her throat.

"If you move your head it's going to cut you," Joe Big said. "Safe the weapon, and put it on the counter."

"The safety is on." They heard a heavy thunk as the .45 hit the counter.

Barney took the .45 from the counter and put it next to the coffee pot. He grabbed Quinn by the front of her sweatshirt, and tripped her over his leg back down to the floor.

Joe Big grasped Mrs. W by the arm and steered her into the office. He pulled out a chair and rolled it in front of one of the desks, and gently guided her into it.

He went to the windows and let the wood shades down, and then turned on a couple of desk lights. He pulled out another chair and sat facing Mrs. W. "Sorry," he said, and showed her a long, slender emery board that he'd taken from the bathroom. "My knife."

Mrs. W smiled. "I am delighted to see that you two have not completely lost your senses."

"You were upstairs?"

"Yes. I was asleep until I heard what I thought was one person come in and make coffee. And then I heard Mr. Lambier talking on the telephone. I should have expected no less from the two of you."

"You've lost your Aunt Jemima accent."

"So I have."

Barney brought Quinn into the room, and made her sit on the floor.

Quinn looked up at Mrs. W.

"It's okay," Mrs. W said to her. She smiled at the two men, her eyes no longer reminding Joe Big of his grandmother's eyes. Her voice and smile were as friendly as ever, but her eyes were like black stones.

"Did you really lose a husband in Iraq?" Barney asked.

"No, Mr. Lambier. I did not. My husband is alive and well, a full bird Colonel stationed at Quantico, Virginia. He commanded a company of grunts headed to Baghdad in the early days of the war. Barely a week in, and he was wounded by a sniper."

"Hey," Joe Big said. "I know your husband. A big black guy. A Major, then. Played football at Ohio State or somewhere like that. Voice like a Baptist preacher."

She smiled, and nodded. "He remembers you and your team well."

"He remembers my team?"

"Of course. You already had a reputation." She smiled.

Barney and Joe Big studied her. An elegant, middle-aged black woman dressed in slacks and cashmere sweater and slip-on shoes. Glasses attached to a gold chain around her neck. Barney knew that Joe Big had been in Afghanistan when the Marines went into Iraq. Big had ad libbed the story about the Major, and she had hitched a ride on it.

Joe Big looked at him.

Barney shrugged.

"Do you know Quinn's old cell phone number?" Joe Big asked Mrs. W.

"I think I recall it, yes."

"What is it?"

Barney punched in the numbers on one of the desk phones, and held Quinn's cell phone toward Mrs. W. The cell phone rang. Barney snapped the cell phone closed, and hung up the other phone.

He walked over to Mrs. W, and opened the phone and selected a picture of the elk.

"This phone was given to us by the bad guys," he said. "Along with two arrows. But not the two that are stuck in the elk."

Mrs. W looked at Quinn.

"I told you I lost the phone when I accidentally kicked it off a big rock I was standing on," Quinn said.

Joe Big walked over to the desk he shared with Barney, and picked up the two arrows taped together. With a quick flick of his wrist and arm, he threw them hard into the floor between Quinn and Mrs. W, the arrows sticking with a solid finality, razors buried deep into the wood.

"As you can see," Barney said. "The nocks are missing on the arrows stuck in the elk. Probably from when it rolled over."

Mrs. W peered at the cell phone in Barney's hand. She looked at the arrows stuck in the floor. "Yes," she said. "The ends are very white and distinctive. I don't see any—what do you call them?—in the picture."

"Nocks," Barney said. He snapped the cell phone closed, and threw it on the nearest desk. "You can hook it to the computer and show it on the big screen," he said. "If you use that enhancement program you showed us, I'm sure you'll see that the arrows stuck in the elk have been mangled by the elk rolling around, trying to dislodge them."

"What are you getting at?" Mrs. W asked.

"One of those arrows stuck in the floor is clean and new," Barney said. "The other has blood on it. The lab will confirm that it is human blood."

"She killed one of them," Joe Big said. He smiled at the rage in Quinn's eyes. "Which might help explain why they did a number on Brianna, and why they tried to do a number on us."

Quinn flushed at the mention of Brianna.

It was hard to believe, Barney thought, that such a beautiful woman —an Irish lass from Boston, no less—had skewered a former Special Forces operator with an arrow. She was beautiful, all right. The same way that a copperhead camouflaged by fall leaves is beautiful. Big was right.

"I wish I could have killed them all," Quinn said to Mrs. W.

"To be sure, child. But as I'm sure these two gentleman agree: knowing you had killed a man would have helped both them and Brianna to better evaluate the motivation of the opposition."

"The opposition," Joe Big said.

"Who are you, anyway?" Barney asked.

She considered him for a moment.

"I'm a troubleshooter," she said.

"For who?"

"I usually operate under the terms of a finding," she said.

"A Presidential finding?" Barney asked.

"That is correct."

Barney looked at Joe Big. Joe Big cocked his head to the side.

"It means she can do any damn thing she wants in pursuit of whatever the finding is about," Barney said. "It's up to the President to inform Congress in a speedy manner." He looked at Mrs. W with new respect. "But since findings are always classified to the very highest level, hardly anyone ever knows about them."

"Do you even have a husband?" Joe Big asked.

She chuckled. "Yes. But he is not in the military." She crossed her arms across her chest, waiting.

A cell phone went off—some kind of Jazz music—on the desk she normally occupied.

"Would you be so kind, one of you, to hand me that phone, please."

Barney walked to her desk and retrieved the phone and handed it to her.

She opened the phone. "Yes," she said into the phone, and waited a moment. "No. They're here now. No. No. Everything is okay. They are being perfect gentlemen." She listened. "Yes. Keep everyone in place, and continue the roving patrols. Thank you." She closed the phone, and smiled at them.

Joe Big sighed, and shook his head.

"We quit," Barney said. "We didn't sign up for anything like this."

"This?"

"This getting shot at and shooting back," Joe Big said.

She frowned. "I'm sorry? The last we heard was that the Flathead Country Sheriff's Department was looking for a car that fits the description of your car. There was no mention of any shooting."

"Let's just go," Joe Big said to Barney.

Barney stared at Mrs. W. "I don't think she knows," he said. "It's not an act."

"Knows what?" she asked. "Okay, here's the deal, gentlemen. As of this moment—Quinn is my witness, as are the recording devices in this room—you two are back on active duty. You are under my command."

"You can't do that," Joe Big said. "We've both been permanently released from duty because of war wounds."

"You were released from active duty, but you are still part of the inactive reserve, and as such can be called up at the discretion of your Government, wounds or no wounds. Sorry about that, sweetie. But look on the bright side. You are now double-dipping as far as pay is concerned." She smiled at them.

Quinn smiled at them.

Two different smiles.

"We killed two men, and knee-capped a third," Joe Big said.

Her eyes widened, and her mouth opened slightly. "My goodness."

"Still want to keep us on?" Barney asked.

"And it's all on you," Joe Big said to Quinn.

"Please explain," Mrs. W said.

Barney looked at Joe Big.

"Be my guest," Joe Big said.

Barney sighed, and for the next thirty minutes explained what had happened from the time they had driven to Harold's house. Mrs. W interrupted only to ask for more details about the men they'd killed and the men who had been in the Chrysler.

Somewhere in the middle of the story Joe Big walked over and undid the cuffs from Quinn's wrists. Her hands were swollen and red. Barney was talking about throwing a flare under the EVO.

"Deal with it," Joe Big said to Quinn. "It wouldn't have happened if we would have known how pissed off they were about you killing one of them with a fucking arrow."

Quinn almost come off the floor at him, but changed her mind when she saw his eyes. Instead, she went to the kitchen to get a cup of coffee.

Joe Big walked through Quinn's darkened office to the front door, and looked out, while Barney continued the story in the other room. A dark shadow stood at the far corner of the porch, head slowly swiveling back and forth. He could make out the bulky outline of an NVD. The street was empty, devoid of traffic.

He turned and went back to the other room.

"And you knee-capped whom?" Mrs. W was asking Barney.

"Patrick Huntington the Third or Fourth, or however many," Joe Big said. "And it was me not Barney who did it."

"Why did you do it?"

"So he couldn't get his hands on me, and so he wouldn't run away. He is a very big, very strong man."

"And what did he say after you shot him in the knee?"

"We didn't have much time to talk. A helicopter landed down the road at his ranch, and let out what looked like a SWAT team."

"He must have told you something."

"He offered us a chance to be on the side of the righteous."

"Ah," She said. "The apple does not fall far from the tree."

"Whatever that means," Barney said.

"His father is a very influential man," she said. "A very powerful man in Washington, as well as on Wall Street."

"A Christian," Joe Big said. It was a statement not a question.

"A Catholic," she amended. "Like me and like you. But an ultra right-wing Catholic allied with rich, powerful, ultra right-wing Evangelical Christians. They'd like to amend the Constitution. They don't believe in the separation of Church and State."

Barney and Joe Big were silent, struggling to digest what she was telling them.

"Religion," Joe Big finally said to Barney.

"American Ayatollahs," Barney replied.

"Technology," Joe Big said. "More money than the GNP of most countries."

"Their own private armies."

"Enough lawyers to populate a small city."

Mrs. W smiled. "You two are forgetting a key element, aren't you?"

"Politics are a given," Barney said. "We don't talk about politics. Ever."

She laughed. "Oh, ye of pure heart."

"Patrick's father owns the company that manufactures the chips we were trying to sell him," Barney said. "Why would Patrick want to buy computer modules that he already owns?"

"He had no interest in the computer modules themselves," she said. "As it turns out, they are obsolete. We didn't know it at the time but his father's company already had a new guidance module in production. They simply wanted to know who was selling them, where they had gotten them from, and for what purposes they were intended. He initially thought that the two of you represented a group willing to sell advanced technology to whoever had the money, even to terrorists. To be fair, he thought he was doing his patriotic duty."

"Who told him we were cops?"

"Quinn let it slip that the local Sheriff's Department had a couple of undercover cops working a case that involved guidance modules—a passing reference at a meeting with their top security people."

Mrs. W regarded them for a moment. "They had plans to capture you, torture you if necessary, and then kill you. When they discovered that you were cops, that put a stop to that nonsense." She smiled. "Unfortunately, Patrick felt the two of you had somehow abused his personal trust. He is apparently a bit of a loose cannon."

"So as far as they were concerned, we were merely a couple of local cops working with the Feds?" Barney asked.

"That's right. They knew nothing about your military background."

"What about Quinn's CI?" Joe Big asked. "The one she killed one of their men over."

"A sad case, that." She shook her head, and managed to look sad without being sad. "There has been a rash of terrorist events around the country attributed to the Earth Liberation Front. Houses burned, very expensive heavy equipment ruined, public utilities disrupted, that sort of thing. One of the subsidiary companies owned by the group that Patrick's father represents was hard hit by some of their shenanigans. The meet was to work out a deal for the purchase of C-4 and solid rocket fuel. The mere fact that Quinn's CI wanted such things was evidence enough to them that Quinn's CI was a serious menace. As you have by now no doubt ascertained, these people have a low opinion of our present legal system."

"Obviously, so do you," Joe Big said.

"Solid rocket fuel?" Barney asked.

"I understand it is quite effective when used to start fires. It leaves no trace evidence whatsoever."

"So let me get this straight," Barney said. "You thought you were dealing with people who had explosives and rocket fuel for sale to the highest bidder?"

"That's right."

"Even to home-grown terrorist organizations, like ELF?"

"Yes, we thought we were dealing with a rogue element."

"And in turn they thought they had discovered an ELF cell," Barney said. "They decided to make an example out of Quinn's CI. Let the cell know that there are people out there who know how to take care of business. Keep messing around and you get dead, that kind of thing."

"You put it crudely, Mr. Lambier. But, yes. That they were able to learn his history of mental instability—which included two previous suicide attempts—only exacerbated the situation."

"No shit," Joe Big said.

"And then Quinn killed one of them," Barney said.

"It would appear so."

"And now we have made a bad situation even worse," Joe Big said.

"No," she said. "Actually, not. You two may have inadvertently done exactly what we hoped you would do. You have forced them to speed up their timetable. You have created exposure."

"Exposure?" Joe Big said. "This is all about *exposure?*"

"Well, that . . . and the fact that there is a good chance they plan to create a terrorist event that uses extremely lethal chemical agents," she said. "Tens of thousands could die."

"So that Americans will be willing to give up even more freedoms in order to win the war on terrorism," Barney said. "It sounds like a bad movie."

"There's more to it than that," Joe Big said. "It's a holy war, isn't it?" he asked her. "Christians against everyone else. Our own special brand of Ayatollahs using the politics of fear to get what they want. Their own private army made up of some of the best, most patriotic men and women who have ever worn a uniform. True believers themselves."

Mrs. W beamed. "You are most astute—both of you."

Barney looked worried at Joe Big. "You don't believe this shit, do you?" he asked.

Joe Big laughed, and shook his head. "Not a chance." He watched as Mrs. W's face turned to stone. "She's talking excuses, is all. If it's about anything, it's about power. The religious thing is nothing more than smoke and mirrors. American Ayatollahs don't exist—other than as a fiction to feed to the Great Unwashed." He looked at Barney. "The 'Great Unwashed' would include you and me."

"I'm disappointed," Mrs. W said to Joe Big. "I thought there was more to you than that."

"Lady—whoever you are—your Machiavellian bullshit has landed one of us and one of them in the hospital, and three of them, including the one Quinn did a Robinette Hood on, in body bags. From the minute we first walked in the door, we've been nothing more than stalking horses to you—cannon fodder, if need be. If Quinn's CI hadn't been looking to buy C-4 and rocket fuel, he'd still be alive. And Quinn would not have murdered one of them." He paused, studying her. "You don't like that word do you? Murder. Well, if Quinn had not *murdered* one of them, then they would not have done a number on Brianna. If they had not done a number on Brianna, then Barney and I would not have gotten involved. And if Barney and I had not gotten involved, then two men who served their country honorably in war would still be alive, *never mind* that they might have been crazy as bedbugs when it came to what they believed is best for this country.

"The sad fact is," he said. "We know them better than we know you. You've sat here behind your desk, a nice Aunt Jemima lady with a sad story about a husband killed in Iraq—a spider spinning a web, with us for bait."

"You were never in any real danger, Joseph."

Barney laughed, and Joe Big stared at her, incredulous.

"I don't know what constitutes "real danger" in your world, lady," he said. "But a hundred and forty plus miles an hour on a crowded highway with no shoulders, bullet holes in the car, and two crispy critters in the forest sort of implies real danger in our world."

She sighed. "The plan was that they would try to recruit the two of you. According to the profilers this would happen. But then—by chance—you met two of them on your way to the Flathead." She looked toward the kitchen and frowned. "I see . . ." she muttered to herself.

She looked from one man to the other. "Whatever you think you know, you keep it to yourself. Do you understand?" There was no mistaking the "or else" in her tone of voice.

Joe Big opened his mouth to speak, and she stood abruptly, surprising them, and walked over to Joe Big. "That is not a request. It's an order." She looked from one to the other. "Button your lips, and keep them buttoned."

"For the record," Barney said loudly. "For all you people listening in on this conversation. We quit. We do not accept, nor do we believe that this woman has the power to reinstate us in the United States Military. As far as we know," he said to Mrs. W. "You are a senior civil service office administrator, nothing more."

"Lieutenant," she said. "Send in the Sergeant, please."

The front door opened and closed, and they heard someone walking through Quinn's office. "Aye, aye, sir," they heard, and a man about their age walked into the light, full camouflage combat gear, NVD attached to his helmet, face blackened, M4 rifle with night sight held in both hands, barrel pointed to his left down at the floor.

"Ma'am," he said.

"Sergeant will you please keep an eye on these two."

"Yes, Ma'am." His eyes did not leave Joe Big and Barney.

She turned and walked to the kitchen.

Joe Big sat on the nearest desktop and crossed his arms over his chest. He could hear the murmur of low voices on the other side of the wall behind him, but couldn't make out the words.

Barney casually took a seat behind another desk.

Both of them stared blankly at the man in combat kit.

Joe Big reached behind his hip and pulled out the Sig, and held it against his right thigh.

The Sergeant thumbed the safety off the M4 and put his finger on the trigger. His eyes glanced toward Barney.

Barney had his .45 in a two-handed grip pointed at the man's head.

The man grinned, his teeth white in his blackened face. He clicked the safety back on, and set the rifle on the nearest desk. He unfastened the strap on his helmet and took it off.

Mrs. W raised her voice in the other room.

Joe Big holstered his weapon, and Barney set the .45 on the desk.

"How many guys you got outside?" Barney asked.

"Sir, enough."

"You don't have to 'sir' us."

"No, sir. I don't."

Barney looked at Joe Big. "Another Jarhead," he said.

"Yup," Joe Big said. "Force Recon. You got any time in the 'Stans, Sergeant?"

"Some." He sat on the desk. "I heard you got your shit blown away in Iraq somewhere."

"He did," Barney said. "Irreparable brain damage."

"Have we met before?" Joe Big asked.

The Sergeant shook his head. "Your team was on the same 53 that was transporting the team I was with. You got out on a ridge on one side of the valley, we got out on a ridge on the other side of the valley. One of the guys asked who the Chinaman was, and somebody else said you weren't no Chinaman; you were an Indian from Montana. I didn't recognize you at first."

Joe Big gestured toward Barney. "Special Forces," he said. "He was on that flight, too."

The sergeant inclined his head toward Barney. "Sorry about that, sir."

"Sorry about what?"

"Sorry about you being Special Forces."

"What's going on around here?" Joe Big asked.

"No idea." The Recon sergeant raised his voice. *"But it's a cluster-fuck, if you ask me.* We're supposed to be guarding against some—he raised his voice again—*bad-ass mercs.*" He shook his head. "I thought I was done with those guys when I left Afghanistan."

"Lot of former Marines and Rangers and SEALS are mercs, these days," Joe Big said.

"When they become mercs they stop being all that, far as me and my team are concerned."

Mrs. W came back into the room. "Thank you sergeant. You may go back to your post."

"Ma'am." The sergeant picked up his helmet and put it on, not bothering to attach the strap. He lifted the rifle in his right hand and left the room. They heard the door open and close.

"Now, then—" she began.

"What do you want with us?" Barney asked. "There's nothing we can do that those guys out there can't do as well or better."

She stared at Barney, as if he was some sort of bug in a specimen drawer.

"She wants us to kill someone," Joe Big said. "Isn't that right Mrs. Whoever You Are?"

"Will you please remove your fanny from my desk," she said to him.

Joe Big stood, and went over to the bay window. He shoved a couple of the plants to the side, and sat.

She took a seat at her desk.

"It seems," she said, taking a sip of coffee. "That there is a very beautiful young woman, half Vietnamese, who owns a deli-bakery in Painted Cliff, Montana. She has a handsome little boy by the name of Samuel. The woman and her son live in a large, expensive house perched on a mountain overlooking village and lake." She smiled sweetly. "How her mother came to be in this country, and how she and her husband managed to parlay a Marine sergeant's pay into a string of car dealerships and other businesses is a matter that, some would say, deserves investigation." She chuckled. "You know those Chinese Vietnamese. They are constitutionally incapable of playing it straight with the taxman, no matter how much money they might have. There are even off-shore bank accounts, I'm told."

She smiled at Barney. "And then there is this cute-as-a-button snowboarder who likes to indulge in drugs occasionally, and who can generally be counted on to supply her friends with whatever pharmaceuticals her friends might desire. A matter for the DEA to pursue, perhaps?

"It would be a shame—" she began, and Joe Big threw a flowerpot at the front of the desk, the pot shattering against the desk, dirt and plants scattering across the floor.

He stood and heaved another flowerpot against the wall to her right, and another to her left, the two pots shattering against the wall, showering her with dirt and shards of clay pot.

Smiling, she brushed dirt from her hair and from the shoulders of her sweater.

Quinn came to the edge of the wall separating the office area from the hallway.

Barney and Joe Big looked at her, and she went back into the kitchen.

"Now we are getting somewhere," Mrs. W said. "Go ahead," she said to Joe Big. "Say it."

Barney stood. "He doesn't have anything to say."

"I want you two young men to go home and get a good night's sleep," she said. "Someone will be along tomorrow or the next day to confirm your reinstatement as full-time military personnel."

Joe Big started toward her, but Barney reached out and grabbed his arm. "Let's go," he said. "We got what we came for."

"And take McBride with you," Mrs. W said. "She will brief you on the mission, and be your liaison."

"Go," Barney said, shoving Joe Big toward the hallway. "Just go."

30
Uncle Ben's Place

"Pull into the Hospital parking lot," Barney said. "We'll leave this thing there."

The three of them were in Quinn's SUV. The streets were empty of traffic, the parking lot and the parked cars stark in the yellowish light from high-pressure sodium vapor lights.

Quinn pulled into a space between two subcompact cars, both covered with pale-yellow frost.

"Leave your cell phone," Barney said.

"Why?"

"So they can't track you," Joe Big said.

"They know where we're going anyway."

"No, they don't," Barney said. "Leave it."

Quinn opened the door and climbed out the driver's side. She turned and tossed her cell phone onto the floor mat.

Inside the hospital, the sounds and colors were muted. Stuffed couches and comfortable looking chairs were arranged in intimate groupings. A heavy-set woman in shapeless clothing looked up from her knitting as they walked through the waiting area. An older, grizzled man slept mouth open on a couch across from her.

"Where do you think he is?" Barney asked Joe Big.

"He's either hitting on the nurses in ICU or reading a book in the ready room."

"Think he'll do it?" Barney asked.

"It's us, bro."

"We're asking a lot."

"He's good for a lot more than we're asking."

Joe Big pushed the button for the elevator.

FIFTEEN MINUTES LATER, they were seated in the LifeFlight helicopter, looking down at city streets sliding past. They'd caught the pilot as he was preparing to fly the plane to the airport. They knew him from their days in Afghanistan—a hot-shit pilot who flew the big MH-53J PavLow helicopter used for special operations groups. The Taliban had been in exactly the right place at the right time—from the Taliban's point of view—to shoot the helicopter down with RPG and heavy machine gun fire. The pilot, a former Smoke Jumper, had managed to extricate himself from the crash site, while the Taliban were busy killing everyone else. Four days later, the Troll had watched through the night scope as the pilot stumbled through rocks and scrub brush about a thousand meters out from their position. He would have missed them entirely if Joe Big hadn't gone out and reeled him in.

His hearing had been permanently damaged in one ear, which made him damaged goods as far as flying for the Air Force was concerned. He'd gone to work flying medevac helicopters for hospitals, ending up back in Montana because his ex-wife loved flyfishing.

The pilot held up a fist and opened two fingers.

Barney gave him a thumbs-up. The pilot was the only one wearing a headset. It was agreed before they took off that there would be no voice communication whatsoever once inside the helicopter.

The helicopter lost altitude in a long, looping half-spiral. The powerful landing light under the nose came on illuminating the field and the drainage ditch in front of Joe Big's place.

Barney slid the door open, and when the skids lightly kissed the field, he jumped out, Joe Big and Quinn right behind him.

Barney slid the door shut. Joe Big, standing in the field beyond the rotor disc, made a circling motion with his right hand over his head, and then made a throwing motion with the same hand in the direction of the empty field and road. The helicopter rose and, tail up, streamed across the field, quickly gaining altitude, the landing light extinguished, as it banked in the direction of the airport.

The house and the barn and the outbuildings were dark in the sudden silence.

"No use sneaking around," Joe Big said. He jogged toward the pasture gate.

"All our shit is in the truck," Barney said, when they were at the bottom of the steps. "What've you got here?"

"A mixed box of grenades. Hunting rifles. A shotgun or two."

"I hate to use my car," Barney said.

"We'll take the old International."

"What about your uncle."

"You can explain it to him, when you meet him."

"I don't think so."

"There's an old Styrofoam cooler in the kitchen," Joe Big said to Quinn. "Fill it with whatever you can find in the pantry. Take only dried or canned food."

"I—" she began.

"If you don't want to come with us, you can stay here. Keys are in the ignition," he said to Barney. "You'll have to put the battery in it. There's a new one on the bench next to the old one. Make sure you put in the new one."

Barney trotted toward the barn.

"Your choice," Joe Big said to Quinn. "Hey, Mouse." He picked up the cat, and draped her over his right shoulder. "Whazhappinin', girl?" He could feel her claws kneading into his shoulder.

Ten minutes later, he had the grenades and guns and an old All Nippon Airways flight bag full of ammunition. The guns and the cooler were a precaution only: in case they could not retrieve the other truck.

They heard the rumble of the old International. And Barney backed it out of the barn, across the yard to where they were standing with the gear.

He shut off the engine, and climbed out.

"What a tank," he said to Joe Big. "You better drive."

Joe Big shined a large flashlight on Quinn. "Give me your weapons and holsters."

"Fuck you."

"Look. You know the drill. We have to make sure you are not carrying a transmitter."

She put her hands on her hips and stared at him.

"We don't have time to argue," Barney said.

She handed Barney her 9mm, and then bent down and removed a small automatic from an ankle holster and handed that to him, too.

"Knives," Joe Big said.

She handed Barney a folding knife.

"Throw your clothes over here," Joe Big said.

Wordlessly, she began to disrobe, the light accentuating her curves and lean muscles and the almost hairless mound between her legs. Her nipples were small, puckered tight against the cold, goose bumps prominent on her smooth skin. Her breasts were perfect ovals—the breasts of a woman ten years younger.

Barney cleared his throat. "Do you have any implants?" he asked. "You know what I mean."

She shook her head, her eyes bright and brittle in the light, not trusting herself to say anything.

"Shoes, too," Joe Big said, walking around her, squinting as he played the light on her hips and thighs and shoulders.

She bent and untied her shoes and stepped out of them.

He threw a medium-size backpack at her feet. "Put this stuff on," he said, and clicked off the light.

He gathered her clothes and weapons and carried them into the house, and threw everything onto the couch.

"You better stay here," he said to Mouse. "There's food on the table, and I left the kitchen window open."

When he returned to the truck, she was dressed in dark blue sweat pants, gold USMC stenciled on the right leg, and a brown T-shirt, Abercrombie and Fitch in white letters across the chest. She was on one knee lacing up the hiking boots.

"How are the boots?"

"They fit."

She stood.

"You're sure you can't be tracked?" he asked. "Because I got to tell you, where we are going, we are the least of your worries if you bring a bunch of Feds down on us."

"Why don't you leave me here, then?"

"You know why," Barney said. "They've lost three men, and you saw what happened to Brianna. We're assuming that based on the pictures in your cell phone they thought you were with Big when the elk was shot. Sooner or later, though, they are going to figure out that it was you, and not Big, who put an arrow into one of them."

"Why do they think it was Joe?"

"Because it was an arrow, and because he's an Indian. Why else?"

"Serve you right, if they catch you," Joe Big said.

"Oh, kiss off. There's no way I could have known what would happen. I didn't even know until two days ago who Mrs. Walker really is."

"You expect us to believe that?"

"I don't care what you believe."

Joe Big leaned his face close to hers. "Brianna," he said.

Her eyes flinched, and she turned away.

"How long have you been together?" Barney asked.

She sighed, and shook her head. "You guys. I don't know why you are wasting your time working for a Sheriffs Department in Montana. Eight months."

"If it's any consolation, one of the guys we killed was the guy who messed her up."

"We're outta here," Joe Big said.

Two hours later, the old International bumped and rumbled down a gravel road alongside the Clark Fork River. They had driven from Joe Big's place into town, and waited in a supermarket parking lot for the sky to lighten and morning traffic to clog the main roads, and then they'd driven to where the brown pickup was parked behind an apartment house. Barney and Quinn were following in the brown pickup far enough back to avoid most of the dust.

To their left, open fields stretched to the base of a massive mountain. Scattered clumps of whitetail deer browsed next to the tree line. The air was crisp, the leaves on the birch and aspen golden in the fall light. The river off to the right moved sluggish, its true speed seen only in subtle eddies and swirls moving across the surface.

Joe Big pulled the truck off the edge of the road twenty meters before a green metal gate. A bald eagle stared down from its nest in a massive old snag.

He climbed out and walked over to one of the fence posts and took a key hanging from a nail on the backside of the post, and walked to the gate and unlocked the padlock that held the gate chain together. He shoved the gate open, and walked back to the fence post and put the key back on the nail.

Barney pulled the Chevy around the International and turned into the gated road and stopped twenty meters in. He climbed out and stretched, and then walked back to the gate.

"You want me to lock it?" he asked, as Joe Big drove through.

"Just wrap the chain around it."

Joe Big idled the International up even with the Chevy. Quinn was asleep, a camouflage fleece jacket cushioning her head against the passenger-side window. Not many people could sleep at a time like this, he thought. They couldn't trust her as far as they could throw her, but she'd be good in a fight. He had no trouble imagining her winging an arrow at someone.

He let out the clutch, and the old truck idled slowly ahead, following a set of dusty tracks through a thick stand of lodgepole, breaking out into maybe ten acres of tall, dried grass. An old farmhouse with a new front porch was directly ahead. On the far side of the house was a new metal workshop and garage that, like the porch, hadn't been there the last time he had visited.

The house felt empty, no steam or smoke escaping from its ancient brick chimney. No dogs. No chickens. No horses. No cattle. No deer in the field. No life at all.

He parked the old International between the house and the new metal building. The brown pickup pulled up behind. He climbed out and walked to the passenger side. Barney leaned over and shook Quinn.

Her eyes opened, immediately aware, not fogged by sleep in the slightest. She sat upright and looked around.

"Where are we?"

Joe Big opened the door, catching the fleece jacket she'd been using as a pillow. "We're at my uncle's. Move over."

"Is your uncle here?"

"Not at the moment."

"There's tracks in and out," Barney said.

"Probably Manfred keeping an eye on the place." Joe Big climbed in next to Quinn. "If Ben was here the gate would've been open."

"Who *are* you talking about?" Quinn asked.

"My uncle."

"I know that. But who is your uncle?"

Joe Big was abruptly happy to be there. It had been years. The metal building and the porch were new, but it was still the same old place. One of the special places of his childhood. A haven then, and a haven now.

"Benjamin Tails," he said.

"I think I heard Mrs. Walker mention that name on the telephone, a couple of weeks ago."

"Is there any more gear from the International that you want to throw in here?" Barney asked.

"I think we've got everything. Just follow the track until I tell you to stop."

They drove past what looked like an old chicken coop and a large pile of firewood split and stacked in even rows, out across the field, following an overgrown track barely seen, high grasses scraping against the underside of the truck.

"Great looking grass," Barney said. "But it looks like a fire hazard, to me."

"It's prairie grass. My great grandfather planted most of it. Ben has it burned off every year. He uses fire the same way Indians used fire. There are no ladder fuels for flames to get into the trees."

"These trees are huge," Quinn said. "There must be a small fortune in lumber here."

"How much land has he got?" Barney asked.

Joe Big shrugged. "I don't know. A thousand, maybe twelve hundred acres, I guess. It goes quite a ways up that mountain ahead of us, and then runs into Forest Service land on two sides. I think he controls the grazing rights for another fifty years or so all the way to the top of the mountain."

"What does he graze?" Quinn asked. "The only animals I've seen are deer."

"Nothing," Joe Big said. "Elk and deer and mountains lions and a bear now and then. You get back in those trees and except for an airplane now and then, you can imagine what this country was like before white men came through and logged it off. There's even a stand of ancient cedars where the creek comes down off the mountain."

"You grew up here?" Quinn asked.

"My dad and I visited a couple of times every year. My uncle let us hunt the resident elk herd. Park the truck over there next to those trees above the creek embankment," he said to Barney.

Barney stopped the truck at the edge of a rocky, washed-out creek bed, a small trickle winding through the rocks in the center.

"There's fish up above in some of the deep pools, or we can shoot a deer for camp meat, if you want," Joe Big said.

"How long you think we'll be here?" Barney asked.

"A couple of days, maybe," Joe Big said.

"Too bad," Barney said.

They sat for a moment, looking at the creek.

"Yeah," Quinn said, the bleakness in her voice surprising both men. "Too bad."

31
Wolves

I saw a wolf this morning," Barney said. "First light. It went through the trees over by the sweat lodge."

"That's probably why the elk are nervous," Joe Big said, staring at the water beginning to heat on the small camp stove sitting on the tailgate. The morning was a uniform gray, the light under the trees the same gray as the sky. The air felt oppressive, free of the heavy frost of the previous two mornings.

"A pack of wolves can wipe out a lot of game in a hurry," Barney said.

"Wolf huggers, tree huggers," Joe Big said. "Even buffalo huggers. I guess these days people need something to hug, no matter how much it upsets the balance."

The pickup rocked, and a tousle-haired Quinn emerged from a shapeless mass of sleeping bag and blankets between neatly piled duffel bags.

"My plants need water," she said.

"That's nothing," Barney said. "My body needs beer."

She edged out from under the topper, her hiking boots looped around her neck, careful to not upset the small stove. She took the boots from around her neck, untied the shoelaces, slipped the boots on, and slid off the tailgate to the ground.

"I had a really weird dream last night," she said.

Barney groaned. "Why is it women always want to tell you their dreams?"

"Something was moving though the trees. It was right outside the truck, watching me."

Barney mimicked the Twilight Zone theme song. "In the back of a truck, next to a stream in Montana," he said, sounding like Rod Serling. "Quinn McBride, a young, female, Special Agent In Charge from Boston . . ."

She smiled, and both men could see that the last two days had relaxed her. Yesterday, she'd taken a long hike by herself to the top of the mountain, and now, tousle-haired and like both of them in dire need of a shower, she seemed to glow with good health. Sitting around the campfire, she'd told stories of growing up poor in Boston; stories about the all-girl gang she'd been in. How her mother had forced her to live with an aunt who had a house in the Philly 'burbs—the best thing that had ever happened to her, even if she didn't know it at the time. She'd earned a full-ride scholarship to Villanova, where she discovered that her street smarts and cynicism were no match for the teachings of St. Augustine of Hippo. She'd planned on the State Department, but the FBI had been too much to resist for a girl who had grown up on guns and violence and adrenaline.

She was beautiful, but they felt no sexual tension when they were with her. Not a coldness, exactly, Joe Big thought. A strange disconnect—an almost monkish insularity, that made her something nice to look at, but that was all. Her sexual synapses simply did not fire with men.

Her stories had been entertaining, but there was no way to tell if they were true or not. Rehearsed was the operative word, he thought. Mrs. Walker, or someone like the woman who called herself Mrs. Walker, had tutored her well, that much was obvious.

"You weren't dreaming," he said.

"What?"

"Check it out." He nodded toward the narrow ledge inside the topper where it was bolted to the sides of the pickup bed.

A tiny red and white origami of a crane was on the ledge, looking toward where Quinn had been sleeping.

She picked it up. "This is really good," she said. "Which one of you did this?"

"Not us," Joe Big said. Barney frowned at the origami.

She looked at him. "Who then?"

"My uncle was here last night."

"I was wide awake my whole shift," Barney said. "Some elk came through in a hurry on the other side of the creek, but that was all."

"I'm pretty sure elk can't do origami," Joe Big said.

"He's pretty slick, then."

Joe Big laughed, pouring coffee crystals into the boiling water. "You have no idea."

"How old is he?" Quinn asked.

Joe Big stirred the coffee with his knife. "Oh, I dunno. He's got to be sixty-something. Hand me a cup, will you?" He filled the cup, using a folded black leather glove as a potholder. Barney held out another cup, and Joe Big filled it. "He can still outwalk me in the mountains, though."

"Is he part Indian, too?"

"The amount of blood he's got doesn't matter." Joe Big tried to take a drink from the stainless steel bowl that he'd used to make the coffee in.

"When did you last see him?"

Joe Big shrugged. "Two years, maybe."

"Big likes practical jokes," Barney said.

Joe Big took another try at the coffee. The edge of the bowl was still too hot.

"I didn't make that crane," he said, frowning at the bowl.

"I can't wait to meet him," Quinn said.

"He puts his pants on the same as the rest of us," Barney said.

"That's exactly right," a voice said from next to the old-growth bull pine five feet or so from the back corner of the pickup.

Quinn squeaked, and spilled some of her coffee on the ground.

Barney whirled around.

Joe Big laughed. "Hey, Ben," he said. "I hope you don't mind."

A tall, lean man dressed in dark gray wool pants and red and black checked wool shirt, a black watch cap on his head, straightened away from the tree, and walked toward them, a scoped rifle slung over his right shoulder. An old scar ran out of the watch cap across the right side of his forehead, down into his sideburn. There were deep furrows at the corners of his mouth and between his eyes. Laugh lines radiated from the edges of his eyes.

A tall, homely man Quinn thought. Most women would find him irresistible.

His eyes were deep blue, flecks of gold in the irises. They seemed kind to her, no hint of what Joe had implied. Certainly not the eyes of the stone-killer sniper described in the briefing.

"Ben Tails," he said, extending his hand.

She grasped his hand, and it was as if the touch of his skin on hers was a conduit to her mind.

He waited, a wry half-smile on his face.

"Oh . . . Quinn. Quinn McBride. I'm sorry."

"Ben," he said, extending his hand to Barney.

"Barney."

"We've got another Barney around here. The Sheriff. He's from the Shenandoah, though."

"It's the accent," Barney said. "We southerners are forever Barney Fife to all the peckerwoods in law enforcement."

Ben smiled. "I couldn't dispute that."

He turned to Joe Big, and they embraced.

He held Joe Big at arm's length. In Mandarin he said, "Long time no see, nephew. What have you gotten yourself into this time?"

"I kind of hoped you might have a better handle on that than we do," Joe Big said in English.

Ben Tails squeezed Joe Big's shoulders, and released his grip. He looked at the three of them for a long moment, his gaze going from one to the other. Both Barney and Quinn felt something dark and not human filter through the trees and permeate the air behind him. They could feel this, but as is the case with most human beings could neither admit nor articulate it. As far as they were concerned, the sky had darkened and maybe snow was on the way. Of the three, only Joe Big knew what it was, and he knew only because he'd felt it many times as a child camping with his father and friends in that very spot.

"I've got some wolves to shoot," Ben said. "Why don't the three of you pack up your gear and head on over to the house. Help yourself to the shower. Make yourself something to eat, if you want. There's plenty of food."

Quinn frowned. "Wolves?"

"A couple of packs have filtered over from Idaho, and are beginning to decimate elk and deer herds around here," Ben said. "The Government is sponsoring a wolf hunt to limit their numbers. Don't worry." He smiled. "I'm authorized."

"I didn't mean . . ."

"Paul Cyr will be along shortly," he said to Joe Big. "He'll be with one of the boys from the Rez." He stared at Joe Big for a moment.

"I—" Joe Big said.

"I don't want to hear it," Ben said in Mandarin. "It's time you got your head out of your ass, and started acting like you know what you are doing. You two are lucky to be alive." He paused, and said in English, "You do know that, don't you?"

Joe Big nodded.

"And that applies to your nonsense about the Tribe, too. Your grandmother must be spinning in her grave."

"Hey—"

"Hay is for horses, son. You give me excuses, and I am going to sic your mother on your bullshit." He smiled at Quinn and Barney. "Sorry," he said. "We haven't seen each other for a while. Family business has sort of piled up in the meantime."

He stared at Barney for a moment. His gaze went to Joe Big.

"Neither of you is involved with this woman, are you?" he asked in Mandarin.

Joe Big shook his head.

"You can't trust her or her boss."

"We know," Joe Big said in Mandarin.

"Have you been to visit your ancestors?"

Joe nodded. "I cleaned the area around the gravestones," he said in English. "Talked to them for awhile."

Ben Tails regarded him for a moment, and Quinn thought maybe she'd revise her opinion about him not looking like a sniper. "Thank you," he said.

Joe Big nodded.

Ben turned to Quinn. "I'm told that Sergeant Brianna Kelsey is up and about and causing all kinds of angst among the hospital staff and the little old ladies in the room next door."

"Thanks," she said, unable to disguise her surprise.

Ben nodded to Barney, "Mr. Lambier."

They watched him walk past the truck and pick his way across the rocks, up the embankment, his figure melding into the trees. Now you see him, now you don't, Barney thought, even though the area under the trees was park-like, and even though he was wearing a red and black checked shirt.

"How does he do that?" Quinn asked.

"Unconsciously," Joe Big said.

"Nothing like an ass-chewing to start your day," Barney said.

"Au contraire," Joe Big said. "He's happy to see me, and glad that I are safe and sound."

"You could tell that?" Barney asked.

"You bet."

Quinn laughed.

"You are so full of shit," she said.

32
Welcome to Ben's World

Late afternoon, and Joe Big was standing next to an old black, kettle-shaped barbecue, watching elk burgers fry on the grill, while he drank a cold Heavy Horse Ale. Thanks to Manfred, his uncle always had great beer. The snow-dusted mountain where his uncle was hunting wolves stood etched against blue sky. The air had that special clarity and dryness that came only in the fall.

Barney came out of the house. He shaded his eyes, looking toward the gate.

"Remember the cookouts we had in Afghanistan?" Joe Big said. "No beer because we didn't want to offend the locals. Dust like talcum powder on everything."

"Vehicle," Barney said.

A white SUV with a green stripe along the side, light bar on the roof, heavy black deer catcher on the front, cleared the trees and came toward them, bouncing and waddling across bumps and swales in the road, dust boiling off the tires.

"Border Patrol," Joe Big said.

Barney picked up the M4 resting against one of the porch supports.

"It's okay," Joe Big said. "It's Paul."

Paul raised his hand in greeting as he drove past and parked on the concrete apron in front of the metal building.

Joe Big used a plastic spatula to take burgers off the grill and put them on a big platter. He handed the platter to Barney, and Barney carried it up the steps to the door. Quinn opened the door and took it from him.

"It's Paul," Barney said to her.

Paul climbed out of the truck. Another man came around the passenger side.

The other man had shoulders so wide he seemed nearly as wide as he was tall. Graying hair in a braid that went half way down his back. Barrel chest, bandy legs. A powerful man who, like Paul, spent a lot of time on a horse, Joe Big thought. Paul was wearing a green Border Patrol shirt, yellow patch on the shoulder; the other man was wearing a dark-brown Tribal Police shirt, gold badge over his heart. Both men were unarmed, leather belts instead of duty belts.

"Howdy," Paul said.

"Howdy, yourself," Joe Big said.

"Barney."

"Hey, Paul."

"This here is Tom Lonewolf," Paul said. "The pretty one is Joe Big Snake Person. The white guy is his partner, James Longstreet Lambier. aka, Barney."

"I see what you mean," Tom Lonewolf said, his voice deep and melodious. Damn, he sounds like Barry White, Barney thought. A Blackfeet Barry White.

"Mean what?" Joe Big asked.

Tom Lonewolf chuckled deep in his chest. "The movie people been at us again, Joe Big. If you didn't look so damn Chinese, they'd probably make you a star."

"Thanks a lot, Paul," Joe Big said.

"Y'all want a burger?" Barney asked. "The Chinese cook just sent a platter into the house."

"Well, I don't know," Tom Lonewolf said. "I wouldn't want to be hungry again in an hour."

The three men laughed.

"Ha, ha," Joe Big said.

"A beer would be good," Paul said. "Long drive over here from the Rez."

Barney picked up the rifle, and walked up the steps and held the screen door for the two men.

"That the new any-kind-of-light scope?" Tom asked, as they went inside.

"It's not a night scope, but it works pretty well in low-light conditions," Barney said, as the screen door slapped shut behind them.

Joe Big found himself abruptly alone next to the barbecue grill, plastic spatula in his hand. A light breeze had come up and he could smell pine, hear the whisper of wind through the high grass, the tick and pop of the exhaust on the Border Patrol vehicle.

Far out across the field, he could see his uncle walking toward the house, rifle slung over his shoulder.

He knew that with the house behind him he was invisible to anyone at that distance. His uncle raised his hand in greeting.

Joe Big raised the spatula in the air, and went over to the steps and sat down to wait.

He had the same taste in his mouth and in his mind that he used to get before a mission. They'd be laagered somewhere, resting up, cleaning their gear or drawing new gear, and no matter the day or the place, the light would change and everything would take on a different reality. They were headed into the land of death. Someone was going to die.

He hadn't felt that way every time they went out. But if he felt it, then one of them died. Sometimes more than one of them.

And knowing that someone, maybe him, was going to die, his vision would sharpen and he could smell things that he normally didn't pay any attention to. Hear tiny sounds. Notice movement: the ubiquitous cats searching for rats and snakes.

It was a feeling that he had never expected to feel here in America. And he hadn't. Not even when they were making buys from biker gangs or from Vietnamese or Ukrainian villains.

But watching his uncle walk toward him, he had that feeling.

He stood, as Ben Tails walked across the yard.

"It's the fear thing again," Paul said. "That's what I think it is. These rich guys think they need to manufacture some kind of terrorist event so that the American people will be willing to give up even more liberty than what they've already given up. The idea is to keep the public thinking that this country is teetering on the edge of ruin. High prices for essentials that shouldn't be anywhere near as expensive as they are mixed with the threat of a major terrorist event."

They were all sitting on the edge of the porch, drinking beer or coffee, letting the burgers settle. Long streaks of golden sunlight illuminated the shadows under the far trees. The porch was in shade, the shadows of the house and the metal building reaching out into the field.

"Sounds like a made-for-TV plot to me," Barney said.

"It's not a movie," Quinn said. "These people—these ultra-conservative Neocons and Theocons—they are true believers. They think they've got Christ and the American military on their side. And they believe that the Constitution should be rewritten to reflect that fact."

"How do you know this," Tom Lonewolf asked.

Quinn smiled at him. "I love your voice," she said. "Sorry. You probably hear that all the time."

"They had him narrate a thing about the Tribe for the History Channel," Paul said. "But his voice is so much like Barry White's, they had to get someone else and do it all over again."

"Girl. I don't know. Don't know why . . ." Tom Lonewolf sang.

Everyone laughed.

"To answer your question," Quinn said. "I've read stacks of journal articles and position papers that lay it all out. These people aren't trying to be secretive. It's all there in the public domain. You can read a lot of it on the Internet, if you want. It's an unholy alliance, if ever there was. Super-rich corporate heads in bed with powerful former officials from Administrations stretching all the way back to the Nixon years, those people in turn mixed with rich, ultra-conservative Catholics and Protestants. You have men who think only in terms of money and the economy in bed with men who think only in terms of Realpolitik in bed with men who believe they are soldiers for Christ."

"Are there a lot of these people?" Tom asked.

"Not really. But because of their money and influence they pack a punch. Between them, they control several of the world's largest security corporations."

"Security corporations?" Paul asked.

She smiled at his voice. "Private military-slash-security companies. Mercenaries, in other words. 'Mobile security teams' who are, and I quote, 'Ready to deploy in support of National Security Objectives, as well as private interests.'"

"That's a bit Orwellian, isn't it?" Joe Big asked. Everyone looked at him: the guy with the big vocabulary.

Ben Tails chuckled.

"You have no idea," Quinn said. "They even have a trade association. The International Peace Operations Association. IPOA. The logo is a sleeping cartoon lion that looks as if it was made by Disney."

"I didn't know that," Paul said.

"Oh, yeah," she said. "Their premise is that society stands to benefit from a regulated mercenary industry."

"And these mercenaries are whom?" Ben Tails asked.

She shrugged. "The cream are former U. S. special forces operatives—SEALS, Force Recon, Rangers, people like that. But a lot of them are drawn from special forces units from all over the world: Chile, Columbia, Poland, former British SAS, SBS, Paras. You name it. Even a few South Africans, even though it's illegal for the South Africans. That's pretty much how it was described to me, anyway."

"Described by who?" Barney asked.

"Mrs. Walker and some of the people who head up Homeland Security. Look. No matter what you and Joe think about her, she and the people she works for are not political appointees. They are not fly-by-nighters. They are not tricksters."

At the mention of the word, trickster, Paul and Joe Big and Tom Lonewolf looked at her."

"What?" she asked. "What did I say?"

"Trickster is kind of a loaded word in the Blackfeet language," Paul said.

"Oh. Well. Sorry. I only meant it in the literal meaning of the word," she said. "The important thing to know is that these ultra-rich Neocons and Theocons are not trying to fool anyone. They are up-front about what they want. Their justifications for curtailing civil liberties are demonstrably patriotic. In their minds, they are the last bastion of American morals and integrity."

"But they are willing to stage a terrorist event," Joe Big said. "That doesn't make sense."

"Not to you, maybe."

"Nothing makes sense to Big," Barney said.

"He who makes light of his opponents is sure to be captured by them," Joe Big said.

"Is that Sun Tzu again?" Barney asked. "Oh, God, everybody. Don't get him started on Sun Tzu."

Tom Lonewolf chuckled his deep, rich Barry White chuckle. "If it looks like a Chinese," he said. "And if it quacks like a Chinese . . ."

Everyone but Joe Big laughed.

There was a long silence, as they watched the shadows lengthen, the snow at the top of the mountain turn to gold. Whitetail had materialized in the field at the edge of the trees, twenty or thirty spread out in small groups or singly in the high grass.

"So why are we having this meeting?" Barney asked. "Or is it just a coincidence that we all showed up here to eat burgers and drink Manfred's beer."

"No coincidence," Paul said. "The plan, near as we can tell, is to make it look like the nerve agent that will be used in an attack on an American city was manufactured and stored on the Blackfeet Indian Reservation here in the United States, and on the Blackfeet Reserve in Canada—which is just across the border from the Reservation. The mules were not going to Canada," he said to Barney and Joe Big. "They were going to the Blackfeet Reserve, which just happens to be in Canada. That might be considered semantics to some, but The People have never paid much attention to the concept of a border."

"Who's going to believe that a bunch of Blackfeet could get their act together enough to do something like that?" Joe Big asked.

"Putting aside your implied insult for the moment, people believe what they want to believe. I mean, people believe that Oswald shot Kennedy." Paul turned to Ben Tails. "You are one of the best snipers ever, Ben. Could you have used that rifle with that ammunition, and fired from that place, and shot the President that fast, that accurately, that many times?"

"No one could have."

"Near as I can tell," Paul said to Joe Big. "There are only a few Tribal members involved. They are being used as part of a front. Included in that front are anarchists, ELFs, even a couple of homegrown, white-guy wannabe terrorists. These people are harmless. All of them. They protest world economic summits, things like that. The worst they do is burn down houses and sabotage heavy equipment. Most of the time, they sit around and smoke dope, listen to bad music, argue philosophy, and thieve from each other. None of them knows what they are really involved in."

"Which is?" Barney asked.

"The primary chemical agent is exactly what you two suspected. A modified form of the VX nerve agent that is even more lethal and less fragile than the old VX. Apparently there was an accident on the trail when they were transporting some of it to the Blackfoot Reserve. We're not sure what actually happened. But that's how the mules were killed, and how, from what we've been able to gather, one of the men leading the pack string was killed."

"Who's giving you this information?" Joe Big asked.

"I am," Ben Tails said.

He smiled, letting the silence stretch.

Joe Big knew better than to try to dig anything else out of him. Apparently, so did the others, even Quinn.

"Well, they aren't going to attack a city with containers of VX on mules," Barney said.

Paul cleared his throat. "One of the companies owned by the people who are masterminding all this manufactures drones for the military. The drones can be outfitted with ordnance of all sorts. I'm sure you and Joseph are familiar with their capabilities. It is important to remember that some of the companies owned by these people have connections woven into all aspects of our military and civilian bureaucracies. The equipment they have access to, especially here in Montana, is state of the art."

He paused for a moment, looking at Ben Tails.

Ben nodded.

"Apparently," Paul said. "They have some new kind of air-delivered weapon that can disperse this new VX over large areas: tiny bomblets that make no noise when they disseminate the chemical, and then disintegrate when they are empty."

"We stole the science from the Chinese," Ben said, "that's how I know about it. This stuff clings to any surface. It doesn't go away. An amount no larger than what could fit on the head of a pin will kill you in a very short time. It has to come in contact with bare skin, though. You could breathe it while it was being dispersed, and it would certainly kill you dead if that happened, but it is not intended to be a gas. Once it is attached to whatever it lands on it isn't going anywhere, not even in a rain or snow storm." He crossed his arms over his chest. "It can be easily transported on pretty much anything that moves. A car, for example, could be covered with it, and the driver not have a clue. Anything that rubbed up against that car would transport the VX to someplace else. As a terror weapon it's hard to imagine anything more effective, especially since the manner of death is ugly in the extreme. Atropine was an antidote for the old form of VX; it doesn't make a dent in this new stuff."

"They got rid of what was on the trail by using solid rocket fuel to start a forest fire," Paul said. "That's why the fire started so fast and so hot, and why the fire guys could find no trace of an accelerant. It takes extreme heat to neutralize this stuff."

"If you know all this, and you know who has it, why isn't somebody doing something about it?" Joe Big asked.

"Like who?" Ben Tails asked. "Who would you like to see go up against some of these mobile security teams that Miss McBride was talking about?"

"I don't know. The Marines, maybe?"

Tom Lonewolf chuckled. Paul and Ben Tails smiled.

"The Marines are first responders on the East Coast for anything like this," Ben Tails said.

"It's not that easy," Quinn said. "If you call the Marines in and you don't find any evidence of this VX stuff, then the proverbial will really hit the fan. There will be investigations. Heads will roll. Platoons of lawyers bearing lawsuits will sprout like evil mushrooms. Generals will be cashiered. Senior civil servants will lose their jobs and along with their jobs their benefits. We need proof."

She looked at Barney and Joe Big. So did everyone else.

"Uh-oh," Barney said.

"Oh, hell," Joe Big said. "This is the reason why you and Walker wanted us in the first place, isn't it?"

"Why all the dicking around?" Barney asked her. "Why didn't you just tell us?"

"You weren't our first choice. With your wounds and your attitudes, we thought there was a better than even chance you wouldn't work out."

"Work out?" Barney asked.

"The idea was to infiltrate people into the organization by way of Patrick. We tried using other people with roughly the same set of qualifications that you two come with, but in every case they went native. These people can be extremely persuasive. Especially when talking to war veterans. Many of them are special forces veterans themselves.

And the people who run their think tanks are as persuasive as they are articulate."

"Not to mention the money," Joe Big said.

"Not to mention the money," she agreed.

"So you told Patrick about us before we went to the meet up the Black—" Joe Big looked at Ben Tails.

"I know all about it," Ben said.

"As it turned out, we thought that Patrick's overreaction was maybe for the best," Quinn said. "Mrs. Walker figured that it would motivate Patrick to try and turn the two of you. We could arrange it so that you were publicly reprimanded—days off, sent back to the SO, that sort of thing."

"So how was it supposed to go down?" Barney asked. "A chance meeting with Patrick and his crew? Loud voices and threats of bodily harm, followed by grudging acceptance of Patrick's apologies and then, after much debate and playing coy, buying into his agenda—allowing ourselves to be gradually seduced by a combination of money and patriotism? We'd end up working security at the company in Kalispell, or out at one of the ranches. From there we could spy on whatever is going down with this new VX. Is that what you had in mind?"

"Exactly," she said.

"Then, like Big said, why didn't you just ask?" Joe Big was watching her—like he'd watched that saw-scale crawl out from the rocks, Barney thought.

"You planned this, too, didn't you?" Joe Big asked. "You and Mrs. Walker, you planned for us to show up at the office, and do pretty much what we did. And then run off somewhere—like here—where you'd have a chance to work on us."

"No." She shook her head. "I mean, yes. We had a plan. But as soon as we realized that you'd killed two men, that plan went out the window. And then when you told her that I had shot and killed one of them with an arrow . . ." She shook her head. "I've never seen her so angry."

"Oh, bullshit," Barney said.

"What's this about killing someone with an arrow?" Paul asked.

"She shot one of the guys who made her CI shoot himself," Barney said. "Skewered him through and through with an arrow."

Paul and Ben Tails and Tom Lonewolf looked at her.

"Really?" Ben Tails said.

"She shot an elk while she was waiting for them to show up," Joe Big said. "And then waiting for the elk to die she lost her cell phone over the edge of a big rock into the bushes. And somewhere between then and when her CI blew his brains out, she lost another arrow in the weeds."

"You didn't tell anyone?" Ben Tails asked her.

"The phone was in heavy bushes," she said. "I didn't think anyone would find it. I was in camouflage. There was no way they could have known it was me."

"And putting an arrow through someone, no matter how well deserved, would have violated all sorts of rules and procedures," Paul said. "You could have lost your job. At the very least you would have been exiled to some Podunk backwater."

"I didn't mess up. I did the right thing." Her eyes challenged all of them. "I'd do it again, if I could, job or no job, rules and procedures or no rules and procedures."

Tom Lonewolf chuckled, and in his deep, melodious voice said, "My, oh my. Ain't this just a crew, though."

"Was this before or after what happened up the Blackfoot?" Barney asked.

"Before," she said. "But I don't think they'd found the phone yet, or if they had, the word hadn't gotten to Patrick."

"And Brianna?" Joe Big asked.

She looked down at the floor, and when she looked up her eyes glistened. "Fuck you, Joe Big. I messed up by not telling Brianna about it, okay? When you become perfect, you come talk to me. Until then, keep your eyes and your opinion to yourself."

"Ouch," Tom Lonewolf said.

"These two have been going at it since they met," Barney said.

"What it *is*," Joe Big said, staring at Quinn. "Is we don't like being blackmailed or otherwise manipulated into doing something we might not want to do."

"A lot of that was Mrs. Walker doing."

"You're saying you would have done things differently?" Barney asked.

"Well . . . not necessarily. She's a smart lady. It could have been more elegant, maybe. But in a world of thousands of possible decisions, the worst one being to make no decision at all, her decisions are always better than most."

"I have no idea what they are talking about now," Paul said.

"The issue here is coercion," Barney said to him. "Mrs. W threatened that all sorts of dire consequences would befall a woman and her family that Big has taken a shine to, if we don't do whatever it is she has in mind for us to do."

"Say what?" Paul said.

"He-lo!" Tom Lonewolf said.

Ben Tails shook his head. "This just gets better and better. Joseph has fallen for someone? Wait until his mother finds out."

"You asshole," Joe Big said to Barney. "I barely know—we just met," he said to Ben. "It's the part-Vietnamese woman who owns the bakery in Painted Cliff," he said to Paul. "Her mother is some sort of marketing genius or something. She owns car dealerships and restaurants and who knows what. But she's Vietnamese Chinese through and through." He looked at Ben Tails. "And you know what that means when it comes to government and taxes and regulations and shit like that."

"Gladys would know all that with a couple of phone calls," Ben said.

"Gladys?" Barney asked.

"Our paths have crossed before," Ben said. "You don't have to worry about your lady or her family," he said to Joe Big. "The company I work for will take care of it."

"It's not that so much, as it is that it's getting a little hard to figure out who the good guys are," Joe Big said.

Ben smiled. "Welcome to my world," he said.

33
The Truth Is Always Unintentional

That's a big ass mule deer," Joe Big said, peering through the spotting scope. "Boone and Crockett, for sure." They were set up at the top of a long steep draw filled with tall grass and bushes and sparse stands of aspen. Blackened spars, the remnants of a long-ago forest fire, stuck out of bushes and tall grass, like artifacts from an ancient civilization. Both were dressed in woodland green camouflage fatigue pants and tree-bark fleece jacket, black SWAT web gear.

According to the scope it was nine hundred twenty two meters to the door of the decayed, two-story ranch house at the bottom of the draw. The barn and several other outbuildings were collapsed into a tangle of grass and chokecherry bushes and five-foot-high Figwort, thistle, and other noxious weeds. Poplars enclosed the house on two sides.

"Figwort was used to treat hemorrhoids," Joe Big said. "Did you know that?"

"Um-humm."

Across the open area from the house was an abused-looking, cream-colored, single-wide trailer up on blocks, rust bleeding down the front. Underneath the trailer was almost certainly home to skunks, Joe Big thought. The plywood skirting was warped and bowed. Narrow rickety-looking wood stairs led up to the door.

Directly below, at the base of the draw, was an old Quonset hut butted into the hillside, metal sheets welded over the windows at the back. Large new-looking circular aluminum vents were set into the top at both ends.

To their left, a long grassy ridge ran downhill behind the old ranch house, all the way down to the beginning of the eastern Montana prairie. The Rocky Mountain Front loomed to their right, like a giant tsunami wave about to break over the prairie below. Far out on the plain, if they looked through the binoculars or the spotting scope, they could see a large cluster of buildings belonging to one of the largest ranches in Montana.

The old ranch below was, near as Joe Big could tell, situated at the very edge of a triangular piece of the Blackfeet Indian Reservation. The big ranch was on one side, National Forest and Bob Marshall Wilderness on the other. According to the GPS, a couple hundred yards down the road from the old ranch and you were off the Rez, and on the big ranch. No telling if the map was accurate, though. Paul and Lonewolf hadn't been sure how large the big ranch was, mainly because it was made up of a patchwork of many former ranches. Ninety thousand deeded acres, Lonewolf reckoned, no telling how many thousands of acres in leased land. But since it was always buying up little ranches on its periphery, "like a giant ranch-eating amoeba," there was no way to know how big it really was. Looking through the binoculars it seemed big enough to be a country, Joe Big thought. For sure, with all the leased land included, it was at least the size of Singapore.

Mountain ranges and massive buttes in the far distance lent depth to a horizon of rolling hills and shallow valleys. Here and there creeks lined with deciduous trees—cottonwoods and poplars, for the most part—cut the prairie. He and Barney were far enough up the hill to make looking out across the plains seem like looking out the window of an airplane.

He caught movement in the bushes below. The rack on the big Muley twisted back and forth, as a small breeze filtered their smell down the hill. When he'd first spotted the rack, he'd thought it belonged to an elk, it was so big.

A hundred meters below the deer was a swampy area. Taiga, the books called this portion of the Rocky Mountain Front. It reminded him of country he'd seen in Mongolia.

Barney grunted and turned on his side underneath the shelter they'd made from a bulletproof blanket they'd stolen from the office a few months ago—some kind of super tough material made out of nanotube threads—whatever nanotube threads were.

All they cared was that it helped to mask their infrared signature, and kept the frost off at night. The dark gray color blended well with the jumble of burned trees and leafless bushes.

Barney turned the page. Like Joe Big, his face was blackened and he wore a green watch cap. The book was a book on gardening and flowers. The only book that Barney had thought to bring. And he was reading it like it was a thriller. That's just wrong, Joe Big thought.

"You know what?" he asked.

"What?"

"This sucks. No one has been here since those two Indian girls showed up in that old truck and beat on the door of the trailer."

"Un-huh. What's your point?"

"My point is that this is supposed to be a secret base for a bunch of terrorists. That Quonset hut is supposed to be filled with some kind of new and improved VX."

"And?"

"And no one is around. There's a whole hut full of VX and no one is around."

"Maybe the place has cameras. Maybe there's someone like you and me hiding out on one of the other slopes, waiting for someone like you and me to get bored and go down and take a look around."

"I've looked at the opposing slopes until my eyes are blurry, and all I've seen are a lot of birds and a few four-legged critters. There's not even any rattlesnakes."

"You make that sound like a bad thing."

"I was thinking of taking a couple back to the office and turning them loose. C'mon, man. Let's go down and take a look. One more night out here, and I'm going to go bug-fuck."

Barney put the book on the ground, and sat up, legs crossed. "You really want to go down there?"

"Yeah. I do. *Especially* since we're not supposed to."

"Patience, grasshopper. Quinn said the place is meant to look deserted. That was the beauty of putting it out in the open, off the big ranch itself. What's that the Burmese say? Slowly, slowly to catch a monkey."

"Screw a bunch of monkeys. And screw Quinn. This place is empty. No one is looking at us. I'd feel it if someone was looking at us. We're out here alone. And it doesn't feel right."

"Well, we've got that giant Muley for company."

Joe Big glanced at him. "Think about it, man. Why would these guys want to use VX on an American city? The more I think about it the less sense it makes. They're conservatives. Conservatives by definition don't want to change the status quo; they want to keep a good thing going. And a lot of them are super religious. No way their religion can justify killing innocent Americans."

"You never heard of 'the end justifies the means'? A Jesuit concept, if I are not mistaken." Barney sighed, and closed the book. "But you're right. I can't see a bunch of former special ops dudes agreeing to attack an American city with a WMD."

"You think Quinn was lying to us?"

"Quinn is sneaky, no doubt about it," Barney said. "She's a Fed, through and through. Plus, she's tough enough to stick an arrow through one of Pick's men—and that's pretty damn tough, you've got to admit."

"I told you she was a piece of work."

"They've been playing us," Barney said. "Quinn most of all. No doubt about it. But I think Gladys or Mrs. W or whoever she is was genuinely shocked to discover that Quinn had killed someone with an arrow."

"Well, think about that, too," Joe Big said. "I mean, here we are. They got us to do exactly what they wanted us to do. We even started feeling sorry for Quinn because of Brianna."

"Man, Quinn has *got* a body—"

Joe Big looked at him, horrified.

Barney laughed. "Got you."

"Don't do that."

"So what is it you think they really want us to do?" Barney asked.

"Start a war between those guys at that ranch out there and the U.S. Government."

"Why would they do that?"

"I don't know."

"It all sounds kind of far-fetched to me. You know what I'm saying? I can see people who are poor and don't know better, like the

Taliban, putting their life on the line, but super rich guys? I don't think so. Not in this life."

"Well, that's the whole point, isn't it? *They* are not putting *their* lives on the line; they are putting the lives of people like *us* on the line." Joe Big squinted down at the Quonset hut. "They live in a world of acceptable losses. All they care about is that the game goes on."

"We've been out here too long," Barney said. "I'm starting to think about Quinn's body, and you're starting to make sense."

"Well, that Quonset hut down there is supposed to be full of some kind of new and improved VX developed by the Chinese Army."

Barney grunted. "If there are a bunch of dead Americans again, the public will believe just about anything."

"Paul's Oswald Strategy," Joe Big said. "I'm not buying that, either. It's too easy to see through."

"People see what they want to see. This country is in a depression. One good shove and things could really go south. Another major terrorist event, and the American people will beg Congress to re-write the Constitution."

Joe Big took off his watch cap and rubbed the stubble on his head. "The problem is, we don't know who has the most to gain. If we knew who had most to gain, maybe we'd know what to do."

"What do you mean?"

"In Iraq and Afghanistan, and just about everywhere else, those mercs answered to nobody but the company they work for." He put his cap back on. "In Iraq, they weren't bound by Iraqi law or U.S. law or even the Uniform Code of Military Justice. I think that's why those guys were so quick to shoot at us, even though they knew we are cops. Long story short, they shot at us because they *could*. If there is some kind of big disaster in America, guys like them, mercenaries, are going to be first responders. Not only will they make a ton of money, but they will also be living proof of why civil liberties ought to be curtailed even more. I mean, security companies thrive on disaster. The more disaster, the more war, the stronger they get. And the stronger they get, the more the Government relies on their services. These are not stupid people, man. They know how to be the good guys when a disaster happens."

"Is that always bad?"

Joe Big was silent, thinking about it. "No," he said. "Not always. Not even most of the time, maybe. A lot of the guys they employ really are patriots, and they really do know what they are doing. A lot of them are former cops. They are well trained to handle war and natural disasters or any combination thereof. They are exactly the kind of people you want showing up on your doorstep when the world goes to shit, but . . . you know . . ." He shook his head, and bent to look through the spotting scope. "It's not natural," he said. "It's not American. The American idea of freedom is based on the American Indian idea of liberty. And that idea cannot tolerate elites. *Everyone* has to agree. And that is light years from what these Neocons and Theocons have in mind. They don't want government by majority. They want elites to rule."

The Muley buck was standing in the middle of a tangle of downfall and old burned logs, its ears rotating like mini-radars.

"If that's true," Barney said, "Then a lot of people in the Government, especially in the big bureaucracies, like the State Department and the Department of Defense, Homeland Security, the intelligence agencies—all those people have got to be nervous. If what you say is true, I wouldn't put it past the people who control Quinn and Gladys to manufacture a reason for getting rid of the people who own that ranch out there."

"You really think the people who own that ranch are big enough to slug it out with the U.S. Government?"

"No way," Barney said. "But they are for sure rich and connected enough to influence the government. Some of them *are* the government. Their companies are threaded through the entire military-industrial establishment."

"Like a cancer beginning to metastasize," Joe Big said.

Barney groaned. "Please don't start with the metaphors again."

Joe Big grinned. "Like a noxious weed in the middle of a field of flowers, spreading its poison through the root system."

"Quit it."

"Mold spores blooming in the bathroom."

"I said, quit it."

"Gangrene entering the blood stream. Blue mold on a bagel. Chronic Wasting Disease in a deer herd."

Barney laughed. "Okay, okay. I get it. But what does it have to do with us?"

"Well," Joe Big said. "I figure there's a lot of skirmishing, both major and minor, going on. I don't *know* this. I have no *evidence* of this. But people are people, especially greedy, power-hungry people. There's got to be a lot of jockeying for power and influence going on, both within government bureaucracies and within the cliques of people who make up groups who want to change our way of life. No way these groups are not butting heads."

"Which means?"

Joe Big rolled over on his back and looked up at the sky. He put his hands behind his head. "Which means that whatever is hidden down there in that Quonset hut is part of a Government plot, and not part of a plot dreamed up by the people who own that ranch out there."

"And to what do you base this amazing leap of logic?"

"I base it on the fact that this whole fucking thing feels way too rinky-dink and half-assed to be something put together by a bunch of ex-SEALS and Force Recon and Delta Force and former cops who were some of the best cops in America."

Barney frowned. "Even the best can fuck up sometimes."

Joe Big yawned, and crossed his arms over his chest, and closed his eyes. "They sure can," he said. He cracked one eye open. "But it sure don't feel that way, this time, *mon ami*."

Barney crawled over to the spotting scope.

"There's another small jet taking off from the ranch," he said. "And a red helicopter that looks like it's headed for Great Falls."

"See what I mean," Joe Big said. "Those guys have got a tower loaded with all sorts of state-of-the-art surveillance equipment. They've got ground radar and Humvees equipped with the LRAS3 surveillance system. And that's just the stuff we can see. There's no telling what else they might have. With the kind of money, and the kind of technology they have access to, they could hide anything anywhere they wanted to, and no one would ever find it. There's flat out no way to get close to that place, if they don't want you to."

"Sure there is," Barney said.

"How?"

"Call in the Marines, like you said."

"That's about the only way, then."

He turned his head to look at Barney. "You think what we find here is supposed to be an excuse to assault that ranch?" he asked.

"Only one way to find out," Barney said, taking his eye from the scope. "You're right. It's time to go see—what're you looking at?" He turned his head toward the ridgeline. "Where did he come from?"

Joe Big was silent, tracking the figure cresting the ridge with the scope on the M14. He pushed the safety off, but kept his finger outside the trigger guard.

"Shit," he said, and snapped the safety back on. "It's not a he. It's a her."

"Her who?"

"Quinn, who else? And she's not even trying to be sneaky."

Barney leaned onto his left side and with both hands picked up the spotting scope and tripod, and moved it so that it was pointing toward the figure moving sidehill along the opposing slope, headed into the draw above them. He squirmed around behind the scope, squinting into the eyepiece, and with his right hand adjusted the focus.

"Camouflage fatigues," he said. "Black SWAT baseball hat. Holstered pistol. Looks like a revolver of some kind."

"No long gun," Joe Big said.

"And no paint," Barney said. "Normal makeup. Earrings. No water. No pack. Hiking stick. She's looking this way with tiny black binoculars."

"The Feds sure have a strange way of teaching their people how to recon."

"It's not that," Barney said. "She's acting like she knows something we don't." He took his eye away from the eyepiece, and stared at Joe Big for a moment.

Joe Big grinned at him. "Makes you *really* want to go down there now, doesn't it?"

Barney peered into the eyepiece again. "She sees us."

"Time to go," Joe Big said.

Barney looked at him. "You don't want to talk to her? See why she's here?"

"What for? She's either going to tell us to go home, or she's going to make sure that we don't get antsy and decide to go down there and check out the place."

"Why would she care so much about that?"

"Because The Dragon Lady told us in no uncertain terms to stay put, call it in, wait for the Calvary to arrive before we went down there."

"Do you really think that she would go to all the trouble of coming out here just to make sure that we don't go down there? That seems like kind of a stretch to me."

Joe Big looked toward the figure watching them. "I'm saying that's a possibility, is all. Could be she's here to tell us it's all a misunderstanding. There's nothing down there except what we can see."

"So why don't we wait and ask her why she's here."

"Because I don't want to get into another argument with her—and then have to go down there just because she says we can't. I mean, fuck, man, people have died."

Barney stood and stretched, hands on hips, arching his back.

"Let's go then. Grab your rifle and pack and leave all this other shit here. We can get it later—or never, I don't care. It all belongs to the Feds, anyway.

In unison, they put on the Vietnam-era Alice packs they both preferred, and picked up their rifles.

"We'll walk upright, like homo sapiens," Barney said. "With the kind of technology that ranch has got, and the Government has got, there's no reason to sneak around—especially not with Quinn wandering around the hillside looking for us." He shrugged. "If push comes to shove, we can lose Quinn no problem, but beyond that, there's not much we can do to hide. For all we know they've tasked a drone or a satellite to keep track of us."

Wordless, they picked their way out of the tangle in the middle of the draw, over to the open slope below the ridgeline. The big buck remained motionless in the tangle of branches, almost impossible to see.

They headed down toward the buildings. Nonchalant. Two hunters walking rifles slung over their shoulders, their hunt finished for the day.

At the bottom they turned to look uphill, but neither could spot her. Joe Big waved in case she was watching.

THE OLD RANCH house was empty of all but an old scarred and nicked wooden kitchen table, and five equally old and scarred, mismatched wooden chairs arranged around the table. Empty beer and soft drink bottles and aluminum cans littered the table and windowsill. An old coffee can filled with sand and cigarette butts and marijuana roaches in the living room. The lingering odor of marijuana. Windows opaque with dirt and grime, sills dry rotted and devoid of all but a few flakes of paint. The wood floors creaked and groaned as they walked through the house, checking empty rooms. The dust on the banister and on the steps leading upstairs was thick and undisturbed. They didn't bother to go upstairs.

Someone had crapped in the toilet, even though there was no water in the toilet bowl. Dust and mouse droppings littered most surfaces in the kitchen. Ancient yellowed linoleum curled at the edges covered the kitchen floor, holes worn in it at the rear door. The stove and refrigerator had been removed, no telling when. The white enamel sink was home to a spider web and more mouse droppings.

On the wall in the living room were large maps of Los Angeles and Las Vegas, Chicago and Philadelphia. The maps were new and had big circles and notations and equations scrawled on them in pink and black and blue felt-tip pen. No other papers or literature of any kind were in evidence.

Barney pulled a small digital camera out of his pant pocket, and started taking pictures of the maps. "Bullshit," he muttered.

When he was finished, they went outside, across the packed dirt and gravel of the parking/turn-around area to the trailer house. As they crossed the open area they could see Quinn standing motionless on the ridge. She had walked back to where they'd first seen her.

The door was unlocked. Inside, there was bedding on the beds, clothes in the closets, a widescreen TV and DVD player, DVDs scattered about. Full ashtrays, empty beer and soft drink bottles, a few dirty plates and glasses and silverware in the sink. Food in the fridge. Food in the cupboards. Dishes and silverware and cups and glasses. No crumbs on the counter. No grease on the stove. No toilet articles in the bathroom. No soap in the shower stall.

Barney took more pictures.

Personal items were in the other bathroom. Razors and blades, a box of Band-Aids, aspirin and Ibuprofen. Shampoo.

The beds were unmade and rumpled, but not slept in. No clothes in the dressers or in the closets. No clutter. No old magazines or newspapers. No garbage.

It went without saying that it was all staged. Joe Big tried the lights. The lights worked. Barney looked carefully for lenses or listening devices. *Nada.*

"I wonder who the two girls were looking for," Barney said.

"Probably paid to bring a message to someone who was never here in the first place," Joe Big said. "Something to keep us from getting too restless."

There was a new Honda generator behind the house, wired into the house wiring, a full tank of gas. It didn't look as if it had ever been run. No need. The trailer had electricity from the power line coming into the property. No carbon or discoloring on the exhaust.

"Stranger and stranger," Barney said.

THE LARGE WOOD doors on the Quonset hut, held closed with an old weathered two-by-ten set in metal hangars, like the hangers on the barn doors at Joe Big's place, proved to be camouflage for a thick, metal door with a key pad instead of a normal lock. Barney took more pictures.

Joe Big stepped over to one of the windows. He pulled on the edge of the metal sheet welded to the wall. The metal plate was firmly anchored to the wall. Barney took pictures of the metal sheeting, and close-ups of the welds.

Joe Big walked to the rear of the building. There were three old shovels and two picks, their handles gray and checked, leaning against the back of the building. Probably left there when the hillside was dug out enough to get behind the building and weld on the piece of metal that covered the rear window, he thought. The concrete pad that the building sat on was old and crumbling in places, the corrugated metal siding rusted where it met the concrete pad.

He set his pack down on the hillside, retrieved the two picks, and walked back to the middle of the building. He dropped one pick to the ground and swung the other hard at the corrugated metal building. The pick sank to the handle in the metal siding.

Barney carried both rifles over, and shrugged out of his pack, and placed the M4 and the M14 on the packs. Both rifles were locked and loaded. He grabbed the other pick, and began putting holes in the side of the building about three feet from where Joe Big was working. In a few minutes, they had punched out the ragged outline of an entrance way.

"Is she still up there?" Joe Big asked.

"Yeah. She's just standing there, watching."

Joe Big gestured Barney back and, reversing the head of the pick to use the broad flat blade, began to connect the holes.

Ten minutes later, they had pried the metal to one side, leaving a hole big enough to easily step through. Joe Big looked inside. Pallets containing plastic weapons cases were stacked five or six feet inside the wall, the curvature of the wall making it necessary to place the stacked pallets well away from the side of the building.

Barney handed Joe Big a flashlight, and Joe Big entered the building. Crouching to avoid the curved wall, he turned left, and walked to the front of the Quonset hut. The front was free of pallets. The only light coming into the building was through the hole they had made in the wall, most of it blocked by the stacked pallets containing plastic weapons cases. The inside of the building smelled moldy. The temperature was only a little cooler than outside. It must have been seriously hot in here during the summer months, he thought, even with the new ventilator fans on the roof at both ends of the building.

He shined the flashlight down the center of the hut. Pallets containing plastic cases lined one side, metal racks containing cylinders about three feet long and a foot in diameter lined the other side. The floor was old, stained with the residue of ranch equipment and ranch vehicles.

"Lot of crates," he called. "Racks of what look to be containers of some kind of chemical weapon. Might as well come in and take pictures. Standing around outside won't help if someone knows we're in here."

Barney retrieved a small LED flashlight from his pack, and stepped inside.

"Shine your light over here," Joe Big said, when Barney had reached the front of the building. He unlatched the catches on one of the cases, and opened it. The case was empty. Barney took a couple of pictures.

"What's supposed to be in there?" He asked.

"An older version of the LAAWS, I think." Joe Big closed the lid, and read the stenciled writing on the top. "Yeah, a LAAWS."

He opened another case at the top of the next stack. Empty.

Barney walked over to one of the cylinders. Yellow and red chemical warfare decals were prominent on each cylinder. Stenciled lettering indicated that they were some kind of cluster munition.

He put the camera in his pocket, and lifted one of the containers out of its rack, and stared at it for a moment.

He hefted it up and down, and abruptly gave a yell, like a karate expert breaking boards and, legs scissoring, did a clean and jerk, holding the cylinder with both hands above his head.

He staggered to the side, back and forth, as if the weight was too much and he was going to drop the cylinder.

"Jesus," Joe Big said. "Watch it!" He moved to help Barney.

With both hands, Barney threw the cylinder hard to the ground. It bounced a few times, the first time nearly to his waist, and rolled toward the back of the building.

"What the fuck are you doing, man?"

"It's empty. Doesn't weigh anything at all." Barney walked down the line hefting other containers with his left hand and dropping them back in their racks.

"All empty," he said. He toppled another to the floor. They watched it bounce and roll toward the first cylinder. "Molded plastic," Barney said. "One-piece, molded plastic. No way to put anything inside."

"Someone went to a lot of trouble for a photo op," Joe Big said.

"Actually not much trouble at all, if you think about it. Plastic containers, a few decals, a stencil and some yellow paint. Used weapons boxes that the Army was probably going to recycle anyway. A couple of sheets of metal and a welder. A heavy-duty door that a lot of ranches use on buildings that house expensive stud animals. And, shazam, proof that the bad guys have WMDs on the Blackfeet Indian Reservation."

Joe Big was silent.

"How's this supposed to work?" he asked. "It took us like twenty minutes to break in and figure out this is all bogus."

They stared at each other for a moment, the light from their flashlights pointed at the cylinders.

"Shit!" Barney said. "Quinn knows us too well. This is why Mrs. W didn't want us down here."

Joe Big turned and ran to the front of the Quonset hut. He ducked behind the pallets containing the empty weapons cases, and half ran toward the opening in the wall, Barney right behind him.

Outside, they did their best to bend the metal back over the opening, but it would bend only half the distance back to the wall.

"Leave it," Barney said.

They picked up their rifles, and put their packs on, and ran up the hill, looping around and then angling up the slope behind the fallen-down barn and the old ranch house, running as hard as they could up the open slope to the ridge, breath rasping, lungs raw by the time they got to the top, across the grassy, rounded ridge, down into a draw much like the one they'd been in on the other side, struggling through a tangle of bushes and muck in the center. A wide, muddy path led up the center of the draw, shod horse prints in the mud.

They hurried across the path, up the far hillside, onto the next ridge. The ridge was rocky, mostly devoid of vegetation.

"Any snakes around here?" Barney panted behind Joe Big.

"Doubt it. We're too high. Maybe a few."

"I didn't see her when we were running up the hill, did you?"

"Nope."

The far side slope led gentle down onto a prairie that stretched rolling to the horizon. The slope was thickly carpeted with small flinty rocks easy to run across, their boots sinking into fine rock and sparse grass.

The ground at the bottom was severely overgrazed, dried cow patties and horse shit everywhere. An empty stock tank sat in the middle of an area that had been churned by cattle and horses watering at the tank, their tracks hardened in the dried mud. A vehicle track led from the stock tank down to a gravel road. Barbed wire fences with skinny metal posts lined both side of the road.

"We're on the Rez," Joe Big said.

"Is that good?"

"It is if we call Lonewolf to come and get us."

They walked, breathing hard, over to the metal stock tank, and shrugged out of their packs, and sat down in the shade next to the tank, rifles propped against the side. From where they sat, they could see up the draw behind the tank, and out across the road to the ranch land on the other side of the barbed wire fence.

"We've got a thermite grenade," Barney said. "Maybe we should go back and fill the inside with some of that old barn wood, and burn the place down. Those containers will melt in no time."

"I vote we wait for the sun to go down, which it's going to do in about an hour, and get as far away from here as fast as we can."

Barney was silent, mulling over their predicament. That they weren't supposed to know what was inside that Quonset hut was a given. The fiction of what was supposed to be in the hut could be preserved as long as they were prevented from telling anyone that it was all bullshit. The hut was a lure, a *raison d'état* for something.

"You think she's going to tell?" he asked.

Joe Big shrugged. "We have to assume so. But it don't much matter, not with that hole we put in the side of the building."

"We could walk over to the ranch, see how long it takes someone to come and get us," Barney said. "Tell them what is in that Quonset hut."

"Oh, yeah. Waltz across the prairie and, hey, Whassup, bro? Sorry we shot two of your buds, and kneecapped the boss's son, but guess what we found."

"They're supposed to be professionals," Barney said. "Cold and calculating and only interested in the money."

"Is that how Pick and his bunch seemed to you?"

"Well, it was an idea."

"Two Federal officers—us—killed while discovering a cache of nerve gas," Joe Big said. "Unbeknownst to the two officers, the place was booby-trapped by the bad guys. Off limits, until Hazmat and Federal investigators are through with the crime scene. But, ladies and gentleman of the press, in the pictures I just passed out you can clearly see from the markings on some of the bombs that were not incinerated that—"

"Finally. The WMD cache that was," Barney said.

"Warrants issued by a secret FISA court, the reasons for the warrants a National Secret," Joe Big said.

They looked at each other.

"Naah," Barney said. "We're being too paranoid."

Joe Big put his head back against the metal tank. "I don't think so."

"How does your uncle figure in all this?"

"He doesn't. He was in Montana on other business, and heard about what happened to us up the Blackfoot. He did a little digging, called in a few favors. Looking out for his nephew, that's all. He wants us to maybe go to work for him, when this is all over. Something about white slavers in Southern China."

"When this is all over," Barney said. "He seems to have more confidence in us than we do."

"He's a force of nature, though, isn't he?"

"Oh, yeah. He is that."

They were silent, gazing at the hillside and up the draw and out across the prairie.

"Imagine what this place was like when it was only buffalo and Indians," Joe Big said. "Herds of elk. Buffalo wolves. Grizzly bears. Grassland all the way to New Mexico."

"Can't," Barney said. "It's too empty."

"Twenty-five million buffalo. The thing that fascinates me is how much time and energy the Indians spent altering the environment so that more and greater herds of four-legged critters could exist."

"Altered how?" Barney asked.

"Fire. They used fire to expand the grasslands, keep the trees and bushes out, to make the land ideal for buffalo and elk and pronghorn. They knew what they were doing, too. It wasn't an accident." He looked out across the prairie, at a distant butte. "These days people want a return to wilderness. Trouble is no one knows what that wilderness might have looked like. For thousands of years, all over North and South and Central America, the Indians had been busy altering the environment—mostly for farming. But on the plains, the great herds of buffalo would have been much smaller if the Indians hadn't used fire to expand and regenerate the grasslands." He shifted to get more comfortable against the stock tank. "Those old Indians proved that altering the environment is not necessarily a bad thing."

"You know," Barney said. "One thing we never considered is that all these assholes are in it together. I mean, both sides win, no matter what. Americans are once again afraid of their shadow. VX, especially the new version, is nasty, nasty shit. For the Government, the freedom to do what it wants increases proportional to the amount of freedom that its citizens are willing to give up. The rich assholes get to re-write the Constitution. It's a win for both sides."

"Expanding the grassland."

"Exactly. A serious WMD threat means more contracts for companies that make surveillance equipment which means more money for the super rich and the super rich-and-religious to promote their agendas," Barney said.

"And more money and freedom for the Intelligence agencies to do what they do," Joe Big said.

"It's kind of like what happened when gas prices went through the roof," Barney said. "The higher the price of a gallon of gas, the more money the government collects in taxes. The extra tax revenue, once used, is factored into new budgets. And the Government suddenly has a vested interest in keeping gas prices high."

"You really think Quinn and Mrs. W and some of the other Feds we've worked with could be in bed with whoever owns that ranch out there?" Joe Big asked.

Barney thought about it for a moment.

"No way. The people who own that ranch might be willing, but there's no way a Federal agency is going to do that kind of business with a private organization. That would be like writing a blank check to those guys out there. No way they'd do that. Whatever they are, Quinn and Walker and people like them are not stupid."

"So why are we running?" Joe Big asked.

"Because that building and what is in it is still in play, that's why. If we would've sat up on that hill like good little boys, and waited for someone to come along that we could capture and interrogate, all would have been cool. Whoever showed up would have been a plant. They would have told us what we wanted to hear, and we would have dutifully relayed the information, and the powers that be would have called in either an air strike or a Hazmat/bomb squad. We never would have been allowed anywhere near the inside of that Quonset hut."

"Oswald stopped in his tracks before he has a chance to do anything."

"Only in this case, Lee Harvey is not a fucked-up former Marine. He is a whole gaggle of very powerful, rich beyond our comprehension, well-connected men and women. Marines would have—might still be used to assault that ranch out there. And given the demonstrably lethal contents of that Quonset hut, the American people will turn into a lynch mob." He paused. "The lynch mob is the key. Without it, there is no touching that ranch out there; no changing the status quo."

"And now there is a big fucking hole in the side of that Quonset hut," Joe Big said. "And Quinn watched us put it there. And we are nowhere to be found. Which means the only way to keep the building in play is to . . ."

"That's right, Kemosabe. Once they realize we've been in there, the shit is going to hit the fan. They are going to do their best to preserve the move they've made against the people who inhabit that ranch out there. Capture will not be their first choice."

Joe Big was silent for a long moment.

"Kind of makes you want to shoot someone, doesn't it?"

"A lot of someones, actually."

"I should have killed Patrick, when I had the chance."

"What good would that have done?"

"It would have inflicted a casualty that was one of them. It would have made it real to at least a few of them." He leaned his head back against the water tank. "But I didn't. And, now, like always, the only casualties are going to be us, or people like us. War all the motherfucking time. Shit."

"Makes you wonder what other kinds of bullshit we've been a part of, and never knew it," Barney said.

"Oh, man. Don't even go there."

"If we can get these pictures to someone who can use them to twist arms and bring the whole shiteree to a halt, we should be okay," Barney said.

"Well, take a nap, for now," Joe Big said. "We'll wait until night to move. If we're lucky, Quinn will keep her mouth shut, and no one will notice that there is a hole in the side of that building."

34
A Murder of Wolves

The moon was an orange dragon's fang coming up on the horizon. They had night vision goggles, but didn't want to use night vision until they had to, preferring instead to follow a serpentine course along the low hills, paralleling as best they could the thin pale line of road stretching to the north.

"What's that down there?" Barney asked. The rocky hillside was ghostly in the dark.

"How are you at riding bareback?" Joe Big asked.

"Why don't we call Lonewolf to come and get us? He can't be too much farther from where we are now."

"Better not take a chance with the phone, until we have to."

"I've never ridden bareback. My ex used to all the time, but I was afraid I'd fall off and look stupid."

"Here," Joe Big said, and handed Barney a couple of small, square packets.

"What's this?"

"Sugar packets from the heater meals. They'll love you."

"How you doin'?" Joe Big asked.

Barney was a dark humped-back shadow on top the buckskin mare.

"Beats walking," he said.

"Sit upright if you can. You're confusing her. If you squeeze with your legs, she'll think you want to go faster."

"Easy for you to say. You been doing this all your life."

Joe Big rode easy, his pack straps loosened so that the bottom of the Alice pack rested on the back of the big bay. He'd chosen well. A mature gelding with a comfortable gait and no problem with a bareback rider. Actually, the horse had chosen him, not the other way around. As he and Barney had approached the small herd, it had cantered out to him. They'd peered at each other in the darkness, and that had been that.

He was carrying both rifles across his back, resting on top the low-slung pack. He didn't like the noise the rifles were making, rubbing and clacking against each other, but there was nothing to be done about it. Barney was having enough trouble without a rifle to worry about.

"This guy is pretty comfortable," Joe Big said. "And he seems to know where he's going. Let me know if you want to switch."

"I'm okay. You're right; this is easier."

"Not a single vehicle has come down that road," Joe Big said.

"You think there's a roadblock on it?"

"I don't know. Maybe. I don't think so. I've got a feeling they think we are still up above the Quonset hut. You sure you don't want to switch? She looks a little stiff-gaited to me."

"I'm okay. She's a good girl."

With his knees, Joe Big urged his horse past Barney, up a slight hill. At the top, he slid off the horse, and walked back to hold Barney's horse while he got off. He lifted the sling of the M4 over his head, and handed the rifle to Barney. "There's a vehicle parked in some trees next to a creek," he said in a low voice. He unslung the M14. "Drop our packs here. Take all your magazines. This doesn't feel right."

His horse nuzzled at his pocket with the sugar packets in it.

He dropped his pack, and took the night vision goggles out of the pack and put them on. They were already set to the night vision setting, but he checked anyway, looking through the scope to make sure the red dot was green.

"What about the horses?" Barney asked, as he put on his goggles. He picked up the M4 and looked through the sight.

"They won't go anywhere."

Crouching low, they moved quickly over the military crest and down the open slope about thirty meters, and sat down. They could hear the horses come to the top of the ridge and look down at them.

Half hidden in the trees and bushes next to a creek, they could see a pickup pulled off the road in what looked like a graveled parking area next to a small bridge. There was no movement.

"Shit," Barney said in a low voice.

"What?"

"There's a body next to the truck."

Behind them the horses started down the hill.

"It's Lonewolf," Joe Big said. He reached up to make sure his goggles were on passive.

Joe Big felt the horse nudge him with its muzzle against his back. The buckskin was behind it.

He stood and turned to the horse. He stroked its neck and muzzle so it wouldn't follow Barney.

Barney spread about twenty-five yards to the right, moving in a crouch, the rifle in his shoulder, slowly pivoting his torso to cover the creek and the bridge and the truck.

Joe Big assumed the sitting position, the M14 in his shoulder, the back of his left arm supported by his knee, left hand holding the rifle in front of the magazine. He pushed off the safety, finger on the trigger. With the scope he scanned trees and bushes to the left of the truck. Two lights winked on about ten meters apart inside the bushes to the left of the truck. He fired two rounds each at the infrared signatures, and was up and behind the horses, swatting them on the ass. "Hee-yah!" he shouted, and the horses took off down the hill, the buckskin tossing and kicking, the bay galloping toward the creek.

Barney ran hard down the slope, running for the trees, not giving his location away by firing.

A muzzle flash strobed in time to the distinctive sound of an M16 on full auto to the left of where Joe Big had put the rounds. The buckskin screamed and went down, skidding on her shoulder and side. Back up on her feet and trying to move to the left. Joe Big waited for her to clear his field of fire, and put the rest of the twenty round clip into the area where he'd seen the muzzle flash, up and running in the direction of the buckskin as soon as the magazine was empty.

He ejected the magazine as he ran, letting it fall to the ground, and tore open the Velcro flap on the magazine pouch at his waist. He pulled out a full magazine and inserted it in the rifle and released the bolt, feeling and hearing it snap solidly forward.

Automatic weapons fire from across the road—another M16—lanced the area where he had been, and out of the corner of his eye he saw Barney return fire.

And then he was in the high grass and bushes next to the creek, behind the buckskin standing spraddle-legged and trembling.

He aimed over the top of her back. She grunted and sank to her front knees, and then collapsed onto her side, forcing him backwards, air and shit expelled from her rear end. The big bay was moving agitated in the bushes next to the creek.

He searched with his left hand and found the magazine pouch with the two grenades, and took out one. He propped the rifle against the Buckskin's back, and pulled the pin, and reared back and threw the grenade in a high arc toward where he'd seen the infrared signatures of two Night Vision Devices.

He dropped face down behind the dead horse. The grenade went off in the bushes, a throaty crack like the sound of rusted pipes coming together, and he was up, rifle in his shoulder, sidling in almost a duck walk through the bushes. He heard the stutter of Barney's M4 on the other side of the trees where the truck was parked. Firing at someone on the road, or on the other side of the road. The M4 fired again, two single shots this time, Barney making sure someone was dead.

A woman in baggy tactical fatigues, a tactical vest on over her fatigues, M16 barrel down in the bushes, was sprawled face up in the grass, most of her forehead missing.

He moved forward, slower. A small movement next to a stand of aspen. He fired three rounds into the movement, and hit the deck.

No return fire.

He raised his head, and then stood, crouched, the rifle held out in front, and edged into the aspens.

A man was crawling toward the creek.

He shot him three times in the spine and neck, and hit the deck again, doing a low crawl to his right, away from the bushes along the stream.

He found two more bodies where the grenade had gone off. All three of the men and the woman were dressed in tactical fatigues, tactical vests on over their fatigues, old-style NVDs. All four had M16s near their bodies, .40 caliber Glocks holstered at their waists, radio headsets and voice mics. A crew cobbled together at the last minute, he thought. Tasked to watch the least likely avenue of egress for him and Barney. SWAT and combat trained, a couple of them, maybe, but without much real-life experience.

He came to the edge of the bushes. The road stretched bright green in both directions.

"I'm at the road," he said.

"Clear," Barney said from the other side of the bridge, in the bushes somewhere.

Joe Big stepped out onto the road and walked quickly back to the pickup, and bent to examine the body they'd seen from the ridge. He could hear Barney jogging up behind him.

"Is it Tom Lonewolf?" Barney asked.

"Yeah."

"Dead?"

"Yeah. His neck is broken, and he's got a big dent in his forehead."

"Fuck."

"Who are they?" Joe Big asked.

"I don't know, but let's get out of here. Sure as hell someone was talking to someone somewhere."

"Take the pickup?"

"No choice," Barney said. "There's a black Suburban across the road in the bushes, but I shot out the tires."

"Knock out the tail lights," Joe Big said. "I'm going to get our packs." He handed the M14 to Barney, and ran back up the hill to where they'd dropped their packs.

The big bay came out of the bushes and galloped toward him, intersecting his path, as he grabbed the packs and started back downhill.

He stopped, and put the packs down, and reached in his pocket for a sugar packet, tore it open, and poured the sugar into the palm of his hand. "Here you go," he said, feeling the velvet muzzle, lips delicate in the palm of his hand. "You go back where we found you." He smacked the horse on the shoulder. "Hyah! Get out of here!"

The horse tossed its head, and neighed, and whirled and thundered up and over the top of the ridge.

By the time he reached the truck, Barney had put their rifles in the cab, and started the truck, and knocked out the taillights—so the brake lights and rear tail lights would not show—and dragged Lonewolf's body to the back of the truck.

Joe Big put the packs inside the cab. "I don't think we can lift him," Barney said. "He's really heavy."

"We can do it."

Barney grabbed the body by the arms, and jerked it forward so that it was sitting upright. They both knelt and slung an arm over their shoulders, and stood, the two of them and the body facing the bed of the pickup. They staggered to the tailgate, dragging the feet and lower legs along the ground. Joe Big leaned as far forward as he could into the bed of the pickup, and Barney dropped the arm he'd been holding, and grabbed the body by the belt and the pant leg behind the knee and pushed, holding the body in place, until Joe Big could drop the other arm, and grab the belt and the other pant leg. "One. Two. Three," Barney said, and they both pushed and heaved, muscling the body up onto the tailgate.

"I've got him," Barney said, breathing hard. The body was on the tailgate to mid thigh.

Joe Big jumped up into the bed, and grabbed the body under the arms and pulled. The body slid into the middle of the bed.

Joe Big vaulted over the side, and Barney closed the tailgate.

"You drive," Barney said. "You know the roads."

They climbed in. Joe Big put the gearshift in drive. "Drive fast," Barney said. "The one I shot has Federal ID."

Joe Big drove fast through a green landscape. An occasional trailer house or a worn, tired-looking ranch house, some with yard lights, some without, went past on either side of the road.

"There's a police radio in here," Barney said. "But we better not use it."

"I've got that one-time cell phone. We'll use it when we get to a paved road . . . which is right now."

He braked hard, the truck slewing sideways, and turned right onto a paved road—a highway.

"Where are we headed?" Barney asked

"Toward Valance. They'll expect us to go the other way—to my parents place near Heart Butte, or into Browning. We've got to get rid of this truck. Everyone knows it belongs to Tom Lonewolf."

"You should turn the lights on if we see traffic coming toward us."

"Roger that. Better call Paul. The phone is in the right side pocket on my pack."

"HEY, PAUL. IT'S Barney. What's happening, man? We ran into your friend, and we're headed out." He paused. "Well, he's feeling about as poorly as anyone can feel, I'm sorry to say." He paused again. "That's right."

Barney glanced at Joe Big. Far ahead a vehicle was coming toward them.

Joe Big turned on the lights.

"A meet would be good," Barney said.

The approaching vehicle materialized into a semi truck, orange running lights outlining the trailer. The semi rocketed past, at least twenty miles an hour over the limit.

Joe Big shut the lights off again.

"I love the way these new NVDs adapt to light," he said.

"Do you know where your grandmother's mother was born?" Barney asked him.

"My grandmother's mother . . . We're almost there."

"We're almost there," Barney said. "Okay. Sorry for the bad news." He paused. "We took care of it."

He snapped the cell phone closed. "He'll meet us in the middle of town. He knows the truck."

"Is there any Internet service on that thing?" Joe Big asked.

Barney opened the phone. "Nope."

"Well, if Paul has his Border Patrol ride, that'll have a link."

"Be taking a big chance, don't you think?" Barney asked.

"Once we write it up, and beam out what we write with the pictures, they'll call off the dogs."

"Why did they kill Tom?"

"I don't know. We were lucky, though. If it had been the guys who were with Pick in the Brew Pub, we'd be dead. Someone would have been up on that ridge with a sniper rifle, and the others would have been set up in a real ambush with interlocking fields of fire, not scattered in the bushes. I'll bet they were an urban team. Fish out of water. The horses confused them."

"They got the one I was riding, huh?"

"Yeah."

"How about yours?"

"I really like that horse, man. If we survive this, I'm going to come back and find him, and buy him from whoever owns him."

"If," Barney said.

They watched the empty road unravel, the hood of the truck following the dotted center line to green infinity.

"What do you want to bet they thought Tom Lonewolf and us are terrorists who plan to attack American cities with VX," Joe Big said. "Five Feds, including one female Fed, sent out to stop us if we came diddy-bopping down the bunny trail. Only a small chance we would come this way, they were told. Feds with no combat experience, defending America against terrorists who are armed with Chinese engineered chemical weapons of mass destruction. One of them lost his cool—probably because he was afraid, and probably because they had been given the latitude to lose their cool. Tom said something sarcastic, and he butt stroked him in the forehead and broke his neck."

He rubbed the side of his face. "Or, I don't know. Maybe he put up a fight. They were Fed's, after all, and he was Tribal Police. The only way they could put him down was to shoot him or hit him with a rifle butt or something. I know I wouldn't have wanted to wrestle with him."

"His time," Barney said. "It don't matter how or why."

"Yeah." Joe Big turned on the headlights, and took his goggles off. "Only it's not supposed to happen here. Not like this. This is worse than being in Ramadi, that time. Want to bet the real SWAT guys are set up on our truck?"

"The problem with the Feds," Barney said, "is they think they can play with anyone they want to play with simply because they are Feds. It's a game to them. Only now it's not. What if we really were terrorists with enhanced VX?"

Farms and houses and mini-ranches, all with orange yard lights, had become frequent. Ahead were the lights of a small community. Valance. White middle-class retirees living next door to one of the poorest Indian reservations in the country, Joe Big thought. Only a few miles from where a member of the Lewis and Clark expedition had killed a young Blackfoot boy trying to steal guns and horses. He gritted his teeth. Somehow the "Expedition" had managed to bumble its way across the entire state of Montana without once running into Blackfeet, and then on the way back to have this one, chance encounter with a group of Blackfeet teenagers.

Fucking guys were so incompetent, it took a pregnant teenage woman to guide them across a country that was full of people going every which way. Trails you could drive a Jeep on going over the passes. Almost a road running the length of the Rocky Mountain Front. Food everywhere, but they almost starved because they would eat only meat. American heroes. Give us a break, he thought. His great, great-whatever grandfather had been right to reckon that white men were not worth the effort.

History might have been different if Lewis and Clark and Company had run into a big Blackfeet village or a large group of warriors headed off to do battle with the Crow or the Snakes or the Flatheads. Not too long before Lewis and Clark had bumbled their way across half a continent, a bunch of Blackfeet had set out to steal horses from the Snakes, and not finding any Snakes, had ended up all the way down in New Mexico, where they had been insulted by arrogant Spaniards escorting a mule train full of gold. The Blackfeet had killed every swinging dick in that mule train.

It probably wouldn't have happened that way with Lewis and Clark. But you never know. It didn't take much to get on the wrong side of a Blackfoot warrior. They were sort of like modern-day Marines: your best friend or your worst enemy.

"What are you thinking about?" Barney asked. "You're grinding your teeth."

"I'm trying not to think about Tom Lonewolf."

He slowed the truck as the highway entered the village.

Amber street lights lit the main street—the highway they were on—all four or five blocks of it. The town was buttoned up for the night. The only gas station was a card-only station. No dogs. No cats. No people. No need to be awake because no one else was awake. One flashing light that marked a crossroads in the middle of nowhere. The town didn't feel empty; it felt impermanent, as if it might float off into outer space when everyone was asleep, leaving only a flashing orange light at the intersection of two highways.

Joe Big slowed the truck to a crawl, and then stopped in the middle of the highway. Another few blocks and they would run out of town. Headlights came on behind them, and a car came up fast and stopped on his side of the truck—a white, nondescript, late 90s Pontiac of some kind, its wheels and side dark with dust and grime. The passenger-side window went down.

"Follow me," Paul said, and pulled ahead.

The white Pontiac turned right at the next corner, and went down a few blocks of darkened houses, and turned right again. They followed it into the parking lot of a stone church with a steep-pitched roof. An old Catholic Church, Joe was sure.

Paul parked the Pontiac. The trunk lid popped open.

Joe Big and Barney climbed out, both of them stretching.

"Throw your stuff in the trunk," Paul said. "Where is he?"

"He's in the back," Barney said. "Sorry, but we needed to get out of there in a hurry."

Paul went to the side of the truck bed and peered in.

Barney and Joe Big silently retrieved their packs and rifles. They threw their packs into the trunk, and Joe Big gently shut the trunk lid. They climbed into the Pontiac with their rifles and spare magazines, Joe Big to the back, Barney to the front passenger seat.

Paul had found a tarp in a box in the back of Tom's truck, and was doing something with the tarp and the body.

He vaulted out of the truck bed, and walked around the Pontiac and slid into the driver's seat and started the car and, wordless, his lips a tight thin line, backed out and turned on the lights. A minute later they were out of town, headed east past large grain elevators.

"One of his nephews is a Sheriff's Deputy," Paul said. "He'll be along in a few minutes to collect the body. Sack out if you want. That cooler back there is full of water and beer." He glanced at Barney. "Get down the both of you if we meet a car or if one comes up behind. Even on the Interstate."

Joe Big passed Barney a water and a beer. "It's all bullshit," he said to Paul.

"Why am I not surprised?"

Barney and Joe Big drank their water and then the beer, silent as they watched the road stretch ahead, the only lights amber yard lights at distant farms or ranches.

Joe Big wedged the cooler into the space between the back seat and the two front seats, and lay on his back across the seat, his head against the door, knees bent upward. Barney put his seat back. He took off the watch cap and rubbed it back and forth across the top of his head.

The car was silent for a long while, only the sound of the tires on the road. Barney started to snore. He snorted once, and mumbled something, and then his breathing became regular.

"Sorry for your loss," Joe Big said.

"I can smell your rifles," Paul said.

"Yeah."

"Who were they?"

"We think they were Feds."

"Feds?"

"They weren't experienced enough to be mercs. And one of them was a woman."

Paul thought about it for a while.

"Better get some sleep," he said.

"Have you got a laptop with you?"

"It's in the trunk."

"We need to download a camera to the Net . . ." Joe Big said, his voice fading.

"I can do it from the car."

"Best if it doesn't come from you."

"There's a truck stop in Helena that has WiFi."

"Sounds good," Joe Big mumbled, and fell asleep.

35
Dancing with Gorillas

"Who else?" Joe Big asked. He'd typed a couple thousand words explaining the bogus nerve gas cylinders, and was making a list of people and organizations to send the pictures and his written explanation to. The idea was to take the two of them and Paul out of the loop. Make them yesterday's news, and therefore no longer a problem, by feeding the story to the right people. Problem was, they didn't know who the right people might be. So they were shotgunning the text and the pictures to people and places who might be inclined to do something about it, but who at the same time would not feel tempted to feed it to the media or to the Net.

"Who've you got so far?"

"The Sheriff, Quinn, that big ranch—I found their web site—the company that Harold works for, both Senators, the Governor, the Blackfeet Tribal Offices, the company your uncle works for, your computer, my computer, the International Peace Operations Association . . ."

"Everyone at once?"

"No. One message per."

"How about our old units?"

"Good idea." He typed in the address for 1st Force Recon, and handed the computer to Barney to type in the address of his old Special Forces unit.

"That ought to do it," Joe Big said, handing the computer to Paul. "We're either going to get killed or we're not."

Paul closed the computer. "As long as you don't accidentally run into anyone in the next day or so, you guys should be okay." He opened the door, and climbed out of the car. "Back in a minute."

They watched him enter the truck stop cafeteria. "I hope we didn't overdo it," Joe Big said.

"Only way they are going to know for sure it was us is if Quinn or Paul or your uncle tell them." Barney yawned.

"What're you saying?"

"I'm saying maybe we need to have a heart to heart with Quinn."

"You want to *talk* to Quinn? Man, at the very least, she knew this was a setup. You *know* she had a hand in creating it."

Barney twisted so that he could see Joe Big wedged against the door and the window, legs stretched out on the seat.

"Can you handle that?" Barney asked.

"Handle what? That you want to *talk* to her?"

"That's not what I *want* to do. It's what I think we *should* do."

"Fuck a bunch of should do, man. They played us—her and Gladys. If those guys were Feds, then Quinn had a hand in putting them there. She scrounged them from somewhere. I'll bet you anything if we'd tried to call out on the Sat Phone it would've been dead. For sure, if we'd tried to get back to the truck, *we* would be dead. Those people are on her and Gladys, not us."

"No argument, from me, bro." Barney squirmed around in the seat so that he could sit half facing the front, half facing Joe Big. "As long as they silenced us—either by capturing or killing us—their little scheme was still in play. By sending those emails we have just permanently un-silenced ourselves."

"What were they planning to do? Call in the Marines?"

"Probably." Barney said. "No joke. They were trying to create a National Security issue. With all the firepower at that ranch, a full-blown assault would be about the only way to shut it down in a hurry. A small team wouldn't get within six klicks of the main buildings."

"They're going to be pissed when they get our email."

"Who?"

"All of them."

"No. I don't think so. Not these people. They'll concede the game, and then set up the pieces for the next one. The way things stand right now, once the emails hit, no one wins, no one loses. Both sides lost pawns. No biggee. Pawns can easily be replaced. They're in it for the long haul. Quinn and Mrs. W will fade away, and reappear somewhere else. My guess is that both sides have won a lot more than they've lost. Otherwise, they wouldn't be willing to play for these kinds of stakes."

"It wasn't a game to Tom Lonewolf."

"Man, you know how it is. It's always a fucking game until it goes down, and then it's never a game. Five dead Feds, and two dead Mercs. The body count is climbing—like it always does. So far we've been lucky. But if this shit keeps up, sooner or later the laws of probability are going to catch up with us."

"Tom Lonewolf and Quinn's CI and Brianna are collateral damage, is that it?"

"Not to you and not to me and not to Paul, they're not. And I've got a feeling some of the mercs and Feds are not too happy, either. From their point of view, we killed friends, destroyed families."

Joe Big was silent.

"Look. Take a step back," Barney said. "We're not anyone's white knights. It was their call, not ours. What's done is done. We didn't start it. We're still here only because we are adept at turning defense into offense. Bottom line is that neither of the two gorillas we've been dancing with has lost or gained more than the other. It's time for us to exit, stage right."

"We've seriously pissed off a lot of people in the last few days, Barn. And we don't even know who they are, except to say that some of them are guys exactly like us."

"Well, that's my point, dude. If we behave in a professional manner, so will they. We haven't done anything that most of them wouldn't have done if they were in our shoes. A couple of weeks, and most of them will chalk it up to business. War all the time, like you said."

"You think this is a war?"

"What else would you call it?"

"We know too much."

"We don't know any more than what everyone knows who gets that email."

"Here comes Paul," Joe Big said.

"Think on it some more," Barney said. "We won't be home for a couple of hours. Whatever you think you have to do, I've got your six, you know that. You might want to give a little thought to Mei and Sam, though."

Joe Big's laugh was a humorless bark.

Barney watched Paul coming across the parking lot.

"You never know," he said.

36
A Good Idea

I am bemused, befuddled, and forever gratified by the fact that we are still alive," Barney said. They were sitting in Joe Big's beat-to-shit Chevy pickup, the engine a dull, uneven rumble, heater on full blast, listening to The Reverend Peyton's Big Damn Band on Joe Big's sound system—a sound system that was worth far more than the whole damn truck, Barney thought—eating croissants and sipping thick dark Rwanda coffee.

Sooty-looking clouds streaked a sullen gray sky. Bone-cold skiffs of yesterday's snow skittered across gray pavement.

"At least if someone decides to sic some of those mercs on us, we'll never know what hit us," Joe Big said.

"That's a good thing?"

Joe Big shrugged. He dusted croissant flakes off his lap. "One minute we're here, the next we're not."

"I can't believe how fast the weather changed."

"Winter is here."

They were watching Quinn going in and out of a house about a block and a half down the street. She was loading boxes into a medium-size U-Haul truck. Two big guys dressed in jeans and sweaters, the handguns on their hips evident even from that distance, were moving her furniture out to the truck.

"Not too neighborly, her leaving without saying goodbye," Barney said.

"She is who she is," Joe Big said.

Barney looked at him. "That's pretty fucking magnanimous coming from you."

Joe Big gestured toward Quinn standing on the lawn talking to the two big men. "She a weapon, man. A beautiful blade that cuts through people and emotions like a sharp knife cuts through paper. I don't know what happened to her growing up in Boston. Part of me feels sorry for her. But don't get me wrong. It doesn't matter how she got to where she is. It doesn't matter *why* she is. It only matters *what* she is."

Barney turned the music up. The Big Damn Band playing Clap Your Hands. They were silent, listening to the music and watching Quinn, both of them unconsciously tapping their feet to the music. "I love this song," Barney said. "How'd you find it, anyway?"

"That old Irish reprobate we met—Colonel Sanders, or whatever his name is—"

"Colonel Kelsey?"

"He insisted I download the vid—which I did the next time our little Federette over there called a meeting. Mouse loves it."

"Ought to be our theme song."

Joe Big laughed. "You should see the vid."

"Sure don't fit her," Barney said. "That's for sure."

"She's the perfect Fed," Joe Big said. "Task her to do something, and the task becomes everything. Morality, ethics, all that good stuff only applies if it helps her to complete the task at hand. And people like us . . . well, she might like us on a personal level, but when push comes to shove, we are merely a means to an end."

"You don't think it bothers her about Brianna?"

Joe Big snorted. "Yeah. It bothers her. But once she saw how it was—with those guys pissed off and wanting a little payback—she went with it, built a whole new scheme that shuffled together everyone involved in a whole new way. She defines the word devious, man. Ask me if I think she gives a shit about the people who have died because of her machinations."

"Machinations? Are those sort of like alien bots?"

"Yeah. Exactly like."

The two big men had climbed into a black Suburban, and were backing out of the driveway. The Suburban headed down the street away from where Joe Big and Barney were parked.

"What do you say we make this simple?" Joe Big said. "Park in the driveway and go in and get her. Take her out somewhere and have a little heart to heart."

"Just like that?"

"Why not? We have to get her attention. Otherwise, there's no telling what she might hatch."

"There isn't going to be a next time," Barney said. "Not for us. I thought we agreed on that? We're done with law enforcement. Maybe go to China and see what your uncle has in mind."

Joe Big smiled. "We *are* done with law enforcement. But we are not done with her. Not yet. With her there *will* be a next time, unless we convince her otherwise."

Barney's eyes narrowed. "You kill her and someone *will* plant our asses."

Joe Big looked at him. "She's responsible for Tom Lonewolf's death."

"And the four guys and one woman who killed him. I know that. But responsible and culpable are not the same thing. She wasn't there, Big. You start killing everyone involved, and sooner or later, probably sooner, someone up the food chain is going to squash us like we are cockroaches on a kitchen floor."

"And you complain about my metaphors."

"You know what I mean."

Joe Big was silent for a moment, looking at her house and the U-Haul truck parked in front.

"Well, I can't promise anything," he said. "I'll do my best."

"Like I said, think about Mei and Sam."

"Stop saying that. There isn't anything there. You know me. I'll end up bailing. I always do. I don't want their eyes on me for the rest of my life."

"Too late for that."

Joe Big looked at him.

Barney shrugged. "Deal with it."

Joe Big put the truck in gear.

"I'm just saying," Barney said. "Don't burn bridges that don't need burning—not with Mei and Sam, and especially not by killing Quinn."

Joe Big eased the truck out into the street. "Sometimes, you're worse than my grandmother was, you know that?"

"Ooh-rah," Barney said.

THE DOOR WAS unlocked. Moving boxes were piled in the entrance way. Two rolled-up area rugs were on top the boxes. The rugs were about seven feet long.

Quinn came through a Mexican-style arch to their left that led to the living room and kitchen, a small box in her hands. Barney hit her in the throat hard enough to make her drop the box and with both hands grab her throat. Her eyes were very large and green.

He grabbed the front of her sweatshirt and threw her face down to the hardwood floor.

Joe Big yanked her arms behind her back and handcuffed her wrists. She coughed.

Barney handed him a long wire tie.

Joe Big wrapped the wire tie three times around her ankles and zipped the tie closed, the end sticking out to the side.

Barney grabbed a handful of her hair, and lightly bounced her forehead several times off the floor. He leaned down, and said in a calm voice in her ear. "If you fight, we are going to stuff something in your mouth. Do you understand?"

She nodded, tears running down her cheeks from the hit to her throat.

Joe Big went back to the entrance way, and returned with one of the rugs. "How about this?"

"Good idea," Barney said.

37
Snow Snakes

Black cold night, snow snakes blowing across the pavement, as the old truck slowly negotiated the same turns they'd taken when they'd driven up the Blackfoot to meet Patrick and Tanya and Harold.

Joe Big turned the truck off the highway, and they bumped and slid over the uneven ground, through small drifts of snow, to the edge of the river, the light from the headlights disappearing into snow-swept nothingness.

They sat for a moment, listening to Groove Armada finish Hands of Time.

Joe Big put the gearshift in neutral, and stepped on the emergency brake pedal. "Too bad we can't," he said.

"Can't what?"

"Turn back the hands of time."

"If you did, you'd lose your memories. And then you'd do everything all over again."

The song ended and Joe Big turned off the headlights and then the engine.

"You want to use the NVDs?"

"Not necessary." Barney shoved open his door and stepped out into the wind and cold and snow.

"I hate cold," Joe Big muttered, as he climbed out the other side.

Barney lowered the tailgate, and climbed up into the truck bed. The carpet was a fat roll dusted with snow. "You are such a candy-ass, sometimes," he said. "Indians are supposed to be impervious to weather. But, nooo. Not you. A little cold and you start *whining.*" With both hands he grasped the end of the rug and pulled hard, the rug unrolling in place, Quinn flipped on her back on the far edge of the truck bed.

Joe Big cut the white tie binding her feet. He put his knife in his pocket, and grabbed her ankles and pulled her sliding across the metal floor. He let go of her legs, and her knees bent over the end of the tailgate, feet and lower legs dangling.

Barney grasped her shoulders from behind and pushed her upright. The night was so dark Joe Big could barely make out her sitting on the edge of the tailgate.

Barney jumped down, and one to either side, they escorted her stumbling over to the edge of the river. The hard slap and wash of water beneath the embankment only served to emphasize how cold it was. She was wearing jeans and a sweatshirt, lightweight hiking boots.

Barney pushed her to her knees.

Joe Big pressed his folded knife against the back of her head; to her it would feel like his pistol.

"Fuck you," she said, her voice husky from the blow to her throat. "You're too smart to kill me. You know what will happen if you do."

"We don't care," Barney said.

"You care," she said. "Joe Big might not, but you do."

"In case you haven't noticed," Barney said. "We come as a pair."

"So shoot me, then," she said. "At least it'll get me out of the cold."

Joe Big grabbed her hair with his left hand to hold her head still, and flicked open his knife and held it in front of her eyes, and then traced a line down the top of her nose from between her eyes to the tip of her nose.

"You bastard."

He stood and wiped his hand down the top of her nose, and then smeared the blood on his hand across her mouth.

She jerked her head from side to side, and spit into the black night.

He leaned close to her ear. "Barney doesn't want me to kill you." He moved his head quickly back as she tried to head-butt him, and punched her in the side of the head, hard enough to rock her off balance. "I want to throw you in the river," he said, his mouth only a few inches from her ear. "I want to spend the rest of the winter imagining you down at the bottom of a cold dark hole. Swaying in the current like some exotic Irish seaweed. Waiting for it to get warm enough for your body to produce enough gas to float you to the top. In the spring, a fly fisherman will find your bleached, bloated body bobbing in the weeds. And Tom Lonewolf will be waiting to escort you to hell."

"I'll leave you two alone for a moment," Barney said. "Don't forget to take the cuffs off," he said to Joe Big.

They heard Barney walk back to the truck. Heard the door open and close, leaf springs creak.

"You played us like we are nothing but characters in a video game," Joe Big said.

"And I'd do it again. So fuck you."

"The end justifies the means."

"That's right," she said. "In this case, that is exactly right. So kill me and get it over with if that's what you are going to do. I'll be the one waiting for *you*."

Joe Big pulled her pony tail straight back from her head, and sliced it off close to her scalp. He dangled it in front of her face. "Hair today, gone tomorrow," he said, and tossed it into the river.

He grasped another handful of her hair, and sliced it off close to the scalp, and threw the handful of hair toward the water, the wind dispersing it before it hit the water. She was silent, as he worked his way around her head, being sure to leave ragged tufts here and there. He could feel her anger, feel the core of her malevolence, and it made him want to do more—made his hand tingle with the desire to pull his knife across the big artery at the side of her throat. But he knew that no matter what he did here tonight, it would not be enough. Tom Lonewolf's body would forever be in the bed of a pickup. They would have to deal with her again, that was a given. Only next time, the where and when and how would be of her choosing. He knew this. But he didn't give a shit. For now, he refused to let himself be anywhere but where he was at that moment.

"This is what the French did to women who collaborated with Nazis in World War Two," he said. "So everyone would know what the women had done, and the women would be ostracized."

"Why are you being so stupid?" she asked, blood dripping off the tip of her nose, thin lines of it on both sides of her nose and mouth. "I came to warn you again not to go down there. But you wouldn't even talk to me."

He cut off the final piece and threw it toward the river. His hands were getting cold. His ears and cheeks felt raw. "Lonewolf died because of your schemes—you and Mrs. W and whoever else helped to hatch them. In a sane world, we'd kill you all. This is to get the attention of that dark thing coiled in your heart. If you come at us again, you die. If I don't get you, Barney will. If he doesn't get you, my uncle will. Or my father. Or one of their friends. Someone."

She was silent.

"We know you now," he said. "*Our* hate, especially *my* hate, is more than *your* hate. If you come after us for any reason, I will know it. I will feel it."

He put the knife back in his pocket, and squatted down behind her, and unlocked the handcuffs and pulled them off, and stood and put them in his back pocket.

"I think it is a mistake to let you live," he said. "I don't think *Gladys* would miss you all that much. She would write you off as battle damage, the same as you figured you'd write us off if things went south." He pushed her back down. "No. Don't get up until we leave."

He stared down at her for a moment. He knew he should kill her. His ancestors, women as well as men, would not have hesitated.

He pulled his pistol from the holster, and thumbed off the safety.

He stepped behind her, and fired five rounds to the side of her head as fast as he could pull the trigger, the stutter of explosions sounding almost as if they were one long, drawn out explosion, flame lancing from the barrel into the darkness.

She screamed, and fell over on her side, hand to her ear.

He set the safety and holstered the pistol, and turned and walked to the driver's side door and climbed in.

He started the truck, and turned on the headlights, and backed away from her on all fours. She stared at the snow swirling over black water.

He put the truck in gear, and they motored, bumping and rattling, back to the highway. He turned onto the highway, and headed back to town.

"She's a lot like us," he said.

"No she's not." Barney put in a CD. Audioslave: Shadow on the Sun. "Do not be believing that shit. You did the right thing. We might have snakes in our brains, but she's not like us. We couldn't even begin to play the games people like her play, let alone dream them up."

"She'll be back. It might take her a while, but one of these days she'll be back."

"Maybe. But I doubt it. She'll get involved in some other scheme, and then she'll get involved in another, and then another, and so on and on, until there is all kinds of unfinished business stacked up. We'll be way at the bottom of the pile by then."

"No such thing as the bottom of the pile with her," Joe Big said. "With her it will be like yesterday."

"Well, we couldn't kill her," Barney said.

"She got a lot of good men and one woman killed."

"She's walking point, that's all she's doing, Big. She's not the one who dreamed up all that shit about VX and dead mules and a building full of nerve gas and a new kind of drone carrying a new kind of puck to deliver it. Only some sociopath with no clue to what happens in the real world could have dreamed up all that. Think-tank wonks, like those idiots we debriefed that time in Kabul."

"It doesn't matter who dreamed up the scheme."

"Oh, did she hurt your feelings? Poor puppy. It's not like we haven't been used before—by people who are a lot more creative about it than she will ever be."

"Well, for her it's personal now," Joe Big said. "We'll have to kill her next time."

"If there is a next time, maybe we will."

"There will be. One of these days when we least expect it."

"We can go back."

Joe Big laughed. "You asshole."

He guided the truck onto the curving on-ramp, and then onto the Interstate. Ahead they could see the glow of the city trapped beneath clouds.

"Might be a good idea to go elk hunting for a few weeks," Barney said. "Get out of Dodge for awhile."

"Okay."

"Now?"

Joe Big shrugged. "Why not?"

They were silent, both of them thinking about hunting elk.

"What're you going to do?" Barney asked.

"What do you mean?"

"This winter, what are you going to do?"

"I don't know. Fix the house a little, maybe. Spend some time with my parents. Maybe help Paul out with some of the kids he's working with—boxing, running, that sort of thing. Read books. Watch movies. Maybe take a class or two . . . We can drive down to Hollywood, visit Roy, if you want." He looked over at Barney, and grinned. "It feels good."

"What does?"

"Being free."

Barney shook his head. "We'll never be free."

"Why not?"

"Too much baggage, that's why."

Joe Big laughed. "Why we have to have baggage, man? Fuck it! We paid our dues. We don't want to be there anymore, *we won't be there anymore.* Keep the memories we want to keep, shitcan the rest."

Barney looked at him. "And then what? Ignore everything that goes on around us, pretend it's not happening?"

"Why not?"

"You're such a bullshitter, Big. You stop to help turtles cross the road. You worry that your cat gets fed."

"At least I don't grow roses."

"Hey."

"Maybe we can be private defectives, or something," Joe Big said.

The truck went around a long curve, out of Hellgate Canyon. To their left the University and the city unfolded toward distant mountains, the Interstate lit with street lamps.

"How you fixed for money?" Barney asked.

Joe Big shrugged. "I've got my disability, and most of my Sheriff's pay. For the past year or so, I've been living off the per diem the Feds gave us."

"Yeah. Me, too. What say we think about it in the spring?"

"Think about what in the spring?"

"Whatever we're going to do?"

Joe Big smiled. "White guys, man. They always got to have a plan."

"I've got a plan," Barney said.

"What's your plan?"

"My plan is to go get some beer. Stop by your place and get Mouse. And then head out to your uncle's and go hunting. We can call the Undersheriff in the morning, and resign over the phone."

"Just like that?"

"Just like that."

"Whoa. Did you see that?" Joe Big asked.

"See what?"

"Three black SUVs went by fast, headed back the way we just came."

"You hacked her hair off."

"I did."

"Cut her nose."

"Did that, too."

"Bad blood."

"*Real* bad blood."

"She put an arrow through someone," Barney said.

"A fact she does not deny."

"Right now she's as mean as a snake shedding skin."

"Meaner. *Way* meaner."

Barney sat upright. "New plan," he said. "Hunting gear and Miss Mouse first, beer on the way out of town."

"Good plan."

38
The Wolf Last Seen

Mid-afternoon on the first hot day of spring, the field in front of Joe Big's place green with new grasses and weeds. Joe Big and Barney sat on the top step, a cooler full of beer and ice on the bottom step, a .243 varmint rifle with a Burris three-to-nine on the porch between them. They were waiting for gophers to show themselves in the field. The idea was that they would drink a beer for each gopher killed. But in the thirty minutes or so since they'd been there no gopher had shown itself. They were getting thirsty.

Barney's new Golden Retriever Lab cross, not much more than a pup, was trying to get Miss Mouse to play, trapping her agitated tail with its paws, and then gnawing on it. It cocked its head to the side, looked at her quizzically, and then trapped her tail again. Through it all, Miss Mouse lay on her side, a perfect model—if not for her agitated tail and black, hooded eyes—of total disdain.

The dog sprang back, face to the ground between its paws, and barked at her.

"Watch this," Joe Big said.

Mouse rolled over, and yawned, exposing her fangs, and sat up on her haunches.

The dog trotted over to her, and Miss Mouse casually hit it in the muzzle and mouth and the side of its face more times than Joe Big or Barney could count, her paws a blur.

The dog squeaked and fell over on its side, and got up and ran to the other end of the porch. It stood, legs spread, head cocked to the side. It whined at Barney.

Mouse lay back down on her side, and stretched her head toward Joe Big and Barney, as if to say the next time that hairball annoys me, what happens is on you.

"What's his name again?" Joe Big asked.

"Totoro."

"What's a Totoro?"

"It's a Japanese cartoon character. A forest spirit. Mickey named him, not me."

"She gave him to you? Why would she do that?"

"He's my consolation prize, while she runs off to snowboard in South America with some hunky snowboarder she met this winter filming totally whack videos of kamikaze runs down impossible slopes."

"You can live with that?"

"Actually, I can. It'll be a miracle if she doesn't kill herself on one of those slopes before it's all over. The way she hooked up with this new guy is they were consoling each other over the death of one of their friends who was killed in a kayaking accident somewhere in South America. There's always one of them dying or breaking bones or turning into a paraplegic."

"The Feds still got surveillance on you?"

"Don't think so. That was a great idea you had to let them put tracking sticks on our vehicles, and bug our phones if they want."

They'd spent two weeks at Ben's place, camped out in the big trees, hunting elk, and using the old sweat lodge. Joe Big had guided Barney onto the track of a really big elk. Maybe an all-time-record elk, he'd told Barney. And Barney had spent three days and two nights tracking the giant elk, doing a low crawl for nearly three hundred meters up a tight, bush-infested draw, through snow and slush and running water under the snow and slush, to find, finally, that for three days he'd been tracking a big old bull moose who was clearly fed up with being followed over hill and dale. The hackles had risen on the moose, and he'd started for Barney. Barney had run for the nearest big tree. He'd spent the better part of a day up in the tree, while the Moose paced below, occasionally wandering off as if it were leaving for good, but hiding out in the bushes uphill from the tree, waiting for Barney to come down.

When Joe Big had come looking, he'd found Barney still up in the tree. Joe Big had laughed so hard, he'd scared the moose off.

"Hey, Bwana. Ain't no elk up there."

"You want an elk," he'd later explained to Barney. "You go get your own elk. I'm nobody's Injun tracker, not even yours."

So Barney had stomped off up the old logging road that went up the mountain, and as luck would have it, a young six-point bull had come sliding down the embankment and stopped broadside in the middle of the road, and looked at Barney as if to say, what the fuck are you doing here, you don't belong here, and Barney had shot it through the heart.

"That's how you do it," he told Joe Big. "Drive the truck right to it."

"The mountain likes you," Joe Big explained. "It watched you play ring around the mountain with that moose and decided you had earned an elk. So it sent this one your way."

Barney squinted at Joe Big. "Do you really believe that shit?"

Joe Big grinned. "You never know."

The Sheriff had been professionally polite, when they handed him their ID and badges. He'd told them they'd done a good job, been some of his best men, he was sorry to lose them. But he hadn't said anything about having their jobs back if they ever decided they wanted to return. The women in the office had been tearful, and hugged them both, but the other deputies had known something was up, and even though they smiled and joked and wished them the best, the more astute among them and the few who had worked with Feds had smiled knowingly.

All in all, it had been surprisingly painless.

Men and women wearing sunglasses on cloudy days, and driving SUVs and sedans with too many antennas, had followed them wherever they went, sometimes parking in front of Barney's house, or in the dirt road that served as a driveway to Joe Big's place. They weren't trying to hide. In fact, sometimes they took their own sweet time moving out of the way. Joe Big and Barney assumed that it was because no one had yet decided what to do with them. People had died, after all. And some of the dead had no doubt been friends of their minders. A senior agent had been found with her hair hacked off, a cut the length of her nose, blood frozen on her face, walking along a snow-swept highway.

Neither one of them blamed the Feds for not being happy. Which of course was not the same as saying they gave a shit about the Feds being unhappy.

One morning, Joe Big had gotten up, and while drinking his morning coffee, had looked out at the black SUV parked at the end of the drive, and he'd gone outside and hopped on his mountain bicycle and pedaled through the snow, down to the truck, and had a conversation with the two Feds in it—an older man, hair streaked with gray, and a young woman all hyper and agitated that he had the temerity to talk to them.

He'd offered to let them put tracking sticks on his vehicle and Barney's vehicle, and GPS locaters in their cell phones, bug the house if they wanted to. A few days later, the same gray-haired guy had shown up alone, and said they were going to accept his offer, would he please sign some documents.

The thing about the documents had been said with a smile, and Joe Big had merely tapped his knuckles twice on the papers—an I-pass gesture—and without further ado the agent had put the documents back in his briefcase, and left.

"I can't believe they already had us bugged," Barney had said. "You gave them a chance to pull the people following us around, is all."

"Somebody's budget is happy," Joe Big said.

"We're already yesterday's news."

"Yep."

"In that case, I think I might give a certain snowboard slut-slash-bartender a call, see if she wants to teach me how to snowboard."

"She's dangerous on a snowboard, man. Don't even try to keep up with her."

"How about you?" Barney had asked.

"How about me what?"

"You know."

Joe Big had looked across the valley, at blue mountains and leaden sky, the trees and bushes skeletal in the waning afternoon light, and hadn't been able to find the words.

The rest of the winter, Barney had skied and snowboarded, careful to not say anything about Mickey, unless Joe Big asked, and nothing about Mei or Sam or eating cinnamon rolls and chili at the deli after a hard day on the slopes.

Joe Big had puttered around the house, cleaning and fixing and painting whenever the weather allowed him to open the windows for most of the day. He'd enrolled in a poetry class at the university, and discovered that as a Tribal member he could attend university free. What a deal. But he'd dropped out about half way through the semester, bored with the students—most of whom were female and full of female angst—and bemused by the instructor who, near as he could tell, couldn't write poetry to save her ass. What he really wanted was someone to teach him how to write a decent sentence; he'd take it from there.

He spent a few days with his parents, explaining what had happened with Tom Lonewolf. His mother had cried, and his father had paced back and forth across the kitchen floor behind his mother. Later, when his mother had gone into Heart Butte for groceries and beer, he'd told his father about the horses and the four men and one woman he and Barney had killed. His father had nodded.

"It isn't over," he said.

"I think it is."

"I don't mean that," his father said. "I mean you and your partner, you are caught in a cycle, a way of life—the same cycle that your uncle is caught in. It's something the old people understood well. You can't break it."

Joe Big frowned. His father never spoke to him about such things.

"The wheel will come around again," his father said. "As long as you live, the wheel will continue to come around."

"My fate, hey?"

His father stared at him for a moment, his eyes sad. "You can joke about it now. It's good you do that. But do not forget that the greatest trickster is yourself."

"Don't lie to myself, you mean? Don't believe my own propaganda?"

"It's more than that."

Joe Big nodded, remembering Barney run up to the car that had gone off the road, onto the hillside, and pour automatic fire into the windows at the figures slumped over the steering wheel and dash; the lance of bright light stuttering from the trees next to the stream where Tom Lonewolf's truck was parked; the grunt and scream of the buckskin.

"I am happy that you have found a partner," his father said. "I mean a partner in the old sense of the word, before reservation life worked its way with The People."

Joe Big frowned.

"When you were a teenager, I thought maybe Roy White Owl was to be your partner. But his heart, though it is a good heart, is not a warrior's heart. You are lucky to have found Barney, and he to have found you."

"Jeez. You make it sound like we ought to get married or something."

His father laughed. "You can steal horses and kill people with him. Talk about anything. The People don't have partners like that any more."

"Who's your partner?"

"I don't have one. I never had one."

"How about Mom?"

"That's a different kind of partner." He squinted at Joe.

Joe Big averted his gaze, looking at the photos and scraps of paper and notices and reminders fastened by all sorts of different magnets to the refrigerator door.

"All my luck is wrapped up in your mother and you," his father said.

Joe Big nodded.

"I hope you will have that kind of luck," his father said.

"Mom put you up to that."

His father smiled. "She wants grandkids, what can I say?"

"Is that why she's got pictures of all her friends' grandkids on the refrigerator door?"

His father squinted at him again. "You got someone in there, don't you?"

Joe Big felt his ears redden.

His father grinned. "Big tough Marine. Hero man."

"You know better than that."

"Yes, I do."

They were silent, both of them staring down at the kitchen table.

"You going to help Paul with the boxing team?" his father asked.

"Yeah. He might send a couple of his kids over to stay with me next fall. Maybe a couple of the cross-country team, too."

"Plenty of room, if you want to move over here for awhile."

"Mom put you up to that, too. Don't say she didn't."

His father nodded. "I know you don't like the Rez much. I don't blame you."

"How about you?"

"I grew up here. I don't much like it, either, but it's in my bones."

"Well, I got plenty of room, you want to live like a white man for awhile."

His father laughed. "We might take you up on that."

"We'll go kill some of Ben's elk. That'll frost his ass."

"You don't want to be frosting that man's ass about anything," his father said. "Which reminds me: he wants his truck back."

Joe Big winced.

He'd snowshoed in to where they'd left the truck, and found it burned to the frame, all the other guns and equipment gone.

Well, it was about what they'd expected. The good news was that it wasn't his uncle's old antique International. The bad news was that he and Barney would have to replace the Chevy with something acceptable to his uncle.

No one had come around to collect the M14 and the M4. Which was fine with them. You never knew when such weapons might come in handy. But he didn't think it likely that the Government would pay a claim for a burned-to-the-frame pickup.

He sighed. No way around it. They'd have to buy Ben a new pickup.

"WHAT'RE YOU SIGHING about?" Barney asked.

"I'm thinking about how much money that pickup is going to cost us."

"No problem, dude. I sold the house."

Joe Big looked at him in surprise. "In this market?"

"The ex offered me a price I couldn't refuse."

"Man, talk about killing two birds with one stone."

"Truer words you have never spoken, *mon frere*." Barney extended his arm, and they bumped fists.

"You want to move out here?"

"I thought I might fix up a room and bathroom out there in the barn, if you think your uncle would go for it."

"Have at it, man. He won't care. It'll only add value to the property. What *are* the gophers doing today?"

"They're playing cards, waiting for us to go away."

They were silent, both of them contemplating the cooler full of beer.

"I got to say it," Barney said. "I can't keep my mouth shut any more."

"Got to say what?"

"Why haven't you been to see them, man? Sam asks about you all the time. He's a good kid. And she's a good person. You could be friends. I know you could. She's no more interested in a heavy relationship than you are."

Joe Big shook his head. "Can't."

"Why not?"

Totoro the dog ran past the front of the house, and continued around the side, panting.

"What's he doing?" Joe Big asked.

"Oh, he gets full of energy and runs around the house, until he can't run any more."

They waited, and the dog came around the corner of the house to their right, running hard past them, on a mission, tongue hanging out the side of his mouth, around the other side.

Joe Big looked at his watch. "Time him the next time around."

"Somebody just turned into the drive."

Joe Big squinted toward the gate at the end of the drive. "Silver BMW. One of the expensive ones." He lifted the binoculars hanging at his chest. "One man."

"An executive," Barney said. "What do you want to bet he offers us a job before he threatens us? Whatever you do, don't shoot him. I'm pretty sure it's not Custer."

Joe Big frowned.

Mouse came up the steps and rubbed against his side. "Hey," he said. "Where you been?"

Miss Mouse purred, and went over and rubbed against Barney. "Out. Out. Vile beast."

"She's trying to say she's sorry for slapping the shit out of your little forest spirit. Where is he, anyway?"

"Now he's out in the field chasing that family of pheasants around."

Mouse tried to climb in Barney's lap, something she never did, but both Joe Big and Barney stood as the silver BMW rattled across the cattleguard, and stopped in front of the steps. She walked to the side of the porch, and sat on her haunches, watching.

The man inside the BMW leaned across to the passenger seat and picked up a bulky-looking leather file holder of some kind. He opened the door, and stepped out.

Late 50s, early 60s, steel-gray hair in a military haircut. Expensive-looking gray suit, but the way he wore it made it a uniform. Pale yellow tie, light blue shirt that matched his washed-out blue eyes. Clean shaven. Lean as a greyhound. A pin that looked like a Navy Cross pin on his lapel.

A wolf last seen in Afghanistan, Barney thought.

"Gentlemen," he said.

Unconsciously they both came to a semblance of attention. "Sir," they both said.

He chuckled. "I take it you remember me. At ease, please."

The last time they'd seen him had been in a hovel in a compound in northern Afghanistan, caked with moon dust, only the area around his eyes where he'd worn goggles free of grime. He'd been a Marine Corps Full Bird then. A leftover from Vietnam and all the wars since. There had been no bullshit in him. No wasted words, when describing the mission. Nickname and call sign, Wolf. Polite and soft spoken and with a sense of humor that had made the mission he'd given them seem a lot easier than they knew it was going to be: the mission in which Joe Big had been hit hard enough to end his career.

The Wolf laid the leather case on the hood of the car, and loosened his tie and unbuttoned the top button on his linen shirt. Smiling with his mouth, but not with his eyes, he took off his coat, and walked to the passenger door and opened it and draped the coat neatly over the seat. He shut the door, and rolled up his sleeves to his forearms. He picked up the case again.

"What've you got in that cooler?" he asked.

"Ah, beer, sir," Barney said. "I can make some coffee if you are so inclined."

"A beer sounds good. It's been a long day." He walked up the steps.

"Let me get you a chair," Barney said. He turned and went inside the house, while the Wolf and Joe Big stared without emotion at each other, emerging a moment later with a wooden straight-back dining room chair.

The Wolf walked up the steps, and settled himself in the chair. He crossed one leg over the other, leather case on his lap. "This is nice out here," he said. "I've got to get myself a place like this." He smiled at Joe Big. "Can't take the little woman out of the city, but I think she'd like the peace and quiet, now and then."

Joe Big opened the cooler, and pulled out an ice-cold, dripping-wet bottle of Summer Honey Ale. He wiped the bottle on his sweatshirt, and popped the top off on an old Coca Cola bottle opener nailed to the porch post, the bottle cap falling into an old wicker fishing basket attached to the post just below the opener. He walked up the steps and handed it to him.

The Wolf raised the bottle in a toast, "Gentlemen," and took a long drink. "Ah, that's good. Real good."

He took another drink, his eyes cold and without humor, assessing both of them over the bottle.

He set the bottle down on the porch next to his chair, and unzipped the case.

"Stand over there next to Sergeant Big Snake Person, will you please Lieutenant."

Barney and Joe Big looked at each other. "Shit," Barney said.

"I beg your pardon?"

Barney and Joe Big were silent.

He leaned forward and handed them each a stapled-together set of papers. "These say that you are officially back on active duty." He handed them another stapled-together set of papers. "And these are a reminder that you are subject to secrecy laws appropriate to your security clearances."

"We have wounds that preclude us from active service," Barney said.

The Wolf reached down and picked up the bottle of beer, and drained it, and set the bottle back down on the porch.

"I hold the rank of Major General, now, Lieutenant. You may address me as Sir, or as General."

"Yes, sir."

He held up the corners of two, very thick folders in the leather case. "According to your medical records, you have both made exceptional, albeit unanticipated recoveries from your wounds. In fact, I have some footage of Staff Sergeant Big Snake Person running twelve or thirteen miles up a road to a ski area located north of here. And an evening of walking, and then riding horses bareback cross country, and then fighting your way out of an ambush, would seem to indicate that you are both less than decrepit. Would I be correct in this assumption?"

They were both silent.

"I see you are not happy with the way this reunion is going." His cold eyes weighed them.

"I work for the Department of Defense, these days," he said. "As you might imagine, the military, especially the Marine Corps and Army Special Forces, is not happy with the mercenary industry. Neither are the President and his Cabinet.

"The President is extremely loathe to use military units within the borders of this country, no matter how small and expert and necessary those units may be." He paused. "Nevertheless, he has made some exceptions. Do you understand?"

"No," Joe Big said.

The General stared at him.

Joe Big returned his stare.

"Well, you haven't changed, have you, sergeant?"

"I'm smarter now." He paused. "Sir."

"Sir, you don't want us," Barney said.

"I don't?"

"No, sir. We are most definitely damaged goods. We would be a drag on unit morale."

The General smiled, the edges of his eyes crinkling in amusement. "And do you also feel that way, Sergeant?"

Joe Big was silent.

The General bent down and from the leather case took more stapled-together pages.

He handed copies to each of them. "It just so happens that I agree with you, Lieutenant. The previous documents that I handed you set the date of your reinstatement to active duty at a day approximately one year ago—the day you were seconded to the Anti-Terrorist Task Force. Included are documents certifying that on that date you were both promoted a rank—to Gunnery Sergeant in the case of Joseph Big Snake Person, Captain, in the case of James Longstreet Lambier. Those promotions were permanent." He paused. "Now, if you will look at the second set of papers, you will see that as of tomorrow at 1200 hours your active duty status has once again been changed to Inactive Reserve status. The length of your Inactive Reserve status, however, has been extended six years. You can be called to Active Duty any time during the next six years."

Joe Big and Barney both frowned.

The general chuckled. "You are wondering why. Well, because it means that everything you've done for the past year has been done under orders from your military command—to wit, under orders issued by my command."

"We were following the General's orders," Barney said.

"That's right, Captain. You were following my orders. And those orders were part of a Presidential Finding issued to my command."

"Then we don't have to worry about any . . . people . . . coming after us," Joe Big said.

"That's right, Gunny. You don't. The crash in central Montana of a light plane carrying five Federal agents is a tragedy, to be sure, but one that the Federals will get over. And the senior Huntington, even as we speak, is apparently dying of a heart attack brought on by the news of his son's death in an automobile accident."

Joe Big and Barney looked at each other.

"Sir, we don't get it," Barney said. "Why bother with us?"

The General looked from one man to the other. He frowned. "Are you two sure you don't want to come back on Active Duty Status? I could use people like you."

"Too much water under the bridge, sir," Barney said.

"Another beer, sir?" Joe Big asked.

The Wolf grinned. "Don't mind if I do, Gunny."

Joe Big fetched three beers from the cooler, and popped the tops. He handed one to the General and one to Barney.

Barney sat with his back against the wall of the house, Joe Big on the top step.

Miss Mouse jumped up on the hood of the BMW, and walked up the windshield and lay down on the roof, her back to them, tail twitching.

Joe Big started to get up to chase her off, but the General said, "It's okay. She's not hurting anything."

Joe Big sat back down. "She?"

"Miss Mouse, I believe," the General said.

Barney shook his head.

"It turns out," the General said, looking out over the pasture at the far mountains. "That they really were manufacturing a new form of VX nerve agent at that ranch. They had modified a drone that one of the Huntington group of companies makes for the Air Force, and they were going to use three or four of those drones to disseminate the new VX. Apparently, they had devised a new munition somewhat akin to a bomb that releases smart pucks—you are both familiar with the kind that I am referring to. Some of the technology is so new that it has not yet been classified. Basically, these new pucks have the ability to direct themselves to the greatest concentration of people or, in lieu of actual people, to a place that people can be expected to gather. The pucks communicate with each other to avoid target redundancy.

"The new VX is practically impervious to environmental or climate extremes. It sticks like paint to anything it comes in contact with, but releases onto whatever living thing touches it. Nanotechnology, I'm told. When it senses human tissue—human DNA—it changes shape and augers into living tissue, like a corkscrew. It's really as much biological and mechanical, as it is chemical. Even the tiniest amount will kill."

He looked from one man to the other. "I do not condone, and the President most certainly does not condone the way Gladys Walker and Special Agent Quinn McBride went about it," he said. "But they were on the right track. There was serious talk of actually using these weapons, and then blaming the attack on a united front of terrorist organizations backed by China."

"China?" Joe Big said. "That's crazy."

The General took a sip of beer. "The whole thing was crazy, Gunny. But it's the kind of crazy that is nothing new. This country has some very rich people who are as fanatical in their beliefs as anyone, anytime, anywhere. This is not the first time something like this has been stopped before it could come to fruition."

"Was there any real danger of them pulling it off?" Barney asked.

"Not really. Some of my men were at the ranch. We had been closely monitoring the testing and production of the new drones and munitions."

"We forced your hand," Joe Big said.

The Wolf smiled, and took a pull of beer. "You forced the *President's* hand," he said. "And I thank you for that. We were able to co-opt the ranch without firing a shot and, unknown to the cabal of men and women who organized this threat, to neutralize both the VX and the delivery systems. You don't need to know how."

"They are being eliminated," Joe Big said. "The people who were behind all this?"

"As we speak. But you don't need to know that, either."

He drained his beer and set the bottle on the porch. He stood and took two envelopes from the briefcase, and zipped it shut.

Barney and Joe Big got to their feet.

"You understand that breathing a word of this to anyone is a violation of the secrets acts that as Active Duty Personnel with the highest security clearances you are forever bound by," he said.

"Sir," Barney said. "We are very happy to get on with our lives."

The General looked at Joe Big.

"Yes, sir. I understand."

"Give my best to your uncle when you see him, will you?" He handed Joe Big one of the envelopes, and shook his hand. He handed the other envelope to Barney, and shook his hand. "Thanks for the beer," he said, and went down the steps to the car.

Miss Mouse jumped off the backside of the BMW.

They watched from the porch as the car made a u-turn and headed back down the road, its tires drumming briefly over the metal cattleguard.

Joe Big opened the envelope and peered inside.

"What is it?" Barney asked.

"It's a check. Our pay for one year of active duty." He looked again. "And another Silver Star."

"Farm out," Barney said. "We're Hero Mens again. Can I have a round of applause?" They both pretended to clap their hands, their hands passing each other without touching. Barney opened his envelope and peered inside. "Damn. People make that much these days?"

Joe Big folded the enveloped in half, and stuck it in his back pocket. He walked down the steps and retrieved a couple of beers, and popped the tops.

The sun was beginning to set, casting long shadows across the fields and across the porch, highlighting their faces. The skin was stretched tight across their cheekbones and foreheads. A thin sheen of oil made Joe Big's skin glisten. Barney's eyes glittered with emotion.

He clinked his bottle against Joe Big's.

"To Thomas Edgar Lonewolf, wherever he is," he said.

Joe Big took a drink, and looked out across the fields.

"Look at it this way," Barney said. "These checks are going to make his family happy."

Joe Big swiveled his head toward him.

"Especially since the money will be given anonymously," Barney said.

Joe Big again clinked bottles with him.

He turned back toward the sunset.
"I just don't get it," he said.
"Don't get what?"
"The games people play."
Barney laughed. "Listen to who's talking."
"Don't say it."
Barney said it anyway.